Prais

At the Heart of the Missing

"It is not every author who is gutsy enough to write in several different genres. Annie Daylon succeeds . . . the written word is in good hands!"
—LYNN LEGROW, AMAZON TOP REVIEWER AND AWARD-WINNING BLOGGER OF FICTIONOPHILE
http://fictionophile.wordpress.com/

"Combines rising suspense with clever puzzles that demand you to keep turning pages. Simultaneously plot-driven and smart."
—MICHAEL HIEBERT, AUTHOR OF CLOSE TO THE BROKEN HEARTED

"Had me in 'can't stop reading' suspense until the last page. Daylon's best so far."
—BEN NUTTALL-SMITH, AUTHOR OF FLYING WITH WHITE EAGLE

Castles in the Sand

"Daylon has written not only a heartwarming tale of loss and redemption, family and love, but also a gripping psychological suspense novel. The plot hits the ground running and never lets up. I was hooked from the first chapter."
—MICHAEL HIEBERT, AUTHOR OF DREAM WITH LITTLE ANGELS

Of Sea and Seed
The Kerrigan Chronicles, Book I

"With the skill of a poet, Daylon weaves the tale of a Newfoundland outport family in the early 20th century. Her mastery of the written word brings the reader into the truths and tragedies of everyday life . . ."
—RON YOUNG, FOUNDING EDITOR OF *DOWNHOME MAGAZINE*

"With insight, wit, and great understanding of the all-too-human emotions of guilt and desire, Daylon draws the reader into a timeless story of yearning and loss."
—PAUL BUTLER, AUTHOR OF *THE GOOD DOCTOR*

"A longing for the sea, and from the sea . . . lives out of control since birth, torn by land and by sea . . . souls steadily whipped by the rhetoric of religion. Pounding rhythms. Exciting."
—DARRELL DUKE, AUTHOR OF *THURSDAY'S STORM*

"You will draw in the scent of the land and the sea, your ear attuned to authentic Newfoundland voices. The old-world characters are compelling in their secretive lives and in acts of love gone wrong."
—NELLIE P. STROWBRIDGE, AUTHOR OF *GHOST OF THE SOUTHERN CROSS*

"I loved the writing. The author captured her characters with whimsy, realism, and a deep understanding. Delightful and poignant . . . I heartily recommend this novel."
—LYNN LEGROW, GOODREADS LIBRARIAN

Books by Annie Daylon

AT THE HEART OF THE MISSING

CASTLES IN THE SAND

OF SEA AND SEED: THE KERRIGAN CHRONICLES, BOOK I

MAGGIE OF THE MARSHES

PASSAGES: A COLLECTION OF SHORT STORIES

THE MANY-COLORED INVISIBLE HATS OF BRENDA-LOUISE

At the HearT of the Missing

"Death is woven in with the violets . . . Death and again death."
~Virginia Woolf

At the HearT of the Missing

a novel by
Annie Daylon

AT THE HEART OF THE MISSING
Published by McRAC Books, British Columbia, Canada.
Copyright © 2017 by Angela Day (N.D.P. Annie Daylon). All rights reserved.

This book is a work of fiction. All names, characters, places, organizations, and events portrayed in this book are either products of the author's imagination, or are used fictitiously. Any resemblance to actual events or persons, living or dead, is entirely coincidental.

No part of this book maybe used or reproduced in any manner whatsoever without written permission from the author, except in the case of brief quotations embodied in critical articles and reviews. For information, please contact Annie Daylon through anniedaylon@shaw.ca or visit her website at www.anniedaylon.com.

ISBN-10: 0-9866980-8-3
ISBN-13: 978-0-9866980-8-8

Cover photo of rose petals copyright © Africa Studio. Cover photo of violet copyright © Kaya. Cover photo of marigold copyright © goodmoments. Copy editing, cover design, content design, and layout by Michael Hiebert and www.professionalindie.com.

McRAC Books Trade Paperback Edition.
First Printing, March 2017.
Printed in the United States of America.

For Ken

Prologue

Friday, May 6th

ROSE STANDS IN THE center of the living room, staring at the opaque, indestructible glass of the window nearest the fire escape. She smirks. *Escape.* There is no escape. The window is painted shut. She fingers her breakout tools—a pair of manicure scissors and a jagged cuticle pusher: scrape paint, raise window, crawl through. But her legs are leaden. It is all she can do to raise an arm to wipe her brow. A whiff of sweat triggers a wave of nausea. Swallowing hard, she glances toward the door.

Time is limited. Yes, he is gone overnight, but at dawn, a jangle of keys will assault her eardrums. She has gotten away with a few tiny deviations from his set of rules, from his idea of perfectionism. But this? This will not go unnoticed. What if she fails? She flinches as she flashes on yesterday: the setting of the table, the misplacement of a water goblet, and the blow to her ribcage.

A sob explodes from Rose's throat. How the hell did she end up here? In this situation? Anxious, she thrusts forward, first one foot, then the other. She is making headway now, inching toward the window, almost there. At the window, she stalls again. What the hell is she waiting for? There is no time for hesitation, no time to question how she got here. But she has to think things through. All her life, she's been completely in control, spiraling upward. All her life, she's maintained independence. Needing no one. Accessorizing with and then casting aside lovers and friends. Her only true allies were blood—her sister and her mother.

But three years ago, her sister Margo vanished. Not a word, not a trace. Gone.

Three months ago, Rose's mother died. Her body battered by cancer, her heart shattered by grief, Violet Harrington just gave up.

The losses left Rose out of touch, alone. Just Rose. A solo, independent woman. Now, imprisoned in front of the opaque window with her makeshift tools in hand, reality knifes her. What she created was not independence; it was vulnerability. Without a support system, she was a target. She was prey. With her porthole of time eroding, with every nerve stretched taut, Rose stares at the window.

How long had he hunted her?

Eight Days Earlier
Thursday, April 28th

One

AM I SUPPOSED TO meet with Rose today? Maybe it's the hospital that's on my itinerary. Is this the last day of the month? Don't know. At the moment, I don't care. The comfortable dent in my pillow owns me. *Thirty days hath September . . .* I mentally recite the rhyme while blinking the room into focus.

The A-frame ceiling looms close, its yellow pine boards glowing in the morning sun. A bulging, black spider rappels from the center beam, pirouetting nearer and nearer to my face. What's wrong with my vision? Everything's too big. I sink deep into my pillow, like a camera operator pulling back for a wide-angle shot. Then, I remember again, as I do every morning, that distance shots are not possible. Things seem big because they are supposed to, right down to the grainy timber and the dangling arachnid. I am in the loft of my two-hundred-ninety square foot tiny forest-green house which sits near the back lane next to the garage and the garbage. The ceiling is barely an arm's length above my head.

Laneway houses—tiny houses—are relatively new constructions, one of Vancouver's answers to housing scarcity in a growing city. This specific laneway house-on-wheels is a solution to the dissolution of a marriage.

It was sudden and lethal, the tragedy that sank Amelia and me. After our six-year-old son died, we couldn't look at each other without triggering agony but we couldn't abandon each other either. Amelia lives in the big house at the other end of the property. The big house faces Turner Street. Amelia owns the big house, or will as soon as I serve her with the divorce papers stuffed in a file drawer at my office. Three sets of papers are waiting there. One for me, one for her, one for the lawyer.

The spider is too close, twirling an inch above the tip of my nose. I swoosh a hand through the air. "Not today, Fred," I say. Aware of the game, Fred skedaddles. He knows I won't harm him. Live and let live. It was my wife who scolded me for naming the infestations and then stomped the life out of Fred's relatives. Not surprisingly, Fred took my side in the separation. "Not today, Fred," I repeat, knowing that this time I'm talking about dealing with the divorce papers.

I'm sitting upright now, comforter and comfort tossed. An eruption of hammering has me swearing at my neighbor. Beer-In-Hand Burt's not a bad guy except for his tendency to operate heavy machinery at dawn. My tiny window is beside me, close like everything else, and I peer out, ready to shake a fist, but there is no sign of Beer-in-Hand Burt, no sign of a jackhammer. The noise continues. I plop my fist on my head. *Damn.* The racket is inside my skull, not outside my window. It's my heart pumping at my newly-awakened brain, battering me over the idea of a visit to the hospital. Maybe I should lie down again, but there's no point. It would be too hard to get back up. My son is gone. Can't change it. The hospital is not to blame. Gotta keep moving. Momentum is everything, especially in my line of work.

I take a deep breath and blow it out. Morning breath. Yuck. I pinch my nose and yawn a growling protest.

I'd swing my legs over the side of the bed, but there is no side of the bed for the bed is a futon on the floor of the loft. A bundle of clothes hunches in the corner where the floor of the loft meets the wall of the house. One jean leg dangles in a suicide threat over the edge, one plaid flannel shirt sleeve reaches in a longing gesture toward me. Does it expect me to wear it a second time? That's not happening. One wear. One wash. I reel in the dirty clothes and stuff them into the laundry bag which hangs by a noose-like rope from the center beam. It's ominous, that rope, but the attached pulley system keeps dirty clothes hidden and keeps company oblivious. Everyone notices the rope, though. I tell them it's never been tested, and I laugh. People don't laugh back.

My phone hums, a hollow sound against the footstool that's doing duty as a nightstand. I reach and pick up a text.

Today. 2:30. Interview fender bender at VGH. Payout pending

I roll my eyes. Freaking insurance forms. Documents are the backbone of the private investigator business, and documents are the lead foot of my working life. The rut is deep. I'm stuck, moving laterally from one set of papers to another. It's not exactly as seen on TV, this profession. No car chases. No drug gangs. No shootouts. At least not in my experience. I don't carry a gun. It's illegal for PIs in Canada to carry guns. Does it matter? I'm a pacifist. Could never shoot anyone. Can't even squash a spider. But I'm pretty good at the firing range. No paper torso has ever escaped my aim.

I unroll from the futon and fluff my pillow. Crawling back and forth, I straighten out the comforter. I spider my way backward down the tiny stairs, much to the amusement of Fred who watches me from a newly-spun strand of silk.

It may be spring but the floor is winter cold. I come to a tiptoe standstill in front of my brown leather loveseat and stare at the wall behind it, at my only piece of art—Bev Doolittle's *The Forest Has Eyes*. A master of camouflage, Doolittle. In this work, a horseman in hostile territory is being watched by thirteen faces peering from rocks and trees. Most days it is easy for me to spot the hidden faces in the print. Today is one of those days. With thirteen accounted for, I hop across the slip of a kitchen. Two hops and I'm in the bathroom.

Encased in white subway tile, the so-called bathroom has a sink with a single tap mounted too high and a toilet with a showerhead hanging above it. I don't know what genius came up with the idea of hanging the showerhead over the toilet, but some days the image creeps me out. Some days, when my wife is traveling, I migrate to the other end of the driveway and slip back in time, pretending that the big shower in the big house is all mine again. But there are times when I perform the three morning esses—shit, shower, and shave—here, simultaneously instead of consecutively. My intention of doing just that is interrupted by a ripple of memory—last night, my wife took the red-eye to Florida. There is no need for further consideration regarding divorce papers today. But one thing I will consider is a luxury shower. This day's looking up.

I turn back to the stairs, to the cupboards under the stairs. Beneath each step is storage space and there are ten steps. The first five spaces hold board games, everything from Backgammon to Yahtzee. Next are puzzles, but no jigsaws. My penchant for five thousand piece jigsaws disappeared with the downsizing. Right now I keep pocket puzzles. My one treat is Mega-Minx, a dodecahedron-shaped puzzle, similar to a Rubik's Cube, but with fifty movable pieces instead of twenty. I avoid the temptation to play with that puzzle. I reach past it, into my tiny closet under the tenth and tallest stair for my day's outfit—white crew neck T-shirt, dark-wash jeans and blue cotton blazer. It is preassembled on a wooden hanger and labeled THURSDAY. I have seven such outfits in my closet. Nothing to do with fashion, everything to do with ease of preparation. I'm all for anything that gets me started in the morning. Gotta get moving. Then gotta stay moving. It all comes down to momentum.

I'm about to dash through the sliding door when I realize that my neighbor, should he appear, would take umbrage at my current appearance. Nudity does not bode well with Beer-in-Hand Burt who, for reasons beyond my ken, has been dogging me since my tiny house rolled into the back lane four years ago. Clenching the hanger in my teeth, I grab an overcoat and wrap myself in it. Ensuring that nothing but Fred is dangling, I head into the sunshine toward the big house. Just as I jam the key into the door—

"Hey, Irish!"

Darn. Almost made it.

I turn. Burt's hairy arms protrude from his sleeveless undershirt, his beer belly hangs down past his waist, eclipsing the top half of his GOT BEER? belt buckle, and yes, the signature beer can is in his hand. The usual scruff of beard is gone. Guess he does own a razor after all. "The name's Flynn," I offer. A fruitless effort. Doesn't matter how many fleas I put in this guy's ear, he'll never get it right.

"Yeah, yeah. Can't marry the two, Irish." He lets out a belch.

I shrug. By "the two" he means my name—Shaughnessy Flynn—and my appearance—brown skin, black hair, and brown eyes. My Indo-Canadian mother wanted to call me Sanjay, but my Irish-Canadian father insisted his only son be named after him. Sanjay got demoted to middle name. Not that I mind, but my ID card is worn to a frazzle. Good man, my father, but he never fully thought things through.

"Where's the wife?" Burt tosses his head toward the big house.

"Visiting her mother for a couple of weeks."

"Ah, yes. Visiting the mother. Makes sense. Mother's Day's next week. Gonna have to buy the wife some roses or something, I suppose."

Roses. That reminds me. I'm supposed to meet Rose. Today? Tomorrow?

Burt takes a gulp of beer. "Oops. Out of fuel. Catch you later, Irish." With a wave of the empty can, he turns.

"Have a good one," I call. I slip into the big house and close the door before Burt can execute his habit of returning with another comment. As I charge up the stairs, I make a mental note: Check schedule. Meet with Rose?

Two

A SURGE OF SEA air greets Rose as she exits her Beach Avenue condo in downtown Vancouver. She strolls along, in no hurry despite the fact that the rest of the world seems to be. A typical city morning. A few days ago, Rose was one with the crowd but work no longer beckons. Still, there are thoughts that nudge about things that need attention. Perhaps she should contact the real estate agent to ensure that the deal on her mother's house has been finalized, or maybe she should check to see that the moving company delivered her mother's furniture to the storage locker. And perhaps she is just guilty of overthinking. There are too many pieces of information crowding her brain.

She scurries from the sidewalk through a parking lot to the False Creek Ferry dock, intent on a trip to Granville Island. She tramps along the gangway, slapping her shoes against the metal grating, feeling its downward slant pulling her toward the water. The little blue ferry is already chugging up to shore. Not surprising to Rose, a regular patron, quite aware that one of the fleet shows up every few minutes.

People are waiting, some scrutinizing the list of fees on the side of the tiny shelter, others digging in purses and pockets for coins. Rose pulls her monthly pass from her jeans and slips into the line forming at the edge of the dock.

The ferry operator, a pudgy, dark-haired, thirtysomething man clad in cargo shorts and T-shirt, bumps the boat up to the dock and hops off. There are no ropes used here to moor the ferry; the schedule is tight, no time for lingering. The operator grabs and holds the boat to eliminate the gap between it and the dock as he welcomes passengers. Once all are aboard, he jumps back on and asks a few people to switch sides for balance. Then he takes his place at the wheel, perched on a high stool for visibility. He collects fares, nods as Rose flashes her monthly pass, and gets underway. Rose settles in for the short ride to the public market on Granville Island.

Rose speaks not a word to the other passengers. Her mother, God rest her soul, told her repeatedly that she spent far too much time on the outside looking in. Her sister Margo had agreed. Others—the people at work—didn't. They only saw what she wanted them to see. Rose had perfected her work mask, that of confidence. She thought about every sentence and paused before giving voice to the words. If she detected a positive reaction to something she said, she repeated it. After a while, she realized that the repetition betrayed her insecurity so she made a game of catching herself in the act. She would stop and readjust her invisible mask until ease slid over her again.

Sometimes Rose wished she could bridge the threshold into everyday conversation. Sometimes she even parted her lips and took a breath, but a glottal stop of sorts occurred. Here on the ferry, thankfully, there is no pressure to make conversation. There are eight other passengers, all focused on electronic devices, their thumbs sliding and tapping on tiny screens. A bespectacled gentleman is about to slip his phone into his pocket when the phone blares the opening strains of Beethoven's Fifth. He rolls his eyes, taps the ignore button, and mutters something about his mother-in-law. Nearby passengers shift slightly on the bench, allot him a few knowing smiles, and then return to their own electronic worlds.

Rose left her iPhone at home. The only thing she wants to focus on is the water as it ripples and glimmers in the rays of the sun. When the operator points out a seal staring back at them with its head popped above water, Rose smiles. A good idea, this excursion. Maybe she should do an entire tour of False Creek with its charming sea village of floating homes, perhaps even visit Science World. She scrunches her nose. On second thought, she might skip Science World; there would be far too many schoolchildren at Science World, a jabbing reminder of the job she just lost. She changes her focus to the traffic on the water.

A sea kayak glides by, its paddler looking quite content with only a thin yellow shell separating him from the ocean. Rose tried kayaking once, even went to training at the local swimming pool, but the first time she rolled the kayak, she panicked. That experience brought her closer to death than she ever wanted to be. She did not go back.

A short distance behind the kayak there is a rowboat. Infinitely more inviting. As it draws closer, Rose can see that there are two young people on the center thwart, giggling and struggling with disobedient oars. There is no sign of life jackets. Perhaps they are stowed in the bottom of the boat? As the ferry judders past, Rose wonders at the audacity of these teenagers who are either confident in their swimming skills or gifted with infallibility. Either way, the lack of life jackets is a blunder. Rose shakes her head. No wonder people get themselves into treacherous situations. One must always be wary.

Granville Island Market opens at nine and she will be a half hour early. She doesn't mind; there's a lot to see on the island. The ferry slows and bumps against the dock, where it bobs in the wake of another water taxi which is just leaving. As she hops off the boat, Rose sees that the island is already bustling with farmers and suppliers who are offloading wares. She ambles around the exterior of the market, listening to the clatter and rumble of trucks, the slamming of doors, and the shouting of vendors. Scavenger gulls circle and flap, landing on the wharf, taking off again, clearly more excited than the vendors to get the day started. Rose sidesteps gull droppings and strolls beside the market to the final entry point near the Seafood City stall. She meanders from the stench of fresh fish to the aroma of fresh-baked bread. When a whiff of coffee wafts up her nose, she follows the smell. She sits on a bar stool facing a window and, while sipping and savoring, stares at the wharf and the water and the boats beneath the bridge.

Once she crawls out of that welcome cup of coffee, Rose heads to the produce section and picks up a shopping basket. She slides along smoothly, squeezing and tapping cantaloupes and honeydews. A subtle bump occurs. Just a nudge from the shopping basket suspended from the crook of her arm.

When she turns to utter a brief apology, she forgets the melon she is holding and blinks into the face of a stranger, a tall, lean man with soft, dark eyes and subtly sculpted features. She rests her gaze. A delightful shiver of want runs through her but she does not telegraph it. Far better that she feign disinterest. Rose clears her throat and takes a step backward.

When he mirrors the action, Rose lets her guard down. He is harmless, respectful. With personal space increased, Rose enjoys a full, head-to-toe view of this man whose posture speaks confidence, and whose attire—sky-blue Ralph Lauren polo shirt, matching cashmere cardigan, chinos, deck shoes—shows style. Definitely appealing.

He extends his hand. "My apologies."

"But my fault." Rose places the melon into her basket and accepts his gesture.

He folds his long, strong fingers over hers. A warm, gentle touch.

She lets her hand linger. The clamor of the marketplace place falls away. She waits in anticipation for him to speak.

"Perhaps I am being too forward," he says in soothing tones. "Then again, perhaps you are just too beautiful."

Any dangling threads of personal restraint vanish, leaving Rose so relaxed that she melts into the compliment. Given the choice, she would have melted into his body right there on the display stand, surrounded by the tang of citrus and squish of grapes. A silly fantasy? Perhaps. But not the awareness that accompanies it. The power here is all his. She waits.

He tilts his head at just the right angle, one that highlights his chiselled features. An unhurried smile forms on his face. "I am Vincent," he says, "and you are . . . ?"

Rose opens her mouth but nothing comes out. She swallows. "Hello, Vin—" Just then, the pyramid of oranges beside them shifts and tumbles and rumbles to the floor. Releasing Rose's hand, Vincent steps back, out of their path.

A silver-haired man, cane in one hand, Sunkist globe in the other, offers a bewildered apology. "I'm so sorry," he says to no one in particular. "I just wanted one orange."

"Not to worry." Vincent scoops up the wandering fruit, restacks the pyramid, and escorts the wiry senior and his single orange to the checkout.

Rose blinks as they disappear into the crowd. He's gone. A moment. A fantasy. A gentleman. And he's gone. Vincent is gone and she didn't even tell him her name. Sighing, she turns back to tapping melons. Her appetite for them seems to have vanished, so she moves to the apple displays.

"As I was saying, I am Vincent, and you are . . . ?" This from over her left shoulder.

Rose can't contain her smile. She turns. "Rose," she said. "I am Rose."

"Of course you are." He nods, an approval of sorts. "Well, Rose, would you like to accompany me in a brief stroll on the pier?"

Rose instantly abandons her shopping basket with its lone honeydew melon, just leaves it atop a mountain of green apples, and trails him to the nearest exit. On the pier, he waits as she moves from behind him to beside him. He sets the pace, his step easy. He sets the tone, his voice calm. She attunes her ear, struggling to hear over the scream of seagulls and drum of her heart. Occasionally, he stops, stealing peeks at her as he pauses to observe a knife-juggling busker or a fish-stealing cormorant. Aware that the glances he casts at buskers, birds, and bystanders are fleeting, Rose experiences a rush of happiness. This gentleman has no interest in anyone but her.

When he puts his cell phone into her hand and closes her fingers around it, she doesn't hesitate. She enters her number and returns the phone. In that instant, she catches sight of a single cloud sailing across the sun. Rose shivers. In the next second, Vincent backs away.

Is he leaving?

Yes, his words are about goodbyes now. Whatever time he has allotted to them, to her, is dissipating. Can she let this happen? She moves closer to him, looks up, her lips parted in mute invitation. He steps back again, a warm smile on his face, a touch of amusement in his eyes. Has she misunderstood? Is she the one who is too forward?

It is with an ache in her chest that Rose realizes he is definitely going away, leaving her standing and staring. Solo once again. Her eyes widen as he steps aboard a yacht. Confident, modest, and rich? Almost too good to be true. As he motors off, she wonders if he will ever call.

Rose meanders, no sense of time or place. Before she knows it, she is aboard a ferry, eyes closed, shutting out the sky, taking in the sway of the tiny vessel. When she reopens her eyes, she realizes that she is not heading home, but going farther into False Creek. Earlier she thought about taking a tour, but she does not recall making a decision to follow through. Obviously, she had stepped into the tour boat line and flashed her monthly pass. A simple mistake or a subconscious choice? She shrugs. It matters little. She engages in being a passenger, staring at the boats and boat houses that slip past, watching their pudgy and privileged owners indulge in morning meals of muffins and mimosas.

Rose wills the boat to keep moving, away, away. An escape, perhaps. She would rather be sliding past other people's lives than be returning to her own. But the ferry reaches its final docking station and retraces its passage. Rose shivers. She is returning to her precious ninth-floor Beach Avenue condo with its ivory walls and stunning view.

Rose debarks and retraces her steps across the parking lot to her home.

The sun gleams through the floor-to-ceiling windows of Rose's condo. It is still early, around noon. So many hours until sundown. Yes, there are things to do, but she sits and stares at life through her window: people walking by, people cycling by, people sailing by. It occurs to her that life at home is not so different from her trip on the ferry. Isolated.

Rose feels a longing so intense that her chest hurts. Is there no cure for this? In an effort to change her mood, she thinks about going to her mother's house to ensure that nothing—not a dust mote nor a thumb tack—is left behind when the property changes hands. But she sighs that thought away. There is no hurry. Whatever has to be done can be accomplished tomorrow.

Until now, she has been exceptionally busy, a needs-must situation, one that served to numb her emotions. Now, there are no urgencies to keep her occupied. In three days, she will take a planned vacation. Three weeks. One in Hawaii, two in Europe. Alone.

The emptiness stretches out in front of her.

Three

MY CHERRY-RED VOLKSWAGEN Golf is a Christmas ornament against the backdrop of my forest-green laneway house, a rather cheery stab of sarcasm. The mismatched driver's door groans as I open it. An overturned garbage can catches my eye. I have to fix that. Closing the car door, I pick up the trash can and park it on top of a dandelion breaching a crack in the pavement. A prolific lot, dandelions. This one displays seeds, which fly through the breeze created by the swing of the trash can and land directly on the balding patch of grass that hugs the side of my tiny house. I slam the lid on the can. Done. There's a feeling of satisfaction in having things where they are supposed to be.

My car, like me, is not fond of morning, but it starts with a couple of turns of the key. With my hands at nine and three on the steering wheel, I head east on Turner Street and turn onto Boundary Road to begin the steep climb to Hastings Street. I hope, as always, that I'll hit the green light at that intersection so I can slide through and ease into a right-hand turn toward my office on East Hastings. No such luck. The car comes to a stop on the incline and rolls back slightly. I congratulate myself on putting in a new clutch which I ride with confidence. There will be no need for the crutch of the emergency brake today.

At the first bleep of the crosswalk signal, a man darts in front of my car. He stops dead and glares at me. Almost instantly, the glare morphs into a grin. I consider the situation. Is he homeless? The image doesn't fit the profile. His face is sculpted, not gaunt. He is tall, over six feet, and has potentially powerful shoulders. His black overcoat—undoubtedly London Fog—doesn't have a stain on it or a button missing from it. The coat hangs open, the belt looped in the back. Why is he wearing a cable knit sweater on a day like this? A pleasing design, the cable stitch. Standard ecru color. His hair is salt-and-pepper, disheveled, but styled with product, not greased by neglect. If there is a mark on his face, I can't tell. A scruff of beard disguises all possible sins. What is this man doing on the street? If he is disenfranchised, he hasn't been so for long.

The man raises his arms and a bucket and squeegee come into view. Ah, a cleaning ruse. Perhaps he is homeless after all. But I can't have him, or anyone else for that matter, sloshing water onto my cracked windshield. Still, the plight of the homeless tugs. Life on the street is hard. I glance at the traffic light. Still red. I excavate a few coins from my pocket and beckon. The man hurries to my window and reaches in, his palm upturned. As I drop coins, I look for distinguishing marks, the habit of a PI. But the sleeve of his cable knit covers the heel of his hand, and I can't see a darn thing.

A car horn blares. I jump. My foot slips from the clutch and I roll back a smidgen. I yank on the emergency brake and slowly relinquish it as I reestablish balance with the clutch. With a cursory wave in the rearview mirror, I acknowledge the driver behind me. The homeless man scurries to cross the street. A car almost clips him, but he makes it safe to the sidewalk. He turns right and disappears behind a white, paneled van parked parallel to the curb.

I release the clutch and move forward. As I pull onto Hastings Street, it occurs to me that the "homeless" man may very well be the owner of that van. Did he get into it? Have I been duped? I shrug. What the hell. It is only a couple of bucks.

Traffic is zooming on Hastings. I'm being tailgated by a behemoth, a Hummer. I let out a snort. Don't understand why people need those things for city living. As my speedometer creeps up to the speed limit, the Hummer speeds by and then cuts in in front of me. I spot the license number: 04SIID.

"Oversized," I say, instantly interpreting the vanity plate. I smile a bit, despite the traffic. Can't help it. Solving puzzles always brings a degree of satisfaction.

I claim a parking spot a block from my office. There's a deli on that block and I make a quick stop to grab a turkey sandwich on whole wheat, hold the cranberry sauce. Why people put cranberry sauce on a sandwich is beyond me. At the drink machine, I automatically reach for a diet Coke but remember something about needing vitamin C, so I opt for orange juice, a choice I know I'll pay for later. Ascorbic acid is a dragon in my gut.

By the time I climb the stairs to the second floor of the dilapidated building that houses my office, both sandwich and juice are gone. I let out a belch and look around to see if anyone notices. Don't know why I'm concerned about that. There is never anyone around. I pull out my key ring. With a click of the lock and a whine from the hinges, the door swings open. I don't even have to nudge the darn thing as it is hung at a lean in the first place.

Here I am, at my place of employment for the last few years. It consists of three rooms: a reception area with a chair waiting for me to hire a receptionist; an office space with a walnut desk, two vertical filing cabinets, a mini fridge, a crime board (currently blank), and an empty room, one which I have no idea what to do with. Right now, it is a junk room where I store boxes of old files that I keep meaning to get back to, cans of paint that I keep meaning to use, and a rollaway cot that I keep falling into when I can't bear the thought of returning home. The only other space is a tiny washroom, not really tiny when I compare it to the washroom in my tiny house. This one actually has a cubicle shower which is small but serviceable. The birdbath-size sink lacks a stopper—another thing on my imaginary to-do list. The mirror on the medicine cabinet has a lightning-streak crack which I make a game of. If I stand in the perfect spot, I have a Harry Potter scar reflection. The toilet works fine as long as I remember to jiggle the handle to keep the water from running. There's a sliding lock on the door. Not that I ever need it. I'm usually the only one here.

I plop down at my desk and open the file drawer to my left. Fingering through, I pull the insurance file I need for the hospital visit. I log on to my laptop, update the file, and print it. After shuffling some more paperwork around, I make a trip to the washroom and grab my briefcase. I'm at the door of the office, just about to leave when someone knocks. I pause. I'm not expecting anyone but my spirits rise at the idea of a delay. Anything to avoid spending time at the hospital. I yank the door open.

"Yo, Flynn!" It's Lee, an old cop buddy of mine. Not that I ever was a cop. Lee was. Still is.

I first met Lee eight years ago during Trivia Night at a local pub. By that time, I had abandoned my corporate career in real estate in favor of a solo stint as a private investigator. I spent countless sleepless hours studying crime and indulged my passion for puzzles by perusing Crime Stoppers and Cold Cases websites.

At the pub that night, buoyed by beer, I congratulated myself on a brilliant idea. I could make my mark as a PI by sharing my insights about unsolved crimes. And who better to share with than the new member at my quiz table, Lee Connors, a compactly-built police officer with a pale, boyish face, bottle-green eyes, and a hint of frost in the tapered sides of his dark-brown hair.

"I can help solve that bank robbery from last week," I told him.

"Is that so?" the officer said, taking a slug of beer. "And just who might you be? The robber, perhaps?"

I shook my head. "Shaughnessy Flynn."

"Shaughnessy Flynn?" His eyes glinted, a mixture of amusement and curiosity. "Your name's Shaughnessy Flynn?"

Experienced with this reaction, ready for it, I slid my ID card across the table. "I saw the grainy stills from video surveillance. Did you notice the robber's shoes? Or, at least, a reflection of them in a plate-glass window?"

Lee looked at me with an affronted frown. "We always notice the shoes, Mr. Flynn. You see," he said, as he toyed with my ID card and tossed it on the table, "any jacket or hat can be disposed of in a hurry. Not so easy to get rid of footwear."

"True." Nodding, I pulled at my collar. "Italian leather, those shoes."

"And . . . ?" Lee threw his hands out to the side, a tell-me-something-I-didn't-know expression on his face.

I leaned forward. "One of those leather shoes is bigger than the other, two sizes bigger. They're not just Italian. They're custom."

"You're kidding, right?" His tone was brimmed with ridicule.

I let the question hang.

"Well?"

"Maybe you left your glasses in the copy room after you changed the toner cartridge today."

Lee's eyes widened. "Excuse me?"

"You have a single, black, powdery smudge on your right ear. Must have scratched it when you removed the toner cartridge. A dirty job, that. As for your glasses, when I told you my name, you repeated it, in question format. Twice. Nothing unusual there. The combination of my Irish-Canadian name and my Indo-Canadian face always arouses curiosity. But you didn't follow through."

Lee tilted his head to one side. "Keep going."

"You didn't read my business card. After one negligible squint, you threw it aside."

A slow smile spread across Lee's face. He fished into his jacket pocket and pulled out a pair of glasses. "I didn't lose these darn things; I just don't like to admit that I need them. Turned forty last week. They say forty's the new twenty. I say forty's a bitch." He retrieved and read my business card. "I'm guessing you're doing well as a gumshoe?"

After that, Lee and I met for a coffee or a pint on occasion. Gradually, conversation rolled into friendship.

Today is Lee's day off, obviously as he is out of uniform. I can never blend the two, his neat-as-a-pin uniform and his ragged jeans and flannel shirt with only one tail tucked in.

I give him the obligatory grin. "Come on in. Didn't expect to see your tired face here today." There are dark circles under Lee's eyes, and his hair, which is more salt than pepper now, could use a trim. What is that mustache all about? An early Movember effort? Or perhaps an attempt to mask that still boyish face? Hard to believe the guy's approaching fifty. In either case, not the usual for impeccable Lee.

"I may be tired but you're looking like something the cat dragged in. Is your forehead getting higher?" He snaps his fingers. "No, wait a minute. That's just your hairline going north." As usual, his eyes glint with glee.

I rake my fingers through my curly mop, releasing a few strands of hair. I hold them up for display. "Can't argue the hairline bit now, can I? But seriously, what's up?" I brush my hands together.

"Lunch. That's what's up. We're supposed to have lunch today, remember?"

I blink at him. "All morning I've been trying to remember if I had a meeting scheduled with someone. I thought it could be Rose. You? Never occurred to me. Sorry."

"Got your phone?" Lee says.

"Huh?"

"Gimme your phone."

I oblige.

"You have to learn to put your schedule somewhere." His fingers are tapping away. "If you can't put it into your phone, perhaps you could use that empty crime board of yours." He lets out a chuckle.

"Humor. Har. Har." My crime board idea came from my penchant for TV crime shows in which display boards are used to advance the story. A single story. A single crime. And, according to Lee, a singularly obtuse concept. Real life detectives don't work one crime at a time. Since criminals refuse to wait for one crime story to be solved before instigating another, real life detectives work multiple cases, all of which would be fighting for space on a display board. "Maybe someday I'll use that board." There's a defensive note in my voice, uncomfortable even to me.

Lee's reassurance is quick. "Truth is, maybe you will. At least you won't have to worry about privacy issues."

"Meaning?"

"Lots of people coming and going at my workplace, including reporters. There's no way detectives are going to plaster profiles and suspects on a board for all to see. No end to the havoc."

"Makes sense."

"Some detectives do use a board system, but keep it in their computers." He passes me back my phone. "There you go."

"Bit late for scheduling, isn't it? I already missed lunch."

"Actually, you've already eaten lunch." He points to the sandwich wrapper in the wastebasket. "But," he adds, "next week we're on a trivia team at the pub, remember? I entered that info."

"Sure, I remember." My face burns with the lie. "I'm pretty good with remembering things."

"Solving things. Decoding things. All *things*, yes. People? Appointments? Not so much."

"Sorry."

He makes a dismissive gesture. "Said that already. And, by the way, you're meeting Rose tomorrow morning. *We're* meeting with Rose tomorrow. Helping her move the mahogany dresser, remember? I just added it to your schedule."

"Thanks."

"Got time for a coffee?"

I shake my head. "On my way to the hospital. Vancouver General. Have an appointment with an insurance client. Papers need signing."

Lee gives me a searching glance. "*Insurance* papers?"

"Amelia is in Florida, visiting her mother."

"What? You're mind reading now?" Lee chuckles as he heads to the door.

"Your eyes went to the filing cabinet before they searched mine. You know darn well that's where I stuffed the divorce papers." I follow him through the door.

"You don't miss a trick, do you?" Lee says.

"Do my best. Could say the same about you. Look, I really am sorry about lunch. If you want, I'll treat you to a sandwich from the deli across the street."

"Stop apologizing. I'm fine."

"Good enough then."

"Later," he says when we get to the sidewalk.

At VGH, I turn into the parkade and brace myself for the often-futile search for a parking space. I go round and round the escalating spiral until I burst from darkness into sunlight at the very top of the structure. I don't mind the climb as I prefer to park at the top. From there, it is only one or two levels down to the skywalk that leads directly into the hospital.

Strolling the skywalk, I cross paths with a variety of people—personnel in scrubs, patients in gowns, and visitors in angst. I search all faces, a habit of mine, and categorize them as doctors, nurses, lawyers, administrators. The easiest to sort are patients and visitors. I once wondered at the lack of worry lines on the faces of patients. But now, sadly, I am enlightened. It is their visitors who wear those lines, permanently-etched, like seams in weathered rock.

A few people hover outside the front doors of the hospital, far enough from the entrance so they can puff a cigarette. Doesn't seem to matter how many tubes people have stuck into them, they still have to add another one. I count my blessings that I had the good sense to quit years back. Still, I find myself seeking out and sucking in secondhand smoke that wafts in my direction.

The automatic door opens and closes behind me. I stick my hand under the first sanitizer machine I see. To this day, I find reassurance in hand sanitizer. That's a holdover, I know, from the tragedy. I fight against germs as vehemently as my son fought for life.

I pass the coffee shop and glance at the snack case. Food can wait. I approach the information desk and stand there. It is sudden, the pall that drops over me. A chill accompanies it and I am back, eight years back. A Jenga scenario, this. One slight push, and I'll crumble.

"May I help you?" The voice jumps me into the present. The receptionist, if that's what she is, wears scrubs. Pretty, pink scrubs, a sharp contrast to her dark complexion and hair. Are those the whitest teeth I have ever seen?

"I'm looking for this patient," I say, showing her the envelope with the patient's name on the front. "Can you give me his room number? I seem to have misplaced it."

"Is he expecting you?"

"Yes." I produce my ID card. "We have an appointment." I open the envelope to display insurance forms.

The receptionist checks her computer. "You can go to the sixth floor and ask about him there. They will help you. The elevator's that way." She points.

With a cursory nod, I head down the hall. This hospital corridor, with its bustling activity, its variety of gift shops and coffee stops, has the appearance and feel of an airport concourse. But behind all those closed doors on the far side of each hallway . . . I abandon the thought.

There is a short wait at the elevator and I step in quickly, hoping I will ride alone. But on my heels, five hospital workers board. All blue scrubs. All wearing stethoscopes and talking symptoms. They are puzzle-solving and I am intrigued. I choose to listen, to ride with them to the tenth floor. I wear a nonchalant expression as they exit, but I'm disappointed. Puzzles are a welcome distraction. This one apparently doesn't belong to me. I push the button for the sixth floor.

The doors open and I stroll up to the counter. Another wait. This time, hospital smells—chlorine and sick and death—creep in. The beep of some IV drip gnaws. The silence of rubber soles on tile taunts. Death has no soul. No child should die with IVs dripping some medicine into his veins. Down the hallway, there is a rumpled shape on a gurney. A sleeping patient. Just like my son. Asleep. That's what I thought. He looked so peaceful. At the time, it relaxed me, the sight of him looking so restful, so much so that I fell asleep myself, his hand in mine, my head resting on the edge of his bed. It was the screams that woke me. My wife's screams.

With a shudder, I disconnect from the memory. Where am I? Oh, yeah. Accident victim. Insurance forms.

Damn. I try to avoid the Vancouver General Hospital. When I have to visit, I try to remain detached. All efforts are in vain. Will healing show up someday? Maybe. But certainly not on this one. I am still broken, the crack in the windshield of my VW Golf a metaphor for my life.

Someone appears at the other side of the counter and I make my inquiry. Minutes later, I enter the insurance client's room. After a few perfunctory words, I obtain his signature. Can't get out of there fast enough. A breeze sails past me as I race-walk back the way I came. Once outside, I take a gulp of fresh air and then hold my breath as I pass the smoking community. I run across the skywalk and barrel up the stairs to my parking level. I throw open the door and as it clunks shut behind me, I step to one side and lean on the wall. After a few deep breaths, my heart stops pounding. Okay. Enough of that.

I head for my car.

Friday, April 29th

Four

AT THE FIRST CHIME of the doorbell, Rose barrels down the hallway of her mother's house and yanks the door open. "About time you got here, Flynn—" She blinks. "Oops. FedEx. Sorry. I was expecting someone else."

The FedEx driver pulls his black cap low and hands her an envelope. Rose angles her head but can't get a good look at his face. She takes a cautious step back.

He clears his throat. "This is for a Mrs. Harrington."

Mrs. Harrington. The name drops like a stone. Rose flinches. Is sorrow always in the wings, awaiting its cue? Mrs. Harrington, her mother, is gone. Rose trembles as she reaches for the envelope.

"Sign here, p-p-please." He holds out a pen.

Rose tucks the envelope under her arm. Why won't the driver meet her eyes? He is tall but stooped like Quasimodo, his brown hair dangling past his shoulders. He's wearing an all-weather jacket, a good idea on a drizzly morning. She focuses on the purple uniform stripe on the underside of his sleeve and follows it from wrist to chest. There's the FedEx logo but no name tag. Don't FedEx drivers wear nametags? She reaches for the pen.

"You don't have a nametag." Rose signs the delivery slip.

"Don't need one."

Rose winces. Had she really said that aloud? "I guess you don't."

"B-b-but you?" He glances at the signature. "What is your name?"

"Rose Harrington." She raises an eyebrow. "Why do delivery people always ask me that when my name is right in front of them?"

He keeps his head low. "Procedure. Make sure we can r-r-r-read the name right, that's all. Not everybody writes neat like you."

Rose smiles. "School teacher."

"Figured as much." He touches his cap and turns away. "Good day, Mrs. Harrington."

"Good day," echoes Rose as she closes the door. She leans against the doorframe and looks at the envelope. It isn't addressed to a *Mrs.* Harrington at all. It is for her, *Ms.* Rose Harrington. Idiot deliveryman. Rolling her eyes, she rips at the seal. It doesn't budge. Scissors. She needs scissors. She goes to the kitchen, the click of her heels echoing through the vacant hallway.

The kitchen cabinets have been stripped of anything that resembles a utensil, but her purse is there, on the granite countertop. She unzips it. When a brief mining expedition fails to produce her manicure kit, she inverts the purse, dumping its contents. Amid the tumbling detritus is a red, leather case. She grabs it, extracts its tiny scissors, and gnaws a hole in the envelope. She then tears a wide slit, fishes inside, and pulls out two tickets.

Ah. Rose nods. The annual gala at the nearby Sylvan Hotel, a charity event in support of conserving heritage homes in Vancouver. A worthwhile event. So many heritage homes in Vancouver were being demolished upon purchase. Rose had done her best to ensure that her mother's house went to a family who planned to live in it. Her mother, Violet Harrington, had always supported this charity event; she must have ordered these tickets.

Rose can't recall when her mother last attended the gala. Three years ago? That would have been just before Margo disappeared. Rose lets out a sigh. She herself was traveling in Europe then. Or was it Asia? The itinerary is blurred, but the timing is accurate. Yes, her mother's last attendance at the gala occurred just before Margo disappeared. But why would her mother have ordered tickets this year? Perhaps, when her cancer went into remission she thought she would be well enough to attend.

Rose flits through memories but there are none of ordering gala tickets. And she would know, wouldn't she? After Margo's disappearance, Rose rented out her Beach Avenue condo and moved in with her mother. From that point on, she knew every decision that Violet Harrington made. Or thought she did. Obviously, she missed some things.

Rose checks the date on the tickets. April 30th. Saturday. Tomorrow. Why are these so late in arriving? Had her mother ordered them as a gift for her? Dare she attend this function? Rose's bags are already packed for a three-week trip, she is meeting former coworkers for lunch today, and she has nothing to wear to a black-tie event. She is about to rip up the tickets when it occurs to her that one of her lunch mates might want them. Shrugging, she returns the tickets to the FedEx envelope and tosses the packet onto the counter. If only Margo were here, the two of them could go off together. The thought is another invitation to sadness. At first Rose resists it, but then she lets it in.

She fingers the yin symbol on her silver neck chain. Margo wore the yang symbol. Rose and Margo, just a year apart in age, were the antithesis of, and complementary to, each other. Rose bore all the characteristics of her Saxon father: blond hair, blue eyes, tall, angular. Margo, although born with a shock of blond hair, grew into a brunette, like her Latin mother, brown-eyed and petite, with a round face. Rose, the elder, was rigid about rules and responsibility. Margo had no such compulsion; she lived to break rules. Rose was usually there to break Margo's fall but Rose was overseas when Margo disappeared. What had happened to Margo? Rose's vision blurs. Would the tears never stop?

She drags her sleeve across her face and begins sorting the contents of her purse, an effort to keep herself busy while waiting for Flynn. She makes a mental note: Put manicure kit into checked luggage. The last thing she wants is to provoke airport security. She groups everything into little piles and returns the piles to the purse, being careful to put the red case on top and the packet containing the gala tickets into a side pocket. When that job is done and there is still no sign of Flynn, she plods toward the stairs.

Rose stops at the foot of the staircase, overwhelmed by emptiness. Time had whipped through the house like a brisk wind, slamming doors and erasing years. How can she start over? How can she go on without her mother? Without ever knowing what became of her sister?

Leaning on the newel post, Rose scans the hallway, one end to the other. Memories are vivid, close. She smiles, visualizing herself and Margo, ages five and four, barrelling down this yellow-oak hallway when Mommy called them to the front door. Mommy gave each of them a huge, soggy Valentine's Day card that had been left on the stoop in the rain. Their names were barely legible on the cards, but the two girls giggled with delight and put the valentines on the radiator to dry. While they waited, they created their own valentines. Big, construction paper hearts, decorated with bits of pink ribbon and white lace from Mommy's sewing box. Rose and Margo made red ones for each other and, together, they made a purple one for their mother because Mommy's name was Violet.

Would that she could pause, rewind, spend time with Margo. Rose turns around, half-expecting to see Margo running toward her. "Like summer camp," Rose whispers.

Years ago in summer camp, Rose and Margo participated in an eight-hundred-meter race, a race Rose could have won. But Rose stopped dead, just before the finish line. She stopped dead, turned, and went back to get her little sister. Hand in hand, they crossed the finish line together.

Rose wipes the corners of her eyes with the back of her hand. What will she do with her memories? What good are memories if there is no one to share them with? Not a single blood relative left on the planet. No one to witness her life. She is completely alone, a single woman by choice. Always so independent. And now? Sometimes she has the sensation that her very soul is evaporating, dissipating like bubbles in tepid bathwater.

Rose clutches the banister as she climbs the stairs. At the top, she pauses and then heads into her mother's room which is almost bereft of furniture. The only thing in the room—in the house, in fact—is a mirrored, mahogany dresser, her mother's treasure. Rose walks across the hardwood floor, her steps resonating to the nine-foot ceiling. She sucks in a deep breath. With that comes a whiff of lavender. Mother's scent, daughter's oxygen. Again the tears well. She raises a hand to wipe them, catches her image in the mirror, and winces. Her fine features are pinched, her blue eyes wounded, her blond hair tangled. Twenty-eight, going on fifty. "Stress will do that to you," she mutters as she amends the fact that her blouse is buttoned incorrectly.

It has been three months since Rose buried her forty-nine-year-old mother. Violet Harrington fought the cancer, even went into remission. It was sudden, her giving up hope, conceding defeat. "Forgive me, Rose, but I can't—" she had said and, without rattle or tremor, just slipped away.

Rose coped with funeral arrangements and estate sales and open houses. Her mother's home sold within five days, forcing Rose into overdrive. She was grateful that the lease on her condo had run its course and the tenants had moved on as this allowed her to reclaim her small space. She had worked non-stop since the funeral, sorting and selling her mother's belongings and preparing the property for the new owners. The mahogany dresser was the only piece of furniture that Rose did not want to part with. Actually, it was the only piece of furniture that her mother asked her to keep. Thank goodness Flynn stepped up, volunteering to move the monstrosity to her condo. Rose glances at her watch. Where the heck is Flynn, anyway?

Five

I STAND ON THE sidewalk, squinting at the SOLD letters splashed across the realtor's sign on the Harrington lawn. Violet Harrington's ash-gray heritage home looms in the background. I rub my forehead, an attempt to banish clutching pain. The headache is self-induced, a nagging reminder of past inadequacy. Maybe I should have popped that Tylenol earlier when I had the inkling. And maybe I should just focus on my purpose today, which is to help Rose, not to chastise myself for my failure to help both Rose and her mother on another day, three years ago. An eternity ago when, despite a lifelong fascination with problem-solving, five years as a private investigator, and many months of effort, I could not find a trace of Margo Harrington.

It, meaning everything, suddenly seems futile. I am thirty-eight years old, separated, and struggling to keep a small PI agency in the black. I drop my gaze to the sidewalk and kick a stone at the SOLD sign. It misses its mark. Typical. *Damn.* I shake my head. Might as well get on with it. This will be my last visit to this house. Still reluctant, I take one final look around.

The street is fairly quiet, cars parked parallel along the sidewalks on both sides. All luxury sedans, each one being a second or third car for most families, I'm sure. A FedEx truck sits in front of the neighbor's house a couple of doors down. Delivering more stuff to an already overstuffed neighborhood.

As I slog my way up the rain-spattered walk, I recall the first visit, the first meeting with Violet Harrington.

The rain teemed that day, plastering my normally springy curls to my head and sending rivulets of water down my neck. At the sight of me, a drowned rat in her doorway, Violet pushed her own problems aside and attended to mine, supplying me with a thick towel. I dabbed the drops from my face, dried my hair, left my soggy shoes on the mat, and trailed her to the kitchen. We sat facing each other, silence hanging between us. A silence that was hers to break.

While I waited, I sensed rather than scrutinized my surroundings—the warm white of the cabinets, the polished sheen of the subway-tile backsplash, and the golden tones of the oak floors—none of which did anything to dispel the cloud of melancholy that surrounded the house. A heritage home, a luxury home. An illusion of happiness. All houses are illusions when it comes to happiness. Or safety. No house can—

"My daughter is gone." Violet Harrington said, her voice barely audible over the hum of air from the heating vents and the drum of rain on the window. "Only twenty-four and she's vanished from the face of the earth. The police . . ." She shrugged. "They've come up empty and I want my Margo back." She leaned in, her eyes drilling mine. "You must find her."

"The Vancouver Police Department does excellent work," I said. "I certainly don't have their resources. I wouldn't want you to think I could—"

She raised a hand, palm toward me. "I know these things. But the police, they work on many cases at one time. And, as I said, they have come up empty. I can't give up. I contacted the Private Investigators Association of British Columbia and they gave me your name. Now Margo is five-foot two . . ." She blinked. "Where's your notebook?"

"Right here." I produced it and a pen from my inside coat pocket.

She nodded, a brisk nod.

I sat up straighter.

"Margo is five-foot-two, one hundred pounds, with black hair, brown eyes, a pixie body, and a pixie hairstyle."

Cute, not pretty, I figured. Probably always be cute regardless of the passage of time.

"Margo just did not come home," said Violet, her eyes glazing over. "I'm a widow, Mr. Flynn. My husband died when the girls were toddlers. Margo, at twenty-four, still lived here with me. Isn't that the norm for young adults nowadays, to live with their parents?" Her tone wavered. She paused.

I offered no response. The question was rhetorical.

"But she didn't come home," Violet said. "She didn't come home."

Silence revisited. Head down, pen scribbling, I waited. When the gap stretched like elastic, I looked up to see her dissolving in front of me. I ripped a couple of Kleenex from the flowered box on the kitchen table and handed them to her. "Take your time. There's no hurry."

Violet nodded. After sniffling and wiping and blowing, she continued. "My two girls—Margo and Rose—did not want to leave me completely alone. Yes, Rose moved out, into a condo on Beach Avenue, an investment of mine actually, but she checked in daily, visited at least three times a week, and kept Margo in line. So independent, my Rose, wanting to visit all the places she read about. She traveled as much as she could.

"When Margo disappeared, Rose flew back from Europe. She was in Italy, I believe." Lines formed on Violet's forehead as she puzzled over the details.

Permanently imprinted on my brain is the image of Violet Harrington in that freeze-frame instant—the crepe-paper brow, the trembling lip, the quivering fingers poking at disobedient strands of salt-and-pepper hair. I guessed her age as sixty then. Later, I uncovered the fact that she was only forty-six. But shock does that, adds years.

Every now and then I pull out the tattered notebook from that day and re-read the details of our meeting. Yes, I transferred the data into a computer file, readily accessible on my iPhone, but I didn't part with that notebook. I like pen and ink. The specifics stay where I put them, concrete, visual. I have never taken to the idea of information drifting like clouds in cyberspace.

I remember watching her reach for her neck like she was about to grab a necklace. "My chain," she said when I asked. "The yin-and-yang medallion. I must've left it upstairs." She stood. "Do you mind? I must get it—something to hold onto, you know?"

I updated my notebook while she was out of the room.

When she returned, I tried to reassure her. "There can be no promises. Details tend to get fuzzy as time passes. Some witnesses disappear and those who remain often embellish details. No promises. But I will do my best."

As always, even in the most uncomfortable situations, there came the necessary contract for services. I sped through this part and left the house to visit the police department.

It was afternoon when I returned to the Harrington house and the driving rain had retreated to a drizzle. It was Rose who answered the door, pulling it wide and standing there, hands on hips. "I'm Rose Harrington," she said, "and I assume that you are Shaughnessy Flynn."

Without saying a word, I fished for my ID card.

She waved it away. "Mother already told me that the appearance and the name don't mesh. I don't need the ID."

I nodded. "Call me Flynn." Darn it all, I recognized her. Somehow I managed to keep a poker face. Did she remember me? I wondered how long it would take for the penny to drop. How stupid was I that I hadn't made the connection between the Rose I had met years before and the Rose Harrington in the family photos?

This Rose Harrington was all business. If she recalled our past, she didn't show it.

I extended my hand.

She ignored it. "How long have you been doing this kind of work?"

"About five years."

"What have you found out about my sister?"

I pulled out my notebook. "Any possibility of my coming in?" I pointed a finger toward the hallway.

Rose stepped aside, grabbed the door handle, and waved me in.

I wiped my feet on the welcome mat. As I crossed the threshold, I slipped into investigator mode, reciting the details of Margo's disappearance.

"I could have told you that," said Rose. "Anything new?"

I blew out a sigh. I needed cooperation, not a wall. If I was going to get anywhere in helping this family, I had to create a pathway. "You don't remember me, do you?"

Rose blinked. "Flynn." She squinted her eyes as if searching. "Flynn," she said again. "I never met anybody named Flynn."

"Probably because I was using my middle name at the time. Sanjay."

Her dark expression rolled away like the stone door to the cave of Ali Baba. "I most certainly do remember you." She wagged a finger in my face. "You asked me out." Her eyes widened. "Weren't you engaged at the time?"

My face felt impossibly hot. My being engaged at the time was only the half of it. The other half? My fiancée Amelia and I were the parents of a four-year-old son. I considered, then vetoed the idea of sharing the latter detail with Rose. Maybe later. Not now. "Yes, I was engaged. That's why I canceled the date . . . eventually."

"Eventually is right. You strung me along for a week." Her eyes were fire, her voice strident. "Why in the name of heaven should I trust you, a liar and a cheat?"

"A liar, possibly. No cheating occurred. I apologized to you. I confessed to my fiancée."

"What happened to her, your fiancée?"

"Married her."

"Oh." Instantly the fire in her eyes vanished, replaced by tears which rimmed, threatened. "How are you going to help my mother and me? How are you going to find Margo?" Her voice broke. The tears flowed.

"Let's go to the kitchen," I said quietly.

My instinct was to take her arm, to guide her down the hall, but men are like that, always trying to fix things, to lead. I subdued the urge. I trailed her into the kitchen. I sat opposite her like I had with her mother earlier that day.

I couldn't help staring, comparing. Just as in our first meeting, I was struck by Rose's fine features, her blond hair, the style of which had changed. She still wore it long, but the cut was layered now, not blunt. A natural beauty, Rose, lean like a sapling, graceful as a trumpet flower. Similar to my Amelia in many ways. And maybe therein lay the attraction. I cautioned myself, putting a halt to admiring thoughts which had nearly led me astray before. It had been a long time since I lied to Rose. My mistake. I owed her.

"I want to help you, Rose. Your mother hired me, but I will tear up that contract and do this for nothing. I just want to help."

After months of investigation, all I knew was that Margo had rented a car, a Toyota, which had been abandoned on the Lion's Gate Bridge, door unlocked, no evidence of foul play. The car was immaculate, not even a fingerprint. Would a rental company have been that fastidious about cleaning vehicles before renting them to customers? I doubted it, checked it, and discovered that I was right. Someone had gone to great pains to ensure that no fingerprints were left in the car. So there was no spoor, no evidence, no witness. And no body.

Margo had last been seen by her mother three days before the car turned up. She had been smiling, happy, her usual self. No signs of depression or suicidal tendencies. She had promised her mother she would return later that evening. Going shopping, she had said. Pacific Plaza. But, if Margo had been in Pacific Plaza that day, there was no proof of it. Every security camera had been checked. Even the street cameras outside Sears and around Robson Square. Not a sign.

The roar of a vehicle brings me back to the present. I press the Harrington doorbell and Westminster Chimes ring out. A flurry of footsteps comes from within, growing louder and halting at the door. Rose must have paused to look through the eyehole. Good. Often, I have chided her about flinging the door wide without checking—

"About time you got here." She grins.

I respond with a fake salute. "At your service, madam." I use a hitchhiker motion to point behind me. "The guys are on their way. They're bringing their own vehicles because they're going straight from your condo to work. One of them has a truck, perfect for this job." I raise my other hand, displaying a bag of mini Mars bars. "For you."

Rose grabs the candy. "Thanks. Come on in. Sorry I can't offer coffee or anything. The place is barren."

"Yeah, I can see that." My voice echoes in affirmation.

"You want a Mars bar?" She waves the bag.

I point at my watch. "At this time in the morning? No sugar for me, thanks."

Rose shrugs. "Good enough." We walk to the kitchen and she tosses the candy onto the counter beside her purse. "I will be glad to have this over with. Selling, I mean. I can't believe I'm leaving today, never to return."

"That's got to be tough."

"Yes. But I have to move on." She leans on the counter and stares past me, a faraway look in her eyes. "There was a time when I thought I was going to explode or implode. Neither happened. But erode? Different entirely. I feel like, piece by piece, I'm being washed away. I have to find my center, my core, before I disappear entirely."

"Answers will come. Just give it time."

"Mom says, I mean, used to say, 'All the answers you seek are inside you.'" She sighs.

A reverent silence hangs between us as we climb the stairs to the master bedroom. For some strange reason, upon nearing the dresser, I latch onto a childhood memory, that of approaching a church altar. The analogy baffles me. If there is a spiritual connection here, it is Rose's, not mine. One look at her tells me I'm right.

Her face wistful, she stares with devotion at the oversized mahogany masterpiece. "My mother adored this dresser. Have to admit that I do, too." Her voice is soft, ghostly, like it is coming from a distant place. She slides open a tiny drawer on the right side of the dresser, one lined with royal-blue velvet and divided into square slots for jewelry. She picks up the one remaining piece of jewelry—a black-and-white yin-and-yang medallion on a silver chain. She curls the fingers of one hand around it and, with her free hand, toys with her own neck chain which holds only the yin symbol, a white symbol with a black dot. I know Rose is remembering her sister Margo and the yang symbol that vanished with Margo.

I wonder if Rose is hanging onto hope. Dare I ask? It can be cancerous, hope. I know that all too well. But the choice to hope is hers. I remain hushed.

Rose blows out a long, low breath. "My condo is too small for this dresser, isn't it?" She tucks her mother's necklace into the pocket of her blue jeans.

"It's not going to be easy getting it down that narrow hallway of yours but we'll manage it." I touch her shoulder. "Look at me, Rose."

She obliges.

"I'm here if you need me."

She steps back, slides away from my touch. "Don't be too kind to me today, Flynn. I'm trying to hold what's left of myself together."

I instantly pull back. "Got it. Back to the task at hand. You could get rid of that black, lacquered armoire at your condo and replace it with this mahogany masterpiece. The guys and I can handle both, this morning in fact."

"I like that lacquered piece," she says hesitantly. "I bought it after my trip to China."

"No room for the two of them." I look around. "Maybe you should have stayed in this place. Lots of room here. Safer area, too. Why you would choose to live in that condo is beyond me. Walking around downtown at night . . ." I shake my head. "The whole area is made up of people looking for trouble and people looking to avoid it. Predators and prey."

"The whole world is comprised of predators and prey." Her voice is low but her words are steel. "Besides, this place is too big for one person and need I point out that it's already sold? How many times have we had this conversation, Flynn? In fact, I had the same conversation with my mother many times. She wanted me to live at home, just like Margo. Then, Margo disappeared . . ." Rose's solid tone fades away. She sucks in a deep breath and turns toward me, a sudden goofy twinkle in her eyes. "What do you want me to do? Spend my life taking self-defense classes and shooting lessons?"

I provide the required grin. "I have to admit that my buddy on the VPD was amazed when I brought a high school English teacher to the gun range."

"Yeah. Well, as soon as things settle down, I'm going back for more lessons, not that I ever expect to use the skill. As for the teacher thing—"

"What about it?"

"It was nice while it lasted."

"What's that supposed to mean?"

"It was a temporary contract, remember? The third one in as many years. I was replacing someone on maternity leave. The leave ended. The teacher came back. Simple as that. Apparently, there is nothing on the horizon for English teachers. The board said something about more money going into science, less to Shakespeare and his cronies."

"They did not say that."

"No, not verbatim."

"What are you going to do?"

"Day after tomorrow, I'm leaving."

I raise my eyebrows.

"Oh, don't worry, I'll be back. A vacation, that's all. I'm going to Hawaii for a week and to Europe for two. When I get back, I'll worry about a job."

"Hmmm." I press my lips together. "Taking off on your own again?"

"I'm quite accustomed to traveling alone, to dining alone, to shopping alone, to attending movies alone, to—"

"I get it." I throw my hands in the air. "But, for Pete's sake, make sure you Skype or something."

"I need to go off the grid, Flynn. I'm leaving the tablet and the laptop at home."

"You're taking your cell phone, aren't you? Have you forgotten how to call? Text? I may need to reach you. What if—?" I drop my voice to a hoarse whisper. "I will never stop looking for Margo."

Rose chokes out a thank you and dabs at her eyes.

My attempt to speak is interrupted by the doorbell. I switch gears and run from the room. "That'll be the guys," I call on my way down the stairs.

Rose listens to the myriad of let's-get-this-show-on-the-road greetings. She steps toward the dresser and opens the top drawer. There it is again. The scent of lavender. It floats up, a miasma, clouding around her, bringing with it her mother's worrying voice. "Are you sure about all this traveling, dear?" her mother had asked, even months before Margo had gone missing. "Can't you find happiness here in Vancouver?" Rose's mother had reached out her hand and tucked in a stray tendril of Rose's hair.

"I'm a grown woman, Mom. I want to see the world, to determine my place in the world."

"I understand," said her mother. "But, no matter how far you go, the answers you seek are here, Rose." She placed a gentle hand above Rose's heart. "Just be mindful. Listen to your inner voice. When it's time to make a decision about the next piece of your life, whatever that is, you will know it. We all meander. Sometimes we land in a dark place, in a desperate place. If that happens, sit still. Be calm. Wait for clarity. It's a freeze-frame moment, clarity. You will know when it arrives."

"You've got to stop watching *Criminal Minds*, Mom," she had said, amused.

Rose cringes. Not funny now. Not funny at all.

Footsteps on the stairs, an army of them, trigger Rose to turn toward the door. Flynn enters, followed by three other men. A rush of musk and testosterone infiltrates, erasing all traces of lavender and sparking something inside of Rose, something that for the longest time she thought was dormant. Until yesterday anyway, when she met Vincent. Rose is definitely in need of sex and Flynn has some pretty sexy friends. But she isn't interested in them. Maybe Vincent will call and then . . . Heat creeps into her cheeks. Her mother would not approve. Sorry, Mom. She slams the dresser drawer. "Hi, guys. Thanks for coming."

Six

I SIT AT THE mid-century teak table in Rose's dining area, an iced latte in hand, watching as she guts both fridge and cabinets in her galley kitchen. I'm comfortable as an onlooker, a good thing since any offer of assistance would be rejected. I'd be no help with the top shelves anyway. I'm five-and-a-half feet tall, a good three inches shorter than Rose. Not nearly as flexible either, but then she has competitive gymnastics on her list of college accomplishments. Me? I joined the chess club. I have myself convinced that someday, somehow, my ability to forecast chessboard moves will come in handy for my PI work. Yep, mental agility is my thing but an exercise class now and then wouldn't hurt. Don't I already have a gym membership? Am pretty sure there's a card in my wallet. Have I ever used it? Perhaps—

A commotion from the kitchen grabs my attention. "Jesus, Rose." I jump from my chair. "Is that really necessary?"

Rose is standing on the kitchen counter, balancing on her toes, peering over the lip at the top of the cupboard.

"Just checking for dust bunnies." She drops to her hands and slips to the floor. "Still have a few things to get out of the fridge."

I blink at the ease with which she descended. The woman would be great at parkour. I shrug away my concern for her safety. Not needed. Reclaiming my chair, I turn my attention to the view.

There is no substitute for being in Rose's condo on a sunny day, staring through wall-to-wall windows at shimmering English Bay. It is blindingly bright. There is not an ounce of shade in the place, with the exception of the windowless bathroom, but the whole point of living on Beach Avenue is the view, isn't it? The condo is small—eight hundred square feet, one bedroom, one bathroom—the walls are bland ivory, but the view? Location, location, location. I can see nothing but dollar signs in Rose's future. I clench my jaw, thinking about my laneway house and my shabby PI office in East Vancouver. I wish I'd had the smarts that Rose's mother had had, investing in a condo like this. Rose, regardless of her recent job loss, will have no problem with upkeep and taxes. Her mother's death devastated her, but the sale of the family home? Rose is set for life. I simultaneously put down my latte and set aside my envy. You make your choices and you take the consequences. With a divorce pending, I'm not about to move anytime soon. Besides, I like my tiny house. It helps keep my world contained. And, when I do have to move? The darn thing is on wheels. I'll just take it with me. I tap my fingers on the table. Still, what I'd give for all this sun.

"Losing patience?" Rose emerges from the kitchen. Her yellow rubber gloves have a spring-green band at the elbow, a band splashed with Shasta daisies and red butterflies. Even her rubber gloves are all about sunshine.

"Would you like me to move in here while you're gone?" I give her my best smile. "Keep an eye on the place?"

Rose peels off one glove, reaches into her back pocket and tosses a key. "That's my extra one. I would certainly like you to check up on the place. Live here, don't live here." She shrugs. "It's up to you."

I pocket the key. "I will check in a few times. Not likely to move in as it's too far from my office. But a man can dream."

Rose glances toward the window, the beach, the ocean. She lets out a long sigh. "It is beautiful."

"No doubt about that. Don't forget your Mars bars." I point at the package of candy sitting on the table. Rose grabs the package, returns to the kitchen, and chucks the candy into the fridge.

"You always do that?" I ask.

"Do what?"

"Store candy in the fridge?"

"Most certainly do. For chocolate, anyway. It's too soon to put that bag into my suitcase; I can live without melted goo all over everything. And"—she grabs her condo key from her purse and whips open the fridge door a second time—"just so I don't forget to take them with me on my trip, I'm going to do this." She puts the key on top of the candy. "I never leave the condo without locking the door and in order to do that, I'll have to get my key from the fridge. Then I'll remember the candy."

"Impressive," I say, nodding my head.

Silence steps in, nothing but the muted sound of traffic from the street below.

The purpose of the visit is complete, the conversation's done, and it's time for me to go. So why is my body welded to the chair? Is something pending? If so, what? Unable to name or explain my discomfort, I dismiss it. "Well, the lacquered armoire is gone and the mahogany dresser has reached its destination—your bedroom—and I have reached my limit. Time wise, I mean." I stand and make a display of stretching. "Gotta go."

"Please thank your friend Lee again for me. I really appreciate his taking the black armoire off my hands."

"No worries. He has lots of lacquered furniture. It was love at first sight for him." I amble to the door and point at her luggage—two bags, patiently waiting in the foyer. "You are probably the most organized person I know." As I shrug on my jacket, it crosses my mind that she is the most independent, too. She is always so independent. So single. So locked into the concept that she can do it all by herself. Career. Travel. No man needed. She may have appreciated Lee taking the lacquered armoire, but she sure as heck would not have asked. Stubborn woman.

Independence is something I respect, to a point. But, because of my impotence in locating her sister, I hover like a helicopter parent where

Rose is concerned. More than that, I promised Violet that I would do just that, hang around, protect Rose if she'd let me. I can't contain greased lightning. But a promise is a promise . . .

"Rose—"

"Here you go." She holds out an envelope.

"What's this?"

"Travel details. Flight numbers, arrival and departure times, hotels. The whole nine yards. Don't tell me you weren't going to ask."

I grab the envelope, quick. Too quick.

"Don't worry, I won't change my mind," Rose says, "but I'll have you know, the only reason I'm doing this is for Mom. She made me promise to . . ."

"To what? Let me keep an eye on you?"

Rose nods. "She made you promise too, didn't she?"

"To watch out for you? Yes. And while we're on the topic, you'll call or text me as soon as you get to Hawaii?"

Rose nods and then takes a deep breath. From the coin pocket of her jeans, she produces her mother's necklace, which she holds high. The yin-and-yang medallion dangles, sparkling as it spins in the sunlight. "Mom knew you did your best," she says, a soft urgency in her voice. With care, she removes the medallion from its silver chain and returns the chain to her pocket. She takes my hand, places the medallion in the center of my palm, and curls my fingers around it. "Mom wanted you to have this."

I picture Violet, fingers white as she gripped the medallion that is now burning into my palm. I shake my head.

"It's Mom's way of thanking you. She knew you did your best in trying to find Margo. No one can ask anything more." Rose locks her gaze with mine. Her eyes are clear, blue as the sea, devoid of blame.

I appreciate her kindness, but, nonetheless, blame abides. I'm good at blame, blaming myself for not finding Margo, blaming my wife for not—

Rose wraps her hand firmly around my fist. "Please keep this."

"This was Violet's symbol of hope. I can't—"

"You can and you will." Rose releases my hand. She takes a step back.

I open my fingers and gaze at the black-and-white symbol.

"You need to let go of blame, Flynn. Things happen. People make choices." Rose pauses.

I raise my eyes to hers.

"Accidents occur," she whispers. "It's nobody's fault."

I flinch. *Accidents occur.* Suddenly this is about my wife? Damn straight it is. Rose is reading my mind, telling me to forgive my wife. The chances of that are slim to none. I shove the medallion into my shirt pocket and clench my jaw to keep from spewing venom.

Rose moves on. "Look at the time," she says, her voice liquid and light. "I'm going to the Lotus Club for lunch. Meeting friends at one o'clock."

"Friends?" I say. A single word can hold a shitload of venom. I could kick myself when I see the pained look on her face.

Rose parts her lips. I brace myself for a clever comeback. There is none, only a sigh. Rose appears flummoxed as she retrieves her condo key from the fridge. She stands there, staring at her purse, key clasped in her hand.

Should I apologize for my gaffe? Rose meant no harm in her comments about blame and she has made no secret about her lack of friends. As I open the door, it occurs to me that Rose doesn't have friends on social media either. Hard to have friends when you don't participate. Relenting, I turn to her. "I'm sorry, Rose. Sorry about that remark. Thoughtless of me."

"No worries," she says, smiling.

"Have a wonderful trip," I say as I exit the condo. The elevator opens as soon as I press the button. Outside, with smog and smell of city traffic closing in, I peel off my jacket.

I sit in my parked car, windows down, sucking in sea air, sinking in self-criticism. Not much of a PI. Couldn't find Margo. Not much of a husband. Can't forgive my wife.

I pull Violet's yin-and-yang symbol from my pocket and stare at it, all the while picturing the withered and grief-stricken Violet. Somehow I feel the need to talk to her, to comfort her. "I haven't given up, Violet. I will never give up on Margo." The words ring true. I clasp my hand around the medallion. This symbol gave Violet Harrington something to hold onto. She chose to leave it to me. And I will hold onto it, too. For Violet. I fish for my key ring and attach the medallion to it. A safe place.

It's time for me to tackle the next segment of whatever mountain I am facing in my search for Margo Harrington. Inch by inch, step-by-step, that's how you conquer mountains. Determined, I plug my car key into the ignition. The engine turns over at the first turn of the key. A good sign.

Shifting into DRIVE, I head for my office and my files.

Seven

ROSE SHOWERS AND CHANGES, choosing a flowing, red linen midi skirt topped with a snowy-white boyfriend shirt. She knots her hair into a chignon, leaving a few strands dangling. She tries on, then discards, her gray gladiator heels. Espadrilles are better for walking. Rose is grateful that the restaurant is just a few blocks away. She can leave her car where it belongs, in the underground parking lot. Driving is not her favorite thing and direction is not her forte. Rose is haunted by the few times she has "misplaced" her car and wandered aimlessly through parking lots, searching. Is she the only woman on the planet who can get lost in a cul-de-sac? Does it really matter? Somehow she always manages to get back on track.

Rose grabs her Prada purse and is good to go. Now where are her keys? Oh, yes. She returned them to the fridge after Flynn's departure.

Outside, a few steps from the door of her building, Rose pauses to take in the ocean view. English Bay is silver under the scrutiny of the sun. A few clouds, cotton balls at best, dot the sky. There is the usual assortment of rusted freighters on the horizon and the expected blur of powerboats in the harbor. A couple of brave souls, clad head to toe in neoprene, are testing their skills at sail boarding. All of this occurs under the watchful eyes of seabirds. Onshore, there are mothers doting and kids digging, patting sand into plastic pails. Laughter and sunshine overwhelm the place. The *brring!* of a bicycle bell turns her attention to the bike path where a bicyclist almost clips a pedestrian who yelps like a startled puppy. Rose winces. That was close, too close. How easy it is for things to go wrong when one isn't paying attention. She refocuses, heading in the direction of the Lotus Club.

When Rose arrives, the hostess escorts her through the bustle and clatter of the restaurant and onto the patio. Delighted, Rose follows along. She much prefers the patio, which practically sits on the beach. A few steps and one can walk barefoot through the sand.

"Rose! So glad you could make it!" Marlene, a vision of office perfection in her gray pencil-skirted suit and black stilettos, rushes forward in greeting. How on earth does that woman achieve such impeccably platinum hair? A superb manager, Marlene, both at the school office and in life, it seems.

Rose supplies the required hug and sits in the chair earmarked for her. Instantly, she looks for the server. Wine is needed here. "Chardonnay, unoaked, please," she says to the young woman who appears beside her. Rose eyes the wine glasses in front of her companions. "Nine-ounce glass, please." She refrains from telling the server to hurry, but she must've intimated it in some way. The hellos are barely out of the way when the wine glass is placed in front of her. After a few sips, Rose calms down, eases in. The social world rattles her, but these are good people. Besides, before she knows it, this visit will be over and these people will be gone, just like everyone else. That is the way of things, isn't it? Her sigh is elongated, but inaudible. There is no need for her to deposit her discomfort on the shoulders of others. She attunes her ear to the conversation.

"And what's next for you, Rose? Do you have another teaching job lined up?" The stentorian voice belongs to Katie, a moon-faced woman around Rose's age, who is glowing in a way that only expectant mothers do.

"No, not yet," says Rose. "Your baby must be due any day now," she adds in a deliberate attempt to redirect the conversation. "You must be very excited."

The maneuver works. What follows is a lengthy conversation about the trials and tribulations of motherhood. Rose smiles, supplying the requisite nods and comments. It is office manager Marlene who suggests they examine the menus. Grateful, Rose complies. She has already decided on a short rib sandwich but, by faking indecision, she can stay safely inside her own head. All the while, she watches the interactions at the table.

In addition to Marlene and Katie, there are two others, both English teachers on permanent contract at the high school which had just terminated her. Jason is a lanky, self-professed member of the literati, whose thick-lensed, horn-rimmed glasses always put Rose in mind of Mr. Magoo. Right now, Jason is fingering his bow tie and bemoaning his fate. "It puzzles me to no end," he says in a chirpy voice, "that I, a meticulous young man, surrendered my heart and soul to a slovenly older one. I do fear that my husband is rapidly becoming the definitive Oscar Madison."

"As long as you love him, I suppose," says Jade, a petite young woman with flawless caramel skin and a decided talent for poking the bear. She flicks back her waist-length black hair.

"No doubt about that," says Jason, "but he seems to be of the opinion that dirty clothes have a second incarnation. He uses them as a doormat. I've actually seen him wipe his shoes on a discarded shirt. Can you imagine?"

"Maybe he expects you to pick up after him," says Jade, her brown eyes twinkling.

"No," says Jason. "I'm quite positive he believes dirty clothes just levitate to the laundry basket."

"Maybe you're just an enabler," Jade adds.

"And maybe you're just an instigator." Jason is never to be outdone when it comes to vocal sparring, but his voice is light and he dismisses Jade with a wave of his hand.

Jade's laugh is musical, like the rise and fall of an arpeggio. She turns to Rose. "Didn't you say you are going on a trip as soon as you finish your contract?"

Rose detects something different about Jade's impish east-to-west grin. "Ah, I see you've had your braces removed."

"Is it that obvious? I can't stop smiling. But . . . your trip?"

"First Hawaii, for one week. Then Europe for two. The tickets are bought and I leave Sunday morning." The mention of tickets tweaks Rose's memory. "Oh yes," she says, reaching for her purse, "I have two tickets for the Heritage Gala tomorrow night at the Sylvan Hotel. A black tie event in aid of preserving heritage buildings. I'm really busy getting ready for my trip and I wondered if any of you would like to attend." She fishes out the tickets and fans them on the table.

"Nice thought, but I'm out," says Katie, patting her ballooning stomach. "At this stage in the game, I need to be home in the evenings and close to the washroom at all times."

Rose looks to Jason.

Jason raises both hands, palms out. "There's not a chance that I would get that husband of mine into a black tie. Thanks, but no."

"I can't attend either, but it is such a good cause," says Marlene. "Can't you possibly take time to go, Rose?"

"Not a thing to wear," says Rose.

"Go shopping," says Jade. "You can zip over to Pacific Plaza today. I'm sure you'll find the perfect thing in no time."

"There's an idea. Maybe I will."

The server is there now, ready to take the orders. While waiting, Rose considers the situation. She could buy a dress. Expensive, yes, and she has spent so much on her trip. It will be a while before her mother's estate is settled. Maybe she could get a dress, keep the tags on it, and return it the next day. Like Margo would have done. Rose grins to herself. That would definitely have been the modus operandi of her younger sister. Rose looks up, half-expecting Margo to chime in but, with a pang, Rose banishes her smile. Margo is gone. Three years. Not a trace. Rose feels suddenly broken, incomplete.

"And what can I get for you, miss?" the server asks, nudging Rose back to reality.

"A short rib sandwich, please," says Rose, as she retrieves her tickets and stuffs them into the FedEx envelope in her purse. "And a second glass of wine."

"Not driving then?" says Jade, eyebrows raised. Always the vigilante, Jade.

Rose is ready for her. "When I say yes to the wine, I say no to the wheel. I walked."

Jade nods her approval and delves into a story about one of her senior students who had gotten himself into a vehicle accident a few days ago. "Not just drinking and driving, but drinking and texting and driving. He came out of it with a broken arm; I told him he's lucky. A cautionary tale, there."

Rose has heard this particular cautionary tale before. So has everyone else. That's what happens when you sit with the same people at lunch day after day. A story sparks, shimmers, and then smolders. Perhaps to fill a void in the conversation or a need within themselves, someone at the table pokes the ashes and the story fires up again, and again and again until it is the auditory equivalent of mold on bread. Today, Rose's companions are patient, polite, nodding at every last detail of the tired and trite. The topic slides away as luncheon plates slide onto the table.

It is a workday, a professional day, for Rose's companions. A short lunch, that's all they have time for. As Rose bids them farewell and accepts their good wishes, she decides to walk in the sunshine to the shopping center. Near the entrance, a horn honks on the street beside her, startling her. She turns. Marlene sails by, smiling, giving her the thumbs up.

Rose waves and enters the mall.

Eight

IN FRONT OF A full-length mirror in a boutique dressing room, Rose models a sleeveless, ebony maxi dress with a flirty front slit. A classic this, a wardrobe staple, whose uniform color and crew neckline make it ideal for everything from lounging to luxury. What accessories would this dress require? A statement necklace, perhaps, or even just her yin pendant with the silver chain. T-strap sandals or stiletto pumps? Definitely the latter with a dash of shoe jewelry. As for a purse? Obvious choice there. Her black clutch with the silver clasp.

As she twirls and examines the dress front and back, Rose becomes more and more enamored with the idea of making an appearance at the gala. What reason does she have to stay away? There is no job to keep her occupied. She has been declared redundant. There is no work for her at home. She has tied up the real estate strings and has finished her packing. And, if she doesn't attend the gala, how will she spend the night? Sitting in a dark room, indulging in a dark mood?

She brushes aside any thought of needing an escort for this potential outing. She doesn't mind going alone. She does everything alone. There is no one she can ask anyway, certainly not at this late date. She sighs as she thinks of one exception.

Flynn would be willing to serve as an escort. However, he would be watching, guarding, taking notes on every man who crossed her path. Over the last three years, he has become over-protective, like an older brother, one who can't help getting in the way. Kind of him, yes, but she needs space.

Three years of emotional parkour—hurdling barrage after barrage of shock, anguish, hope, despair, loss, grief—has left her drained, an empty vessel. She needs time to process, time to feed her physical needs, and time to play. The presence of Flynn would remind her of loss. She shakes her head. No Flynn. If she's going, she's going alone.

The Heritage Gala could signal a fresh start. Not only would she begin meeting her own needs, she would also be honoring the memory of her mother who fully supported this charity. And this dress? The fact that her libido leaped to life yesterday—at the Farmers Market of all places—made her realize she was interested. Maybe she would not hear from Vincent again but, should an opportunity arise, she would be prepared.

Rose stands, hands on hips, staring into the mirror at the determined glint in her own eyes. She's definitely buying this dress.

Saturday, April 30th

Nine

HEART THUDDING, ROSE LURCHES from sleep. What time is it? Why is it so cold? Touching her hand to her chest, she discovers that she has sweat through her pajamas. No wonder she's shivering. What made her perspire so much? A nightmare, perhaps? Unsettling, that thought. Tossing both it and the duvet, she sprints from bed, strips off her polyester pajamas, and shrugs on her terrycloth robe. As she deposits the pajamas into the bathroom hamper, she wonders if she should discard them entirely, perhaps replace them with wicking sleepwear. She's still chewing on the idea as she runs the shower.

All cares are forgotten when she steps under the warmth of the spray. No better way to ease into the morning than with the gentle caress of the newly-installed rainfall showerhead. A good investment, that. Her hair is dripping and plastered to her head before she remembers that there is no need to wash it. Today is spa and salon day. Massage, manicure, pedicure, shampoo, trim, and style, in that order. Laughing at her forgetfulness, she squeezes a globule of shampoo into her hand. Sometimes life dictates that you change the order of things. Shampoo now. Trim and style later.

It is a decidedly red day, as far as nail polish is concerned. She has a penchant for all shades of red, from blush to blood. Today's choice of color will be . . . what? She feels a smile crease her face. Red. Rose red. What could be more appropriate?

Rose's spa of choice covers an entire floor of the Sylvan Hotel, the same venue as this evening's Heritage Gala.

All seems well as she is about to enter the building, yet a spider of anxiety causes her to shiver. Is someone watching her? She looks around. No. No one. Just her. She continues through the door to the elevator and presses the call button.

As soon as the elevator reaches the designated floor, a soothing scent—eucalyptus—wafts in. Rose inhales deeply, then crosses the corridor to a frosted-glass door. It glides open; she steps in. There she pauses to take in her surroundings.

Natural light pours in through floor-to-ceiling windows, burbling water glistens in the featured water wall, and the tufted, buttery-leather couch in the waiting area is so inviting that Rose immediately aims for it. She exhales a contented sigh the second she sinks into it. Ease enfolds her. She has booked a session in the sauna, a soak in the mineral pool, and a stress-relieving massage—three hours in the stillness of this oasis.

Rose is humming as she changes into the spa's white robe and slippers and secures her belongings—cell phone included—in a locker. Cell phones are verboten here. Spas are about the soothing of souls, not the staccato of phones. This will be a stress-free morning topped off with lunch from the spa's own lifestyle cuisine—perhaps a Caesar salad with crispy chicken. She smiles as she heads for the sauna. There's beauty in the downtown life, she decides. Despite Flynn's concerns about safety, everything is so accessible.

After lunch, Rose strolls to the waterfront, to her hair appointment at Beauty Bee on Beach which is set in a crook on the seawall overlooking the marina and opposite Granville Island. For Rose, Beauty Bee is another highlight of living in this area. Customers come from both sides of

English Bay, traveling by bicycle, car, transit, or even sea bus. Stylists and clients always chat away. Rarely is there a void in conversation, never is there pressure to join in. Always, there is a glass of wine or a mug of coffee for patrons.

As Rose arrives at the salon, she spots a dark sedan parked nearby. She pauses, her hand on the door handle. The car pulls out and drives off. Is it a coincidence that as soon as she eyed it, the car left? Rose shrugs and heads into the salon.

Coiffed, coddled, and back at her condo, Rose stares at her reflection in the bathroom mirror. Should she walk to the gala? Not in stiletto heels. Should she drive? No. Her car is happily tucked away in the parking garage and will remain so until her return from Europe. What then? With a shrug, she settles on hailing a cab at the curb.

Rose whips open a drawer in her mother's mahogany dresser, a dresser which now contains all of Rose's things. The scent of her mother's perfume wafts. Rose shivers, grabs her sought-after hosiery, and closes the drawer tight. The scent lingers. As she dresses, Rose feels a fluttering in her stomach. Is there a message here? Is she missing something? Should she be going to the gala alone? Her mother was always so concerned about such things. Especially since Margo . . .

Rose thrusts disconcerting thoughts aside but can't banish the sudden queasiness she feels. Perhaps a light snack will offset her upset stomach. Covering her dress with a towel, she toasts a single slice of whole grain bread, thinly coats it with butter, and nibbles it while hovering over the kitchen sink. Feeling better, she brushes her teeth, discards the towel, and touches up her lipstick. She grabs her clutch and plops her cell phone into it. Is she forgetting anything?

Rose glances around. She smiles when she catches sight of the FedEx envelope she had tossed onto the dining room table earlier. Of course. The tickets. She removes one ticket from the envelope and deposits it into her purse. Shrugging, she tosses both the spare ticket and its FedEx packet into the recycle bin under the sink. She grabs her keys from their resting place on top of the Mars bars and then heads to the lobby of her building.

The air is warm, the breeze light, and the sky blushed in the dying rays of the sun. There is a flurry of activity, people scurrying to their evening events. Rose smiles. A typical Beach Avenue Saturday. She steps to the edge of the sidewalk and beckons an approaching taxi. It pulls over.

The taxi driver is a sixtysomething man who turns to her and smiles, tweed cap bobbing, false teeth dancing. "You be careful now," he says, for no reason that Rose can determine, as he drops her off and accepts her cash payment.

Entering the Sylvan, she veers left, produces the required admission ticket, and walks down the hall. At the door of the ballroom, she stands, wide-eyed, staring at the centerpiece that dominates the room—a fully-functional fountain made entirely from champagne glasses. Fascinated, Rose heads straight for it. In her effort to get a closer look, she bumps into someone. She pivots, apology at the ready, and ends up eye level with the satin lapels of a black velvet tuxedo. She raises her head, blinks, and nearly drops her clutch purse. "Vincent," she whispers.

As he takes her hand to kiss it, he subtly reaches his other arm around to the back of her dress. She shudders. A slight sensation of fingers near the zipper and the immediate realization of their purpose sends heat surging to her face. Dear God! Did she really forget to tuck in the price tags?

"A stunning dress, made more beautiful by the creature it enfolds." He releases her hand and steps back. "If you'll excuse me for a few minutes . . ." A slight bow, a radiant smile, and then he turns and walks away, blending into a sea of tuxedoes.

Mouth gaping, intent on escaping, Rose retraces her steps to the hallway. There she spots the powder room and dashes toward it. Once there, she gazes into the mirror at her scarlet face. How could she have been so stupid as to leave the price tag visible? Yes, she had intended to return the dress tomorrow as there would be enough time before her flight. This whole debacle was a feeble attempt to pay tribute to her sister, but she can't fathom how Margo ever managed to pull off things like this. And that man, that charming man, must think her an absolute moron. She turns her back to the mirror, swivels her head, and examines the area around the zipper. Yes, he had pushed the tag inside. There is nothing visible now but a sliver of plastic thread which she hides, checking and double-checking to ensure that nothing shows. She faces the mirror again, examining every nook and cranny of her face. The makeup is perfect, every strand of her upswept hair is behaving itself. She actually looks pretty good considering her assessment of that same face yesterday when she was at her mother's place. A definite switch from appalling to appealing.

Now what? Does she want to face that man again? Maybe she should just leave and have done with it. "Margo," she says aloud to the mirror, "this is all your fault. You would have done this, not I. I can't carry this stuff off."

"Sure you can."

Rose wheels around. A toilet flushes, a stall door swings open, and a silver-haired teapot of a woman emerges. Her attire is plain: black A-line skirt, white long-sleeved blouse, sensible black shoes. No adornments other than a nameless VOLUNTEER tag.

"Sure you can," the stranger repeats. "Whatever it is. Obviously, it's something you want to do, or you wouldn't be talking to the mirror. Who's Margo?"

"Margo is my sister." Present tense, Rose notices. She had almost said *was*, but, no, she said *is*. She couldn't contain her smile. Hope. She still has hope.

"And your name?"

"Rose. I'm Rose."

"Well, Rose, I'm Matilda." Matilda approaches the sink and makes eye contact with Rose in the mirror. "It's been my experience, darling, that the things we try to talk ourselves out of are the things we want the most. If you don't do it now, you'll regret it later. Whatever it is, give it a whirl. Never know where it may lead. That's a lovely dress, dear. Be a shame to waste it. Toodaloo!" With that, she spins on her heel and scurries through the door.

"Well, Margo," Rose asks the mirror, "you agree with Matilda, don't you?" *Damn.* She misses Margo. Together they would have laughed and strolled right back into the ballroom. Such a free spirit, Margo.

Rose nods. "Well, I'm here, Margo, so I might as well see this through." She takes another deep breath and does a slow exhale as she exits the powder room. She marches back into the ballroom and stands, eyes searching the crowd. When she catches sight of Vincent, her heart thrums. Rose starts toward him and then veers toward the bar.

The brawny bartender smiles at her as she approaches. "Who took the wind out of your sails?" He lowers his head and tugs at his cuffs. His biceps bulge beneath his crisp, white shirt.

Rose tilts her head. She catches herself picturing those biceps in a skin-tight, compression shirt. A gray one, maybe. "Am I that transparent?" She smiles as she searches his shirt for a nametag. Nothing but the generic VOLUNTEER tag.

"Like a pane of glass."

"But glass can be transparent or translucent. Opaque, even."

"It's transparent from this angle, lady." He leans on the counter with one hand and adjusts his black-framed glasses with the other. "You want something to drink?"

Rose lets out a sigh. "Any of that champagne available for consumption?" She indicates toward the bubbling fountain.

"I think I can manage that."

"Make that two, please." The smooth baritone voice flows into her ear like the opening strains of Ravel's *Bolero*, subtle, subdued, a beginning. Rose's heart responds with an immediate flutter, her loins with a flash of heat. She inhales sharply, taking in the scent of musk. A tremor slips through her. She turns and blinks into his face.

"I see you've sorted things," he says, glancing at the back of her dress. He reaches behind her, taking two champagne flutes from the bartender, and passes one to her. "Rose, isn't it?"

"Rose," she whispers, taking pleasure in wrapping her lips around the word that he has just said. "Yes, I am Rose."

Vincent brings his champagne glass to his lips. She raises hers. He pauses before drinking and places his fingers on her arm. "Wait. Let's not waste this opportunity." He raises his glass. "To the beauteous Rose, royalty among blossoms."

She beams and brings her glass to his, creating a glockenspiel clink of crystal on crystal.

He sips.

She mirrors him.

He smiles.

She wants him.

And then, Rose, the English teacher, who often produces an apt phrase or a poignant quote, is tongue-tied. Apparently, her libido has eclipsed her vocabulary. While Vincent's sculpted, six-foot-something frame hovers over her, Rose becomes devoted to the consumption of her champagne, sipping, sipping, until she has drained every drop.

"A dance, Rose?"

She nods.

He removes her glass from her hand, places it on the bar, and offers her his arm. She floats beside him to the dance floor. When she turns to face him, he embraces her and apologizes for perhaps being too forward.

His words are familiar, niggling. Didn't he apologize in the same way on their first encounter? Wasn't it she who bumped into him, both times?

"I cannot help but succumb to the temptation that is your beauty," he says.

A hint of incredulity pierces her thoughts. *Too good to be true. Too good to be true.* The phrase repeats and repeats . . . She lets out a whoosh of breath, dismissing flashes of contrived scenes from soap operas, popping them all one by one like fireworks in the night sky. With warning images blown to smoke, she leans into him and follows his steps. It is comfortable here, her head resting on his chest. She will just stay long enough to stop her head from feeling woozy. Not good, drinking that one glass of champagne on an almost-empty stomach.

"Would you care to spend the evening with me, beauteous Rose?" His voice is a gentle murmur in her ear. His fingers toy with a disobedient tendril of hair on her cheek. His free hand brushes down her back to her waistline. He draws her closer.

Rose lifts her head to meet his gaze, which is as intense as her longing. "I must catch a flight tomorrow," she says. A giggle of disbelief rings in her ears. Is she really going to do this?

"I'll get you where you need to be. I'll get you there on time." He smiles.

After another couple of glasses of bubbly, she is leaning into him again, this time while standing at the door of a black car. Has she seen this car somewhere before? He opens the door, and she hesitates for a nanosecond. Rose takes a deep breath and can almost swear she smells her mother's perfume. That is impossible. She blows out a breath and shakes her head.

Rose steps into the car. Vincent closes the door and whips around to the driver's side. Her mother's voice is chattering inside her head, but she can't make sense of the words. The driver's door slams. Her mother's voice disappears.

Rose melts into her seat. She has the sensation of being strapped in. That's just Vincent, she realizes, putting her seatbelt on for her. Considerate of him. A gentleman. The car jerks forward, on its way to . . . Rose doesn't know where.

Sunday, May 1st

Ten

ROSE AWAKENS, HER MIND fragmented, a scattered piece of a jigsaw puzzle. She blinks repeatedly. Where is she? In bed. A strange bed. Naked. Wrapped in a black satin sheet. Dear God. What has she done?

She jolts to a seated position. A deep breath brings the cloying fragrance of flowers, rose blossoms. Gulping, she skims her right hand across satin until her fingers meet velvet. She plucks a soft item and brings it into her line of vision. Eyelids fluttering, she examines her find. A rose petal. She looks around. She is adrift in a king-sized bed surrounded by a pool of rose petals, bloodred rose petals. A blurred memory drifts in. She clings to it, focuses it.

As the puzzle pieces fall together, Rose falls back, smiling. She puts her hands behind her head and, in a lazy, feline motion, stretches her entire body. So huge is this bed that her fingers do not locate the headboard, her toes do not meet the footboard. Yawning, she props herself up again and surveys her surroundings.

Other than the rose petals, the room is a stark blend of black and white, punctuated by stainless steel. This man certainly likes silver: sleek bed frame, legs on the white-leather chaise longue, and art-deco sunburst on the wall. The room shimmers in sunlight which makes its way into the room through a series of sun tunnels. They are so high. How high is that ceiling anyway? Sixteen feet? Two stories? The tunnels seem to be the only source of daylight. Not a sliver of light makes its way through the drawn curtains. Blackout curtains, obviously. The whole thing reeks of high end, minimalist decor which is not particularly her style.

Rose thinks of growing up in her mother's traditional house which had crocheted antimacassars on each upholstered chair and of her own eclectic condo which has everything from a Victorian mahogany dresser to a mid-century modern dinette set. This place is a whole new experience. Vincent may not have her taste in décor, but in bed . . .

She tries to recall the events of the previous evening. The details elude her, and her head aches. But her body? It is there, that relaxing sensation that comes in the aftermath of love-making. She remembers his hands stroking her, her inviting him in. She smiles. Yes, there was definite pleasure there. And she definitely had had too much champagne. Way too much. It was Vincent who had accepted the champagne flutes from the bartender; it was the bartender who repeatedly refilled them before retreating into the shadows. Yes, too much champagne. She searches her soul for regret but can find none. Does it matter? She wanted adventure. She wanted sex. Apparently, she got both. One question concerns her: Where in the metropolis of Vancouver is she?

She pauses, struggling to recall her trip from the gala to this place. Readily available visuals are the dance floor and the sedan. Then what? What time is it anyway? Surely, it is Sunday morning and she is scheduled to fly out of Vancouver Airport today. She tosses the sheets aside. She'd better get some clothes on. Where is her dress? There will be no taking that thing back to the store now. Of that, she is certain.

Rose does not have long to consider these things because Vincent, clad only in black satin pajama bottoms, appears in the doorway, breakfast tray in hand. Rose is oblivious to the contents of the tray, but she does take in bulging biceps and the top of a very promising set of washboard abs. She pulls the sheet over her and then, after a slight reconsideration, tugs it off again.

His approach is slow, deliberate.

In silence she studies him, her eyes roving, her body tingling.

She pats the bed.

He smiles, places the tray on a bedside table, and sits beside her.

She touches his arm and turns it toward her, her attention drawn by a glimpse of a black-lettered tattoo, one that extends from elbow to wrist.

Diabetes Type I

She looks at him questioningly.

"Easier than a bracelet," he explains. "Can't lose a tattoo."

She nods. "That's the wisest use of ink I've ever seen."

He smiles. "I'm glad you approve." He reaches toward the tray. "I took the liberty of liberating your cell phone from your purse. I thought you might like to call someone." He passes the phone to her.

"Not really necessary, but not a bad idea. Thoughtful of you. A text will do. Just to let Flynn know . . ."

"Flynn? Someone I should be concerned about, this Flynn?" A playful light twinkles in the depths of Vincent's dark eyes.

Rose laughs. "Not at all. And you know what? I can call him later, when I get to Hawaii."

"Hawaii, is it?" Vincent runs his fingers up and down the nape of her neck.

Rose shivers with pleasure. "Yes. Waikiki. My flight leaves in a few hours." She tosses her phone aside.

Vincent leans in, clamps his hand gently over her trembling chin, and brushes his lips against hers. She feathers her fingertips over his shoulders. For a moment, he pulls back, his gaze riveted on her face. "Perhaps you would consider postponing your trip?" He curves his lips into a disarming smile.

Rose can't help but beam in return. "Can you think of any reason for my staying here another day?" She leans back, waiting.

He rakes his eyes over her body. "I do believe I can," he says.

"Then I do believe a delay can be arranged," says Rose. She reclaims her phone and calls the airline.

Eleven

I'M KEEPING MY PROMISE to Rose, that of checking her plants. Upon entering her condo, I note that the suitcases are gone. Yep. She's winging her way to Hawaii already. Guess I should check everything while I'm here. I tour the place. That doesn't take much effort. The hallway is long and narrow, almost a shotgun layout. To the left are the dining room, the kitchen, and the living room. The right is just one long, solid wall, a photo gallery containing pictures of Rose, Margo, and their mother. The only interruption to that wall is one door that leads into the cubbyhole bathroom. At the end of the hall is Rose's bedroom which holds a queen-sized bed flanked by mismatched night stands, and the mahogany dresser. A small, ecru leather recliner and a brass floor lamp occupy one corner. A litter of books lie on the glass-topped table beside the chair, a mixed bunch, many genres: thriller, historical fiction, Shakespeare's plays. The sign on the wall above—BOOK NOOK—is redundant, but Rose likes it.

Rose lives on the ninth floor. I approve of that; it is more secure than ground-level apartments. The walls are paper thin, and I'm sure that both Rose and her neighbor know each other's habits. Right now I can hear the neighbor's stereo, "Where Have All the Flowers Gone?" Somebody sure likes folk music and likes it loud. I am more of a classic rock man myself.

I trot around and stick a finger into the dirt of all plants, mostly fern and ficus, and one African violet. All are fine for another day or two. In the galley kitchen, I move past the fridge door to create enough space to swing it open. I peer inside and raise my eyebrows. Rose's precious Mars bars are there, unopened. Strange. Didn't she say she was going to take them with her? Yes, she said she would leave the condo key on top of them so she wouldn't forget them. The key is not there. She must have chosen to abandon the Mars bars. I close the fridge door and pause to ponder. Then I return to the living room where I do a slow pivot, taking in the whole space.

I conjure up a visual from the past—the past being my visit on Friday—and overlay it with what's now staring at me. Everything is just as I remember it, with one exception. On the dining table, there is a jagged strip of paper. Nothing of importance, just something ripped from an envelope. Something for the recycle bin. As I pick it up, I swipe the side of my hand over the table top, shaping an arc amid specks of paper dust. I dutifully carry the scrap of paper to the kitchen, open the door under the sink, and drop the paper into the recycle bin. I'm about to close the door when I catch sight of something else in there—a FedEx packet. Curious, I pull it out, open it, and wander back to the dining room.

I dump the contents—one ticket to the Heritage Gala—onto the table. This is an event I'm familiar with. Rose's mother was a philanthropist whose main concern was the preservation of heritage homes in Vancouver. In fact, she always ordered two tickets to the Heritage Gala. An expensive purchase, about five hundred bucks a ticket, if memory serves. Whether Violet Harrington attended the gala or gifted the tickets, I don't know, but she always bought two. Never one. There should be two tickets.

The inconsistency jars me. Is there a problem here? Problems are meant to be sorted. If a problem exists, I don't know what it is, never mind have a solution. Did Rose order just one ticket and toss it? Or did she order two tickets and decide to attend solo? Would she go to a major event on the eve of her travels? Possibly. Rose would have wanted to support this cause; it meant a lot to her mother. Is there something for me to be concerned about here? Probably not. I have this no-stone-unturned philosophy when it comes to Rose, or maybe what I have is no end to the guilt about not finding Margo. Shrugging, I return the ticket to the envelope and the envelope to the recycle bin.

"Where Have All the Flowers Gone?" is still blasting through the wall as I leave the condo. Somewhere between the elevator and the door of the lobby, I subconsciously change the song title to "Where's the second ticket gone?" The newly-formed lyric plays on a loop in my head. Great. An earworm. That darn thing will haunt me all day.

Twelve

ROSE IS ALONE.
She is uncertain as to Vincent's whereabouts, but he has promised a swift return. In his absence, she is to pamper herself with a luxurious bath.

Bath bombs and bath soaps and body lotions—her favorite brands—sit in a row on a floating shelf, as if in anticipation of her arrival. In her current adagio frame of mind, she doesn't question that. She immerses herself in the soaker tub, leaning into its sloped back, extending her arms on its dual armrests. She lingers until the water temperature drops from hot to tepid, then cautiously steps out and wraps a thick towel around her torso. Padding her way into the bedroom, she sheds the towel in favor a white dress shirt, one which Vincent selected for her. She cinches her makeshift dress with a crimson silk tie, another choice of her thoughtful ... *what*? What is Vincent anyway? Boyfriend? Inamorata? One-night stand? Rose shrugs the questions away. Deliciously clean, definitely cozy, she wonders what to do next.

It is inexplicable, her choice, that of making a diagonal trek through the living room which is shiny to the point of sterile. There is not a scuff mark nor a dust mote, neither of which could hide under the scrutiny of the sunlight, which floods the room. Conscious of each minuscule movement, Rose crosses the floor in a steady heel-to-toe pattern, head down, like a walking meditation. She maintains course until she encounters a barrier, a closed door. She places a hand on the doorknob, then stops. What right does she have to continue? Why does she feel that she must? Hesitant, she looks behind her. There's no sign of Vincent. She turns the knob and nudges the door which arcs open in silence.

The room revealed holds no surprises. It is just an office, a den really. Directly opposite the door are white bookshelves, not crammed, but lined with books. Black leather covers with gold-lettered spines. On the left is a desk with an acrylic top and stainless steel, tubular legs. Its chair, again acrylic, is barely visible. A ghost chair. There is no clutter of phones or notes or computers or files. The room is devoid of color. With one exception.

On the wall above Vincent's desk, spanning the width of Vincent's desk, is a large, unframed print of two small girls clad in white dresses and lighting paper lanterns. It is set in a country garden dominated by greenery and splashed with flowers: pink roses, white lilies, and yellow carnations. Rose is both drawn to the print and puzzled by its presence. An anomaly, this painting of girls and flowers in a loft of stark and steel. Rose approaches the painting, seeking the name of the artist—John Singer Sargent. Captivated, she lingers.

A whisper of breath on her neck causes Rose to jump. She turns.

"Vincent! You scared me half to death."

"Why are you here?" Vincent's face is grim, his body rigid.

"I-I don't know." Rose feels her cheeks burn. "I was waiting and wandering and I wound up here." She shifts from one foot to the other. "It's so beautiful, the painting. My mother would have loved it."

"Ah, I see," says Vincent, relaxing his stance. "My mother loved it too."

Past tense? Rose's thoughts change from "caught" to concern. "Has your mother—?"

"Died. Her heart. She suffered for a long, long time." His words are drawn out as if he is reliving slow-motion agony.

Rose aches for him. "I'm so sorry—"

"What's this?" Vincent raises his right hand. In it, he holds the towel Rose used.

With her concern brusquely curtailed, Rose blinks in confusion. "Excuse me?"

"Mother taught me to love flowers," he says, his face stone, his voice monotone. "She taught me many things, including good manners. Wet towels belong in the hamper."

A shiver of apprehension sweeps through Rose.

Slowly, Vincent smiles. "Mother also taught me a sense of humor," he says, a playful twinkle in his eyes as he swats her with the towel.

Relieved, Rose grins into game-playing mode.

It is with reluctance that Rose mentions her upcoming trip. "I have to return to my condo. My luggage, my traveling outfit, everything I need is there."

"Ah, but you rescheduled your flight, remember? Tomorrow, you fly. As for today?" Vincent offers an arresting smile. "A surprise awaits you."

A bubble of delight sweeps away Rose's thoughts of leaving. Is there anyone more thoughtful than this man?

"Dinner is on its way as we speak." He extends his hand.

As Vincent's fingers fold over hers, Rose's delight overflows into a grin.

He leads her to the bedroom where she waits, as instructed, not moving an inch nor making a sound while caterers slide in, set up, and slide out. When Rose emerges from her hidey-hole, a lavish meal awaits—planked salmon with rissole potatoes and romaine salad.

Dinner is a quiet affair with candlelight and chardonnay after which Rose again trails Vincent to the bedroom. She is still clad in Vincent's pajama top, which he takes pleasure in peeling off. Flowers need to show their raw beauty, he tells her. She allows for this. Clothes are superfluous here.

As his hands explore her body, she abandons herself to a whirl of physical sensation. Right now, in this moment in time, Rose is experiencing exactly what she had craved. Escape, attention, sex. Perhaps she should consider forgetting her travels entirely, just staying here.

On Sunday night, contented, she sighs into sleep.

Monday, May 2nd

Thirteen

SLEEP ELUDES ME. THE few moments of drowsing I experience are overrun with images of violets and dandelions blanketing the lawn in front of Violet Harrington's newly-sold house. It's not the floral images that trouble me; it's the white fountain in their midst, a fountain gushing petals of red.

I toss and turn but I can't explain the dream. So I do what I usually do. I get up and start pacing, counting my steps. There's a problem with pacing in a tiny house. There is literally nowhere to go. Four tiny steps, turn, four more tiny steps, like a tin duck in a shooting gallery. When my body winds up instead of winding down, I get dressed and head for my office. It is only four o'clock in the freaking morning. No doubt I'll pay for this decision later in the day when my ass is dragging along the ground. What the hell. You can sleep when you're dead. There's a problem here, something I need to solve. The second problem is that I don't know what the first problem is. One thing is for sure: I'll be the only moron out and about at this time of day.

I'm wrong. There are others, but the streets are mostly hushed. The motor of my VW is annoyingly loud.

At the office, I scramble for coffee. While it burbles into being, I retrieve my Margo Harrington file box from my spare room and park it on my desk. I pull out the first file containing the details of the case, just like I did on Friday when I found nothing. What did I miss? What am I missing?

Two coffees and two hours later, I've read all the interviews pertaining to the case and I've found nothing new. I need a break, a diversion of some kind, before I tackle the remaining reports.

I rinse my coffee pot, locate a fresh filter, and dump in two scoops of coffee. While the coffee maker churns, I wander into my spare room and glance at the paint cans. Definitely a diversion tactic there. This place could use a coat of paint. I sit on that idea for a minute and then I shake my head. Nope. Not going to paint a darn thing. What about the insurance file boxes? I count them. Seventeen boxes. *Damn.* Where did they all come from? Is this the time to go through them?

With a shrug, I start in, retrieving dusty files, placing them into file cabinet drawers, and breaking down boxes for the recycle bin. I'm about halfway through when I come upon a box labeled "Sanjay." That one literally knocks me on my ass and I just sit there, staring at it.

I reach a tentative hand, lift the lid, and drop it to one side. One by one, I pull out things my son treasured: six shells, seven Transformers, a well-thumbed copy of his favorite book, *The Story of Ferdinand,* and an egg carton, each section containing a piece of a jigsaw puzzle. Like me, Sanjay loved puzzles. I wonder what happened to the box for this particular puzzle. I examine the pieces and the memory comes. There was no box. This "puzzle" was originally a photo of my red VW Golf, one that Sanjay and I glued to Bristol board and cut into jigsaw pieces. How many times had we assembled this puzzle? Countless. I smile. No wonder I cling to that darn vehicle. I close the egg carton and gingerly set it aside. I'll keep that puzzle for a while yet. The VW Golf too.

The next thing I choose from the box is a family picture: Sanjay, Amelia, me. Sunny day, blue sky, ocean backdrop. Sanjay is in the middle, skipping along, hand in hand with his mommy and me. His mommy. Amelia. The sight of her tears open an old wound. Some mother she was. A good mother doesn't let go of a child's hand in order to get a closer look at a coveted pair of Jimmy Choos spiraling on a silver stand in a department store window. Amelia, with her wavy blond hair and her singularly sweet smile. I rip the picture in two. I crumple the part containing her image and fling it into the waste basket. Then I just sit there, twitching, while the anger ebbs to emptiness.

With mechanical movement, I return each of Sanjay's treasures to the box, replace the lid, and push the box into a far corner. I breathe in, long and slow, and give that box one extra push. Done. I turn toward the remaining file boxes. My interest in organization has vanished. I leave them untouched and trudge to my desk.

What about the clutter of Margo Harrington cold case files here? Should I start back at them? Probably, but I'm gutted at the moment. Grief does that, creeps in and eviscerates. My thoughts filter back to the day I met the grief-stricken Violet Harrington. The image of her shattered face takes hold, floods me with empathy. Upturned on my desk, still attached to my car key ring, is Violet's yin-and-yang medallion, a visual prod. My promise to her jumps to the fore. *I will never stop looking.* Sighing deeply, I drop into my chair and stare at the files.

Finding solutions to puzzles sometimes involves doing nothing other than staring at the same information over and over again. Even when I walk away, my brain percolates. Eventually, inevitably, solutions appear. There's more process than prestidigitation, more measure than magic, to puzzle-solving. I start in, determined to lose myself again in this work.

Margo Harrington disappeared in May, three years ago, almost to the day. Around Mother's Day. Maybe even on Mother's Day. I glance at the calendar. Mother's Day is approaching—May eighth. I think about my soon-to-be ex-wife and am grateful that she's in Florida. I sure as hell can't deal with being anywhere near her on Mother's Day. That scalpel of a thought triggers an erratic heart rate. *Stop thinking, damn it.* After a few calming breaths, the thought is severed. I revert to reviewing the case file.

I read the details surrounding the discovery of Margo's abandoned rental car. Nothing. So, what next? To profile a criminal, you profile the victim. What had Margo done before her disappearance? I focus on minutiae. Everything that Violet reported is here, all the events, step-by-step that led up to Margo's disappearance. Who would have, could have harmed her? Is there anything I didn't notice before?

Two words pop from the page. Heritage Gala.

One week before she vanished, Margo Harrington attended the Heritage Gala with her mother. Why hadn't I pinged on that before? Maybe because, before, there was nothing to hang that piece of information on. Now? Now there is the fact that Rose received a ticket. There was only one ticket in the envelope at Rose's condo. Why would she order only one ticket? And why hadn't Violet Harrington told me about the gala? That she had attended this specific gala with Margo? It was here in the police report. Was Violet hiding something from me? Maybe I should be profiling Violet Harrington. I smirk at that, a throwaway thought. But perhaps I shouldn't toss it. Hmm. The late Violet Harrington. Why *didn't* Violet mention that she had attended the Heritage Gala with Margo?

Abruptly, the questions stop. With no direction from me, my mind has gone dark, as if crashed like a computer during a power surge. There's nothing for it but to wait. One second, two seconds, three—

With a jolt, the questions whir again, this time swerving in a new direction.

What about Rose? Did Rose attend the gala on Saturday? Maybe I should ask her about that. Sorry to interrupt your vacation, Rose, but . . .

I pull out my phone and call her. I drum my fingers on the desk while the phone rings and rings and rings . . . and then goes to voice mail.

Fourteen

SUNLIGHT FILTERS IN ON Monday morning. Vincent and Rose lie enmeshed in each other's arms. Vincent is attentive, all ears, encouraging Rose to share her stories. Memories gush like the waters of Niagara. She holds nothing back . . .

The early years: Mother's lullaby, *Hush Little Baby, don't say a word* . . . The squishy brown teddy bear with the pink bow tie. The alphabet blocks stacked into a pyramid. The shiny, new, black patent-leather shoes that pinched her toes. The fun and games with her little sister Margo—You're It and Simon Says and Hop Scotch. Kicking high on swings, wind tossing their hair. Reading Dr. Seuss, rhymes tripping their tongues. Making mud pies, dirt blackening their fingernails.

School Days: The whisper of lead pencils, sliding across paper. The specks of chalk dust, dancing in sunlight. The ping of the desk bell, relaying "time's up." So many multiplication tables, repeated like bird song. The very first poem—"The Little Turtle." The piano recital—Beethoven's *Für Elise*. Weekly choir practice—doh, re, mi, fa, sol . . .

On and on, through primary, elementary, junior high . . .

At this point, Rose pauses, regarding Vincent with curiosity. Should she continue?

Vincent peers intently at her, his gaze as soft as a caress. "You can't stop there," he says with quiet emphasis.

Rose nods and natters on.

High school: The giggling and dating. Meeting boys. Loving boys. Dropping boys. Dropping prom dress for promise of everlasting love. Promise broken, heart broken, moving on to cap and gown.

Adulthood: Still more school. Two universities. Two degrees. A career in teaching. Learning her craft. Paying her dues. Guiding her students—laughing, wide-eyed children—in the ways of confidence and independence.

Here, Rose's monologue comes to a halt.

Vincent leans toward her. "What is it, my beauty? Why are you suddenly so sad?"

Rose shrugs. "I love teaching," she says. "But, like so many things in my life, I've lost that, too." The thought jolts her from the joy of remembering to the sadness of same. She must abandon those thoughts, at the very least circumnavigate them. She needs to move on. That is the very purpose of her planned vacation, isn't it? To move on. Still, she's reluctant as she whispers, "Vincent, I am enjoying our time together, but I really feel the need to get on with my plans."

Vincent is silent.

"I will happily visit you upon my return."

The silence continues, an eerie stillness.

A fluttering occurs in Rose's chest. It is sudden, her awareness that she is naked, vulnerable, in bed with a stranger. It is strange, the mixture of amusement and avarice in his eyes. Her heart in her throat, she waits, hoping for soothing words.

Vincent's face curves into a slow, easy smile. "But, my lovely," he says, "there is no need for you to rush. There are hours before your plane departure. There is nothing for you to do but simply *be*."

Rose exhales, an outpouring of tension. She hadn't even realized she was holding her breath. Instantly, her discomfort drifts to a backburner. "You have a plan?" she asks.

"To start, why don't you have a quick shower? Freshen up?"

Rose leans her head back and gazes into his eyes. "I haven't a thing of my own to wear, you know. Perhaps I should hop over to my condo and grab my suitcases?"

"Ah, but you have yet to sample all the shirts in my wardrobe." Seeming very pleased with himself, he stands and sweeps his hand through the air. "This way, madam."

Together, laughing, they run to Vincent's walk-in closet which contains row upon row of freshly-laundered shirts. This time, she opts for a blue shirt. This time, he chooses a belt from a drawer which contains only belts, all rolled in concentric circles, all placed neatly one beside the other. His choice is a fine, black leather strap with a silver buckle and a metal-tipped tongue, tooled in a floral design. He extends it to its full length and loops it around her, using it to draw her to him. He leads her to yet another drawer, this one filled with ties, all neatly placed, lined up with military precision.

"The belt is fine!" Rose ducks down to release herself from the loop, grabs the belt and shirt, and skips toward the bathroom.

When she returns, refreshed, sporting his blue shirt and leather belt, she discovers that Vincent is sorting his outfits, mixing and matching and hanging them on a pullout rack. "What do you think?" he says, stepping aside. "Which is your favorite?"

Rose scans the lot, five in total, and chooses gray upon gray — suit, shirt, tie, and pocket square. "There is sophistication in monochrome," she says.

Nodding, Vincent returns all but Rose's selection to their proper places in the closet. "I shall certainly keep this outfit in the running for our last meal together," he says.

Something clicks in Rose's mind. Last meal? "That sounds ominous."

Vincent offers no details. Choosing a casual shirt and Levi's, he dresses. "You have not yet had a proper tour."

"Oh," says Rose, the last meal comment forgotten. She is wriggling with discomfort now at the memory of being caught exploring. "I'm sorry I went into your den yesterday—"

"No need to apologize. It is I who am at fault here. I neglected my responsibility as host and now I will rectify that. Let me show you around."

She follows him from room to room, absorbing and appreciating the details of the open plan loft. The living area is stark with white leather mid-century modern sofa and chairs. Its coffee table—rectangular, transparent glass on sturdy, chrome legs—is a diminutive twin of the dining table which, Vincent explains, can expand to seat eight or ten. The dining chairs, also contemporary, are softer in design with tall curved backs. Rose cannot resist running a hand across the top of one—white leather, buttery soft. Vincent instantly obtains a dusting cloth and wipes the chair. "Oops! Sorry," says Rose, giggling at his fussiness.

While he busies himself with that, Rose examines the sideboard, a boxy, lacquered, four-door creation that appears to float. Again with the white. The sideboard almost disappears into the white wall. There are no legs visible and no knickknacks on the top. Come to think of it, there are no knickknacks anywhere. This could be a staged model, all set for buyers.

She scans the open space. This place is beyond flawless, especially the kitchen, their next stop. Vincent opens the door to the completely stocked pantry. All grocery items are in *ABC* order, literally. Every label on every jar and every can faces front, and the lid of each can gleams. Mounted on the wall beside the pantry door is a steel towel rack which accommodates two ironed linen dish towels with silver stripes on the edge. They hang perfectly straight, bottoms aligned. The stainless steel appliances are immaculate; the French-door refrigerator is unblemished by fingerprints or magnets or to-do lists. Even the cutlery drawer, utensils nested in shiny groups of eight, is impeccable, not a crumb to be seen.

"I have a penchant for cleaning," says Vincent. "You can help if you like, or just sit at the counter and watch."

Watch, she does, fascinated by Vincent's ability to kill an entire morning unlocking and relocking doors and drawers in pursuit of dust bunnies and breadcrumbs. Through her smiles and nods, she is aware of something niggling at her brain. Isn't this all a bit twisted—this compulsion for cleanliness? Maybe. And maybe it's just an idiosyncrasy, harmless. Pensively, she looks around. Should she attempt to learn more about this man?

"What about you, Vincent? Do you have any family at all?" she asks. She cringes as she recalls, that Vincent, like she, has lost his mother. "Oh, I don't mean to bring up sad—"

Vincent waves away her concern. He looks at her, a dark flicker in his eyes. "Of sorts. I have a brother with whom I don't see eye to eye. I avoid Gideon at all costs. As for my father, he is dead."

Rose meets his gaze full on. "What happened?"

"My father crashed his car on the Sea to Sky Highway. A terrible tragedy," he says with no sign of emotion.

"I'm so sorry for your loss." A sudden awareness hits her. "We are not so different, you and I. I lost my father to tragedy many years ago. My mother died of cancer," she says. "Just three months ago," she adds, unable to hide the longing in her voice.

He looks at her. "I'm sorry for your loss, for both our losses."

Rose nods. "I think my mother started dying when my sister vanished. That was three years ago. Mom never really admitted as much, but I gathered that she somehow blamed herself for Margo's disappearance. I'll never understand why."

"There are more things in Heaven and Earth, Horatio, than are dreamt of in your philosophy."

Rose melts. "Shakespeare. You surely know how to win the heart of an English teacher. Thank you for that." She sighs. "I guess I'll never know why my mother blamed herself." Feeling renewed, not knowing why, she leans toward him. "May I help you with your chores?"

Vincent supplies her with rubber gloves and cleaning utensils. Alongside him, she scrubs, buffs, and straightens. It occurs to her that Vincent has not inquired about the disappearance of her sister. Most people land and linger on that topic, delving like vultures for morsels. A considerate man, Vincent. A wave of gratitude envelops Rose; she doesn't want to talk about Margo. She smiles as she shines the already-gleaming stainless steel fixtures.

When the cleaning is finished, he laughingly inspects. She plays along. He congratulates her on passing all scrutiny.

As they are shelving cleaning supplies, he leans in and draws her close. They are on their way back to bed.

"What have you done with my gala dress, Vincent?" Rose asks casually as she lies at his side. "I hadn't intended to use it as a traveling dress but it will do in a pinch. I will barely have time to dress, gather my things, and get to the airport." She lets out a lazy yawn.

Vincent offers no response.

Rose props herself onto her elbows. "Vincent? My dress?"

"You are not leaving," says Vincent in a smooth baritone voice, his face expressionless.

A tingling sensation arises in Rose's gut. Is something amiss? Of course not. Vincent revels in her company, that's all this is. She flicks any semblance of concern into a corner of her mind. "Yes, I *am* leaving. I must leave. I have travel plans. My flight departs this afternoon."

Vincent offers an arresting smile. "I simply mean that you are not leaving *yet*." He casually reaches to the bedside table and tugs its drawer open. "Don't worry. I'll get you to the airport on time." From the drawer, he pulls a pair of shiny handcuffs. "I thought we could indulge in a little fantasy of mine." He casts a seductive glance over her whole body.

Rose looks up at him. His eyes are serene, compelling. Dare she engage in this? Reluctant, she reaches for the rumpled silk sheet and covers her nakedness. The shield of a sheet does nothing to erase her raw sense of vulnerability. "It's not that I don't appreciate your company," she says, aiming for an even tone. "This has been wonderful, but I really must go. I do have travel plans." She's repeating herself, an old habit, one that crops up under stress.

Vincent slowly peels off her protective sheet.

Rose shivers as cold steel skates across her nipples.

"You will enjoy this." Vincent grabs one of her wrists and clamps a handcuff on it.

The hair on the back of Rose's neck stands up. "What are you doing?" Her voice is too high, too thin.

He faces her, a wounded look in his eyes. "As if you don't know. I offer you the gift of my presence and you have the effrontery to refuse?"

Sheer, black fright sweeps through Rose. Was this the dark place her mother had warned her about? Her heart battering her ribcage, she edges into a protest. "But you can't—"

"I'm afraid you've left me little option."

Rose blinks in disbelief as he tightens the handcuff around her wrist. Somewhere in the back of her mind she registers the clink of metal on metal.

Vincent jumps to the floor, unraveling his body until he towers over her. He plods to the foot of the bed and paces in silence, back and forth, back and forth. He stops, turns to her, and glowers down. "As I said, you are not leaving."

Completely numb, Rose looks from Vincent to the stainless steel headboard. Why is she shackled to the stainless steel headboard?

Fifteen

ASSUMING THAT ROSE MAY have attended the gala on Saturday, I Google images from the event. I click on the most recent of many hits, scanning all photos, looking for Rose. Coming up empty, I click on the event from three years earlier, the one attended by Margo. This time I have better luck, finding photos of both Margo and Violet. I scrutinize these pictures. Did Margo or Violet have an escort? Apparently not, although there is one image of Violet Harrington seemingly staring at the back of a man in a velvet tuxedo.

So, there's no evidence that Rose attended the Heritage Gala. There's no evidence of any mishap, mistake, or misconduct, and no apparent connection between Margo's disappearance and the Heritage Gala event. Am I concerned about nothing? Totally possible. I've been at my office for hours, accomplishing zilch. But something is niggling at me. What is it? Wait a minute. Wasn't Rose supposed to phone or text me when she arrived in Hawaii? Yesterday?

I call Rose's cell, hoping that she'll answer and dismiss my concerns with some kind of "get a life" phrase. But, just as before, the phone goes to voice mail. I sag with disappointment. "Rose, just checking in," I say, foregoing the urge to mention the gala. No point in worrying her without solid cause. "Give me a call or shoot me a text when you can," I add, keeping it casual.

My coffee pot emits a sputtering sound. I respond, unplugging it and emptying its muddy circle of dregs into the tiny bathroom basin. I hold the pot under the faucet. As the water pours in, my thoughts pour over everything I saw in Rose's condo yesterday. Did I miss something there? Should I go back? Check that FedEx envelope again? I shrug. Why not? I have nothing else pending.

I return the clean coffee pot to its home and head for my car.

Sixteen

ROSE IS FULLY AWARE that Vincent is towering over her, but she doesn't react. Not yet. She cannot react. Everything—motion and emotion—is stopped like a broken clock.

Vincent leans in. "What? You have no words? No soliloquy? An English teacher such as yourself." He sniffs in disapproval.

Her body taut, Rose grabs a quick intake of breath and then releases it in a series of shallow gasps. She wants to stay in the nothingness of shock, to pretend that none of this is happening, but fragments of truth are flitting in.

Rose has been snubbing truth since she met this man, certainly since she arrived at his loft, a loft located somewhere in Vancouver. *Somewhere in Vancouver.* Clutching her chest, Rose stares past Vincent and does a visual sweep of the bedroom. The ceiling sun tunnels are inaccessible and the windows are shielded by blackout curtains. Why had she never attempted to open those curtains? Are there windows behind those curtains?

Her vision blurs and acid erupts in her throat. Clamping her lips, she swallows a glob of vomit. She yanks at the handcuffs. The pain is acute. Emitting a sob, she yanks at the handcuffs again. Nothing changes.

She looks at Vincent, whose face is set in an air of conquest. Fear skewers her.

An image of her cell phone flashes to mind. Where the hell is it? Yesterday she tossed it onto the bed. Panic-stricken, she now uses her free hand to rummage the sheets. "Where is my phone?" Her voice is razor-edged.

Vincent rubs his hands together. "You have no need of a phone, my beautiful Rose. Your phone, if you'll pardon the cliché, is sleeping with the fishes."

Rose ceases the search. She tilts her head to look at him. Is she hearing correctly? Why does she feel like she's under water? She shakes her head.

"I couldn't risk having the phone pinged now, could I?" he says. "And you, my dear, expressed a clear desire to go off the grid. Wasn't that what you said? To recuperate from the pressures of life?" He steps back and bows like he's taking a curtain call. "Your wish is my command." He smiles.

Rose blinks. She searches her brain. "Flynn will find me," she says, more to herself than to Vincent. "He'll see that I did not pick up my suitcases. Flynn will find me."

Vincent's smile morphs to outright laughter. "Your suitcases are here, as you will soon see. And why would Flynn even consider looking? You were going on vacation. Your private investigator friend has no reason to search for you."

Rose's fear ratchets up.

"I'll let you sit with this for a while. The handcuffs are necessary, but there is no need for you to be shackled to the bed. If you come to see things my way, I will allow you to wander freely." He retreats to the bathroom.

As soon as he is out of sight, Rose crabs her way to the headboard, curling her fingers around the stainless steel railing. She rattles the handcuffs. She stops. Has the noise drawn his attention? At a hiss of gushing water, she jumps. Heart slamming, she cocks an ear to the bathroom. She hears the patter of shower drops on tile, steady at first, then interrupted. Has he stepped under the spray? Rose takes a deep breath. Yes. He is in the shower. In the shower. That gives her time. Time to make sense of this. Is there sense to this? What the hell was she thinking, getting into a car and jumping into bed with a stranger? *Stranger danger. Stranger danger.* The warning taunts like a playground chant. Rose curls her free hand into a fist and pommels a pillow. How could she have let this happen?

She stops, fist in the air, at a wisp of memory. What was it her mother had said about dark places? *Wait for clarity.* Rose takes a deep breath, then another, and another. Where the hell is clarity when you need it? Nowhere yet. If she can't achieve clarity, she'll try for calmness. Panic will own her if she lets it. She takes more deep breaths. All the while, she listens for the background, the drum of the shower, the hum of Vincent. Yes, he is humming, like one does on an ordinary day. He's humming some folk song, vaguely familiar to Rose. He's repeating its refrain. Over and over.

Abruptly, the hum and the drum stop. Rose shivers. The shower door opens. What is that squeaking sound? Is he wiping fog from the mirror? The sonic toothbrush whines. The electric razor whirs. She hears the pad of bare feet, the murmur of hangers sliding on rails. He is choosing clothes. With a start, she realizes that earlier she had helped him choose an outfit for their last meal together? *Last meal.* Why had she dismissed those words? She wraps her free arm around her knees and stares at the closet door, waiting, hoping his is not wearing the distinguished monochrome gray upon gray she had picked for their last meal.

Vincent reappears, sporting a Polo shirt, a cashmere sweater, and khaki slacks. He appears calm; she experiences hope. Perhaps his violent actions were an anomaly. Perhaps his civilized self has returned. Perhaps she can bargain.

"If you remove the handcuffs, I'll do whatever you wish," she says. An offering.

He doesn't respond.

"Please, Vincent." Her plaintive plea is alien to her. The independent Rose Harrington does not beg. Somewhere in the back of her mind, she registers fact: Independence is illusion. Delusion even.

Vincent scrutinizes her, his eyes grazing over her every pore.

Keeping her gaze on him, Rose tugs at the satin sheet, bringing it up to cover her naked body.

"No," he says with lethal calmness. "You are not ready. And I must leave for a time. My garden awaits." He strides across the room.

A scream claws at Rose's throat. She throws her head back and releases it, a piercing cry.

Vincent pauses, rocking back onto his heels.

She holds her breath.

He spins around.

She watches each purposeful step he makes.

At the bed, he stoops, expelling a blast of freshly-minted breath into her face.

Rose blinks but doesn't turn away.

"Go ahead and get the screaming out of your system," he says, spitting the words. "But, be advised that you are wasting your strength." He stands. "Sound cannot penetrate these walls. No one will ever hear you." He whips around and marches out.

There are shuffling noises which go on for seconds, many seconds. Perhaps minutes. She must figure a way to keep track of these things. She starts counting, Mississippi seconds. She's up to sixty-three when she hears the front door slam. What about the locks? Hope quivers.

Click go the locks.

Hope tumbles.

Silence drops.

Seventeen

AT ROSE'S PLACE, I thrust the key into the lock and step through the door. I head down the hall, first to the bedroom, then back to the bathroom. There is nothing amiss. Not that I expected anything to be. I go to the living room and draw the blinds. A sunny day, a stunning view, a shimmering sea. As usual. In the kitchen, I check the recycle bin. There it is, the FedEx envelope. I reexamine it. Again it spits out one ticket. Nothing else. One ticket, which I pocket.

As I turn, I open the fridge door. There isn't much inside. Except the abandoned Mars bars, an uncovered dish of butter, and an opened container of skim milk. Inexplicably annoyed, I hunt through drawers until I locate a roll of cling wrap. Ripping off a lengthy strip, I create an airtight seal around the butter dish and stash the dish in the freezing compartment. My annoyance increases as I remove the skim milk from the fridge and pour it down the drain. Seriously? Who leaves an open container of milk in the fridge for three weeks? And why the hell am I irritated by it? It occurs to me that the source of my irritation has nothing to do with abandoned chocolate, naked butter, or sour milk. It has everything to do with the fact that Rose promised to contact me. She hasn't.

I yank out my cell phone and punch in her number, determined to give her a talking to. When it goes instantly to message, I leave a voice mail. "Rose, call me." I then text the same message. I pull her travel information from my jacket. If I can't reach Rose via *her* phone, I'll just call the darn hotel in Waikiki. I punch in the number.

Not a single ring travels to my ear, just an instant thank-you-for-calling message, followed by a stream of inquiry directives. "For reservations, press one, for change in reservations, press two . . ." I choose the all-other-inquiries option and pace the floor while listening to a second stream of instructions. Finally, after punching in another number, I hear a ring, two rings—

"My name is Kevin," a chirpy voice cuts in. "Who am I talking to, please?"

I identify myself. "I'd like to speak with a guest at your hotel. Her name is Rose Harrington."

"Room number, please?"

"I'm sorry. I don't know the room number. Again, the name is Rose Harrington, H-A-R-R-I-N-G-T-O-N. She checked in yesterday evening."

"Please wait while I locate the information." After a short silence, Kevin returns with a single sentence. "There's no one here by that name, sir."

"Excuse me? She had a reservation."

"Yes, sir, but she did not check in."

Stunned, I say nothing.

"Is there anything else I can help you with, sir?" Kevin says, voice slightly raised.

An effective cue. "No," I say, in a raspy, almost inaudible tone. I clear my throat. "No. I don't think so. Thank you for your time." I disconnect.

Thrown off balance, I wander to a chair and sit, my mind buzzing around this unexpected detail. Rose didn't check into the hotel? Why didn't she check in? What about her flight? Did Rose make her flight? A fleeting thought occurs. Call the airline and ask. A useless and naïve idea, that. They won't release information from a passenger manifest. Not unless there are special circumstances, such as a missing person's report. Too soon for that, isn't it? Without special circumstances, even

Lee could not acquire information about a specific traveler on a specific flight and he has the clout of a police badge. Privacy laws reign supreme. What then?

Sometimes I need to go quiet inside to hear the next thing tapping at me and the next thing is the Lotus Club. Just before I left here Friday, Rose mentioned she was having lunch at the Lotus Club with friends. Yep. Rose mentioned friends and I made a joke. Why hadn't I just shut up and asked her about those friends? Now I have to find them.

I Google the Lotus Club. Pacing, I punch in the number. I start counting my steps. It seems I am always counting something: footsteps or stair risers or cracks in the sidewalk. As I shift to counting my breaths, I stop and take a deep one.

"Lotus Club," says a smooth contralto into my ear. "How may I help you?" Her question is hurried. Perhaps someone is prodding her, impatient for a table.

"Good afternoon. I'm looking for someone who dined there at lunch on Friday." There is silence so I add, "Friday, April 29th."

"I'm not sure I can give you any information, sir."

"I'm sorry. I should have identified myself. I'm a private investigator, Shaughnessy Flynn, and I'm working a case." White lies are allowed here. "I'm looking for Rose Harrington who was scheduled to have lunch there on Friday with friends."

"Oh, I see." After a brief pause, the voice adds, "Sir, I am looking at the list of reservations for that date and there is no one of that name here."

"I see." I take a beat. "Is the manager available?"

"Would you like to schedule an appointment with the manager?"

I roll my eyes. Sometimes restaurant personnel are too damn well-trained. "What I would like is to speak with him now, please." Internally, I kick myself. Maybe "him" was a "her" and I'd be instantly rejected, chastised for bias.

"One moment, please. I'll put you through."

Good. She bypassed my *faux pas*. And now I'm on hold. My life is on hold. The music from the Lotus Club, a *Jeopardy*-type theme, clashes with the folk music blaring from the condo adjacent to Rose's. I ignore both and start counting seconds.

"R. G. Chang here. How may I help you?" A male voice, crisp and resolute.

"Are you the manager, Mr. Chang?"

"Indeed I am."

"I would like to speak with you on a matter of some importance. Is it possible to set up a meeting?"

"And you are . . . ?"

Okay. So no skipping corners. "My name is Flynn, Shaughnessy Flynn. I'm a private investigator and a friend of mine appears to be missing. On Friday, she was scheduled to have lunch at the Lotus Club, and I want to find out for certain if she attended."

Maybe it's something in my voice, worry or whatever, but the response is positive. "Sir, if you can drop by the Lotus Club, I can fit you in."

"I'll be there within the hour."

As I head for the door, I become more aware of the folk tune emanating from the neighboring condo, the same melody I heard here yesterday—"Where Have All the Flowers Gone?" The music suddenly increases in volume, telegraphing the fact that Rose's neighbor is home. On the heels of that realization comes another: Maybe Rose's neighbor knows something about Rose. I can toss a few questions at him or her and then continue to the Lotus Club. I shove my phone into my pocket, exit Rose's place, and approach the neighbor's door. There is no point in ringing the bell as its *ding* will not pierce the music's blare. I knock, not a tap but a pound. I wait. Seconds tick. I pound the door again.

Abruptly, all falls silent.

"I'm coming. I'm coming." The door creaks open and a hunched man appears, his spine so curved that his face is parallel with the floor. He's wearing a denim shirt, frayed jeans, and a broad-brim Tilley hat, and he's leaning into a white cane.

Physically and visually challenged. There's no end to the tragedy life inflicts on some people. I take a respectful step back.

"What's all the hammering about?" the man wheezes. "You scared the bejesus out of me."

"I'm sorry to disturb you, sir. My name is Flynn and I'm checking up on my friend's place." I point to Rose's door. Abruptly, I drop my hand. Stupid idea, using a visual indicator with someone who is visually impaired. Not that he could see me anyway with his eyes aimed at the threshold. "Rose Harrington. Your neighbor. She's away, as you probably know. Have you seen her lately?"

"You got a brain in you, sonny? Can you see this cane?" He taps it on the tile. "I can't see nothing. Never met no neighbor. What's her name? Rose, you say?"

"Yes, that's right. Would you mind telling me your name?"

The man raises his cane and wiggles it in my general direction. "I'm not telling you nothing." He closes the door, or attempts to. Anticipating his action, I stick my foot into the opening. *Damn.* That hurts. But it's effective.

The neighbor opens the door again.

"Well, sir, if you remember anything or notice any strangers milling about, will you please give me a call? Here's my card." I draw out my wallet and fish for a business card.

The neighbor snatches at the air until he latches onto my card. He pumps his arm up and down, up and down, in a seemingly deliberate show of trying to bring the words into focus. "No, still can't see a damn thing." With that, he tosses the business card at me and slams the door.

I shake my head. Nice going, Flynn. Could you have handled that any better?

With a sigh, I pick up my card, retrace my steps, and again check Rose's condo for signs of an intruder. Nothing. I pull out my cell phone and snap a picture of Rose's gallery wall, one very specific section of the wall. I check to make sure my shot is in focus. Yep, there they are. Rose and Margo, arm in arm, smiling. After one more look around, I leave.

As I am on my way to my car, it occurs to me that perhaps I should check in with Lee. Do I have enough information to be concerned about Rose? I can see Lee shaking his head, perhaps offering for consideration the fact that Rose might be staying with a friend or an acquaintance. So, first, the Lotus Club.

Then, if necessary, I'll talk to Lee.

Eighteen

VINCENT MEANDERS THROUGH THE gardens of the Lord estate. An overhead screech breaches the stillness but he is not alarmed. Accustomed to the cacophony, he casts a casual glance toward a flock of gulls skimming the sky. Benign creatures, really. Stalkers and scavengers, yes, but the birds are just living their lives. Aren't people the same? Nodding decisively, Vincent continues his circuitous walk through the sprawling floral gardens of his family's coastal estate.

An especially warm spring, this one. The crocuses and daffodils are gone, as are the tulips, the festivals for which just ended. The cherry trees snowed their blossoms weeks ahead of their assigned festival. There were a few late bloomers. The evidence is here, in the fallen blossoms peppering the flowerbeds. The sight causes Vincent to frown. Mother would not like this. A place for everything, everything in its place. No lost or lonely blossoms allowed.

Vincent gathers the errant petals and deposits them into the compost. Probing his pocket, he extracts a container of sanitizer and squeezes a globule into his hand. It is satisfying, the acrid smell of alcohol and the resulting death of bacteria. Brimming with contentment, he continues his adjudication of the gardens.

Pink and white petals of magnolia trees are drooping, rag doll-like, their purple stamens exposed to the world. Rhododendron bushes, rich in red and white and periwinkle and purple, are towering, almost forming a floral canopy. Azaleas splash in front of him, a stunning array of pink.

A sweet fragrance beckons, the scent of roses. Inhaling deeply, anticipating pleasure, Vincent goes to the heart of the rose garden. Once there, he sweeps his eyes over a myriad of blossoms, following a stream of color, everything from white to peach to fuchsia to . . . The visual flow stops at an empty plot which has been stripped of its shimmering red floribunda roses. Nothing remains but furrows of dirt. Vincent lets out an audible sigh. No red roses. Mother loved red roses. Sadness tugs.

His late mother, Annabel Lord, an ardent floriculturist, dedicated her life to landscaping this property. Vincent spent hours here, laboring with her, learning from her. Now he spends hours here alone, grieving for her. With Mother's Day in the offing, he plans on gifting his mother with a bed of roses, red roses, in the fallow plot. Before long, with the new roses installed, his garden will rival the work of God in the Garden of Eden. He smiles at the comparison.

Sorrow assuaged, Vincent notes that the sun is already more than halfway across its trajectory. He must go soon. Reluctant, he meanders, pausing to inhale the scent of hyacinth, to caress a petal of iris, and to eye a glittering of hummingbirds. He throws his vision out of focus until his gaze is a rainbow blur.

He doesn't hear footsteps, doesn't need to hear footsteps, to know that Gideon is on the scene. He is all too familiar with the stealth of his brother. Vincent doesn't turn, doesn't speak.

"You wanted to see me, Vincent?"

Vincent sighs. There had been times when he wanted to see Gideon, when he even welcomed Gideon. But those times were long past.

"Mother sure had an eye for flowers," says Gideon.

Longing to ignore Gideon but priding himself on etiquette, Vincent slowly pivots. He can't look at Gideon though. He refuses to look at him. "You must be mistaken, Gideon. I really don't want or need you for anything at the moment."

"I saw you staring at the rose beds. Thinking of a change in plans? You can't do that without me. You're useless without me."

The words burn through Vincent like acid. Why must Gideon be so reproachful? Vincent struggles to maintain a calm surface. "Mother gave me *carte blanche* when it came to house and gardens." He angles away from Gideon. In the far corner of the estate, he eyes the waving tendrils of a willow tree, a tree which survived a windstorm that felled his sturdiest oak.

A windstorm. What an apt metaphor for his brother. Blowing in, creating havoc, taking leave. Amused, Vincent turns his head to hide his smirk. If Gideon is the wind, then Vincent will be the willow. "Mother taught me well, the art of fine flowers, the art of gracious living." He cautions himself not to boast. Boasting makes him a target. Gideon is a marksman. Vincent waits a beat and then adds, "My only plan is to honor her love of blossoms." There. Gideon can't find fault with that.

"You just like things to look pretty. Sculpted. Like you."

Vincent clenches his jaw. How could he think, even for a second, that Gideon would not find fault? While reining in rage, Vincent stares at a single azalea petal. Pretty. Pink. Perfect.

"All chisel and charm on the outside," Gideon continues as usual, drilling deep. "A draw for the ladies, I'll give you that. But inside? You're a mama's boy. A weakling. Craving attention like flowers crave water."

A bead of sweat trickles down Vincent's brow.

"You want to get rid of me, don't you?" Gideon lets out a contemptuous snort. "You haven't got the guts. I'm the one with the strength. You need me, little brother."

Vincent struggles with frustration. Do all younger siblings suffer this baiting process? And, more to the point, should he take this bait? Mother always said one must pick one's battles. "The plans for the new rose bed are progressing nicely," he says. Ease falls over him, an indicator that he has chosen his words well.

"We will accelerate those plans. I'll be here when things need doing." Gideon's departure is swift and soundless.

A small triumph, Gideon's sudden retreat. Vincent doesn't pause to ponder; he just sprints to his car. Lingering could be misconstrued. Gideon might re-appear. Besides, Vincent has errands to run. Perfunctory matters. Then he will return to the loft.

Rose is waiting.

Nineteen

I'M ABOUT TO TURN my ignition key when I realize I'm well within walking distance of the Lotus Club. I exit my VW and stroll along Beach Avenue, imagining Rose taking this very same route three days earlier on a similarly sunny day when the area would be buzzing with activity. Intent on seeing everything she saw, I eye my surroundings. Typical Beach Avenue crowd. Bicycles zoom. Cars honk. All west coast fitness buffs or tourists with cameras. Skirting traffic, I cross the street and enter the cramped restaurant.

Directly in front of me is the hostess station. Squeezing past me are greeters and servers, dressed in black, mostly female. How the heck do they manage to spend all day in stiletto shoes? A bane for feet, a boon for podiatrists. Not all of the servers wear six-inch heels. Some heels are four, five inches. tops. While waiting, I search feet until I find one server wearing flats. The common sense one. That's the one I want to talk to. I make a quick note to do that before I leave.

I don't have to wait long at the hostess station. A beauty greets me. Long, dark hair, a dress so tight that it leaves little to the imagination. Is everybody into teeth bleaching these days? Maybe it is just the purple lipstick that gifts her with the appearance of snow-white teeth.

"Lunch for one?" she asks.

"Not today, thanks." I produce my card.

She ignores it.

"I'm Shaughnessy Flynn, private investigator, and I'm looking for information about my friend who may have dined here on Friday."

"Shaughnessy Flynn?"

At some point, I'm just going to give up and legally change my name.

I wave my ID. This time she notices it.

She nods. "You called earlier?"

"Yes. I spoke to the manager and he said that he would squeeze me in for a meeting."

"I'll let him know you're here." She disappears.

"I'll wait," I say to no one in particular. I step aside to allow a couple behind me to gain access. The hostess returns, mutters a quick apology to me, and escorts the couple to a table. I watch as she distributes menus and then heads to the bar where she talks to a short Asian man with a spiked crew cut. She points at me. He turns his angular face in my direction, nods, and heads my way, his stride resolute.

"I have been expecting you to stop by." He extends a hand. "I'm the manager, Mr. Chang. I understand you are making inquiries about someone who ate here a few days ago?"

"Flynn, and indeed I am." I shake his hand. There's something satisfying about our matching heights, about looking into this guy's face and not at his chest. His iron-brown eyes tell me that if there are answers to be had, he has them. I produce the picture of Rose and Margo. "The blond lady. Her name—"

"I am not in a position to give information to just anyone," he says, folding his arms.

Out comes my ID card again. "I understand but this lady is my friend who was supposed to fly to Hawaii this past weekend. She did not check into her hotel in Waikiki."

Mr. Chang eyes me, deciding whether or not to help. Hoping that the concern in my voice trumps the doubt in his mind, I keep talking. "I believe my friend ate here on Friday. She said she was having lunch with friends at the Lotus Club."

The manager scrutinizes the card. He runs it back and forth across the splayed fingers of his left hand, reminding me of the way I used to stick hockey cards in the spokes of my bicycle when I was a kid. "Let's go to my office," he says, grabbing the reservations list for Friday. "Follow me."

Mr. Chang's office is a hole-in-the-wall affair; my own place of business is a palace by comparison. He parks himself in the swivel chair behind his walnut desk and points me toward one of the two gray folding chairs in front of it. "What is the name of your friend?" he asks.

"Rose Harrington."

He runs his finger down the reservation list. "No such name here."

"Yes, sir. Your hostess said the same thing. But perhaps the reservation was in someone else's name? She was a teacher at—"

"Oh, the teacher group. I remember that. I took that reservation myself. What was the caller's name again? Mary? Marilyn?" He again runs his finger down the page. "Marlene! That was it! Definitely Marlene. I don't have a last name."

"Can you give me a number?"

"In this day and age? Not a chance. Not without permission."

I nod, understanding. Should have contacted the school first.

"The other option, of course," says Mr. Chang, "is that I can call her and ask permission to share her number."

With a wave of my hand, I dismiss the idea. "Not necessary but appreciated." I take out my notebook. "Since I'm here, can you tell me anything about the group? How many? Distinguishing features?"

"Let me think. There were four, I believe. One was pregnant, very much so. One ordered a large glass of wine as soon as she sat down. Very pretty blond lady wearing a red skirt. I believe she was the guest of honor."

That was Rose. "You have an eye for detail."

"It pays to remember your clients in this business. Besides, they had all been here before. The aforementioned Marlene . . . I think she's an office manager or something."

"Any snippets of conversation?" I ask.

"No, no. I remember seeing them at the end table on the patio. The server for that section is here today. You want to speak to her?"

Before I finish nodding, the manager is on the phone. Seconds later, a perky server appears. Amanda. Long brown hair, black nail polish, radiant smile, and little black dress, emphasis on the little. Her thigh muscles are taut. I am willing to bet that she cycles to work daily. When I eye the shoes, I smile. Flats. The same server I'd made note of earlier. The one I wanted to talk to.

She gives me a cursory look before turning her attention to her boss. "The hostess said you wanted me." There are question marks in her eyes, curious but not worried. A confident young woman.

"Yes, Amanda. Take a load off for a minute." He waves toward the third chair opposite his desk. This man must be accustomed to meeting in trios.

Amanda flicks her hair back, sits on the edge of the chair, and steals a glance at the door. I bet she is thinking about the tips she is missing.

"Do you remember anything about a party of teachers who sat at your station for lunch on Friday?"

Amanda scrunches her face. Not a pretty look. "I'm not sure," she begins.

"They sat at the far end of the patio," prompts her boss. "A blonde. A pregnant lady. A man with glasses—"

"Oh, yes." Amanda's grimace morphs into a grin. "I remember them now."

"Do you remember anything about the group?" he asks.

I throw in a few words. "Perhaps what they talked about?"

"I'm not sure. I'd have to think about it. What's this about anyway?"

"One of the party is missing," I say.

Amanda sits even straighter. "I see." Her tone is serious now. "Let me think. One of them seemed in a hurry to get her glass of wine."

"Established." The manager looks at his watch.

"Yes. Well, they were a chatty bunch. Pretty happy to be together. I brought wine to the blond lady. The rest already had their drinks. I went back after a bit to take the orders and had to wait for a minute or so. The blond lady had put tickets on the table and was asking anyone if they wanted them."

"Did you say tickets, plural?" I ask.

Amanda nods. "There were two tickets. Anyway, they all said no. They encouraged her to use them. When she said she had nothing to wear, the Asian lady suggested she go shopping, at the Pacific Plaza."

"What were the tickets for?" I ask, already knowing the answer.

"The Heritage Gala. They were just sitting there, crystal clear. While I was taking the blond lady's order, she picked them up, put them into a FedEx packet, and put that into her purse."

Amanda pauses. "Is she the missing one? The blond lady?"

"Why do you ask?" Sometimes people are more aware than they realize.

After a quick shrug, Amanda says, "She seemed kind of like lost. Sort of there but not there, if you know what I mean."

I nod. No words necessary.

Amanda leans forward. "She was having a lovely time."

"Thank you, Amanda," I say.

The manager stands.

Amanda and I follow suit.

"That's it then," says Mr. Chang. "Thank you, Amanda. You may return to your station."

I offer a card to Amanda. "If you think of any more information—"

With a swoop, the manager intercepts my card and passes it back to me. "If you think of anything else, Amanda, let me know and we will deal with it."

With a reassured nod, Amanda leaves.

"She's young," says the manager. "I have an obligation to protect my employees. Promised her mother, you see."

I nod. Indeed, I do see. I promised Violet Harrington.

I leave the restaurant and hang around near the bicycle rack in the front while I Google the high school Rose worked at. There they are, the phone digits. I punch them in. The street noise interferes and I plug my finger into my other ear while I wait. I glance at my watch. Not likely to get a response this late in the day, am I? One ring, two rings . . .

There's an abrupt hello.

I'm not bothering with formalities. "I'd like to speak with Marlene, please."

"Marlene is gone for the day," reports a singsong voice. "Please try again in the morning."

"I wonder if—"

"Tomorrow morning, sir." The line goes dead.

I redial. After four rings, the phone goes to voice mail. My turn to disconnect. Now what?

Morning seems a long time away. I glance at my watch and sigh my way to my car. Nothing I can do but wait. I reassure myself that by tomorrow morning, Rose will show up and I'll go back to filing insurance claims.

For now, I'm heading to my tiny house and leaving worries outside the door.

Twenty

IN THE AIR-CONDITIONED comfort of his soundproof Audi, Vincent absentmindedly turns on the radio. The forceful strains of an atonal symphony invade the stillness, rattling him. He switches off the radio. He needs silence. He needs to contemplate.

Vincent had felt a glimmer of triumph in today's encounter with Gideon, but there was no triumph, not really. There was, there *is*, only a grim reality which hangs like a millstone: Gideon is in charge.

Vincent tightens his grip on the steering wheel. Damn that Gideon. It was Vincent who lured Rose. It is Vincent who should decide how long he keeps her. Why should Gideon have any say in the matter?

The answer hammers away. Gideon has say, and sway, because Vincent allows it. Why can't he thrust Gideon aside? Just erase him like a digital photo? *Click. Delete.* It should be that simple, shouldn't it? A decisive blink? But it isn't. Reluctantly, Vincent cues the memory which is always waiting in the wings. As real as now . . .

He was ten. He was sitting like a mouse in a sterile office and listening, powerless, to a sharp-nosed, deadpan, thin man in a white lab coat—a child psychologist.

Sitting beside Vincent was his father, William Lord, jaw clamped, fists clenched. Huge fists, the sight of which made Vincent shiver. Vincent closed his eyes so he couldn't see those fists. What instantly popped into his mind were blotches of color—marbled hues of purple, yellow, blue, and black. The very blotches which now painted his back and his chest and his buttocks and his legs. Colors created by his father's big fists.

The psychologist made a pronouncement. "I fear, Mr. Lord, that the death of your wife triggered turmoil in your son. The paranoia, the depression, the selective mutism, the mood swings—all symptoms which may abate with the passing of time."

Vincent's father accepted advice about kindness and patience. "Yes, Doctor. Whatever you think is best, Doctor," he said as they left the office.

But at home, William Lord scoffed and taunted and mimicked Vincent's skittish behavior. Then he formed his hands into fists. Vincent ran.

In his room, Vincent locked the door and fled to the security of the darkness under his bed. He covered his ears to mute his father's roar. The walls vibrated from the pound, pound, pound of fists upon the door. Vincent couldn't control the shudders that racked his body. Cornered, helpless, he uttered a pain-filled cry, "Mommy, come home!"

The door to his room flew open. He stiffened. A gasp spat out of him when daylight sliced his hiding place. He peered out.

"Hey, little brother. Wanna play?" It was Gideon, decked out in a clown costume, wearing whiteface makeup and a rainbow wig and a big red nose.

Vincent reached a tentative hand. He tweaked Gideon's spongy nose. It squeaked. Vincent smiled.

After that, Gideon always showed up, in some kind of get up, to distract, to entertain, or to comfort. When Vincent needed a big brother, Gideon was there.

As the Audi hums, Vincent sighs, resigned. He owes his life to his big brother. It was Gideon who engineered the death of William Lord, at a convenient time, a time when Vincent was old enough to inherit everything. No money worries. Thanks, Gideon.

A stab of guilt hits Vincent. In the past, he always welcomed Gideon's presence. But now? Gideon is an intrusion. Demanding. Overbearing. And yet, Vincent allows Gideon to plot and plan every aspect of his life, their lives.

Vincent lead-foots the gas pedal. Damn it all. Gideon isn't getting Rose until Vincent is ready to release her. A police cruiser passes, cuing Vincent to check his anger, to ease his foot off the accelerator. To this point, he has managed not to draw too much attention. It wouldn't do to risk a speeding ticket.

At the door of the loft, he places his shopping bags on the floor and then fumbles for the correct keys. A vexing process, disengaging four locks in sequence, a process aggravated by his compulsion for repetition. He shoves the gold key into the first lock.

Unlock, lock, unlock. *One.* Already he feels relief. Next the silver lock.

Unlock, lock, unlock. *Two.*

Unlock, lock, unlock. *Three.*

Unlock, lock, unlock. *Four.*

He sighs as process trumps annoyance. Rose must be beside herself in anticipation of his arrival. However, everything has an order. After Vincent locks the door, he pauses, listening.

All is silent.

He proceeds to the kitchen and stows his purchases. A place for everything. The take-out containers remain on the counter. From those, he makes a plate of beef and broccoli, chicken fried rice, and a vegetable medley. He arranges the food so that the servings do not touch each other. He sets cutlery and a napkin on a rose-patterned place mat. There will be no wine this evening. Coffee, perhaps? He glances at the Keurig and shakes his head. Too late for caffeine. His Rose will be in need of water. When all is ready, his excitement increases. He heads into the bedroom.

So wide-eyed, his beauty who is hugging the headboard, her body shielded in a black satin sheet. So eager, her face.

"My apologies at having kept you waiting." Regret twinges at the sight, the severity, of the handcuffs. "I trust you have not been too uncomfortable."

Rose says nothing, just stares.

"Surely you must be ready to roam more freely?"

"Y-y-yes."

It is curious, her struggling for a simple word. "Your voice is raspy. A sore throat, perhaps?"

"I'm fine," says Rose.

Nodding, Vincent removes the cuff attached to the headboard. Grabbing her free wrist, he cuffs her hands together.

Rose blinks. She skitters to the other side of the bed and jumps off.

Vincent takes a deep breath. This is it, the game. His gait easy, he follows Rose during her helter-skelter sprint. She is searching, like they all do. He has learned to let them. There's no point in making announcements about the lack of phones or computers. She won't listen. They never listen. Wouldn't life's lessons be easier if we listened?

As she whizzes past him for the third time, he comes to a standstill. He cringes when she claws at windows. There is no concern about her getting through them because they are painted or puttied shut. But he does detest scratches. He sighs at the futility of her pounding on the steel door, her hammering at all four locks. Holding up the keys, he jingles them to catch her attention.

She turns her head.

He pockets the keys and pulls out earplugs at the onset of the screams. Sometimes he wishes he had lowered the ceilings a touch in order to rid this place of stairwell acoustics. Perhaps Rose didn't have a sore throat earlier, but she will soon. Vincent props himself against a pillar. When he sees her body sag against the front door, he removes his earplugs. He doesn't like the next part, the show of force, but familiarity has taught him of its necessity.

With purpose, he walks toward her. She flings herself at him, cuffed hands raised, fingers formed into claws. In a lightning move, he snatches a handful of her hair and yanks her into his arms. He clamps a hand over her chin. Narrowing his eyes, he spits words. "You will not question my authority." He drags her, and drops her onto the white leather sofa, and presses a knee into her chest. She thrashes.

Vincent waits a few seconds before selecting the fluffy, black pillow with the red piping and lowering it until it blocks her breathing. "This is unfortunate, I fear. There is no way out, Rose, unless I choose it. You already know that this residence is completely soundproof."

Her body flags beneath him. Giving up so soon?

He lifts the pillow but she sets in again, glaring, flailing, screaming. He shoves the pillow into her face a second time. "Let me detail it for you further. The windows are opaque. Light enters through lamps or sky tunnels. There is no way up. The ceiling is sixteen feet high. There is no way out. The windows are unbreakable and the door is steel. You've already encountered the locking mechanisms. You will be here until I bid you leave. Now, are you ready to behave?"

The wriggling mass stills itself.

He raises the pillow.

Rose pulls her body into a fetal position, puffing and panting. She looks up, face drained of color, eyes bright with fear.

Almost done. He slowly lowers the pillow.

Rose holds her hands in front of her face. "No," she says, her voice clear. "I understand."

"You understand what?"

"That there is no way out."

"Unless I choose it."

"Unless you choose it."

Nodding, he extends a hand.

Timidly, she reaches.

He kisses her cuffed hands and folds her into his arms. "I have brought dinner," he says.

Tuesday, May 3rd

Twenty-One

I DON'T PHONE AHEAD. I just arrive outside Rose's former place of employment early Tuesday morning. I say outside because I circle the perimeter, checking every door. The place may be a secondary school but it's locked down like Fort Knox. Is it a holiday? The explanation clicks like handcuffs. *Read a tweet, idiot. Watch a newscast.* Security. Mass shootings abound. Schools are no safe haven.

I resort to my phone and punch in the office number. This time Marlene answers the phone. I launch into a terse explanation of who I am and why I'm here and she gives me directions to the only unlocked door, the one nearest the office. She will meet me there.

I make my way to the designated door and catch sight of students through an adjacent window. Sitting at study carrels, earbuds attached, all on devices. Not a personal interaction in the room. The joys of technology.

The door rattles, then flies open so fast I execute a side maneuver. "Mr. Flynn? I'm Ms. Marlene Denton." There is beat, a pause in which she scrutinizes me. Ms. Denton, in her blue power suit and pumps, is both office manager and security guard. She nods. "You are a private detective?"

I pull out my card.

She takes it, pulls reading glasses from a pin on her lapel, and reads it. After a minute, she nods. "You may come in."

I step through the door and stand on the mat, waiting for the authority that is Ms. Denton to give direction. Yes, she has platinum hair and an electric blue, pencil-skirted suit, but she comes across like she's clad in a black veil and matching robe. I look at her waistline, expecting to see a gigantic black string of beads and a dangling cross. Being educated by nuns does that to you. I always doff my hat to authority.

"This way, please," says Ms. Denton.

I follow her to the hallway, a vacant hallway that smells of sweat socks, perhaps even a vague scent of skunk. I know what that is, but I'm no narc. A bell rings, not a *brrrring* bell I recall from childhood but a high-pitched shriek that should be allocated as a secret language for tracking beloved pets. I jump but Ms. Denton doesn't waver. Hallway doors fly open. Kids trickle, rush, and swarm. I pick up my pace, hugging the heels of Ms. Denton lest I am lifted and swept away in the crowd.

Ms. Denton leads me to the head office where a student sits at a reception desk. "This is my desk." She nods at the student in passing. "Students do reception work when I'm not available. We can use the VP's office; he's in class."

I don't acknowledge the student and she doesn't acknowledge me. Ms. Denton and I just keep moving. In a few more steps, we are in an office. A blank-walled office with a desk and two chairs, the plastic student-variety chairs. Bright orange. There's nothing welcoming about this place. The students must love this.

"The vice-principal is hardly ever here," Ms. Denton says. "He sees no need for décor."

I can feel heat in my face like I've been caught doing something improper. Should have known Ms. Denton in the power suit would be aware of everything, including my thoughts.

Ms. Denton points toward a chair. She sits and I sit. She stares again at my card and places it on the desk. "How may I help you? What's all this about Rose?"

I produce my notebook. "I understand you had lunch at the Lotus Club on Friday?"

"Yes, yes, I did. Four of us met Rose there." She waves a hand impatiently. "What's going on?"

I jump straight to it. "I think Rose is missing. I'm hoping you can help me find her."

"Rose went to Hawaii, didn't she?"

"She didn't check in to her hotel in Waikiki."

Ms. Denton leans forward. "How can I help?"

"Do you know if Rose attended an event on Saturday evening? Or perhaps if she decided to stay with one of her lunch friends?"

"The answer is no on both counts. Obviously, you've tried to contact her?"

I nod. "I've phoned Rose. No answer. I've texted. Again, no answer. And she did promise to keep me in the loop."

Ms. Denton looks at me questioningly.

"I'm a friend," I offer by way of explanation. "I was friends with her mother who died recently."

"Rest her soul."

A respectful pause.

"And . . .?" Ms. Denton prompts.

"Well, I promised Rose's mother I would take care of Rose."

"After Margo's disappearance, you mean?"

No words are needed here and I don't offer any.

"Well, I do know about you, Mr. Flynn. Rose referred to you many times during our conversations. You helped her move her mother's antique dresser on Friday morning, didn't you?"

Why is there a lump in my throat? I glance down and put pen to notebook. Nothing to write but my eyes are filling.

Ms. Denton moves the conversation forward. "Well, here's what happened on Friday. You know we were at lunch. Rose showed up looking glam, as usual, wearing a skirt the color of a maraschino cherry and a basic white shirt. She could win a next top model show."

"What did you talk about? What did she talk about?"

"She mentioned that she would be traveling."

"Hawaii and then Europe?"

"Yes. She talked about that, about the tickets already being bought." Ms. Denton points a finger at me. "Tickets! There's a reminder. Rose pulled two tickets from her purse and put them on the table. They were for the Heritage Gala and she did not want to attend. She offered them to us."

"But nobody took them?"

"Nobody took them. We tried to convince *her* to go. To have some fun. When she said she didn't have a thing to wear, someone—Jade, I think it was—suggested she hop over to some little boutique in Pacific Plaza."

"Boutique?"

"Mitchell Crown's, I believe."

I jot down the name of the store.

"I don't know if she went to that particular shop, but she did go to Pacific Plaza."

I glance up, eyebrows raised.

"I drove past the Plaza and saw Rose enter."

Nodding, I add Lee's name beside the name of the store. He can check Rose's credit card purchases, although I know she isn't much for credit. Debit either, for that matter. The woman uses cash. If it weren't for the fact that she carried herself in such a no-nonsense way, she'd be a target for muggers.

When I look up again, Ms. Denton looks at her watch. My cue to stand. "I won't take up any more of your time." I close my notebook.

Ms. Denton rises from her chair. "The others who attended lunch on Friday are here at work today. I can arrange for you to talk to them, but I don't think you'll learn any more than I told you. Rose was the first of the group to leave the Lotus Club that day. The rest of us returned here."

I nod. It's time to go but I'm wavering. I clutch my notebook so hard my knuckles turn white. "One more thing . . . Did Rose seem out of sorts, upset, during lunch?"

Ms. Denton pauses, then shakes her head. "Not at all. She was quiet. Pleasant. The norm. Never a great conversationalist, Rose. But she showed no signs of distress."

My fingers relax. I breathe more easily as I put my notebook into my pocket. "Thank you. I'll come back if necessary. Now, however, I need to follow Rose's path. Mitchell Crown's and, if need be, the gala venue."

"Can't you just check her credit card records for the dress purchase?"

"Rose has this habit of paying cash for everything."

"Oh, yes. If I recall correctly, Rose pulled cash from her wallet on Friday, as if we'd let her pay for a lunch that was in her honor. She certainly had enough cash to buy a cocktail or party dress."

"Good to know." I extend my hand. "Thank you. You've been more than helpful."

She shakes my hand, a surprisingly firm grip. She looks me in the eye. Worry lines arch her brow. "The words 'you're welcome' or 'anytime' don't fit. But, if you need me, I'm here."

"In the meantime—"

She releases my hand. "I intend to meet with the teachers involved, ask them about their memories of the day. If anything new comes up, I will let you know."

I nod. We are silent as Ms. Denton escorts me back the way we came. The halls are catacombs. Lockers and doors are closed. Class is in session.

In the parking lot, I call Lee.

The phone goes to voice mail.

Twenty-Two

ROSE CAN'T KEEP TRACK of time. A simple thing, the tick of a clock. But there are no clocks. No clocks. No phone. No watch. Is time gridlocked? If it is moving at all, it is moving by infinitesimal increments or in fluid slow motion, like a wading-through-water sensation. One hour, two hours, she doesn't know.

Vincent has granted her free run of the loft. *Free run.* The phrase evokes images of chickens flapping and pecking in an open plan barn. Content to roam in their prison. But Rose doesn't roam. Stripped of any bodily covering, she cowers on the stark white sofa, her feet tucked under her.

He lurks, watching.

Independence eroded, Rose hovers on the edge of an abyss. She toys with the desire to fall, to let the darkness take her. The feeling is familiar.

When Margo disappeared, darkness was a boa constrictor, squeezing the life out of Rose. Informed that she was experiencing shock, assured that shock would pass, she functioned day by day, hour by hour, minute by minute and, most days, by putting one foot in front of the other. For at least two months, that's what she did, coped one step at a time. Eventually, Rose shifted into the reality of life without her sister.

But now? Maybe shock cannot sustain, but does it have a time frame? In her dazed state, would she even recognize its retreat? All she knows is that two months is unthinkable. Can she accelerate the process? If she is to survive, she has to recover. Fast.

Rose sucks in a decisive breath. She propels herself away from the abyss. Darkness will not own her today.

What can she do? Attempt to reason with this man? Maybe she can cajole him, feign interest in him. She has fed him many details about her life, her loneliness. Maybe he too is lonely. Possibly she can tell him she acted hastily earlier in trying to escape. And maybe she's an idiot. Has trauma completely clouded her thinking?

Again she hears whispers of her mother's wisdom. *Wait. Wait for clarity.*

There it is, the time factor again. *Wait.* Can she wait? Dare she initiate? She lowers her feet to the floor. She stands. The indignity of her nakedness floods her face with heat. Still, she pulls her shoulders back and pads her way to the kitchen. She feels no pain, despite being shackled. She feels no cold, despite being barefoot. Perhaps the floors are heated. Perhaps shock numbs both emotional and physical sensation.

Cautiously perching on a kitchen stool, a hard fist of fear in her stomach, she raises her arms to the counter, registering the resulting clink of handcuffs on granite.

He turns, his dark eyes stirred, questioning.

Silence stretches, a tightrope. Rose summons her courage. With her heart beating wildly, she stutters into conversation. "V-Vincent . . ."

Instantly, he is at her side. "Yes, my beauty. What is it that you wish?" His voice is happy and eager.

Rose takes a relieved breath. He's coming back to a sense of reason. This is the man, the gentleman she bumped into at the market. She inhales and blows out a long, steady breath. She widens her eyes and meets his, square on. She lets her words tumble. "Vincent, you need to think about what you are doing here."

Vincent stiffens. The flash in his eyes is lethal.

Has she awakened a giant? Rose braces herself.

Vincent returns to his place behind the counter. His pacing is that of a caged panther. Halting, he turns to her. A slow smile creeps across his face. "How dare you question me a second time?" The voice is unruffled. "Under no circumstances do you question me, beautiful Rose. Didn't I make myself clear?" He tilts his head.

Rose waits, nerves taut. Dare she try again? Maybe a gentler tactic? "Perhaps you can reconsider—"

So sudden the blow. Open-handed, yet powerful. Splayed on the floor, staring at an impossibly high ceiling, Rose has the sensation of disappearing. Is she injured? She feels nothing. She is melting into a heated floor. Is this real? Maybe she's in some kind of film.

The room fades to black.

Twenty-Three

BY THE TIME I get to the police headquarters, my body's dragging. But I need to be here.

Most of my PI work is in civil law which deals with problems involving inheritance, insurance, and family issues. Criminal law is a different animal. Is there something criminal going on with regard to Rose? I'm not sure.

If Rose did not go to Hawaii, where is she? Possibly still in Vancouver. But where in Vancouver? Do I even have grounds to report her missing? I don't know, but something's off. Yeah, something's off.

I need advice and Lee's the one to ask.

As mandated at headquarters, I report to the public service counter. Lee's out on shift but due to arrive shortly. He spends his lunchtime here, working out. A lot of cops do that. There's a top-of-the-line fitness facility here. A personal trainer, too. And a counselor. Emphasis these days is less on blowing off steam by chugging beer with the boys, more on dealing with things by crafting a sound mind in a sound body. I hope Lee doesn't mind missing today's workout.

I take a seat in the front row of three rows of blue chairs beside the service counter. It's all about blue here, heritage blue. From my pocket, I excavate a granola bar, my emergency food of choice. As I munch, I gaze across the lobby at the interior blackness of the fingerprint room. To my left, beside the exit, is a table flanked by two chairs. On top of the table, there's a phone and three well-thumbed telephone books. People still use phone books? I shrug. To my right are the elevators. Periodically, their doors open and groups in blue swish by, their black shoes strong and silent, steel-toed and rubber-soled. Chatter swirls and echoes from voices that are light, noncommittal. All men's hair is trimmed, all women's pinned. Every uniform is crisp and creased. Are the women wearing perfume? It's undetectable. But aftershave? The air staggers from the weight of it.

Every single officer notices me. Every one sizes me up without acknowledging my existence. Fascinating—eyes which are aware of everything, yet reveal nothing.

Suddenly Lee is in front of me, a quizzical look on his face. "What's up?"

"I tried to call."

"Yeah. I was on the job. Just picked up your message. You okay?"

I wave a hand through the air. "I'm fine. It's Rose I'm concerned about."

"I'm listening." Lee folds his arms.

"You missing your workout?"

"No worries. Ran a marathon this weekend. Need to recover. Now, what's going on?" He plops into a seat beside me.

I let out a sigh.

"Not trying to rush you, bud," says Lee, "no workout but there is paperwork. You know the score."

"Got it. I think Rose is missing."

He's instantly on alert. "Details?"

I spill what I know, all the while realizing it isn't much. "I'm trying to track her steps. I know—"

"Give me the details again. First, she didn't check in at her hotel, right?"

"Right. She did specify that she wanted to go off the grid but she promised to call or text me when she arrived in Waikiki. When she didn't follow through, I phoned the hotel."

"Did she make her flight?"

"No way to find out."

"You're right about that. At this point, anyway. What else have you got?"

"Rose had two tickets to the Heritage Gala. I don't know if she attended. She had lunch at the Lotus Club on Friday. One of her lunch companions, Marlene, said she may have attended the gala, and that she may have shopped for a dress at Pacific Plaza after lunch."

"Want me to run a check on her credit cards?"

I nod. "But I'm pretty sure she paid cash."

"Do you know the store? At Pacific Plaza? Have you been there?"

"Mitchell Crown's. That's my next stop."

"Good enough." Lee stands. "As you likely know, there's no wait time on filing a missing person's report. The whole forty-eight-hour thing? Total myth. But there has to be a solid basis for filing." He paces, his right hand stroking his chin, a habit of his when he's processing. When he turns to me, his eyes are clear. "And I think there is. I sure as hell hope you're wrong, but I trust your instincts. Is there anything else I should know?"

I nod.

"Out with it."

"Remember Rose's sister?"

His eyebrows instantly shoot up. "Margo?"

I let out a sigh. "I may be jumping the gun here, but—"

In an instant, Lee's sitting beside me again. "But what?"

"The Heritage Gala? Three years ago, one week before she went missing, Margo Harrington attended that event."

"You think there's a connection?"

"Don't know. Can't shake the feeling the gala and the disappearance are connected."

Lee stares at me, long and hard. "Should have led with that. Let's file a report immediately. When that's done, I'll find out whether or not Rose made her flight."

"You'll let me know?"

"Absolutely. In the meantime, you check out the boutique."

Pacific Plaza is a masterpiece in urban planning. From the outside, it appears to occupy minimal space but it houses a hundred or more stores, most of which are underground. It is with hope that I march through its arched glass entrance and up to the store locator map. The place is crowded. It's still within peak shopping hours. I pinpoint the store I'm seeking and thread my way through the swarm to the lower floor.

Minutes later, I'm winding my way back. A wasted effort, it seems. The employees on shift today were not working on Friday. Not a one. As I blow through the exit of Pacific Plaza, I blow out an exasperated sigh.

Yet another tomorrow. More waiting.

Twenty-Four

ROSE IS ON THE white couch again. This time clad in satin. A pajama top of Vincent's in a deep shade of red, one that matches her fingernail polish. She looks around. It's daytime. Afternoon? Evening? The last thing she remembers is lying supine on the floor. Did Vincent slap her?

"Ah, there you are, wide awake at last."

Rose cringes.

Vincent moves in, too close. He pats her head. "Shh, precious Rose. You are safe." He scrutinizes her face. "I did my best to stop the swelling. Ice packs and whatnot. Even held you under a cold shower for twenty minutes, but you were gone. I figured it best that you sleep it off."

He extends his fingers and palpates her face, his touch surprisingly tender. "The bruises will fade. You really must be more careful. I don't know how you managed to fall from that stool." He grabs her handcuffs and pulls her to her feet. Rose says nothing as he leads her to the kitchen counter. When she doesn't sit, he gently lifts her and places her on a stool. "You will eat while I attend to the cleaning."

Rose can't move a muscle. She doesn't know why, but she is stuck, a fly on flypaper.

"You have full run of the loft, my darling Rose, if that's what you are wondering."

Yes. Yes. She knows that. Full run. Free run. Like the chickens. Perhaps she should try to run like the chickens. She attempts to raise her cuffed hands from her lap but her hands won't cooperate.

The aroma of coffee infiltrates. Her mouth waters as she looks at the tray in front of her. Whole grain bread. Peppered, scrambled eggs in ridged ramekins. Strawberry jam and orange marmalade in single-serve packets. Breakfast. Or is it brunch? Her stomach growls. She needs this food. But is this food safe?

"You need not worry. The food is safe."

Rose blinks. Is he reading her mind?

"I have no need for drugs." Vincent brushes a dismissive hand through the air. "I have learned over the years that detailed planning and irresistible charm are sufficient. There is no subterfuge now. I have attained my goal. You are here, aren't you?" He strokes her arm and goes about his business.

Rose again attempts to raise her hands. This time, they comply. She picks up a fork and samples the eggs. She tastes nothing foreign. Could she tell if drugs were present? She doubts it. Does it matter? She continues to eat, all the while eyeing Vincent who is immersed in activity.

Vincent's cleaning is precision-based, a millimeter at a time. When he opens a kitchen cupboard, she sees its contents in a glaring new light. This is not just organization; it is perfectionism in the extreme, OCD perfectionism. Could Vincent tolerate even a tiny deviation from this perfectionism? She looks around and eyes two kitchen towels hanging in perfect alignment. Folded the same. Width the same. Length the same.

"I hated my father," Vincent says. "He killed my mother."

Chilled, Rose fixes her gaze on him.

Vincent laughs as if elated by her reaction. "I thought that might catch your attention. Do not fear. I was speaking figuratively. But my father did break my mother, heart and soul. It was his fault she died."

Rose offers no words.

He continues.

"William Lord berated my mother, belittled her gardening." Vincent blows out a resigned sigh. "Flowers blooming, Father badgering, Mother weeping. Those are my childhood memories."

Rose leans in. Is there something else? She dares not breach the silence.

Vincent raises his head and stares off into space. "Mother tolerated everything, as best she could. When William Lord bedded another woman, Mother gave up. Died. That's when the beatings started."

Vincent curls his hands into fists, his lips into a sneer. "Squandered effort on his part. I didn't retaliate. No, it wasn't me. It was Gideon who did that, the retaliation. It was Gideon who exacted vengeance."

For a few seconds, Vincent falls silent again. "Sometimes one needs an older brother," he says quietly.

Gnawing on a triangle of toast, Rose watches transfixed as Vincent's posture exhibits a slow change. He suddenly appears taller, tauter. She swallows. A morsel of toast sticks in her throat. She coughs. She grabs the glass of water from her tray. She gulps. She breathes.

He is beside her now, massaging her neck. She squeezes her eyes tight. Is this it? Is this the end? She swallows the howl lurking in her throat. Seconds pass. The sense of danger disappears. Rose opens her eyes.

In a transformation as quick as the click of a toggle switch, Vincent is again calm, unassuming. He moves toward the towel rack. He removes the dish towels, refolds them, and returns them to their place. "I was away when Gideon arranged my father's demise. A tragic accident, they said. The Sea to Sky Highway can be treacherous." He pulls a bubble level from a drawer and checks the edges of the towels. Smiling, he looks toward her, waving the level. "Perfection." He puts the level back in its place—a drawer which he locks.

The hairs on the back of Rose's neck stand up. Why hadn't she noticed that *all* the drawers have locks?

Vincent continues cleaning and talking. "I cared for no one after my mother died. That is, until I met a girl whose name, Lily, triggered something my mother said. 'Pick all the flowers, Vincent. Enjoy them while they are young, while they are in full bloom. Don't give them time to develop a hatred of their own reflection.' I invited Lily to stay here for a few days. I had a bouquet of her namesake flowers delivered. When the bouquet faded, I passed Lily to Gideon. What happened from then on..." Vincent shrugs. "Gideon tends the gardens. The gardens need fertilizer."

A new fear creeps in on cat paws. Rose cannot allow it to surface. Yet, she must be aware and wary. She must prepare. For what, she doesn't know. Rose focuses on the towels that Vincent has just realigned. Just how attuned to perfection is he? What if she moved a towel? Would he notice? Can she test him, find a weakness? Maybe leave a small piece of tissue on the bathroom floor, then try the towels? Step-by-step, inch by inch...

What was it he said about a bouquet of lilies? About the bouquet fading? Shivering, Rose glances around, looking for a bouquet of roses. Is there one? No. No roses. She exhales.

Looking at her plate, she chooses another piece of toast and a forkful of eggs. There is no physical hunger now. But she must eat. She will not survive unless she eats.

Wednesday, May 4th

Twenty-Five

TOMORROW BECOMES TODAY AND still I am waiting.
I'm sitting in the lounge area in the foyer of the Pacific Plaza, killing time by staring at gloomy clouds through a domed-glass ceiling. When the minute hand on my watch edges toward opening time, I head toward the boutique Rose visited. I stand outside, eyeing the clerk inside, wondering if she will consider opening a bit early. But, no. She catches my eye and doesn't even smile. Why should she? The leather purses on a nearby counter are not lined up properly. She attends to them.

The tiled floor in this mall is shinier than a bald pate. My shoes, with their scuff marks, are an embarrassment by comparison. A few people mill about, all playing a waiting game like me. Some are carrying coffee and the odor pervades. A quiet lot, these shoppers. None are fully engaged in the day yet. There is no white noise chatter, only the incessant drone of elevator music.

The awakening of the mall is abrupt. Simultaneously, locks click open and metal gates collapse into accordion pleats and judder into slots in walls and ceilings. I am the first into my store of choice and I march up to the checkout counter.

The albino-skinned beauty at the register has ginger hair. Not ginger, actually, some deeper color of red, a bottle kind. Conservatively dressed in black and white—the apparent uniform of the well-appointed store clerk—she looks at me with a little surprise, or is that annoyance? She's not ready for the first customer of the day.

"Good morning, Sabrina," I say.

She appears startled at the sound of her name. Perhaps she thinks I am a mind reader. The only thing I am reading right now is her nametag. "I'm Shaughnessy Flynn." I present my card. "I'm looking for information about Rose Harrington whom I believe shopped here on Friday afternoon. She was in search of a dress for a gala on Saturday."

Sabrina's expression now switches to one of puzzlement. She takes my card and fingers it for a minute while she looks around the store. Finding what she wants, she nods. "I can't speak to you about this. Excuse me, please. I'll get the manager."

I'm not surprised. Everyone needs to get the manager. I lean on the counter. Another waiting game.

The manager is all smiles when she approaches. She is older, not old (I never say old anymore in reference to women.) She is heavyset with cropped silver hair and an affinity for gold, as attested by the multitude of fine chains dangling from her neck, each displaying a trinket: a cornucopia, a crucifix, a cantilevered stack of books. So, she's grateful, religious, and a bibliophile? She exudes joy. I enjoy pegging people. Beneath all the chains is her nametag. Obscured.

"Good morning, Mr. Flynn," she says. "I understand you want information about a customer. I'm not sure that I can help you with that." She passes back my card.

Okay. So it's cut to the chase time. "I understand that. People are sometimes reluctant to give information in this situation. Permit me to explain . . ." My trailing off is deliberate. This is a woman who likes to be in charge. Even though there is a ticking clock on my need to know, I need to let her make the choices here.

She folds her arms. "Go ahead."

Good. I'm in. Well, not quite in, but I have a foot on the threshold. "Rose Harrington, my client and friend, was scheduled to fly to Hawaii but she did not check in to her Waikiki hotel. I have been told that she may have shopped here on Friday."

"We have a lot of customers, Mr. Flynn. You'll have to give me more than that." She's tapping one finger on the sleeve of her striped black-and-beige cashmere sweater. In my head, I'm hearing strains of "Ebony and Ivory."

I'm making headway here so I keep a poker face and spill the details: time of day, description of Rose as a tall, long-haired blond, slender. It's when I get to that part of the story that Sabrina, the reticent cashier clerk who has been hanging within earshot, steps forward.

"I remember her," she says softly, standing at the elbow of the manager who turns.

"Okay, Sabrina, what can you tell this gentleman?"

"Exactly what he said. A tall, blond lady, late twenties, I'm guessing, came in to look for a dress for the Heritage Gala."

"Did she buy a dress?"

Sabrina nods. At that point, another customer approaches with a question and Sabrina, with a nod from the manager, scurries off to help. It is sudden, her stopping and twirling about. "Oh," she says, "the blond lady mentioned that she was going to have a spa day on Saturday: hair, nails, massage, the whole bit. We both go to the same hairdresser—Beauty Bee on Beach. Don't know what spa she uses." Sabrina turns away. "I'm coming," she calls to the waiting customer.

The manager's phone rings and she glances at it. "I have to take this. I assume we are finished here?"

"Yes, thank you," I say as she veers off. I pause, pull out my notebook, and glance at my list of questions. The only relevant one was "Did Rose go to the gala?"

My phone blips. A text message. Could it be Rose? I whip out the phone. My sigh is one of disappointment. It's Lee.

Looked for receipts.
No credit card expenditures by Rose.
Not a one.

Tell me something I don't know. I type in "Thanks" and exit the store. The mall, which short minutes ago was practically vacant, is now swarming. A reversal of yesterday's high school scenario. Where did all these people come from? And where the hell is Rose?

Twenty-Six

A FUG OF STEAM rises from the silken water of the ergonomic bathtub where Rose sits, almost fully immersed. There are no bubbles. She is not allowed that shred of privacy. Bubbles and bath bombs would only hide her beauty and Vincent will have none of that. There is only oil, baby oil, for his young and beautiful blossom. He insists that she spread her arms, palms up, on the armrests. She obliges. Not that she has much choice. Vincent used zip ties to bind her wrists to the acrylic safety handles.

Vincent is not here now. But he will be soon. A flat sound emanates from the direction of the kitchen, a steady scrape. Is he scraping food from a plate? Rose fixates on the metal-on-metal sound until she can match it with an image. Vincent is sharpening a knife, a steady drawn-out rhythm, a ping-and-whistle tone which pares her nerve endings. She begins and maintains deep breaths, feeling her body slowly become one with the eerie cadence. Abruptly, the sound ceases. Her adrenaline kicks in. She cannot stop trembling. She squeezes her eyes tight as she hears him approach.

He is beside the tub now, at a full stop. A clatter occurs. She pops her eyes wide and jolts at the sight of a black-handled knife on top of the vanity, just an arm's distance away. Instantly, she turns her attention to the mirror above the sink.

A haze blankets that mirror and tints Rose with gratitude. Without condensation, that miracle of science, she would see his reflection. It is enough that she feels his eyes crawling over every part of her body.

How long will she be forced to sit here? The overbearing presence beside her stoops. Her fingers curl into fists. His lips to her ear, he blows a gentle breath. "Almost done, my beauty. Almost done." He tilts her torso forward and steps into the tub behind her. Rose lets out a sob. He lowers himself into the water, pushing her head under, holding it there, and tugging it up again. She gasps. He repeats the procedure. When she resurfaces, he pulls her body close until she is resting against him. She is aware of a fragrance. What is it? Soap? Yes, a bar of lavender-scented soap. Her mother's scent. A scent Rose often lingered over in the high-end bath shop she frequented, just to have a moment of remembering. The memory is a treasure, eclipsed now, as Vincent waves the soap under her nose and slides it over her body.

Rose experiences a peculiar phenomenon. She is standing outside the tub. She is wiping condensation from the mirror and humming a tune. Perhaps she is not here at all. She is in her own tiny bathroom, checking her face in the mirror, looking for that slight breakout of acne that occurs every time she encounters an irresistible square of Belgian chocolate. Perhaps she is loading toothpaste onto her electric toothbrush and gearing up for a little dance to quicken her toothbrush's programmed two-minute timer.

As Vincent soaps her and toys with her, she stays outside of the reality. She is safe on the outside. It is only when he steps from the tub and uses the knife to slash the ties binding her wrists that she steps back into her body. Violated. Yes, but she is still alive. He returns the steel cuffs to her wrists and leaves momentarily. She hears him in the kitchen, unlocking a drawer, perhaps concealing the knife. Upon return, he grasps her underarms and lifts her from the tub. A strange swish of gratitude floats through her. He doesn't plan on drowning her. The sucking sound of water. The swirl and whirl as it evacuates the tub. Using a towel, thick and gruff, he blots her body, drying every pore.

Upon command, Rose deposits the towel into the hamper. Upon command, accompanied by a syncopated chink of handcuffs, she scours the tub and shines the fixtures. On hands and knees, she scrubs the bathroom floor. A whack of the toilet brush on her rear stops her. What has she done wrong?

"Missed a spot."

Rose backtracks, making tiny circles with the blue-handled plastic scrub brush. She lingers there, which apparently appeases him.

He leaves the room.

Breathing more easily in his absence, Rose ponders Vincent and his perfectionism. What if? What if? What if she were to try a small test? Would he notice a tiny change? As she dries the floor with a chamois, she recalls her idea of dropping a minuscule piece of tissue. Should she follow through? It is while shaping the hanging square of toilet paper into a *V* that another idea occurs. How adamant is he that the toilet paper be hung to unroll from the front? What if it unrolled from the back? Heart pounding, she rips the last square and flips the roll. Stuffing the shred of evidence into her mouth, she folds the end of the roll into a perfect *V*. A perfect *V* for the perfect Vincent. She sneers, an action that brings a smidgen of comfort. He hasn't broken her. Still, as she cleans the tools of her new trade as a maid, she has concerns about the piece of toilet paper in her mouth. She can't just create a spit wad and let it fly. Instead, she swallows it.

Vincent chooses that instant to march up behind her.

She steadies herself. Inspection time.

Vincent peeks into every nook and corner. He glides a finger along the top of the toilet tank. He checks for spots on the faucets. He smiles.

And she is safe. He hasn't noticed the toilet paper turnaround. A small triumph, but a triumph nonetheless. Rose hides the hint of a smile that threatens her face as she puts the cleaning equipment into its storage place. It's late afternoon now and her stomach is growling.

Vincent perks an ear. "Hungry, little one? Well, you'll just have to live off the fat of the land." He pats her rear end. "Not that there's much there to begin with, but you had breakfast. That's enough food for one day." He runs a hand through her hair, entwining it in his fist. "Such flaxen beauty," he says, drawing her to him.

Rose cringes.

He looks around, a final inspection. Everything gleams, the tang in the air is Mr. Clean. Still, Rose wonders if he will find fault.

He does not. He merely nods his approval and drags her to the bedroom.

"I have a few chores here," says Vincent. "Then, sadly, I'll be gone throughout the afternoon, perhaps overnight."

Dropped onto the edge of the bed and ordered to stay, Rose focuses on her toenails, the bloodred polish on her toenails. All that time in the tub and there's not a chip in her nail polish. Was it only Saturday that she had a manicure and a pedicure? They do excellent work at Beauty Bee.

"I will be but a minute," Vincent says.

A minute? What's he up to? Will there be another bout of abuse? At this point, it doesn't matter. All she knows is that she wants to live. The padding of bare feet is the mark of his reappearance. She has the sense that he is raising his arm and she cowers, covering her face, closing her eyes. Something falls on her, yes. But it is not painful. It is soft. She opens her eyes. Clothes. He has tossed clothes. She stares at the alighted objects. These are her clothes, her very own clothes, the ones she had packed for her vacation. Bizarre, that. He really is in possession of her suitcases, just as he said.

"You may get dressed now." Again the handcuffs come off. He watches while she pulls on a thong and a bra. She rushes into jeans and a T-shirt. It feels so good, this idea of being clad. She runs her hands, wrinkled like raisins, up and down the thighs of her jeans. She raises her head. Something in the corner of the room catches her eye, something new and shiny.

A tremor forms in her core. Questions swirl. Why is that here? That stainless steel dog cage? Where did that thing come from? When did he move it into the room? She remains mute.

"You must need the facilities by now." Vincent escorts her to the bathroom and stands over her while she lowers her jeans and sits.

Rose keeps her back straight and her head high. What could he possibly take from her anymore? She urinates. She wipes. As she stands and pulls her jeans up, she presses the lever. A simple thing, the flush of a toilet. Familiar. Real. On some level, it grounds her, strengthens her. Without apology, she edges toward the sink. He bars her path. She does not back down. He angles his body, allowing her access. She washes her hands, dragging the action out. In her head, she is singing the "Happy Birthday" song. That's how you know how long to wash your hands. The length of the "Happy Birthday" song. Everybody knows that germs are dead if you wash them long enough to sing "Happy Birthday." What can she do to get out of this? What can she do to make him dead? How can she do that? What the hell can she do? She turns off the water, dries her hands, and pivots toward the door.

He clamps a hand onto the waistband of her jeans, jerking her to a halt. He slips past her and turns to face her. "You may have noticed the special treat I bought just for you." He handcuffs her again and then runs a finger along the outline of her chin.

Rose jerks her head away. In doing so, she catches sight of her face in the mirror. Reddened. The imprint of his hand on her cheek. Her eye is swollen, turning dark. A hideous image. The face of a victim.

He forces her head back and again traces the outline of her chin. "I trust you will forgive the severity of the cage," he says in a low monotone, "but I do have a penchant for shiny objects." He wraps an arm around her and steers her toward the dog kennel.

Rose draws back and stops dead.

Gripping her arm, he thrusts her forward. He slams her into the cage.

She lands in a heap on a dog pillow in a three-foot square metal cage, blinking in disbelief at wire walls.

He kicks her leg which hadn't fully made it across the threshold.

She retracts, a snail retreating.

He closes the door of the kennel and pads his way across the room.

Pinched and cramped, her heart battering her eardrums, Rose remains motionless. There are shuffling sounds, perhaps the slipping on of shoes, the shrugging on of a jacket. Strange, the idea of a coat on a hot spring day. Is it a hot spring day? It was a hot spring day when she met him.

He returns. "I'll be gone a while," he says, "but you will be safe in your little room." He heads toward the exit. With a quick snap of his shoulders, Vincent turns around. "One thing that puzzles me . . ." He rushes back toward Rose, coming to a halt in front of her prison, dropping to his haunches.

Rose doesn't want to look at him, but she can't stop herself. She raises her head and glares.

"Your sister?" he says, his voice clipped, his eyes cold. "Mar-i-gold." He raises the corners of his mouth into a menacing smile. "Marigold is a peculiar name for a brunette, don't you think?" His laugh is quick, a pistol report.

Stung, Rose sinks onto the dog pillow.

Still laughing, Vincent strides toward the door.

Rose doesn't listen for the telltale sounds of his departure. Instead, she clenches her fists, digging her fingernails into her palms. She had told Vincent many things, too many things.

But she had never once referred to her sister by her full name: Marigold.

Twenty-Seven

IT'S MIDDAY WHEN I get to the gala venue. I considered going to the hair salon first but figured it was pointless. Yes, I can backtrack if I need to, but it is obvious now that Rose did attend the gala so this is my next step. Stupid of me not to head here first.

The lobby of the Sylvan breathes tradition in its abundance of dark wood, paneled walls, and cubby holes for mail and messages. A heritage building, certainly appropriate as a Heritage Gala venue.

"How may I help you, sir?" the uniformed desk clerk asks. He tosses his head, a habit no doubt, one that he could break by cutting the thatch of black hair hanging over his left eye.

"I'm seeking information about an event that was held here Saturday night. The Heritage Gala?"

He nods. "What would you like to know?"

"How do I find out if someone attended that gala?" I show my card, which he takes. I hurry into details. "I'm looking for a friend and client. Her name is Rose."

"Umm. Private investigator." He returns my card, his expression blank. "There's not much I can help you with."

"I know that it's not policy to give information to strangers but I can put you in touch with a reference at the police department—"

"It's not that. I would normally just refer you to the events manager, but she's not here today." He's already looking over my shoulder at a group of people standing behind me. He returns his gaze to me, both hands on the counter, all business now. "I doubt if the events manager could help you, anyway. All she did was book the event. The gala was run by volunteers. You may want to talk to the bartender, perhaps even the servers, the valets . . . no, not the valets. No valet parking for that." He shakes his head. "You'll have to contact the events manager. Here's the info." He presents me with a business card.

"Thank you for your time." I take the card and start to turn.

"Sorry I can't be more help," the clerk adds. "Have you Googled the gala? If your friend was there, she'll show up on the net. Everything and everyone does, eventually. That event was covered by the press, you know. Probably tons of pictures on the web. Have you checked the web?"

"Yes, I have checked Google, but maybe I missed something. Thanks. I'll give it another shot." I shove the card he gave me into my wallet and head for the exit. A single glance back shows me that he has moved on, to the next customer, the next question, the next toss of his head.

What do I move on to? I'm exhausted beyond my ability to think. What time is it? Lunch time. A sandwich, some salad, and next? Revisit the Google gods.

Twenty-Eight

MY PLAN IS TO go to the hotel restaurant and refuel while I Google. I'm dragging as I head to the parking lot to retrieve my laptop. My lethargy evaporates when I spot a man, possibly six feet tall, walking the perimeter of my vehicle. Instinctively, I call out. A dumb move. On the alert, he stiffens for a millisecond, then bolts. I give chase but it doesn't last long. He is a jaguar and I am a tortoise. I pause to catch my breath and he vanishes between two skyscrapers. Passersby glance, shrug, and then go about their business. I go back to my car and check it. Nothing seems out of order.

What the heck would anyone want with my jalopy? Ages old. Nothing of value, except my laptop. I hastily unlock the trunk and rummage through the folds of the ragged, flannel blanket in which I conceal objects of potential interest to criminals. I sigh when I realize my subterfuge worked. My laptop is still here. I pick it up and close the trunk. I stare in the direction of the escapee, wondering if I had missed anything about him. Anything familiar there? Nothing comes to mind. Should I report this incident? I shrug it off. I'll mention this non-incident to Lee later.

I've lost the urge to go back to the hotel. Instead, I trot to the closest coffee shop, looking back occasionally to check my vehicle. If it could, it would likely roll its eyes, or its headlights. The darn thing's been left on its own and survived on more than one occasion. It'll survive without me during lunch. I move into the coffee shop.

With lunch, latte, and laptop on a tray, I choose a table and sit with my back to the wall, eyeing my car in the parking lot across the street. It is not until I have eaten the crust from the sandwich that I open the laptop. While I log in, I munch walnuts from my salad, one at a time. H-e-r-i-t-a-g-e, I type. Google offers suggestions and I click on the one marked gala.

Heritage Gala. April 30th. There are a variety of sites, hundreds of pictures. I click with the right hand, pluck walnuts with the left. Seems to help concentration, that steady action. Every few seconds, I glance at my car. No one lurking. I work through the links.

Yes, hundreds, maybe thousands of pictures. Not a one of Rose. No surprise there. I already Googled it earlier. If Rose were in any of these links, wouldn't I have seen her? Temporarily defeated, I close the laptop. Maybe I just need to mull things over. I nibble on my BLT as I root through my salad looking for walnuts. This time, as I pick them out, I put them on the plate. Before I know it, I have formed a frame, the outer edge of a puzzle, at the center of which is the plate's floral design. A pretty flower, the lily. Just three petals. I like threes, groups of three, the rule of three. Three. Vi, Margo, Rose. Three. I flick at a walnut and the pattern disappears.

What the hell am I doing thinking about numbers? And flowers? The only flower I should be concerned about is "Rose." What am I going to do about Rose? I've hit a dead end. So has my sandwich apparently. Nothing but crumbs.

I reopen my computer and reacquaint myself with Google. Perhaps I missed something the first time. The first *two* times, idiot. But, I remind myself, that's the way puzzles work. You stare and stare. You leave it. You go back. Miracles emerge.

Every nook and corner of that ballroom was photographed that night. I click on every picture. Am about to give up when I catch sight of something, not inside the ballroom, but outside, in front of the venue. The foreground is a picture of a couple. No one I know. Irrelevant. It's the background that grabs me. In the background, at a seven o'clock position, there is a shoe, a single shoe, a stiletto heel with a red rose on the front. Rose's shoe. I was there when she bought that detachable rose. Shoe jewelry, she called it. That is Rose's foot. That is Rose, getting into a car outside the gala venue.

All that is visible of the car is a wedge of fender and an arc of interior, enough to see that the vehicle is black—a lustrous ebony—and the seats are leather, a carefully-crafted quilted pattern in a rich, sandalwood hue. I scrutinize the photo. I enlarge it. There is no logo visible. How do I find out what kind of car, whose car? No doubt there was no end to the number of expensive vehicles lining the streets for the gala, some hired, some owned. No valet parking.

Who the hell did Rose get into a car with? Did she have a date for the gala? How do I find out? I reread my notes from the mall boutique. Rose went to a hair salon called Beauty Bee on Beach. Maybe she mentioned the gala to her stylist.

Laptop in hand, I lunge for the door.

Twenty-Nine

THE LORD ESTATE, MASKED by ten-foot boxwood hedges, is accessible by a wrought-iron gate which responds rapidly to a click of Vincent's remote. Once inside, he idles his vehicle, waiting the few seconds it takes for the gate to close behind him. After a resounding *clank!* and a glance at the rearview mirror, he drives on. One can never be too careful. No one else has access—by key, remote, or code—to this property. Except Gideon. Gideon has access to everything.

Vincent follows the circular path of the cobbled driveway, past the green-tipped white hydrangea spheres and lush, pink azalea bushes, past the columned entrance to the mansion, toward the parking lot. He pulls into a slot beside a white, paneled van and casts a glance toward the driver's side window. Unoccupied. Vincent shrugs. Did he really expect to find Gideon that easily? He shifts into REVERSE, driving comfortably backwards until he comes to the front entrance. There, he puts the car into park. He steps out.

The house is a Victorian master with fish-scale tiles, gingerbread trim, and a wrap-around veranda which is a jewel, the charcoal of its newel posts and columns forming an anchor for the light gray of the steps and landing. It was Gideon who suggested painting the front door in those same two shades of gray. He said it would lend an air of sophistication. In this, as in most things, Gideon was right.

Vincent walks slowly up the steps. He unlocks the door and deposits his keys in the brass receptacle on the mahogany table in the foyer. The sound echoes; Vincent shudders. Does he want to be here? This is his family home, yes, but he prefers his loft. He considers leaving, avoiding ghosts, but dismisses the idea.

Why hasn't he heard a word from Gideon? An annoyance, Gideon, but he is still family. Vincent needs to talk to Gideon, needs to persuade him to stick with the script. Vincent depends on Gideon. One should depend on an older brother, shouldn't one?

Vincent roams. The house is sheathed in darkness, all drapes drawn. Should he open the curtains, fling the windows wide? Not necessary. He gets enough sunshine through those sky tunnels in his loft. One never knows what evil can enter through open windows.

Finding no trace of Gideon, Vincent meanders into the library and clicks a toggle switch. Light fills the room, not an overpowering light, but a warm invitation. Vincent glances at the shelves of leather-bound books and lets out a contented sigh. This is the only place in this house where he likes to be. A good thing, since he will apparently have to wait for that brother of his.

A visit to the bookcase, a selection of a book, a comfortable reading chair. That's all he needs. Wait. Vodka. He needs vodka.

He opens a nearby cabinet and pours a single, no a double, and takes a sip. Instantly, warmth travels down his throat into his body. He nods in contentment.

Before he settles in, he switches off the overhead light and turns on the brass floor lamp beside his brown recliner, a lamp with a horizontal shade, a lamp which is set at just the right height so that light floods the page, not blinds his eyes.

Vincent chuckles as he turns the book over and over in his hands. How his father would have hated this book, would have sneered at him for reading any book about floriculture. But Vincent loves flowers. Mother taught him to love flowers.

Vincent drops the book into his lap. It falls open to a full-color illustration of a single red rose. He smiles.

Perfect.

Thirty

A DOORBELL CHIME ANNOUNCES my entry to Beauty Bee on Beach. As I step into the roomy, white, rectangular salon, I'm inundated with the sounds of giggles and chatter. A pungent odor—coffee mixed with chemicals—permeates.

Directly ahead is a white portable fireplace, a classic design with inset panels and a decorative dentil molding. On top of its rectangular mantel sits a crystal bowl flanked by two candles, red in silver holders. Centered on the wall above are two square prints, identical close-ups of a single red rose blossom. The electric firebox is black now, turned off as one would expect, like a TV on a hot summer day.

The fireplace is dead center between two stylist stations, each containing a full-length mirror with a beveled looking-glass frame and a white leather stylist chair. There are three more such stations in the room, two on the left, and one on the right. To my left is a stained-glass divider, painted with roses. I look at the mat under my feet, again a rose pattern. I can instantly visualize Rose in this place. It's almost as if it were designed for her.

I scuff my feet and poke my head around the divider. Ah, a desk. No computer on top. No one sitting in the acrylic chair. No real evidence of business, except perhaps for the red phone and the large, open appointment book. I approach the desk. All appointments are penciled in.

It's not long before a petite, brown-haired stylist approaches, comb in hand. She's wearing a flouncy, flowery blouse over black, cropped leggings. And flip-flops. Can't help but notice her toe ring—opal. An October birthday? Her toenails are bright, tangerine. "I'm Sue," she says, smiling. This woman smiles a lot. Her face is creased in all the right places for a smiler. "How may I help you? An appointment, perhaps?"

I know she's eyeing my hair and I run a hand through it. Not the best idea because a few hairs leave with every touch these days. I avoid looking into the mirror behind her. "I was wondering if I might ask about a client of yours."

She takes a step back. I pause, assuming that she is going to ask for the manager.

"Well," she says, "I'm waiting. You can't just stroll into a business establishment these days and make such a request without at least producing some identification."

Ouch! Didn't see that coming. Instantly, I pull out my ID. "Sorry. I'm just so accustomed to people saying they have to call their managers."

"I am the manager." Sue takes my card and scrutinizes it. "Flynn. The name sounds familiar." A look of awareness crosses her eyes and she opens her mouth as if to drop a tidbit of information. She stops. "Hmmm. And just who are you asking about?"

"My friend, Rose Harrington. She's--"

"I know Rose. She's my client. She's in Hawaii."

"She's *supposed* to be in Hawaii."

A worried look falls over Sue's face. "What do you mean?"

"She didn't show up."

Sue opens her mouth like she's about to speak. She says nothing. She lowers her head.

"So I'm searching for her."

Sue looks up and locks her eyes with mine. "What can I do?"

"Rose had an appointment on Saturday?"

Sue nods.

"Did she say anything about changing her plans?"

I see something in Sue's eyes, a thought forming. "Follow me," she says, and leads me toward a door at the back of the salon.

As soon as we are inside the break room, which is big enough to contain my entire laneway house, Sue closes the door.

"Sit." She says, pointing toward a rectangular table. Again, I obey. She chooses a chair directly opposite.

"Rose was in on Friday for a trim," says Sue. "I suggested she try a curly look for a change, but no, Rose knows her mind. She likes the layered look. She doesn't need dye, that's for sure. That hair is naturally flaxen, the envy of all—" Sue stops dead. "Sorry. I natter when I'm nervous. What do you need to know?"

"Did she say anything to you about the gala she was planning on attending?"

"Only that she was going. And that she was going solo."

"Are you certain about the solo detail? Did she say anything at all about meeting someone?"

Sue shakes her head. "We see a steady stream of clients on Saturdays. Most of them are excited to share their plans for showing off their new hairdos. I hear lots of stories and have to admit that my recall of details is sometimes as blotchy as a first-timer's bottle dye job. But this time? Rose was adamant about going alone."

Despite Sue's confident response, I persist, hope upon hope. "Perhaps she made arrangements to meet one of the friends she had lunch with on Friday?"

"Not a chance. Yes, she spoke of them, but in a wistful fashion, if you know what I mean." She gives me a knowing look.

Clueless, I blink. "Enlighten me."

Sue casts her eyes skyward and I know she's losing patience.

"Please," I add hurriedly.

"Typical male. No offense."

"None taken." I grin. "In my experience, women read subtext. Men only see what's in front of them."

Laughter explodes from her throat and she spreads her hands, palms up. "Okay, then. She spoke of how happy they are, how they seem to know what they are doing with their lives: one of them, the gay one, is recently married, another is having a child, and another is in charge of things at her place of employment, yadda, yadda, yadda. I'm pretty sure Rose is searching, looking for something or someone. I'm sure she could use a love interest but she refuses to throw herself into the Internet pool. She'd love to meet—" Sue stops in mid-sentence and stares past me. Her eyes shift from left to right, like she's reading a book. "Rose did meet someone," she says slowly. "Not on the Internet. Not on Friday. It was before that. Thursday. It was Thursday. She went to Granville Island on Thursday. Hadn't intended to. She was taking a walk and just wandered to the False Creek Ferry dock. She meandered and decided to pick up some produce. She bumped into some guy there. What was his name?"

There is another pause. I wait, pen poised.

Sue snaps her fingers. "Vincent. His name was Vincent. And she was a smitten kitten."

"Did she go anywhere with him?"

"No. No. She walked with him for a while but he left Granville Island before she did."

I sigh. Nothing there. "Is that all?"

"She gave him her phone number."

"Oh?"

Sue nods. "Yes. In fact, she entered it into his phone."

"Did she get his number?"

"I don't know. I don't think so." She puzzles over it for a few seconds. "No, that's all I remember." Her eyes glaze as she stares at me. "I know all about you, Flynn. Rose values your friendship. She loves to tell the story of her Indo-Canadian friend with the name of an Irish redhead. Anything you need, anything you can think of, you call me. And keep in touch, please."

I nod.

A voice calls to her from the salon. She jumps. "Darn it all. Customer waiting. Must run." She scurries to the door, holds it wide, and waits for me.

"Thank you for everything." I hurry past her.

Thirty-One

FLUMMOXED, NEEDING TO THINK, I walk to Sunset Beach, just blocks from the beauty salon. It is soothing, the shimmer of sea and sigh of waves, but it does nothing to clear my thoughts. Maybe what I really need is someone to help me think. Someone like Lee. Why haven't I heard from him? It's been twenty-four hours since we filed a report with Missing Persons. Shouldn't he have some info for me by now? And wasn't I supposed to meet Lee this evening anyway?

I pull out my phone and check my calendar. Ah, there it is. Trivia Night. I call Lee. The phone goes straight to message. No patience for that, I thumb a text.

> **Stuck. Any info? Not up for trivia.**
> **Meet at watering hole at 7? Thx.**

Not long after I press Send, the response comes.

> **No trivia? No worries. Yes to watering hole.**
> **Need to chat. See you then.**

I wonder what "need to chat" means but I'm not going to fixate. Still, I have time to kill, so I stroll to a nearby bench and plop down. To my right, there's a lumpish man toting a metal detector, searching the sand in a line pattern, back and forth, back and forth. Such steadiness and patience should result in treasure. But life is not always like that. I watch for a while, then look to my left.

Adjacent to the False Creek Ferry gangway is a curved stretch of sandy shoreline dotted with rocks and driftwood. Three dogs are playing, swimming, and digging there, clearly oblivious to the NO DOGS PERMITTED ON BEACH sign. One of them, an aging golden retriever, runs onto the asphalt path between me and the beach. The dog stops dead in front of me and shakes, releasing water droplets like a lawn sprinkler. I'm grinning as I turn away from the incoming spray.

"Sorry, Mister." This from a brown-haired boy, a teenager with a blinding smile who has run up behind the dog. A middle-aged man—lean, lively, and somehow familiar—joins the teenager.

"Bobby, you know you're not supposed to let Lady off leash," the man says.

"It's Bob, Dad." The boy's smile is gone now, replaced by an exasperated look. A typical teenager. "Bobby's a little kid's name."

The father grins. "Got it. But there are rules." He points to the sign.

Bob shrugs. "Lady loves the beach, Dad. She's not getting any younger, you know."

"I know, son, but the last thing I want is to pay a two thousand dollar fine." He turns to me then and extends his right hand. "I'm Justin, Justin Wentworth," he says. "And this here is my son, *Bob*. Our apologies."

I shake his hand. "Flynn. No problem. A few drops of water never hurt anybody." As I release his hand, a memory ripples. I know this guy.

Justin looks at me curiously. "Have we met?"

Darn. I hoped he'd forgotten. Justin and I had met through our children, at a realtors' family event in a city park a long time ago. "Are you in real estate?" I ask, determined to keep it vague.

"Yeah. You?"

"I used to be. Got out during the last boom, ahead of the downward curve."

"Smart man. I lost a lot in the crash."

I nod. "A tough time." I take a beat. I have no desire to revisit the crush of my past. I have to slip out of this before Justin asks me about my family. "It's a booming business now, though."

"Indeed it is, but I'm much more cautious these days. I've got a family to support." He glances toward the parking lot behind me.

I follow his gaze. A woman and a little girl—perhaps six or seven—are waving at him. "Justin! Bobby!" the woman calls.

"Coming, Sarah," Justin calls back. He turns to Bob. "Let's go, son. Your mother and sister are waiting."

Bob puts a leash on the retriever. "Bye!" he says.

I watch as they cross the bike path to the parking lot, a sensation of envy pulling at my gut. I turn back to my ripple of memory, a colorful ripple, the ripple of a rainbow-colored parachute. My son, Sanjay, met Justin's Bobby when they were standing beside each other in a huge circle of kids, all gripping the edge of a rainbow parachute. Amelia and I were holding hands and smiling as we watched the children play.

One game involved the use of cotton balls in the center of the parachute, cotton which bounced like popcorn when the children jiggled the edges of the chute. In another game, the children raised the parachute, the parachute ballooned, and designated players scurried to a free spot on the other side before the parachute could float to the ground. The memory of Sanjay's bright smile bubbles through me.

Sanjay and Bobby played together all afternoon that day, a sunny afternoon when Bobby was content to be Bobby, when both boys were four. At the end of the day, Amelia and I met Justin and Sarah and talked of arranging a playdate. It never materialized. What's that expression about life happening while you're making other plans? It's true. Life happens.

So does death.

My mood instantly darkens. Why should that man have his family while I do not? My wife is not waiting for me. My son—

A police siren screams, piercing my thoughts, stopping them cold. I shake my head, ridding myself of residue. I've got to stay with what is. The whole Rose issue has me down one rabbit hole. I don't need to drop into another one. I glance at my watch. Better move before I lose all impetus. I head to the watering hole on Davie Street.

The watering hole, an Irish pub, is basically a wide corridor flanked by a long bar on the left and a line of tables on the right. Little light makes its way through the tiny windows at the front. The walls are dark wood with the exception of the far wall, the focus wall, which is exposed brick. The floors are wooden planks which amplify every scrape of a chair or clunk of a boot. I crimp my nose as I adjust to the pervasive smell of beer and sweat.

It's still early. No sign of Lee. Would be easy enough to spot the lanky Lee even though the place is crowded. I like it when it's crowded. It's the people—regulars whose taut faces and steel-toe boots are pockmarked from the labor of life—who give this place a cheery atmosphere. It's here that they hang out or hide out, as the case may be.

I weave my way along the bar until I find a free stool. The bartender shows up pretty fast. A new guy. Tall like Lee. I often wonder what it would be like to be on the other side of six feet.

"What would you like, fella?"

"Tonic water," I say, despite my craving for a pint. I glance at his hands. Why would a bartender have dirt under his nails?

"Wouldn't you prefer a Harp's lager?"

"Yes, I sure would. Working, though." My curiosity is peaked. "What made you think I would choose that brand?"

He uses a hitchhiker thumb to point to the chalkboard behind him. "Irish pub. Lots of Irish beer on tap." He maintains the position, his ribbed, muscle-fit, long sleeve shirt expanding to accommodate his expanded bicep. The guy must spend hours in the gym. Big guns. Taut chest. Big head, too. Bulbous nose. Bald. Looks like he's wearing a skull cap, but I can't tell for sure in this dim light. Eyes black like coal. I glance at the chalkboard. "Tonic water," I repeat.

"Good enough then." Seconds later, he plunks the drink on the bar. "Anything else?"

"Not for the moment." I glance toward the door.

"Meeting someone?"

"A friend." This guy may want conversation, but I'm not interested. "Thanks." I pick up my drink, drop cash on the bar, and head to a newly-vacated table. Gotta grab it before someone else does.

Just as I sit, I spot Lee lumbering through the door. I wave.

"Be right there," he calls as he heads to the bar. I watch the bartender fill Lee's order without saying a word. Frothy glass in hand, Lee pulls out a chair across from me. "Sorry if I'm late, bud."

"You're not."

"Wanted to meet you earlier, but work . . . you know what it's like. Okay, give me the four one one." Lee looks at me, his face radiating concern.

The overhead fan whirs to life. I'm surprised that I can hear it over the din of voices. I pull out my notebook and start in with the details. It's a relief to retrace my steps, to give voice to my search. When I finish, I wait.

The muscle-bound bartender is nearby now, wiping down a table. I catch his eye. He abruptly returns to the bar.

"Sounds like you got a lot of info from that stylist," says Lee.

"Yeah, she was pretty chatty. Busy too. She had just told me the name of the guy Rose met when she got called back to work."

"You say that Rose left Granville Island alone?"

"That's what Sue the stylist said."

"This guy, Vincent, he left before her?"

I nod.

"Did she walk with him to his method of transportation?"

"Not a clue." I'm irritated with myself for not thinking to ask.

"Perhaps Rose mentioned that she and Vincent parted at his car, bus, boat?"

"Sue didn't say."

"You should ask her."

"Damn fine idea." I jump to my feet.

"Where do you think you're going?"

"To the hair salon."

"No, you're not," he says, his voice a steel reprimand. "Park it." He points to my chair.

Taken aback, I sit, my gaze fixed on Lee. Why hasn't he taken even a sip from his beer? Is the beer a ruse to make this seem like a normal trip to the watering hole? "What the hell is going on, Lee?"

He runs a finger up and down the outside of his beer glass, drawing parallel lines in the condensation. "You told me Rose wasn't distraught, right? That she specified going off the grid?" His tone is low now, somber.

"Right." I inhale, deep. Air stalls in my lungs and I let out a single cough.

"You know," Lee says painstakingly, like he is having difficulty shaping the words, "that since Rose wasn't distraught and since she specified going off the grid—"

"You're repeating yourself."

He ignores my interruption. "—it is possible, *likely* even, that she will show up of her own accord." He gives me a penetrating look.

My heart quickens. I impulsively fling my hands up in a halting gesture but instantly pull them back. Nothing's going to stop what's coming. I fold my arms across my chest. "Out with it."

"Good enough." Lee straightens in his chair. "Your instincts were spot-on. Rose Harrington was not on Sunday's flight. In fact, she rescheduled her flight to Monday."

A nervous laugh escapes me, jars me. "I hope like hell you're saying I've been worrying for nothing. Are you saying she checked into her hotel in Waikiki a day later than planned? Rose checked in on Monday. That's it, right?"

Lee shakes his head. He reaches across the table and rests a hand on my forearm. "I'm sorry, Flynn, but Rose did not show up for the Monday flight, either. From what I can tell, Rose Harrington did not go to Hawaii."

I'm trying to snatch hold of his words, to make sense of his words. Isn't this what I suspected? *Exactly* what I suspected? That Rose is missing? Yes, but suspicion and reality are different beasts. My arms are still folded tight and I'm rocking back and forth, tiny movements.

Lee's hand tightens around my arm. "You okay, bud?"

"Where the hell is she, Lee?" My voice is foreign, high-pitched, its edges rough with panic.

"I wish I knew. What I do know is that you can only sit with this for a minute. No time to process. Not yet." He shakes my arm. "Flynn, are you with me?" He leans back in his chair and waits.

I swallow hard, unfold my arms, and knock back the tonic water, wishing it was something stronger. "Yeah. Yeah. I'm with you."

"You have a personal connection here, Flynn. You also have options. If this is too big a conflict, just drop back. Let us handle it."

I shake my head. "Not a chance. Promised Rose's mother I'd take care of her. Can't hand this off. The VPD can do what it has to, but I'm in this and I'm not backing off."

"Good enough. Moving on. You up for taking the next step now, talking to Sue the stylist? I can do that for you."

"No. No offense. I'm sure Sue will talk to you but, right now, I'd prefer to do it myself."

Lee nods. "Understood. As long as you know you're not alone in this." He points at his watch. "But you'd be wasting your time going back to the salon now. It's eight o'clock. No chance it's still open. Did the stylist give you her card? Can you call her?"

Lee takes a photo of Sue's business card while I call her number. The phone goes to voice mail. I leave my name and number and ask her to call. "I have an important question," I add. As soon as I disconnect, it occurs to me to text her.

Lee throws me a puzzled look. "Who are you calling?"

"I think I should text the question to Sue," I explain. "It'll give her time to think before she responds."

Lee nods. "Good idea, allowing time between stimulus and response."

"That doesn't sound like your usual police jargon," I say, grasping at any opportunity to stab holes in the uneasiness shrouding us. I manage to throw in a grin.

"It's not. It's Steven Covey, from *Seven Habits of Highly Effective People*."

"Excuse me?"

"What? I *read*." He points at my phone. "Go ahead. Text the question."

I thumb in the text. "Now there's nothing to do but wait. Why don't I go get you another of whatever you're drinking? Club soda?"

"Tonic water."

"Tonic water it is. When I get back, we'll hit the details again." Lee heads for the bar.

I slump in my chair, gutted. Typical pub sounds swarm around me: the murmur of voices, the clink of ice, the scuff of barstools. A blender whirs, a patron swears. I glance toward the bar. There's no sign of the muscle man. Must have been at the end of his shift. Doesn't matter. I watch as Lee turns from the bar and clomps across the room, floorboards creaking under his weight. He sits down and I sit up, straight and tall. Work time.

It's a while before Lee and I leave the watering hole. He heads to his home. Me to mine. As Lee said, there's nothing now but the waiting. I wonder what Rose is doing. Is she waiting? I stop the wondering there because anything else is unthinkable. Another rabbit hole.

The sun is sagging on the horizon as I pull into my back lane. Beer-in-Hand Burt pops up at my driver side window, scaring the heck out of me. When my heart stops thundering, I roll down my window.

"Switched to lite," he says, waving a beer can. "Wife keeps at me about the weight. Too many calories."

"She may have a point," I say and then cringe. Why did I respond? The threat of conversation looms.

"Yeah. The family doc agrees with her. Says if I don't stop pumping beer, I'll be pumping insulin." He raises his other hand. "Brought a beer for you. Haven't seen you in days. What's new?"

There it is, the dreaded conversation invitation. And I'm stuck. The man is blocking my car door. With a sigh, I accept the beer and follow him to his back porch.

I listen, or pretend to, as he informs me about all the movement in the neighborhood. Someone has a new puppy, someone has a new baby, and someone has new boots under her bed, boots that belong to someone else's husband. Beer-in-Hand Burt is the neighborhood snoop.

When he asks what's going on with me, I shrug. "Nothing." And that's true. There's nothing new with me. Just with Rose.

And Vincent, whoever the hell he is.

Thirty-Two

VINCENT AWAKENS TO A sharp pain above his brow. Too much vodka? He blinks. How long has he been here? The reading lamp is cold. Did he turn it off? He fumbles for and flips the switch. Nothing. Repeating the procedure does not alter the outcome. He slaps at the rectangular shade which swivels until it is parallel with the arm of his chair.

Just what time *is* it anyway? He glances at his watch but the room is so dim he can't see the time. Why didn't he wear the Rolex with the luminous dial? Why did he leave his cell phone in the Audi? Perhaps he *should* have flung the curtains wide upon arrival.

Groaning his way out of his chair, he stumbles over his book, his precious book, which lies facedown, open on the rug. A word of apology falls from his lips as he retrieves it, reshelves it. Staggering to the entrance of the library, he switches on the overhead light and raises the dimmer until the room is lit like New Year's Eve. His eyes widen. Is that mud on the floor?

"What the hell?" Instantly, he claps a hand over his mouth. He mustn't swear. Not here, in Mother's house. She never liked it when he said bad words.

But the floor is caked in mud, long dragging lines of mud that stream like vacuum tracks. Vincent looks down at his own clothes, which are also smeared and dirty. "Damn that Gideon," he says, Mother's preferences forgotten. "What has he done now?" Anger flares, a fire in Vincent's gut. He must find that brother of his.

But before he checks for Gideon, he checks his anger, setting it aside long enough to head for a shower. The body must be clean. Nothing can be done until the body is clean.

The Lord home is a mansion but the plumbing is decrepit, desperately in need of updating. The showerhead offers a strangled trickle, not a waterfall gush like the shower at the loft. As Vincent strips and steps in, he remembers yesterday, helping the dead weight that was Rose into the loft shower after she fell in the kitchen. How clumsy of her to tumble from the kitchen stool like that. Maybe he should plan another shower with Rose, one where she can be a conscious participant. He must do that before Gideon takes her away.

Vincent grins. Gideon is jealous, that's the problem. Jealous because Vincent has Rose. Rose picked Vincent, not Gideon. That's why Gideon dumped mud all over the place. Gideon is sick with envy.

Vincent hums while he soaps and rinses and towels. He tosses his muddy clothes into the hamper and, from the adjacent walk-in closet, chooses a new outfit—a two-piece gray Armani with wine shirt, silver tie, wine and silver argyle socks. His slate-gray wing tips are a perfect match. A glance in the full-length mirror has him smiling. Clothes make the man. He's ready to face Gideon now.

Vincent heads for the patio, stopping dead when a single thought pierces his mind and guillotines his confidence. What if Gideon has already gone off script? Would Gideon do such a thing, change the plan, go rogue?

It is with reticence that Vincent heads into the sunshine and down the cobblestone garden path, the usually immaculate garden path which is now a mosaic of stone and mud. He follows the mud, sidestepping every blotch to avoid splattering his suit. Summoning his courage, he patrols like a beat cop, aware of every nuance. If there is an anomaly, he will find it.

It is at the periwinkle patch that he comes to another halt. Why is there a strip of flowers ripped from the periwinkle groundcover? This is not part of any plan.

Vincent's gut churns. What is Gideon up to? Is he burying some dark secret? Perhaps Gideon is up to nothing. Perhaps he is just planning on planting a tree.

Vincent shrugs. Perhaps he shouldn't dig into this too much. He chuckles at his unintended pun and keeps walking.

A few feet from the ripped up flowerbed, Vincent finds garden implements: a long-handled spade, muddied work gloves, and a pair of hedge clippers. Vincent bites the inside of his lip and looks around. He isn't worried about the rounded spade or the gardening gloves. As for the clippers? Yes, Gideon needs them, a standard tool. But Gideon should not have access to sharp objects. Vincent locks every kitchen drawer at the loft for that very reason. Gideon with a knife in hand? The thought is unnerving. It's bad enough that Gideon has access to Vincent's insulin kits.

Maybe he should confiscate Gideon's keys, give him access to nothing. Maybe he should broadcast that fact to Gideon, as soon as Gideon shows up. Vincent's knees start to wobble. Why do thoughts of Gideon induce weakness? The truth hits and hurts. Gideon is the strong one, that's why. Vincent sighs. He gingerly picks up the clippers and stashes them into a box in the nearby toolshed. He locks the box. He locks the shed. Pointless endeavors both, as long as Gideon has keys and codes to everything.

Vincent ambles to the patio, to a white wicker chair with a floral printed cushion, and sits, waiting.

With Gideon, it's all about the waiting.

The sky slips from blue to purple to indigo. The solar garden lights glow into the night. Vincent drifts in and out of sleep. Still the waiting. Then, suddenly—

"What's with the Armani?" Gideon is standing behind him. "Preparing to make an impression? Afraid your meager self needs body armor?"

Vincent makes no effort to turn around, every effort to remain calm. "What are you up to, Gideon?"

"Are you watching that Flynn fellow?"

"Flynn?" Vincent is jolted off course, like a car on black ice. But he doesn't move from the chair. "Why would I be doing that?" he asks, his innards quivering.

"Better than reading those filthy books about flower sex. Don't you know Flynn's looking for her?"

Vincent ignores the taunt and the question. "Why is there an extra flowerbed, Gideon?" Good. He's back on track now. Asking what he wants to ask.

"Did anyone see you with Rose at the gala? You weren't stupid enough to tip the bartender, were you?" Gideon stoops and whispers in Vincent's ear. "Did you do that, Mama's boy?"

Vincent jumps to his feet. "Why is there an extra flowerbed, Gideon?" His voice is loud; his mouth is dry.

Gideon slowly rises, a Goliath unfolding. "It's not extra, little brother. It is supposed to be there."

"No. It isn't. It is not in the plan."

"Part of the plan lies in dealing with the past. No concern of yours. It's handled."

Vincent parts his lips to protest, but his throat closes up on him.

"Now, back to this Flynn fellow," says Gideon. "Are you aware that he's looking for her? He's closing in on you, Vincent."

Vincent shrugs in acquiescence. "Makes sense, I suppose. Flynn is a friend of the family."

"I doubt he'll get very far in that decrepit car of his."

Vincent sits erect, quick like a meerkat, his mind pierced with the memory of William Lord's automobile accident on the Sea to Sky Highway. Would Gideon attempt such a thing again? "You're following Flynn?"

"Someone's got to." Gideon's voice is pointed, a missile.

Vincent slouches into his chair. No amount of persuading or pleading will stop Gideon now. Vincent internally scoffs at his earlier idea of confiscating keys. That's not going to happen. But he must continue to conceal sharp objects. And he must be wary. At the loft. Especially at the loft.

"I guess you're right. Someone's got to keep an eye on Flynn." Vincent clears his throat. "Are we on schedule then? You'll deliver the flowers tomorrow?"

"They're already clipped, trimmed, and in a vase."

Vincent frowns. "Our rose bush, the shimmering-red floribunda, it died, didn't it? Wasn't it supposed to be a hardy variety? Where did you get red roses if ours died?"

"You're such a simpleton, Vincent. Have you not heard of florists?"

Of course, the florist. As always, Vincent didn't think things through. He pulls at his collar. "Is there any way to trace the flowers?"

"As long as that Flynn fellow is kept in the dark, no one will ever know."

"How are you going to keep Flynn in the dark?"

Gideon laughs over his shoulder as he walks away. "Don't worry about that. I'll handle it."

Alone again, Vincent struggles from his chair and lumbers through the house en route to his car. Halfway there, he stops, switches on a hall light, and checks his watch. One A.M. Where did the time go? He has been here for hours, too long. He really should check on his precious Rose. But there is still mud in this house. Mother wouldn't like having mud in her house. And Rose is contained, so there is no need to rush. He glances down at his exquisite outfit. Sighing, he trudges to the bathroom and changes back into his muddied clothes.

A few minutes later, he is on hands and knees in the library, scrubbing, scrubbing, scrubbing. The detergent bites his skin, but he won't wear rubber gloves. He deserves punishment. Yes, it was Gideon who dragged dirt into the house, but it was Vincent who promised his mother he would care for this house. There must be no dirt in Mother's house. What a waste it was putting on that Armani suit. Never mind. He will wear it to the loft. Rose has already chosen a suit for their last meal together, hasn't she? Perhaps she would prefer the Armani. He will give her the choice. Then he must arrange the evening meal. He must return to the loft soon so he can properly invite Rose to dinner.

Perhaps he should call it supper. A Last Supper of sorts. Yes, that's it, a Last Supper.

Thursday, May 5th

Thirty-Three

ROSE BLINKS INTO WAKEFULNESS. Why can't she see anything? Oh. Nighttime. An attempt to raise her head brings a surge of dizziness. Did Vincent lie to her about drugging her? Does it matter at the moment? There's something else she needs to deal with, something else trying to pierce the fog in her brain. What is it?

When the answer comes, a long moan grinds from her core. *Vincent knew her sister's name.* Rose had only spoken of her sister as Margo, yet Vincent knew her sister's full name.

"Mar-i-gold," Rose says aloud so she can feel the weight of the word on her tongue, so she can articulate each syllable. When they were little, Margo couldn't pronounce the three syllables. "Margo," she would say. The name stuck.

How did Vincent know the full name? Had he researched Rose's life? Stalked her perhaps? The questions mobilize a rush of dread. Rose shapes her fingers into claws, grips the wire wall, and throttles it. The result is a rattle of handcuffs against steel, high-tensile steel. How can she get out of a steel cage? A padlocked steel cage? She falls back onto the pillow.

What time is it? She has no idea. Could he still be here? She perks an ear toward the door of the bedroom. All is silent. She lets out a relieved breath. What should she do, just lie here, caged, until he gets back? Trooper wouldn't do that.

Trooper, a border collie cross, was a beloved member of the Harrington family when Rose and Margo were children. That dog never, ever stayed in his cage. Trooper was an escape artist.

Rose sits up, bumping her head on the top of the cage. If Trooper escaped, she can, too. She can break out of this kennel. Can she do it without raising suspicion?

She and Margo had set up a video recorder and watched Trooper. His trick was not to push the door out, but to pull it in, on the hinged side. A brilliant dog, Trooper, but Rose does not have to go to such extremes. She can undo slide bolts. Her problems lie with the padlock and the handcuffs. Can she bypass those?

In the blackness, Rose examines the cage, running her fingertips over every inch of every wall. There is not one door, but two, each of which is closed with slide bolts. Yes, there's a padlock on the front door, but Vincent did not lock the second door, the one adjacent to the wall. How did a detail man like Vincent miss that? How the hell did *she* miss it? Rose brushes the questions aside. The important thing is that she can get out. It will be tricky, trying to navigate slide bolts while wearing handcuffs, but she can exit this cage.

Rose latches onto the wire cage and bounces it away from the wall. The cage moves slowly, a tortoise of a thing, but it cooperates. When she has created a sufficient gap between the cage and the wall, she disengages the bolts, spills into the room, and lies there, panting. Aware of the crunch of time, she toils to get to her feet, a process aggravated by the hours she spent curled like a pretzel. While stretching, she considers her next step.

Escaping the cage was easy, but can she escape this loft? Doubt sits heavily. She's already pounded on every door and window.

She inspects the periphery of the loft. There is one exit and it has four locks. Deadbolts. Double-keyed deadbolts. Rose is familiar with the sound of the deadbolts, with Vincent's *click-click-click* pattern with the deadbolts. *Unlock-lock-unlock*. Three times for each lock. Four times three is twelve. Twelve clicks mean that Vincent is leaving or that Vincent is returning.

Swallowing hard, Rose glances at the first lock. No movement. No click. And no sign of any keys. Of course not. Vincent has the keys. Whether he's on his way in or on his way out, Vincent needs the keys.

She moves on.

The interior of the loft is modern, but an assessment of the opaque windows proves that the building itself is not. There are no full-length windows, no modern-day sliders which would indicate the presence of a balcony. All windows are tall rectangles, their sills three feet off the floor. Only one—the dining room window—has a traditional sash with a latch. At some point in time, the latch would have easily turned, and the window would have slid up with a slight push. Now the latch is rigid, and the window is caulked into its casing. But this window was once used. A fire escape exit, perhaps?

Rose examines the caulking on the window; it appears new. Has it been disturbed recently? Has the window been opened and then re-sealed? If she finds a tool, can she scrape enough caulking to loosen and lift the window? Possibly. Maybe she can loosen the window a little at a time. She can hide slivers of caulk in the zippered lining of the dog pillow. Would Vincent notice? Maybe. Maybe not. The dining room is located at a diagonal from the kitchen and, as long as she is mobile during the day, she can distract him. But he is a perfectionist and a neat freak. Maybe he notices every deviation from the norm. Did he notice when she changed the direction of the toilet paper? He didn't say. He displayed no tells. And, she reminds herself, he used only one padlock on a cage with two doors.

Rose grapples with her thoughts, not knowing what to do next. If she can't escape now, perhaps she can locate a tool, a weapon of some sort. Later, she can buy time by slipping back into the cage and bouncing it toward the wall. Rose refuses to contemplate the consequences of possible floor scratches. Instead, she focuses on the now, on noting her every movement, and on leaving no evidence of that movement.

En route to the kitchen, Rose reminds herself not to pilfer anything that might be noticed. That proves easy because there is nothing to take. Everything is locked. Every cupboard, every drawer, even the cutlery drawer in the kitchen is shut tight. Not a utensil in sight, just like at her mother's a few days ago when she was seeking scissors in an empty kitchen. The only tool she could find that day was her manicure scissors. She comes to a standstill. She had put her red manicure kit into her suitcase. Maybe Vincent didn't remove it from the suitcase.

The focus of her hunt changes from tools to luggage.

After a thorough search, looking behind every table, in every closet, even under the bed, Rose comes up empty.

Okay, so no tools. Now what?

How can she get out of here when she has no tools? Even if she did have tools, would she have time to remove all that caulk tonight? Her gut responds with a pang of discomfort. A crystal clear no. Rose trusts the instinct. So, if she's not getting out of here tonight, what else can she do?

Perhaps another test to see how much she can get away with? When her eyes fall on the kitchen towels, which are perfectly aligned on their stainless steel rack, she changes the position of one towel, making it about an inch lower than its twin. Will he notice? Perhaps she should switch it back. She shakes her head and moves on, toward the den.

She tiptoes in. It is exactly as she remembers: acrylic desk and chair, bookshelves meticulously lined with leather-bound, gold-lettered books. No phone. No computer. No way to make contact with the outside world.

On her first visit to this room, she headed for the painting of the two girls in the flower garden; now she goes to the bookcase. If the titles are an indication, Vincent's interests lie in two topics—gardening and guns. Despite his affinity for floriculture, he has not blessed this place with a single plant, not a single flower, unless she counts herself. She sniffs.

What about guns? Does he have a gun?

Rose moves her finger along the spine of every book; she tips each book and peeks behind it. No tools, no weapons, not even a speck of dust. She strolls the room, examining the periphery, inspecting every corner. Coming up with nothing but feeling as though something is beckoning, Rose pauses. Where should she look?

The painting catches her eye and she angles toward it, instantly, inexplicably choosing to glance behind it. She discovers a ledge, just two finger-widths from the edge. When she flattens her cuffed hands and slides them along the wall, the painting arcs up enough to allow her access. She shoves her fingers into the alcove, latches onto a metal object, and pulls it out. As the painting *tap-taps* back into place on the wall, Rose lets out a wisp of a sigh. No damage done. She glances at her hands.

Sweet Jesus. A handgun. Adrenaline in overdrive, Rose's body trembles. The weapon tumbles to the floor. She jumps back, instinctively raising her hands to cover her face. When there's no pop, no explosion, she lowers her hands and steps toward the gun.

She stares at it. A riff of hysterical laughter erupts from her, followed by a series of short gasps. She sucks in a breath and holds it. Is the gun loaded? Without picking it up, she eyes it, checking for a magazine. There is none. She reaches behind the painting again, running her hands along the niche in the wall. No. There's nothing else there.

Where is the ammunition? If he has a gun, he has bullets. She can't use the gun without bullets. Gingerly, she picks up the weapon, holding it by its grip, checking for the safety. Once she has a feel for it, she returns the weapon to its hiding place and scours the room again. Nothing. She goes back to exploring the entire loft.

After a long search, gifted with a precise knowledge of every nook and cranny, Rose shakes her head. The ammunition must be here, somewhere. What has she missed? She heads back to the den. This time, she walks directly to the acrylic chair behind the desk and collapses into it. The view is different here and yet completely the same. Nothing.

Succumbing to the futility of her search, she pulls the chair in, drops her elbows to the surface of the desk, and holds her head in her hands. Her knee begins bouncing, an involuntary motion. When it nudges something, she jerks back. What the hell? She runs her fingers under the desk. A button, invisible to the eye and almost level with the underside of the desk. She presses it.

She jumps when a panel in the bookcase opens, revealing a hidden room.

Rose is edging toward the opening when she hears it, the first click of the first lock.

Vincent is home.

Thirty-Four

I CHECK MY MESSAGES. Still no response from Sue the Stylist. Too early to call? It's only eight in the morning. I am about to call anyway when the phone rings and there she is. Serendipity in action.

"Sue, I was just about to call—"

"Flynn, that Vincent fellow left Granville Island in a yacht."

I pause as I blink the image into my brain. "A yacht? Are you sure about that?"

"Absolutely. Stupid me. You think that I would've remembered that gem of a detail yesterday. Like I told you, so many clients, so many stories."

"No worries, Sue." I take a beat and fire off another question. "Did Rose happen to mention anything about the yacht having a name?"

I am met with dead silence. "Sue?" I prompt.

"Sorry. Just trying to jog my memory. To the best of my knowledge, Rose did not mention a name."

"Did Rose talk with anyone else in the salon?"

"Now, there's a thought. I was with her a while, but I did take a few phone calls. Come to think of it, she had a mani-pedi here, too. I remember her stunning rose-red nail polish. Want me to ask around, see what comes up?"

"Would be appreciated."

"Will do," Sue says. "Anything else?"

The chime of the Beauty Bee doorbell sounds through my cell. "That's my cue," I say. "Can't thank you enough, Sue. Get back to me if you learn anything."

"As soon as I can. Promise. Gotta run." Sue disconnects.

I instantly text Lee.

> **Apparently, the guy Rose met on Granville Island left in a YACHT. Name of yacht not known. Any way we can check into this?**

As soon I click SEND, I contact the events planner at the gala venue. A pleasant woman, if a melodious voice is any indication, one who has been informed about my earlier visit to the hotel. I learn that one of the event servers is a regular worker at the hotel, that she is on shift this morning, and that she will happily talk to me. I immediately tell the planner that I will be there in a half hour.

At the hotel, I make my way to the counter. The clerk with the thatch of hair over his eye spots me, points a finger at me to indicate that I wait, and pages someone named Matilda. Obviously, this someone has been hovering, waiting to be summoned, for when I turn my head, Matilda is standing beside me, hand extended.

Matilda is a silver-haired, rotund little woman with a stubby nose and a sunshine smile. She is clad in a hotel uniform, blue like standard hospital scrubs. "I've been given a few minutes to chat with you," she says.

"Your events planner is certainly cooperative."

"Well, we were informed that you would show up. By the police, I mean."

I smile to myself. Lee's been busy.

I take out my phone, thumbing and sliding images until I locate the photo of Rose and Margo. As I raise the phone toward her, she waves it away.

"Let's sit first, shall we?" she says.

As anxious as I am to pepper her with questions, I oblige, glancing at her shoes as I follow her to a nearby grouping of brown club chairs. Those are no-nonsense shoes, tasseled, black leather brogues which are crinkled and worn down on one side of the heel. Is that from pronation or supination? Doesn't matter. The bottom line is she spends lots of time on her feet and she needs this break.

I again raise my phone and display the picture.

Matilda's gray eyes light up. "Sure, I remember her. The blond one, I mean. I saw her in the powder room early in the evening. A beauty, she was. Sleek dress, black as night, slit to the hip. She was having a grand conversation with herself."

"Excuse me?"

"She was staring into the mirror, trying to convince herself to do something. Don't know what. But she was sort of talking to someone else, too . . . I think it was her sister. Yeah. Mary or Marty or something."

"Did you see her after that? In the ballroom, I mean?"

"I think she was at the bar for a minute or two. Then some guy approached her. The next time I looked, she was gone."

"What did the guy look like?"

"All wearing tuxedos, mister. All looked the same to me."

"Was he white? Black? Green?"

Matilda giggles. "Oh, I see. White, definitely white."

"Tall? Short? Fat? Thin?"

"Tall. Six feet, perhaps. Not thin. Built."

"Do you remember anything about his hair? Bald? Thick? Black? Blond?"

"Definitely not bald. Short on the back and sides. Longer on top. I guess it was what you might call a classic cut. Not sure of the color because the room was dimly lit. Brown or black. Definitely not blond."

"Did he have a beard or mustache?"

"No beard. I guess he could have had a mustache. I didn't get that close to him."

"I know it's unlikely given what you have already told me, but were there any identifying marks?"

"If you mean a tattoo or scar, I really don't know, Mr. Flynn. As I said, it was too dark to tell. But I remember watching them sip champagne. They linked arms and clinked glasses, you know—"

"Did they get champagne from a bartender?"

Matilda shrugs. "Maybe. Some did. Lots of servers working the room, too. Attendees lifted champagne flutes from trays which floated past. The place was a sea of black-and-white uniforms and black-and-white tuxedos, punctuated by the occasional pop of color from the gowns."

"Well put."

Matilda blushes, seemingly pleased with herself. "I watch all the red carpet awards shows," she says, patting her hair. Anyway, after that . . ." She shrugs. "I headed back to the kitchen. The next time I went into the ballroom, I looked, but there was no sign of them."

"You mean they left early?"

"I mean I didn't see them. That's all. I got busy and forgot about them. I have no idea what happened to either of them."

I nod, knowing that this avenue of information is at an end. "Is there anything you want to add?"

Matilda bites her lip. "I'm sorry I can't be of more help."

"Thanks, Matilda." I give her my card. "If you think of anything more, please call or text."

She pockets the card. "Happy to oblige, and if I'm to be honest, I'm grateful to you for showing up. It's a joy to get off my feet even for a few minutes," she says, confirming what I already knew. With a reluctant sigh, she pushes off the arms of the club chair to stand. "Gotta get back at it." She extends a hand, gives mine a firm shake, and launches into work mode. She zips across the expansive lobby to the elevator. She pushes a button. She paces.

I watch her, amazed at her energy. Not a lazy bone in that body. Like Matilda, I'm ready to launch into the next work thing. Unlike Matilda, I don't know what that next thing is. As she disappears into the elevator, I am stuck in the gap between now and my next step. For a few seconds, I spin the hodgepodge wheel of information in my head, shards of which are jockeying for position. Where to go? What to do? Rose? Sue? Lee?

I flip through my notebook and stop at the notes from Pacific Plaza. The store clerk mentioned a spa. Rose was going to a spa. On a whim, I grab a brochure from a nearby rack. I'm right. There *is* a spa here, one that covers the entire fifth floor. It's worth a shot. I tread in Matilda's footsteps to the bank of elevators.

On the fifth floor, I get out and am almost knocked out by some acrid odor. What the hell is that? I cross the hallway, enter the spa through sliding doors, and slip into a world of gurgling water features and soothing flute music. My pace automatically slows as I make my way to the counter, on top of which sits a plaque engraved with the word "Concierge."

"How may I help you?" asks the smiling, well-scrubbed lady behind the counter, a lady with an elfin face the color of liquid honey. Her voice is calm, almost a whisper.

"I'm checking to see if a friend of mine booked an appointment here on Saturday," I whisper back, echoing her lead.

She gives me a quizzical look.

I pull out my ID and state my case. My words are set now, a routine. A convincing one.

She checks the appointment list. I'm waiting, staring at the crown of her head, at the two dark lines running beside the center part, parallel like train tracks. A clear betrayal. Not a natural redhead, this young lady. Time for a dye job.

She runs her finger down a page, stops, and looks up. She nods. "Yes, she spent three hours here on Saturday."

"Any chance I can talk to the people she had appointments with?"

"Certainly, but there was only one person. Your friend spent time in the sauna and the mineral pool; then she had a long massage. Her masseuse is here, but I doubt she'll be much help."

I raise my eyebrows.

"Our clients come for the silence and sleep through the sessions." The concierge smiles. "If you'll excuse me . . ." She slips away from the counter through an arched doorway and returns seconds later. "The therapist will be right with you." She points me toward a couch.

I sit and sink into soft leather. Immediately, I move forward, to the edge of the seat. Can't get too comfortable. I'm exhausted and strained and I have things to do. I glance repeatedly at my watch.

Soon, I'm back on the elevator, plowing my fingers through my hair. The spa concierge knew what she was talking about. Other than basic pleasantries, Rose had revealed nothing to the masseuse before drifting to sleep on the table.

I'm getting nowhere. It's time to pull back and take a hard look at accumulated data. That means heading to my office.

Lee was right. I do have the opportunity to put that empty crime board to use. I'll set up a display and then I'll make a choice, the most likely of which is to take another look at Rose's condo, even if it's just to pamper her plants. You never know. Perhaps I missed something there. I bounce the heel of my hand off my forehead. *Damn.* I'm jumping from one thing to another, playing "what if", accomplishing nothing. First, my crime board. Then, my next step. On second thought, first, caffeine. Then crime board. Then the next step.

I charge through the doors of the hotel, grab a coffee at a nearby vendor, and head for my car.

Thirty-Five

THE FIRST CLICK OF the first lock jolted Rose, firing her into overdrive. She pushed the button to close the secret door, bolted for the kennel, and now she's lying still, body curled, muscles taut.

Dread descends when she realizes that the gap between the cage and the wall still exists. How can she move the cage without being heard? She grabs the wire enclosure and bounces toward the wall. The noise is thunderous. But if he is still outside the door, he can't hear her. This place is soundproof. She bounces again. The wall is closer.

She sucks in a breath and holds it, straining to hear his approach. If only her heart would stop walloping her chest, pounding her ears, obliterating the clicks of the remaining locks. Nothing. Is he inside already? She exhales slowly and listens for the sounds of the locks being reactivated. No such sound occurs. Where is Vincent? Why hasn't he come into the bedroom? What's the hold up?

She is caught off-guard by the peal of the doorbell, a floral melody. What the hell is that song? And what does it matter? *Someone's here. Will Vincent open the door?*

"Good morning," says Vincent.

Rose emits a gasp. Who is he talking to?

"Good morning to you, Vincent." A different voice, flat, inflectionless. Is there familiarity in it? Has help arrived?

Rose sucks in another breath. "Fire!" Her scream is explosive, a high-sonic stiletto. Startled at her choice of word, speared by a sliver of memory about people responding to that word faster than they would to "help," she repeats it. "Fire! Fire! I'm in here. Somebody help me." She erupts into shrieks, releasing feelings she had bottled up for days, all the while bouncing the cage toward the wall until it is back where it started from, completely aligned. She maintains the shrill tone until she can sustain it no longer and the screams fade into guttural rasps.

There is no response.

"Here are your roses, as requested, Vincent." The stranger's voice adapts a sarcastic tone.

Flowers? Rose's hope disintegrates. A flower delivery. Her namesake flower. Lilies for Lily. Roses for Rose. And that voice. Where had she heard that voice before? Had she recently heard that voice? When? When? *When?*

"It'll soon be my turn with this one, Vincent," the voice says. "A lively one, by the sound of her."

"You'll have to excuse Rose, Gideon," says Vincent. "She's overwhelmed by all this attention, I'm sure."

Rose scans her brain. Gideon. Vincent's brother, Gideon.

"I'll give her lots of attention," Gideon says.

"It is not yet your turn." Vincent sounds sulking, defensive. "You are pushing the timeline. Look at this vase. These blossoms are at their peak. The placement of a few buds would have given me a bit more time. You're not getting her today, Gideon. I'm not finished. You always want things your way."

"You know the rules. When the flowers die, the flower dies." A triumphant laugh accompanies the sound of retreating footsteps. The door slams. The locks are activated, three turns each—first, second, third. It is the fourth—the final *thunk!*—which stirs the defeatist in Rose's soul.

Tears flood, streaking her vision, causing the wire walls to morph into silver waves. In a daze, Rose curls into a ball. Her brain fires a catalogue of reprimands: Why hadn't she called the gala organizers to ask who had ordered the tickets? Why hadn't she called Flynn to let him know where she was? Why had she, the ever-vigilant Rose, relaxed her watchfulness the instant she met Vincent? What was she thinking by going home with the first man who offered? Why had Vincent mentioned Marigold?

It's her sister's name that brings the rampant brain activity to a halt. Stillness blinks, then a new thought stirs. Does all this have anything to do with the disappearance of Margo?

Rose trembles as Vincent unlocks the door to the cage. He extends his hand to her. "Time to get up, my lovely."

Hesitantly, she complies. She scrunches her nose as the odor of chlorine assaults her nostrils. What has he been cleaning? In a sideways glance, she notices his Armani suit. Why is he smelling like bleach and dressed to the nines? Feeling she is on the cusp of something, something that defies logic, Rose summons her courage and looks at him straight on. On the day she met Vincent, had she sensed a connection between him and Margo? Is she here because of her sister? Possibly. Maybe. Yes?

He smiles calmly. "Come, see your flowers," he says as he grips her bicep and leads her to the living room. There, on the transparent coffee table, sits a silver vase that resembles a Roman urn. Vincent picks it up by its two vine-tendril handles and holds it directly under her nose. The roses are long-stemmed and bloodred. Stunning flowers at their absolute peak, their scent sickeningly overwhelming.

Beads of sweat form on Rose's brow. Her breath quickens. "How lovely," she says, as her knees threaten to disown her. Through dizzied vision, she scrutinizes the bouquet for any sign of an unopened flower. There is not one bud in the vase. She counts the flowers. Two dozen roses, all in full bloom, blossoms on the verge of falling away.

Rose's heart sinks.

She remembers her mother's talent for prolonging the lives of cut flowers. How did her mother do that? Something about vodka or 7-UP. How could Rose prolong the lives of these condemned roses? How long do they have? Two days? How long does *she* have? Two days? Suddenly aware that Vincent is talking, she tunes in.

"A rose is the most beautiful of blossoms, don't you think? Much prettier than a lily or a chrysanthemum or a marigold."

There it is again, her sister's full name. Is it a taunt? Rose closes her eyes. It is lightning quick, the image of Margo that crops up. Accompanying it is razor-sharp clarity. The key to Margo's disappearance is here, in this place, with this man. What has he done to Margo?

Rose opens her eyes wide, then tapers them to slits as she observes her captor.

Vase in hand, Vincent heads toward the kitchen. As if in answer to her query about prolonging the life of flowers, he unlocks a cupboard and brings out a bottle of vodka.

Rose remains glued in place, alert, wary.

Vincent pours two fingers of vodka into a glass and sprinkles in a teaspoon of sugar. "This will delay the growth of bacteria and prolong the life of the blossoms," he explains as he adds the mixture to the vase. He returns his ingredients to their respective cupboards and parades the vase back to the coffee table, twisting and turning it until he is satisfied with its placement. Then he wraps one arm around Rose and draws her close. "Such beauty, don't you think?"

Rose stiffens. "Y-y-yes," she manages.

Thirty-Six

FOR THE FIRST TIME, I'm grateful that my office has a shower. A short stint under the spray is all it takes to stimulate blood flow. Refreshed, I stare at my crime board, a white board, a blank slate.

I consider doing a linear timeline—dates across the top, events along the side—but some instinct kicks in and has me drawing a circle in the center. Guess I'm opting for hour-and-minute, wheel-and-spoke, or flower-and-petal. Pretty much all the same.

A clock face it is. In the circle, I print the name "Rose." Then I draw the first spoke, or radius, to the twelve o'clock position of an imaginary circumference. At this position, I print the starting date, Thursday, April 28th, and a clockwise arrow. I continue creating radii until I have the illusion of a clock, and place dates at each hour position until I am up to today. That makes eight days and four blanks, to be used as, *if*, needed. It is in the pie segments between the hours that I make notations.

On April 28th—one week ago—Rose met a man on Granville Island. A moneyed man. A man with a yacht. I make my first notation.

Rose meets Vincent.

Beside the note, I add a dollar sign and an outline of a boat.

The next day, Friday, I went to the Harrington house. A fact, but one I'm willing to bypass. No need to have it on the board if it is not relevant. I shrug. Was there anything unusual at Violet Harrington's house that morning? No. I was there to help Rose move the only thing she wanted from that house: the mahogany dresser. Her mother's favorite piece of furniture. My understanding is that Violet insisted, on her deathbed, that Rose keep it. I wonder why. Maybe it is germane. I make a notation.

Mahogany Move.

On that morning, did Rose say anything to me about the events of the previous day? No. What about Friday afternoon? Rose met friends for lunch; Rose shopped for a dress at Pacific Plaza.

Lunch at Café. Pacific Plaza for Dress.

I nod after I write those in. I had followed through on both of those leads.

What happened on Saturday, April 30th? I flip through my notes. Rose visited the hair salon. Ah yes, easy to sum that up.

Hair Salon. Sue.

I smile as I add Sue's name. Another avenue I can check off. Been there, done that, talked to Sue. Further info pending? A possibility. I amend the notation.

Hair Salon. Sue. More info?

What else? The salesclerk at Pacific Plaza mentioned the spa. She didn't know what spa. I do.

Spa. No Data.

The most important thing Rose did on Saturday? She attended the Heritage Gala, the same gala that Margo attended three years ago.

Heritage Gala. Margo, Three Years Ago.

I'm back to wondering why Violet Harrington didn't tell me she attended that gala with Margo. Is there a link between the gala they attended and the one Rose attended, a connection other than the obvious charity represented? Nothing pops up, so I move past that idea and fill in all the steps I have taken from Sunday until today.

Then I study my board, waiting for connections to appear. I grind the details until I am fatigued, hungry, and dizzy. It occurs to me that the dizziness may be caused by the absence of covers on my whiteboard markers. The odor is acrid, stomach churning. I cap the markers and return to my puzzle. It's still a jigsaw, pieces missing. The largest gaps come with the name Violet Harrington and with the mahogany dresser.

What is Violet Harrington's part in all this? *Does* she have a part in all this? Why did she insist on Rose taking that mahogany monstrosity to her tiny condo? Yeah, yeah, I get the emotional connection. Still . . . no stone unturned.

I'm back to wondering if I should be profiling Violet Harrington.

I stare at my starting point, the center circle on my clock face. Under Rose's name, I add another. "Violet."

Now what?

In the absence of other ideas, I'm heading to Rose's condo. Perhaps I did miss something. Perhaps I should scrutinize every inch of that dresser. Why did Violet want Rose to keep it?

Thirty-Seven

ROSE HAS BEEN GRANTED permission to remain near the bouquet of roses, to admire the bouquet of roses. This is no hardship for she can barely drag her eyes away. What happens if petals fall? If one petal falls? Are watched petals like a watched pot?

When she hears Vincent approach from behind, she sucks in a breath, wishing him away. A useless endeavor.

"My dear," he says. "I've forgotten to seek your opinion. Which suit would you prefer I wear to dinner this evening? This one?"

When Rose doesn't look up, he bends and cups her face in his hands. "I expect you to pay attention." He steps back and executes a runway turn. "This suit? Or the other which you chose for me?"

The girlfriend experience? Rose reigns in a frenetic urge to laugh aloud. Vincent wants the *girlfriend experience*? Straightening her back, she adapts her best Scarlet O'Hara persona. "That is a fine suit, but I would be ever so grateful if you would wear what I chose for you." She swallows quickly, hoping he hasn't noticed the hint of the South in her voice. She mustn't go overboard. No southern lilt. No sense in treading dangerously. Bide her time. Play his game.

"Why, of course. How thoughtless of me to even suggest an alternative." He steps up to her, leans over her.

She does not cringe.

"Come with me, my flower." He reaches a hand.

What is it he wants now? Rose takes his hand and follows him to the dining room.

"We must perfect the art of table setting. Later we will use the appropriate linens. This is merely a training session, a rehearsal if you will."

Rose widens her eyes as he marches into the kitchen. She almost forgot that she had misaligned the dish towels. She stiffens. Will he notice? Without hesitation or comment, Vincent slips past the stainless steel rack. He opens a drawer and pulls out a tablecloth.

Relief slides through Rose.

Vincent goes to the dining room and spreads the cloth on the table. Rose observes, all the while feeling like she is in a bizarre dream. When he pulls china plates from the floating white sideboard, she comes to grips. As surreal as it is, this is no dream. He is determined to demonstrate table setting. Perhaps this is a blessing. This will give her the time she needs, the time to process. She must multitask; she must pay heed while making plans.

Rapt in whirling thoughts, Rose loses concentration. When Vincent uses a ruler to display the correct distance from the dinner knife to the water glass, she doesn't catch the exact measurement. As a result, she misplaces a water goblet.

Vincent doesn't parade disapproval, but disapproval pervades the air. For seconds, he is still.

Rose mirrors the stillness.

The jab to her ribcage is sudden, there and gone, like lightning.

She folds. "My apologies," she whispers, breathing through the pain. She unravels her body and pastes on a smile. "I'll get it right this time. I promise."

Vincent pats her on the back. "I know you can do it."

Rose takes the plastic ruler he passes her.

"Exactly one inch from the tip of the dinner knife," says Vincent.

Her handcuffs rattle as she places the ruler on the table. She commands her hands to stop shaking and they comply. He will not break her.

Thirty-Eight

AT ROSE'S CONDO, I steer straight toward the mahogany dresser, tear open all its drawers, and pluck out all their contents. I cringe at the impropriety. These are Rose's silk and satin undies I'm tossing about. Am I a barbarian now? Gut instinct tells me I must keep going.

At the end of the search, there's a mound of garments on the top of the bed. Just clothes. Nothing else. What did I expect? I don't know what the hell I'm looking for, anyway. Scowling, I prowl the condo.

There's nothing out of sorts in the whole place except for the plants whose stems are arced from thirst. *Damn.* I should have attended to them yesterday. I hurriedly supply water, all the while chatting with fern, ficus, and violet, hoping the resulting carbon dioxide will aid their recovery.

Back in the bedroom, staring at the dresser, I launch into a soliloquy. "Okay, Violet Harrington. I'm here." I raise both arms to the heavens. "Help me out. Tell me something. Tell me anything. Why were you so insistent that Rose keep this piece of furniture?" I lower my hands and run them across the top of the entire dresser, right to left. Then, with the tip of my index finger, I reverse the direction, skimming across the intermittent dark and light stain, noting the richness and depth of the mahogany grain. Splaying my fingers, I press hard against the surface as if trying to squeeze out secrets. "Why, Violet, why were you so adamant? You must have known Rose would choose to live here, in this tiny condo, not in your big house. This is a minuscule bedroom. This dresser is a monstrosity." I lift my hands and watch the ridges and whorls of my fingerprints fade to nothingness.

With a sigh, I raise a hand to rub my aching jaw. I must have been clenching my teeth again. A longtime habit, that. Clearly a symptom of frustration. Got to stop it. Eventually.

For now, I choose to take my annoyance out on the dresser by yanking at an open drawer which promptly abandons its track and drops to the floor. I stoop to examine it, bottom, sides, and top. Nothing. I repeat the procedure with the other eight drawers and come up empty. Maybe I'm done with this. Maybe my instinct is on hiatus.

The dresser is hollow now, dark and foreboding, a cave. I access the flashlight app on my cell phone and go spelunking, aiming light into the recesses of the cavity. Nothing on the left side. I repeat the procedure in the center section. Nothing there either. I move to the right, scanning the top, middle, and the bottom. I'm about to click off the light when I detect a shadowy rectangle in the back, in the lower right-hand corner at the back. It's darker than the wood—a blotch of paint, perhaps? But why is it there? I extend my right arm. When I poke the rectangle, it gives a little. When I pull back, it springs back into its original position. An air pocket? I slip one fingernail under an edge of the shape, creating a tiny slit. I retract my finger. What's this? A chip of black paint is lodged under my nail. I reach in again, this time creating an incision down one side. Then I put my fingers under it, and tug.

With a rip that sounds like a sigh, the dresser releases the rectangle. I draw the rectangle toward me, into the light.

It's with a sense of awakening that I stare at what I'm holding, at the envelope I'm holding. I turn it over and over in my hands. It is tightly sealed, painted black, and was painted to the interior back of a dark dresser.

"What have you been hiding, Violet?" I whisper. The question evokes an image of Violet as I last saw her, a woman ravaged by grief, withered before her time. "Whatever it was, you couldn't tell Rose, face-to-face. But you wanted her to know, didn't you?"

I rip at the envelope. It resists, then gives. I reach inside and withdraw the contents.

Instantly, I'm hit by a rush of awareness so powerful it leaves me breathless. I'm holding Margo's necklace.

Margo's yang pendant went missing when she did; it was never recovered. Until now.

I stare for what seems like an eternity. My hands are trembling as I reexamine the envelope. I blow into it to create a pocket. At the bottom of the pocket, there is a tiny square of paper, creased so many times it threatens to crumble as I retrieve and unfold it. When I finally spread it flat, it reads:

Vengeance is mine, sayeth the Lord.

"What the hell did you do, Violet Harrington?" I whisper. "What the hell did you do?

Thirty-Nine

WHEN THE SHOCK EASES, restlessness seizes me. I need to do something. I need to review my notes. Not my new crime board notations but my handwritten notes which, for the first time in a long time, I have left at my office.

It's not the info about Margo's necklace that I need to read. I'm crystal clear about the fact that I'm holding Margo's necklace. What's gnawing at me, what I need to check on, is something Violet Harrington said. Something that will help me make sense of my discovery, particularly of the note attached to the discovery.

I pull out my cell phone. Now, finally, I'm grateful for the technology that I've shunned for years. All my notes are accessible on my cell phone.

I click through my files until I locate the file dated three years ago—my first interview with Violet Harrington. I plop onto the bed, on top of the pile of Rose's underclothes and accessories, and start to read.

On the day of the first interview, I queried Violet Harrington about her history.

"My husband died when the girls were very young," she said, the first thing out of her mouth.

I asked if she had dated again.

"Not for a long time. The girls needed my attention." She paused there and bit her lip.

I remember thinking that she wasn't going to answer my question. I was wrong.

"There was this one time," she said, "when the girls were teenagers, that I met a man. William was his name." She stopped there and put a hand to her mouth. Another hesitation. "William," she said. "Lord, what was I thinking? He was married." She shook her head.

"We all get lonely," I said. Eager to ease her discomfort, I immediately went to the next question.

As I read this now, I come to a halt. I read it again. Is there something here? Nothing strikes me as problematic or revealing, so, just like I did on the day of the interview, I move past it.

This time, I don't get far. There's a sudden tightness in my chest that causes me to wince. What the hell? I pause. I breathe. I thumb back a page on my cell and I read one particular sentence out loud. "William. Lord, what was I thinking?" Then I let that same sentence run across my mind like a news crawl on a TV screen. *William. Lord, what was I thinking? William. Lord, what was I thinking? William . . .*

I jump to my feet. What if there is a mistake here, not in her words, but in my interpretation, in my punctuation?

What if she had said "William . . . Lord. What was I thinking?"

The thought detonates an explosion of data at digital speed. I clutch my cell phone in my right hand and the yang necklace in my left and stare from one to the other as I do the mental equivalent of pumping brakes. I need to slow down. I need analog speed. Not digital. I need to grind through all the information and to give this new detail its due. A freaking punctuation mistake. Is that what I'm looking at?

I suck in a breath and hold it. I wait until everything slows to a halt.

And there it is. A clear picture. A flawlessly clear picture.

Violet Harrington had an affair with a married man. That man was William Lord. Margo Harrington disappeared without a trace and someone, possibly named Lord, possibly named William Lord, had returned her yang necklace. Accompanying that necklace was a note of revenge.

Margo Harrington was kidnapped out of revenge.

What about Rose? Dear Jesus. My brain ramps up again. Rose disappeared. Is there a connection between the disappearance of Rose and that of Margo? Did Rose know this William Lord person? Is there a connection?

Is there a revenge play in effect here? One that includes my friend Rose Harrington?

Forty

WHEN THE TABLE-SETTING lesson is complete, Rose sits at the kitchen counter while Vincent gathers all paraphernalia—cutlery, cloth, and china—and systematically puts it away. His is a solo performance now, as practiced and showy as an operatic aria. Rose watches as he subtracts each place setting, piece by piece. After he tugs linen napkins from silver rings, he refolds the napkins and returns them to their home in a drawer. In mere minutes, the dining room has reverted from adorned to austere.

Vincent moves to the kitchen counter.

"Look at me," he says.

Without comment, Rose swivels.

"There will be pancakes for brunch, with blueberry syrup, crisp bacon, wheat toast, and orange juice," he says.

Rose blinks. Is she expected to cook? No, obviously not. In the next second, he is opening drawers again. He is like a sous chef now, making preparations, filling ramekins with marmalade, blueberries, butter, salt, and pepper. He brings out a Pyrex mixing bowl, one with both spout and handle, and pours in a measured amount of pancake mix. "Next we need eggs and milk." He turns to the fridge.

As he opens the fridge door, Rose eyes the butter knife he left on the counter, a tiny knife, ideal for prying caulk. Without as much as a second guess, she pilfers the small, perfect tool, and slips it into the side pocket of her jeans. Heart pounding, hoping the slight *clink* from her handcuffs had not betrayed her, she places her hands back on the counter.

"There we go," he says, putting the milk beside the mixing bowl. With one hand, he expertly cracks an egg on the edge of the bowl and releases its golden yolk into the mixture. He repeats the procedure and then grabs the butter. "Now, where did I put my butter knife?" Vincent casts a glance toward her.

Rose doesn't move. Should she feel fear? She doesn't. It's fury she's choking back, pulse-pounding, heart-throbbing, fist-clenching fury, but she remains immobile, like still water, the pilfered butter knife pressing into her gut.

He selects another knife from the cutlery drawer.

Rose sighs an inaudible sigh. Her eyes are burning, her muscles screaming. She is suddenly empty, drained.

Butter plops into a white ceramic frying pan. It sizzles. Rose salivates. When had she last eaten? Is the food contaminated? She has to eat. She has to rebuild her strength.

Tonight she has a mission: find ammunition. Perhaps she will work on that window, on getting the caulk out of that window. It is the only possible route out of here. The gun alone might not be enough. The idea of the weapon causes doubt to creep in. Is she even capable of shooting him? What kind of person can just shoot someone point blank? What if she misses? What if he wrestles the gun from her hands?

She is so caught up in thought that when Vincent places a meal in front of her, she jumps. Upon instruction, she picks up her fork. Although tempted to gobble the pancakes, she cuts them into bite-sized pieces. She toys with the food on her plate. When he eats, she follows suit. Not wanting to draw attention to the missing knife, Rose avoids the butter. Is she going to get away with stealing the knife? It seems so. Perhaps Mr. Perfectionist is not so perfect. He didn't notice that the cage had been tampered with and he didn't notice the towels had been realigned. It is quite likely that he hasn't noticed the missing knife, either. Feeling more confident, Rose straightens her posture.

Vincent pushes the ramekin of butter toward her. "Where is the butter knife?" he asks.

Rose slumps. He knows. He knows she shoved the tiny knife with the rounded point into her pocket. She swallows.

Vincent places his knife and fork on his plate and rests his hands on the counter. "Put it back," he says, his face a dark cloud.

Rose slowly pulls the knife from her jeans and passes it toward him. She pauses halfway, knife extended, handcuffs rattling. When he makes no effort to reach for the knife, she leans and stretches. The round point of the knife is within an inch of his plate when, with the swiftness of a Venus flytrap, he grabs both her hands.

She gasps.

He compresses her hands in a vise grip.

She cringes.

He lets out a laugh, loosens his grip, and pries the knife from her curled fingers. He draws her hands to his lips. "Such beauty. Such naiveté." He kisses her hands before releasing them.

Rose drops her hands into her lap. She keeps her head low. This is a setback but she is not defeated. She must continue. She raises her hands and resumes eating.

The meal is protracted and silent, save for the occasional scrape of tine against plate and clink of cuffs on counter. Rose appreciates the silence. As it extends, she regains her composure. She retraces her thoughts, dwelling on dilemmas. Can she find ammunition? Can she shoot him point blank? Can she shoot him if challenged? Will she be here tomorrow? She wonders what time it is now. Midday perhaps. It's difficult to tell. The light from the sun tunnels is bright.

The only thing she knows for sure is that the sun is shining.

Forty-One

I'M STUCK, BUFFERING LIKE a computer as I try to make sense of a swarm of data. Is there a connection between the disappearance of Rose and that of Margo? Should I call the police?

It's the sound of Lee's voice, yelling at me through my cell phone that clues me in. I already called. I don't remember doing it, but I already called.

"Flynn. Flynn! Are you there?"

I stare blankly at my phone.

"Flynn! You called. What's going on?"

I raise the phone to my ear and clear my throat. "Lee, I found something hidden at the back of the mahogany dresser." I stammer through the details. Just facts, all facts.

"Any connection to Rose there, Flynn?"

"Trying to figure it. The necklace. Violet had both symbols. Margo had the yang. Rose has the yin. Other than that . . ." My voice shudders as I let the sentence trail away.

"I'm on it," says Lee. Then he's gone.

And I'm left waiting, wondering what to do next.

It's as quiet as a crypt here. No sound. Not even traffic. But it wasn't traffic that punctured the silence on recent visits. It was the neighbor's flower music—*Where Have All the Flowers Gone?* Where, indeed, have the flowers gone? Where is the music? I'm wondering at the stillness. I'm aggravated by the waiting.

Waiting is the enemy. It disrupts momentum. Why should I wait? I'm a private investigator. Does the lack of badge make me impotent? Does it mean I can't help my friend? If I could help Rose, what would I do next? I haven't a clue.

I sigh my way to the door. Momentum doesn't matter if I'm out of options.

As I lock Rose's condo, I glance at the neighbor's place. Why is his door ajar? I step over to the door and raise my hand to knock. At the first rap, the door swings open. The hallway, like Rose's, is long, almost a shotgun layout, and it is completely empty. Not a table, a chair, a plant. Was it this way the last time I was here? I focused on the resident then and barely got a foot in. This time? Despite the fact that I have a visual of Lee wagging a warning finger, I'm going in. Yes, I'm breaking all kinds of laws here, but I don't give a damn. I step across the threshold. I don't touch anything; I just make my way down the hall. The place is as empty as a church on a Monday morning. I pull out my phone and call Lee again.

"Lee, I need you to run a check on something else. Rose has, or had, a neighbor. Don't know the name. The guy seems to have disappeared and the door to his condo is wide open."

"And I assume you went in?"

I say nothing.

"There'll be a police unit there shortly. You should stay put, and by that I mean get the hell out of that condo. Consider it a no-go zone. Wait in the hallway."

"Got it." I walk backward as I leave the neighbor's place, as if that gesture can undo my footprints. In front of the elevator, I pace in a figure-eight pattern, an activity that both revs up my anxiety and makes my head spin. I need to move, but I must feel like I'm getting somewhere. I press the elevator button. The elevator instantly opens. I ride to the lobby and charge through the exit. Then I'm in the sunshine, squinting and waiting. I start pacing again, on the sidewalk, making figure eights around the bus stop and the fire hydrant.

It occurs to me that I could leave. The police will arrive shortly to check on the neighbor's condo with the wide-open door. Maybe I will be here when they arrive. Maybe not. What would I accomplish by leaving? Where would I go? I shrug. Perhaps I should stay. Those are my shoe tracks on the freaking carpet in the neighbor's condo. Idiot. How stupid was I to enter? Should have called the cops. Another shrug. At least it wasn't *break* and enter. Should I leave? What can I do?

A single thought jumps to the fore. *Google William Lord*. I pull out my phone.

I find an address in West Vancouver. Dare I go? On my own?

A police car roars up, blinking and braking.

Guess I'm not going anywhere. Yet.

Forty-Two

I'M STANDING IN THE hallway outside Rose's neighbor's door, trying to explain to a twentysomething, exuberant officer why I chose to trespass. The words "gut instinct" are not going over well with this guy. It doesn't help that he's over six feet tall; kind of tough making eye contact when I'm eye level with the flap on his shirt pocket. In a side glance, I see his partner, inside the neighbor's condo, talking to the building superintendent—a graying, frog-faced woman with a blunt haircut and a square, squat body, a woman whom I have never set eyes on before. I sidle toward them, but eavesdropping is thwarted.

"Let us handle it, sir." The officer in front of me crosses his arms and plants his feet shoulder width apart.

I refrain from telling him I had met the sightless neighbor with the S-shaped spine. No input wanted here. None given. I'm still straining to hear the super, though. The only thing I manage to catch is a reference to a tattoo. Not much help there. Tattoos are ubiquitous. But perhaps there is something distinguishing about this particular tattoo.

My second effort to edge closer is no more successful than the first. Fortunately, the elevator pings and Lee steps out. He waves his badge. "Do you have all the information you need, Constable?"

When the officer nods, Lee grabs my arm and yanks me into motion. We're in the elevator before he releases his grip.

"What the hell, Lee? I want to talk to that super. Maybe she knows something about Rose's neighbor."

"Let the officers handle it. They know what they're doing." He presses the lobby button. "I'll keep you informed."

"But—" I start to reach for my cell and catch myself. If I share my discovery about the West Van address, I'll be in watch-and-wait mode again.

Lee raises his eyebrows. "But what?"

"Nothing," I say, lowering my glance. The ding of the elevator triggers my adrenaline. "Later," I say and step forward as soon as the door opens. When the door closes, I execute a fist pump. Sorry, Lee. I'm going to West Vancouver, to the last known address of the Lords.

I exit the elevator and march through the lobby. Lee's Honda Accord is parallel parked in the NO PARKING ZONE, dead in the middle of two flashing police units. When the hell did the second police car show up? Not relevant. I make my way to my own vehicle, farther down the block.

I strap in and turn on the car. I check my side view mirror to ensure that there is no sign of Lee or any other cop and then I revisit Google, the address of William and Annabel Lord. West Vancouver. The British Properties. I Google the names individually and come across obituaries. Dead? Seems so. Both of them. Annabel a couple of decades back, William a few years later. Then who the hell sent the vengeance note? The note was folded and creased, but it was not that old. Who sent it?

A new resolve shoots through me. I turn off the phone, drop it into the cup holder, and focus on pulling from the curb. The street is clogged with cars and bicycles and buses, the result of drivers slowing to gawk as they guide themselves around the police units. Unable to contain my excitement, I begin talking to myself. "So, if they are both dead, who owns the property? And the yacht? Is there an heir?"

I nod my head. "Logical. But who the hell is it?"

I honk in acknowledgment of a driver who makes room for me. I inch into the traffic stream and begin the painfully slow crawl along Beach Avenue.

Twenty minutes and a few blocks later, I pound the heel of my hand on the steering wheel. This is going to take forever. I busy my mind by plotting my route. An easy task. My vehicle doesn't have the luxury of GPS, but I don't need that anyway. Don't need my phone either. Good thing about the latter as I wouldn't Google and drive, or text and drive, or drink and drive. Multitasking is fine when there is no risk to life and limb, mine or anyone else's.

I keep my eyes on the road while I conjure up a mental image of a map of West Vancouver's British Properties. Four thousand exclusive acres across the Lion's Gate Bridge. This should be a twenty-five minute drive from Beach Avenue to destination. "Not in this traffic. Settle in," I tell myself.

Just then traffic eases up. I smile and depress the accelerator.

My smile is punctuated, and eliminated, by a crash up ahead. "Great. A fender bender. I'll be here forever."

Forever is not long. After a few seconds of parking lot status and a few feet of creeping along, I'm back at the speed limit. I'm again wondering if I should rethink, go back, get Lee, but I guillotine those thoughts. All I'm going to do is check out the house and canvass the neighbors. That's what I do, right? I'm a private investigator, for Christ's sake.

The fender bender that caused the delay isn't as bad as it seemed; when I motor past the site, the cars involved are already at roadside and the drivers are exchanging information. After that? Regular stop-and-go city traffic flow. At a red light, as the car idles, my mind becomes quiet. No more second-guessing. "Good enough," I say as the light turns green. I'll call Lee later.

Then I'm on the Lion's Gate Bridge, praying that there will be no problems. Any accident, major or minor, on the center span of the bridge, could delay me for hours. The Fates are with me. In short order, I pull up in front of the Lord house. I take one look at it.

Excuse me, the Lord *mansion*.

Forty-Three

I PARK BESIDE THE visitor intercom and press the buzzer. No response. I get out of my car and stand outside the wrought-iron gates, peering in at the cobblestone, circular driveway, and the manicured hedges. The air is fragrant with hints of lilac and jasmine. The owners of this place may be deceased, but someone certainly lives here. And someone on the premises is a gardener. Likely a full-time hired hand.

I need to explore, but I can't just climb the gate, as tempting as that might be. Ethics stand in the way. Not to mention alarms. The police already questioned my judgment in entering the condo next door to Rose's. Two incidences of trespassing in the same day would not bode well. How do I manage this?

I'm scratching my head for a solution when it, or rather *he* appears. It's the sound of a twig snapping that triggers me to do a one-eighty and come face-to-chest with a man. I take a step back. Don't know where the hell this guy came from, but he is long-limbed and sinewy, clad in a plaid button-down shirt and faded Levi's, which are tucked into black rubber-soled ankle boots with neoprene uppers. His golden buckskin gardening gloves are cinched at the wrist. Due to his oversized, black-rimmed sunglasses, there is not much of a facial visual, but he is thin-lipped and clean-shaven. His hair is short, on the sides anyway. The top of his head is shielded by a black baseball cap with an uncharacteristic lack of a logo. He's standing in front of me, too close, before he says a word.

"What in tarnation are you doing here?" he drawls.

"My name is Flynn, and I'm a private investigator," I say, reaching for my ID card. "I'm looking for the residents of this property."

"Mr. Lord ain't here. I can't let you onto the property without his permission." He folds his arms.

"And your name is?"

"I'm just the gardener, mister. Gardener and gatekeeper."

"What's this Mr. Lord's first name and where is he?"

"*Mr.* Lord could be in Vancouver. Could be in Europe." He shakes his head. "Mr. Lord don't share the details of his comings and goings. I just get my orders in the email and I show up regular. Pruning and watering today." He lifts and drops his shoulders, a shrug as drawn-out as his voice is drawled.

I'm getting nowhere pushing questions at this guy. I change tactics, nodding my head toward the gate. "Took the liberty of looking in. Some great work on the gardens. I bet those flowers are a showy bunch. What am I smelling? Jasmine? Lilac?"

The gardener lifts the corners of his mouth into a controlled smile. "You want to see my gardens, mister?" He holds the grin like he's playing with the idea.

That's exactly what I want but I can't appear too anxious. I glance at my watch. "I've got a little time. If it's not too much trouble . . ."

"Good enough, then. Leave your vehicle here. Follow me."

That's the only prompt I need to jolt into motion. I'm on his heels as he strides to the keypad at the right of the gate. He tugs off one glove so he can key in the code.

I smile to myself. *Finally.* An advantage of being short. I'm eye level with a triangular space—the gap created by his bicep, his torso, and his armpit. Through that space, I can see his hand, specifically his index finger, as he punches the numbers. Six digits. Easy-to-remember digits, from the Fibonacci sequence.

The gate swings wide. He ambles through.

I follow, pondering the passcode. Familiar numbers. One, one, two, three, five, eight. The Fibonacci sequence is a specific series. Each number is the sum of the two preceding numbers. Anybody with half a brain can memorize them. Why would a gardener, or the owner of this place, use Fibonacci numbers?

Perhaps the answer lies in the gardening. The number of petals in a flower often coincides with a number from Fibonacci: Buttercups have five petals, lilies and irises have three. Perhaps the answer is as simple as the gardener or the owner—someone who loves flowers or studies flowers—assigning the sequence.

Someone like Violet Harrington. She loved flowers. I love numbers. Private investigating is often about building relationships; floriculture and Fibonacci gave us a connection. There was another connection there, unspoken. The loss of a child. It was a long time before Violet and I broached that subject.

"This way for the grand tour, Mister," the gardener says.

I refocus, watching his every move.

He pulls on his gardening glove and cinches the wrist. Can't fathom why, but he then removes his other glove and puts it back on. Before he completes the second half of that move, I notice the tail end of a tattoo on his left wrist. Is that a capital letter "I" or the number "one"? I'm not sure. I don't ask.

He leads me directly to a path on the near side of the mansion. I try to get a closer look at the house but, before I know it, we're through a wrought-iron gate and on a step-stone path beneath a canopy of purple clematis. On the right, in the shade, is a row of variegated hostas, the depth of color of their huge, unscarred leaves providing clear evidence that this is one well-tended garden. Further affirmation comes when we mount a series of steps leading up to the deck at the back of the house. On the deck, the gardener steps aside and waves a hand through the air. I stop and stare. Against the backdrop of ocean, sits a multi-tiered garden, awash with color, alive with birdsong.

"You must be one heck of a gardener."

He says nothing, just waves me on. We cross the deck and descend the stone stairs into the first terrace. As we step onto a path, a hummingbird zooms in, hovers, makes a lateral move, swoops upward, and lingers again. Before it rockets away, I spot its vivid red throat, flashing like a warning sign. A shiver runs through me.

We approach two lengthy rows of laburnum trees whose leafless, yellow-pea flowers dangle like gold chains. Flowing like a river beneath the trees is a groundcover of periwinkle, interrupted only in one section where a long segment of tiny purple flowers is missing, stripped away. A curious breach. I want to ask, but let it pass.

Continuing the tour, we come upon a clearing where a carpet of forget-me-nots is flanked by a riot of colorful pansies. I gaze to the end of the carpet, to a life-sized garden statue of a woman who is posed, arms folded, a wreath of flowers on her head. "In memory of Annabel," I say, reading the plaque beside the statue.

"She watches over the flowers," says the gardener who bows his head and then moves on.

"Who's Annabel?" I ask and then remember. "Oh, it's the owner or former owner. Right?"

He shrugs and walks on, past a spouting fountain whose droplets plop into a circular pond. We arc around the pond and enter another path. "This is the rhododendron walk," the gardener says. We are instantly surrounded by leathery-leaved shrubs with plump clusters of blooms in white, gold, variegated pinks and reds. "Most people don't know the difference between rhododendrons and azaleas." The gardener sounds like he's giving a lecture. "The most common distinction is that rhododendrons are evergreens while azaleas are deciduous." The tone of his voice gives me pause. Is it my imagination or is his southern accent fading?

At the end of the rhododendron path, there is another clearing, a circular one containing a stone bench and a cluster of cherub statues. And surrounding this are the rose gardens. I inhale the perfume and gaze at blossoms of peach, white, yellow, and pink. "What, no red?" I say, not expecting an answer.

The gardener points to a gap in the visual flow, an empty bed, earth turned.

"There will be a new bed of roses any day now," he says.

I nod. Am I missing something? If so, what? I'm becoming eerily self-conscious. Why did I come here alone? Perhaps I should have listened to Lee after all. I shake off the discomfort. Perhaps there is something here I need to know.

We carry on, climbing, descending, climbing again, eventually returning to the deck at the back of the house. I pause to scan the scene—a grand-scale garden, a circular sanctuary with a serpentine layout configured in switchbacks and tangents and figure eights. A well-tended masterpiece.

The gardener leads me back to my car. "Satisfying tour?" he asks in a tongue-in-cheek manner.

"Stunning. You do remarkable work." I'm feeling safe now, in front of the house, and I want to ask more questions. How far should I go?

"You be needing anything more?" the gardener asks, his southern accent evident once again.

"You could tell me your name."

"You the cops?"

"No, not the cops. As I already told you, I'm a private investigator—"

"Why are you investigating this place?"

"I'm looking for a friend."

The gardener doesn't move a muscle.

"You want to tell me your name?" I'm stalling now.

"You don't need to know my name, mister." He waves me toward my car. "You should just get into that little red vehicle of yours and be off."

I oblige. In my rearview mirror, I can see the gardener, standing, staring as I drive off, his eyes hidden by dark glasses.

It is with mixed feelings that I ease my way onto the road. I'm relieved. That much I know. Relieved to be safely out of there, relieved to be rid of the gardener. I'm troubled too. Is there something here that I need to know?

Maybe the neighbors can enlighten me.

As I pull into the neighbor's gravel driveway, my phone rings. Startled, I grab for it. My car rolls backward. *Damn.* I drop the phone and yank on the emergency brake. The car comes to a standstill and I search for my phone, which has landed between the bucket seats. I shove my hand down and, with index and middle fingers, manage to lock onto the phone and draw it up from its hiding place. I glance at the screen. It's Lee. *Good.* I'm ready to share my discovery. I manage to connect before the phone goes to message.

"Lee! Good to hear from you. There's a mansion in the British Properties—"

"What the hell are you doing?"

I ignore the question. "You wouldn't believe the gardens at that place. The estate belonged to William and Annabel Lord. Listen. I want you to check out the gardener for me. The guy won't tell me a thing. I'm about to canvass the neighbors—"

"You'll do no such thing," Lee says. "I want you here, at the cemetery, at Violet Harrington's gravesite. You know where that is?"

My breath catches. "Yes. But why—"

"Violet Harrington's body is missing. Someone robbed her grave."

Forty-Four

THERE IS ONLY ONE cemetery in Vancouver. It consists of about ninety thousand graves divided into sectors and it honors all parts of society from mayors to first responders to military to citizens. I've attended funerals there, twice. The more recent was Violet Harrington's. The first was that of my six-year-old son.

I glance at my watch. Two-thirty. The cemetery is a half-hour drive from the British Properties, rush hour is descending, and I'm stalling, still parked in the Lords' neighbor's driveway. I'm absorbing the shard of information Lee provided and trying to make a connection between it and another fragment that is bouncing around in my head. Problem is, I am uncertain as to what that other fragment is. Perhaps the missing splinter will surface and the fragments will collide during my drive to the cemetery.

I put my car into FIRST. The front wheels barely make contact with the asphalt when a black car flies past me. *Damn.* Good thing I was easing out of the driveway. My ramshackle vehicle couldn't have taken a hit by that speeding bullet. I don't catch the make or the plate of the offender. I just shrug off the experience and flick on my right-turn signal indicator.

A quick glance to my left reveals a surprise—the gates of the Lord mansion are open wide and closing fast.

Do I go to the cemetery or go back to the mansion? That's a no-brainer.

I switch my signal indicator from right to left and pull out timidly, still a bit shaken by the fly-by car. There's no need to rush through the gate before it closes. I know the passcode. The Fibonacci passcode.

In the driveway of the Lord mansion, I pause, taking a moment to visualize the garden. Everything in it was perfect: mature trees, meandering paths, a kaleidoscope of flowers. But something haunts, an anomaly. Yes, there was a gap in the rose bushes, but there was something else, too. What was it?

I reimagine the garden tour—the starts, the stops, the stunning views—until the answer surfaces. It was the flowerbed, the one with the flowers removed. The periwinkle flowerbed. The gape in the purple flowers was long enough, wide enough . . .

Jesus. Periwinkle is another name for violet.

Forty-Five

SOMEHOW, TIME HAS ESCAPED Vincent's notice. It's not that the events of the day are compressed; it's that, try as he might, he doesn't recall them. Three hours of his life have vanished into blackness. Vincent wants that time back. An impossible task. So, in lieu of that, he wants more time, more time with Rose. And to get that, he has to negotiate with Gideon.

Vincent arranges a meeting, choosing as a venue a restaurant in the very hotel which had played host to the Heritage Gala. The gala where Vincent lured Rose. The gala where Vincent, not Gideon, was in total control.

It is approaching three o'clock, the appointed meeting time. Vincent will be late returning to Rose, but he reassures himself that she will understand. She enjoys her little kennel, and hearts do grow fonder through absence.

Vincent parks parallel to the sidewalk across the street from the restaurant. He exits his Audi and glances at the ivy-covered, brick hotel, itself a heritage building. A heritage building that held a gala in support of heritage buildings, the restoration of which was a passion of Rose's mother, therefore a passion of Rose's. Vincent knew she would show up at the gala. He amends that last thought. It was Gideon who knew. Gideon is the one who keeps track of those things.

Vincent heads for the crosswalk and waits. Standing just in front of him, eyeing traffic, is a young, shiny-haired brunette. Vincent takes a deep breath so he can inhale her perfume. Chanel. Captivating. Vincent does like the classics. As she planks a sandaled foot onto the crosswalk, a lime-green convertible coupe whips past, a woman at the wheel, blond hair streaming, metal music blaring.

The brunette pulls back to the sidewalk. "It's a crosswalk, bitch," she utters under her breath, a phrase clearly meant for no one's ears but her own.

Vincent leans in. "My sentiments exactly," he says.

When the brunette smiles at him, he returns the smile, offers her his arm, and escorts her across the street. Safe on the other side, she looks up at him, her dark eyes shining with interest. Vincent merely bids her good day and watches her walk away. A lovely morsel. Sadly, he cannot be all things to all women. Monogamy is a sign of a strong moral center. Vincent's current one-and-only, Rose, is waiting for him. Still, he can't help but stare after the lanky brunette, imagining all kinds of entanglements with those long legs.

The legs are forgotten when a different beauty catches his eye. A classic four-door sedan, a Rolls Royce Phantom, is zooming toward him. In the lane adjacent to it is another stunner, a contemporary three-wheeled motorcycle, a Polaris Slingshot. He watches these exquisite pieces of machinery as they drive past him and turn the corner. Worthy of notice, both vehicles.

Vincent glances back at his own car and nods in approval. His sleek, black Audi A-6 is high-performance and luxurious, yet unobtrusive. He has selected stealth over show. As much as he admires eye-catching machinery, he cannot indulge in same. It would be a grievous error to simplify life for eyewitnesses.

As he climbs the stairs to the restaurant at the Sylvan Hotel, Vincent hopes he has arrived first, hopes he can be seated at a table with a view. There is nothing like a beautiful day enhanced by the sight of English Bay.

The door to the restaurant is spread wide, an apparent effort to usher in patrons and sunlight. The idea works for patrons as the place is relatively full, but not for lighting. The interior is dreadfully dim, its walls paneled in dark oak.

Vincent pauses while his eyes adjust to the gloom. He climbs to a landing and nods in approval as a hostess approaches. "I'm meeting my brother here," he says, glancing around. "Oh, never mind," he adds, waving a dismissive hand, "I see him."

The hostess smiles and scurries away. Vincent slips toward a booth in a shadowy corner, the sight of which makes his spirits sink. How silly was he to have hoped for an ocean view? Gideon has planted himself in the dark like roots in the soil. There is no point in suggesting a move. Gideon will not comply.

Vincent plops down and picks up a drink menu. "You want me to order?"

Gideon shrugs. "It's time."

"Time for what?" Out of the corner of his eye, Vincent sees a server approaching—a gangling, blond youth with a well-practiced, glacier-white smile.

"May I get you a drink to start?" the server asks, pad and pen poised.

"Just a coffee and . . . a water," Vincent says, waving him away.

The server nods. He stuffs both pen and notepad into his waistband and hurries off.

Vincent returns his attention to Gideon. "I repeat, time for what?"

"Time for a certain flower to be put to bed."

Vincent sits up straight. "It's too soon. There's no rush."

"That private investigator is homing in. He visited the gardens today."

"Who the hell let him in?" Vincent's knee is bouncing erratically. He presses a hand on it, forcing it to be still.

Gideon hikes his shoulders a second time. "I rather enjoyed toying with him."

"How could he possibly have found the place?"

"Doesn't matter. Only time matters now. Your Rose has become a thorn. You must transport her from the loft to the estate before Flynn returns with cops in tow. You must prepare the rose bed. Tonight's the night, Vincent."

Vincent shakes his head. "I thought you were going to handle Flynn. And prepare the rose garden."

"I'll do the latter, if necessary. But I think we can complete the mission without slaying the sleuth." Gideon's laugh is sinister.

Vincent stiffens. "You shortchanged me with the bouquet of roses, Gideon. No buds. All blooms. Already drooping. That is not fair play. I'm keeping her. One more day is all I ask. That was the plan. The final meal is tomorrow, not tonight. Then you can have her."

"Tonight. It must end tonight. The finale occurs tonight. Remember the vow? We must annihilate the family. Margo Harrington is in her final resting place. Violet Harrington is where she belongs now. Only Rose remains."

Vincent frowns. "Violet? Where she belongs?"

"You'll thank me later."

"Thank you? What the hell are you talking about?"

Gideon lifts the corners of his mouth in an ominous smile. "You're smart enough. Figure it out."

Instantly inundated with images of the mud-filled mansion and muddied garden walkway, Vincent points an accusing finger. "You moved Violet Harrington's body? Why? She was already dead. Why would you move her body?"

"All a part of the plan, little brother. But don't worry. I stuck her deep. The violet bedding plants are waiting beside Violet Harrington's new grave. You can plant them tonight, on top of Violet, after you dig up the rose bed."

The strength oozes out of Vincent. "Mother would not like having all that mud in her house." He shakes his head.

The server is approaching, tray in hand, a cue that Vincent must move this conversation along. Vincent gathers enough fortitude to squeeze out his predetermined request. "One more day. That's all I'm asking," he says. Standing, he pulls out his wallet. In a desperate stab at control, he adds, "No. Not asking. Telling." Vincent nods his head decisively and tosses a twenty-dollar bill on the table. "Goodbye, Gideon."

He thunders past the wide-eyed server who spins like a turnstile to avoid dropping the tray.

Outside, Vincent pushes a button on his car key fob and the Audi responds with a beep. He bounds across the street to the car door. There he pauses and glances toward the ocean. As he watches a gentle wave slip to shore, a sense of longing filters through him. He strolls to a nearby park bench and sits to gather his strength.

After a time, soothed by the sight and sound of the sea, Vincent returns to his car.

Waiting in the passenger seat is Gideon.

Vincent chides himself for not relocking the vehicle. Reluctantly, he opens the driver side door and gets in. He has no words for his brother.

"You really should learn to lock your car doors, little one."

Vincent cringes. He hates being called that, little one. Gideon is putting him in his place.

"You know I'm right, Vincent," Gideon says. "Besides, this is Thursday. Didn't the Last Supper occur on a Thursday? Tonight's the night."

Vincent turns away, closes his eyes, and allows defeat to seep in. "Tonight's the night," he says.

When he reopens his eyes, Gideon is gone.

Forty-Six

I'M PARKED IN THE Lords' driveway and I'm struggling to wrap my head around a horrific notion. I know that Violet Harrington's body was moved from its grave. Is it a coincidence that there's a space, the shape and size of a grave, in the periwinkle bed at the Lord mansion? I stab at the idea, trying to poke holes in it. The image remains stalwart.

There's no coincidence here.

I know I should contact Lee. Instead, I turn off my phone. No more waiting. This needs to be handled now. I'm on to something here. I can feel it. Got to keep the momentum going.

I exit my car.

At the gate, I key in the pass code: *one, one, two, three, five, eight*. With a *clank* and a whine, the gate swings inward. It crosses my mind that I will need a shovel. That's not a concern. There's a shed here, likely full of gardening tools.

I go straight to the gardens and retrace the path to the violet beds. Earlier, I had merely glanced at the breach, the missing rectangle of flowers. Now I squat down and lean in. That breach has occurred within the last couple of days. The dirt in the bed is crumbled in some places, compacted in others. Dug up, refilled, and slammed down by the back of a shovel. Sitting along the outer edge of the breach is a line of bedding plants—violets—waiting to enter the soil.

I glance around and head to a nearby shed. A padlock. There's no point in wasting valuable seconds picking the lock so I kick in the door. I pause, waiting for some screaming mark of intrusion. None occurs. I enter.

On my immediate right is a wall mount, lined with tools. I grab a shovel.

Then I'm back at the bed of violets. I gouge the soil, plunging the shovel deep, excavating the first scoop. As I twist to throw the dirt, my back resists with a warning twinge. I repeat the procedure—stab, scoop, toss—over and over, focussing on the middle, on depth at the middle. I'm digging and digging and hoping I'm wrong.

I'm not.

The shovel thuds, and I freeze. Seconds pass. With the tip of the tool, I scrape away soil until the source of the sound is revealed. A rotting skull. Overcome, I move the shovel to my side and lean into it. A deep inhalation is a mistake, for with it comes the stench. I struggle to repress the urge to vomit. I turn and, shovel in hand, pull myself away from the plot.

I'm sobbing at this point. I extricate my cell phone from my pocket and call Lee.

"Where the hell are you?" Lee's voice is adamant.

I take a deep breath and blow out the information. "I'm at the mansion. There's a body or the remnants of one. It's likely Violet Harrington."

"Jesus, Flynn. I wanted you to wait. Look, the police are already on their way." He pauses. "You know you're crossing boundaries here."

"Yes, but I had to check." A sudden panic hits. "Dear God. I should check the rose beds, too."

Sirens wail in the distance.

"The police. Wait for the police. They will check the rose beds."

I don't respond.

"Flynn. Flynn! Are you still there?"

"Yeah, but . . ." I plop down beside the shovel. "Rose's sister, Margo, her full name was . . . *is* Marigold. Did you know that?"

"And . . . ? Did you see marigolds there?"

"No, but that doesn't mean . . ."

The police cars are at the gate now. Voices shouting, footsteps slamming.

Without disconnecting, still clutching the phone, I jump up and run all out. I don't know where the marigolds are but I remember the rose beds. I can hear Lee yelling at me through the phone. *Damn.* With a punch of my thumb, I shut the phone off. I jam it into my pocket.

I have to check those rose beds.

Forty-Seven

YES, GIDEON HAS AGAIN pulled a vanishing act and Vincent is sitting in the car alone while the city swirls around him. He starts the engine and lets it idle.

Vincent detests being on his own. After his mother passed away, he tried to stand up to the world. When he failed and withdrew, a psychiatrist labeled him with borderline personality disorder, a diagnosis which confounds Vincent to this very day. Just what does it mean, this disorder? Does it make him neurotic?

Vincent contemplates his obsession with routines, his constant cleaning of counters and floors, his repeated locking and unlocking of doors. He shakes his head. There's nothing phobic about those behaviors. Germs and jeopardy lurk everywhere. One must be vigilant . . . but is he overly so? Vincent reaches out a hand in front of him. It's trembling again. Probably just a reaction to his disappointing encounter with Gideon. That's all it is. A normal reaction. He gives his hand a shake and plants it on the steering wheel, gripping tight. With a toss of his head, he dismisses the idea of being overly fearful. That doesn't belong to him at all.

What about psychosis? Is he psychotic? Vincent sniffs. He's not crazy. He's methodical, thoughtful, and kind to everyone, including the flowers he gathers. If anyone's crazy, it's that brother of his. If the police knew what lay beneath Gideon's flower gardens, they would incarcerate him in a heartbeat. *If the police only knew* . . . Alarmed, Vincent stops the thought. He shouldn't be thinking about informing on his brother. What would people say about that? Is there anyone else here? Nerves taut, Vincent glances in the rearview mirror. There's no one in the back seat. He swivels his head and sweeps his eyes across the car's interior, double-checking. Definitely no one else here. Good. On the heels of relief, he releases a snort of laughter. No one can hear his thoughts, can they? No one will ever know. *But if the police knew* . . .

All it would take to stop Gideon would be a well-placed word. Perhaps Vincent could do that, just drop an anonymous message to the police. Yes, Gideon is Vincent's brother, but why should Vincent worry about Gideon after all the evil things Gideon has done? It was Gideon who put this revenge play into effect. It is Gideon who is demanding the premature disposal of Rose. Why should Vincent put up with that when, with a single phone call, Vincent could dispose of Gideon and then keep Rose forever? One simple phone call. Can he make that call? Should he betray his brother? And who would stop him anyway?

Mother would, that's who. Mother would frown at this. She would not tolerate betrayal. Can he defy Mother? Vincent has never defied Mother. Can he do so now? Instantly, the word "no" falls from his lips. An impenetrable wall, his loyalty to Mother. With a pang of disappointment, Vincent dismisses all thoughts of betrayal.

"But what about Rose, Mother?" he asks, a sliver of hope in his heart. Now he can visualize Mother and she is shaking her head. She will not entertain the idea of extending the timeline with regard to Rose. *One should select perfect blossoms, shower them with attention, and release them before they wilt.*

Vincent sighs as the vision of Mother fades. He has always applauded Mother's philosophy regarding flowers. In fact, he lives that philosophy, doesn't he? Isn't every woman a flower? He does indeed shower his flowers with attention and, to this point, has been willing to release them before their beauty fades. As for his precious Rose, shouldn't she be given equal treatment? Shouldn't she be disposed of before she learns to despise her own reflection? How long would it take for her to indulge in hating her own mirror? Can he allow her to experience such agony? He slowly shakes his head. He cannot permit that to happen to such a stunning flower.

Steeped in sadness, Vincent sighs again. Mother was right. There is a time limit for all blossoms. And doesn't that make Gideon right, too?

"Tonight's the night," Vincent whispers, an affirmation. He shifts the car into gear. He must focus, not on the loss of Rose, but on the joy of the coming event, their Last Supper. He will set a textbook table. He and Rose will have a picture-perfect evening.

Vincent can feel his mood lightening as he pulls away from the curb.

Forty-Eight

I'M ON MY BUTT beside the gap in the rose beds, totally sapped after an all-out sprint and exhaustive search. After digging and sifting, using my fingers as a sieve, I found nothing, not a damn thing. The gap is just that, a gap, not a grave. Rose isn't here. Rose isn't dead.

I stumble to my feet and, sagging with relief, I meander from the garden, through the front gates, and continue to my VW Golf. I get behind the wheel and am about to start it up when a police vehicle pulls in front of me, blocking me in. I let out an elongated sigh. Where the hell was I going anyway? I look up at the mansion. Perhaps this is where I need to be, but I can't access that house, not yet. I grab my phone and call Lee.

"Rose is not in the garden," I say. "I have to get into the house."

"That's another no-go zone," says Lee. "I'm almost there. You have to wait. You hear me?"

"Yeah, yeah, I hear you." I disconnect and exit my car.

Two police constables pepper me with questions, why-are-you-here and how-did-you-get-in type of questions. Impatient, I shift my weight from one foot to the other. While one officer phones Lee to check me out, the other watches me. I'm watching the house. I need to get into that house.

The officer pockets his phone. "Mr. Flynn, please wait on this spot for Sergeant Connors. He's on his way."

I nod.

When both officers move away, I make my move toward the house. I'm barely past the gates when my attempt is foiled by a yellow-vested member of the Vancouver Police Department who escorts me back to my starting point. I stand where she tells me to, and this time I stay put, executing slow rotations so I can take in everything.

A hand touches my shoulder.

I turn my head. "Lee. About time."

"Can't make sense of this one," Lee says. "You attended Violet Harrington's funeral, didn't you?"

"Yes."

"Any ideas why someone would move her body to this place?" Lee's looking at me, straight at me.

I hear his words all right but I'm more interested in whatever thoughts are flickering behind those green eyes of his. Sergeant Lee Connors knows something I don't. I'm not asking, yet. "I don't know why someone would move the body here." I'm telling the truth, or I think I am. But, as the words leave my lips, a conflicting flinch hits my gut. There's meaning there. Guts don't balk at truth. What am I missing? I frown.

Lee looks at me quizzically. "Are you sure?"

"No. Something's bugging me. Obviously, the Lord family has something to do with this."

"Have you been in the mansion?"

I sniff. "Tried. Foiled by cop." It occurs to me that I hadn't informed Lee that I was heading here, to the estate. Would it be wise to spotlight that sin of omission? Maybe not, but I do it anyway. "How did you know I was here?"

"The hairstylist called me."

"Sue called you? Why?"

"Because, like you, I asked her to call if she remembered anything. FYI, I also asked her to say nothing to you about the name of the yacht."

"You know the name of the yacht? Why would you keep that from me?"

Lee shrugs. "Figured you might jump the gun."

"You got that right, obviously. But I'm not apologizing. Can't wait around where Rose is concerned."

"So, I'm guessing you Googled William Lord?"

"The Google gods know everything," I say.

"What exactly did you find?"

"Found out William was married to someone named Annabel. Found the last known address."

"And . . . ?"

"Didn't look anymore. Locked on the address and hit the road."

Lee is silent, his jaw clenched.

"Clearly I missed something. You want to enlighten me?"

"Just give me as much detail as you got, Flynn."

"All I got is that William and Annabel Lord owned a house in the British Properties." I wave an arm in the direction of the mansion. "This house."

"Owned? Past tense?"

"Both dead."

"Who owns this property now?"

I shrug. "The gardener was here earlier. Said a Mister Lord owned it. Said he didn't know where Mister Lord was. And he wouldn't tell me even if he did."

"Did the gardener tell you his own name? Did he tell you Mister Lord's first name?"

"No on both counts. Believe me, I asked. Repeatedly."

Lee reaches into his pocket. I assume he's going for his phone, but what he retrieves are his glasses. I brace myself. Lee has something serious to say. Before he speaks, Lee pulls out his phone and begins searching, searching. "Flynn, I could let you go on about this but . . ."

I'm losing patience. "Are we going into the house?"

He nods. "The discovery of the body on the property warrants entry. You know that."

"What the hell are you holding back from me? Whatever it is, say it."

Ignoring me, Lee walks toward the house. I follow like a foot soldier. He lets out a sigh, one which I can hear over the ruckus of footfall and voices and engines, even sirens. When we reach the steps to the house, he turns to me. "Flynn, you don't usually miss details, but sometimes personal involvement—"

"What are you talking about? What did I miss? "

"Instead of rushing, if you'd actually read the obits . . . you'd know they had a son."

"Son? What son?"

"William and Annabel Lord had a son named Vincent."

I slump onto the steps like I've been shot. I plant my elbows on my knees and drop my head into my hands.

"It's all connected, Flynn," Lee continues. "The yacht Vincent left Granville Island on? The name of it? It's the *Annabel Lord*."

I sit still. "Anything else?"

"Nothing yet. We will search the yacht. As for you, I want you to wait here for a bit," Lee says.

"Not a problem. Won't move a muscle."

"I'll check out the building and bring you inside later." He heads up the steps.

I say his name. Not loud. Not loud at all. Yet, despite the din, he hears me. "Yes?"

"There's one more thing." I fumble in my pocket and drag out the envelope, the one I found hidden in the dresser.

I hand him the envelope.

He sits beside me, opens the envelope, and examines its contents.

"I told you about this earlier," I say. "The yang necklace? Definitely Margo's. I found it in the mahogany dresser. On the inside. Painted to the back."

"Do you think Rose put it there?"

I shake my head. "I think Rose knew nothing about it. It was Violet who insisted Rose keep the dresser. Violet hid this necklace. Not Rose. Violet."

"Any idea why?"

"Guilt, I'm guessing."

"How so?"

"I think she did something that caused all this. I think something was as simple as dating William Lord. But whatever it was, Margo's disappearance was just the beginning."

"I admit that this isn't looking good," says Lee, "but Rose is an intelligent woman, a competent woman. Athletic too, if I recall. Great hand-eye coordination."

"Point being?"

"Rose has skills. Remember the time you took her to the gun range?"

"She couldn't shut up about the adrenaline rush."

"If there's a way out, she'll find it. And we'll do our damnedest to find her." Lee pats my shoulder before he stands and walks away, leaving me on the steps of the Lord mansion, remembering Rose, remembering her at the gun range, remembering how she wanted to go over and over the steps in using a nine-millimeter handgun.

Forty-Nine

ROSE IS ON ALERT. She dare not escape the kennel, not yet. Vincent said he would be gone a short time this afternoon. She counts seconds, then minutes, and then loses track. How long is a short time? Should she get out of this cage now and search for bullets? What if he shows up? She can't fight him without a weapon. She needs bullets for that gun, that nine-millimeter gun. If she finds bullets, can she figure out how to use them? She sifts through the memory of the only time that she had handled a firearm: her trip to the gun range with Flynn.

She and Flynn had arrived early. Other than one female clerk, Rose was the only woman there. No surprise. She expected testosterone. She focused on watching the clerks unload guns from black cases.

As the firearms emerged, the room acquired a vague scent of gunpowder. The clerks efficiently removed trigger locks and lined up guns—mostly semiautomatics—in a glass showcase. All the while, people, single or in clusters, entered. Soon it was standing room only. Rose noted that there were many women, of all ages and ethnic groups. Lesson learned. Not a male-dominated activity after all.

The system for service was "take-a-number" and Rose and I were number seven. When called, we, along with eight or ten others, were escorted into a side room for instruction by a tall, skinny twentysomething man who seemed anxious to get things going. He set in and rattled off his pre-shooting spiel. Clearly a pro at this. I was sure Rose could relate because she told me about giving the same grammar lesson repeatedly. After a while, the words just flew. No thought. No meaning.

Rose and I chose our paper targets—the standard, torso outline. We donned safety goggles and protective earmuffs and lined up at the entrance to the indoor shooting range.

Our instructor, a stocky woman with a chestnut ponytail, spoke calmly as she led us to our respective booths. I glanced at Rose who was bobbing with excitement.

"Just pick up the gun like you were shown," the instructor said to Rose. "Your finger is your safety. Keep your finger on the barrel of the gun until you are ready to pull the trigger."

Rose lifted her gun, which felt heavy, not cold. Why had she expected it to feel like an ice pack? She picked up the magazine and looked at it.

The client in the booth next to her fired his first shot. Rose recoiled.

The instructor smiled at her. "Loud, isn't it? It's okay. Pick up your gun."

The blast of the neighbor's gun had detonated Rose's adrenaline.

"Go ahead." There was no end to this instructor's encouragement. "Load it. Make sure it's always aimed at the target."

Rose pushed the magazine into the handle and it clicked into place. What she could not do, with her heart whacking her chest, was pull back the slide.

"Don't worry," said the instructor, who was rapidly becoming Rose's new best friend. "Just use the slide catch." She pointed at a small lever. "Push it down."

Rose did as she was told and caught herself grinning when the gun clicked into firing mode.

"Now, stand with your feet shoulder-width apart and aim, using your front and rear sights. When you are ready, take your finger off the barrel, place it on the trigger, and squeeze it."

Rose followed instructions and fired. With the kick of the gun, her adrenaline gushed, sending her entire body into overdrive. A tremor started in the core of her being and travelled into her fingertips. Her heart pounded in her ears and her hand shook so badly that her shot missed the shape of the target completely. Bullet holes appeared beside the neck of the body outline. The magazine contained ten rounds and, by the time she put the gun down, only three holes appeared where they were supposed to be. She switched places with Flynn who shot ten rounds, accurate rounds. Rose took two more turns, but could not stop shaking.

As we were leaving the gun range, I watched Rose strut across the parking lot.

"Pleased with yourself?" I asked.

She turned and grinned. "It was exhilarating, like the time I rode a rollercoaster. With the roller coaster, once was enough. But the shooting range? I want to go back. Have to admit, though. The adrenaline shocked me. I couldn't stop shaking."

"You can learn to control that. You're an athlete, a performance gymnast. You can control the rush and the result. What do you call it in sports? Controlled aggression? You can control the adrenaline. The way to do that is through repetition."

As Rose lies curled in the dog kennel, she realizes that if she finds the bullets, if she can load and shoot, she will have to control the adrenaline. What did Flynn call it? Controlled aggression? Yeah, that was it.

Rose begins to breathe slowly, steadily, controlling each breath, checking her heart rate, all the while imagining herself holding and aiming a semiautomatic handgun. Over and over and over. The only way to gain control is through repetition.

Yes, the memories I have of Rose at the gun range, of Rose as a person, are those of a strong, independent woman. "I think I need to give Rose credit," I say, to no one in particular. To my surprise, Lee responds. How long has he been standing beside me?

"Yes," he says, "you do. She's a capable woman. Whatever she's gotten herself into, she'll do her best to get out."

I nod. "Thanks, Lee."

I'm still sitting. I'm still remembering that day at the shooting range. I remembering being worried that day, worried about how Violet Harrington would react to my taking Rose to a gun range. I'm remembering emptying the magazine into the paper torso and pushing a button. I'm remembering the paper target zinging toward me. I'm remembering the attendant passing me the target.

"A flower lover, are you?" the attendant had said, grinning.

I looked at the torso. Center mass was full of bullet holes, outlining a flower. I had no idea why I had outlined a flower, a violet.

On that day, I just shrugged it off. But now, the memory gives me pause. I shake my head. On some level, long before the discovery of the yang necklace, I had known that the key to Margo's disappearance was Violet. And today, when I put Violet's name at the center of my crime board, I knew that the key to Rose's disappearance was Violet.

Why didn't I make the connection earlier? It seems so obvious now.

At the heart of the missing is their mother, Violet Harrington.

Fifty

VINCENT INITIALLY CONTEMPLATED USING his mother's bloodred-rose-patterned china for his Last Supper with Rose, but the idea rattled him. Yes, the whole flower mission had its roots in honoring his mother, but Mother's ornate china would have contaminated the austere elegance of his loft. There were practical considerations as well, ones that mitigated any hint of guilt. It would take time to unearth Mother's china, time to transport it, and time to clean it. Gideon had set the timer and the clock was ticking. There was simply not enough time. Mother would have understood. As for Gideon?

Gideon doesn't care about china patterns. He cares about conclusion: the faster the petals fall, the better he likes it.

Earlier, Vincent taught Rose how to set a proper table. A rehearsal, that's all it was. It is now time for the main event.

With Rose assisting, Vincent prepares. Rose manages quite well despite the constraint of handcuffs; she almost misplaces a goblet again but, this time, she self-corrects. Vincent nods in approval. No punishment required. They finish the job in silence. Vincent puts an arm around her and they step back to admire their creation.

Everything is perfect.

The glass-topped table, cushioned with a fleece pad, is draped in ivory damask. The plates are delicate—ivory porcelain with two platinum bands, a wide one at the rim, and a thin one at the point where the center meets the rim. The ivory theme is maintained in the choice of napkins. Vincent had considered punctuating the palette with red dinner napkins, but dismissed the idea. The red is sufficiently present on the ruby lips of Rose and in the blood velvet of her rose bouquet, which he has moved from the coffee table to the center of the dining table. White tapers in silver holders flank the floral bouquet. Ivory napkins are cinched by silver napkin rings whose etched rose motif adds depth. The silverware is as it should be: sterling, aligned outside-to-inside, soup spoon, teaspoon, and dinner knife on the right; salad fork and dinner fork on the left. The dessert spoon sits perpendicular at the head of the plate.

Vincent scrutinizes the crystal stemware: a glass for white, a glass for red, and a water goblet, aligned diagonally from the tip of the teaspoon to the point of the place card. The embossed rose on the place cards speaks volumes. This is Rose's time. Her Last Supper.

As he is about to turn from the table, he glances at the bouquet of roses. They are certainly at, even stretching beyond, their peak; one particular stem is slouching. Its petals will drop soon. He sighs. He must make the best of things now while he has the opportunity.

"It's time, Rose," he says.

Fifty-One

SEATED AT THE DINNER table, clad in the sleeveless dress she wore to the gala, Rose fixates on the centerpiece—the bouquet of roses. Though aware of the threat they represent, she feels no panic. Panic is an alarm, a warning of danger; initially, it owned her but then it peeled away. She feels numb now. The goosebumps that pebble her arms are not fear-based; they are a result of the frigid temperature of the loft. Vincent cranked the air conditioning, explaining that roses last longer if they are kept cool.

Rose prays he's right. Her emotions may be dulled, but her brain is wired. She's been watching those flowers like a sentry. Some of the blooms look hearty, but others? Their velvet petals are brown-edged and wilting and willing to drop at the touch of a finger. She looks away in an effort to take her mind off the threat but her every hitching breath brings with it the sickening scent of roses.

As Rose shifts in her chair, pain clutches her ribs; she breathes through it. Are her ribs broken? Possibly. It doesn't matter. She'd had practice dealing with pain during her days as a gymnast. Under pressure, athletes become diamonds or coal dust. Pain can be acknowledged later. Not now.

Now she's perched, preparing to flee at the right opportunity. As her thoughts whirl, her hands tremble, creating a repetitive clink of handcuffs against her dinner plate. Vincent has cautioned her about doing damage to the china. Damage to his china means damage to her body. She lifts her hands. The clinking stops.

Vincent looks at her with a curious glint in his eye. She reaches for her water goblet, her cuffed hands working in awkward tandem. Bringing the glass to her lips, she meets his gaze. Vincent is preparing to light the slender candles which flank the flowers. Grinning, he produces a barbecue lighter, shaped like a gun, releases the catch, pulls the trigger, and offers flame to wick. Success is instant. He lights the second taper.

Rose takes a long, deep breath. He's occupied. She's safe. For the moment. A memory ruffles, that of summer storms on the prairies. The air grows heavy and humid. Clouds gather and darken. Heat rises, closes in. The skies light up. Thunder cracks. Rain pours. People flee.

She's seen the thunder in Vincent and doesn't want a recurrence. But storm or no storm, tonight she will flee. A moment of doubt penetrates. How can she get out without tools? Should she steal another knife? Should she wait another day? How can she get past this vacillation, this indecision?

As Vincent withdraws his hands from the second candle, his sleeve makes contact with the roses. A single petal shudders, then flutters down, down, alighting like a butterfly on the ivory damask. Rose gulps as her fear flares up. Quivering, she returns her water glass to its place. The water sloshes but remains contained.

Vincent turns to set the lighter down on the sideboard.

She reaches, pilfers the turncoat rose petal, and pushes it inside her dress. She lowers her hands to her lap and angles her head down, checking her neckline for telltale signs of red. There are none. There is only the sensation of the velvety smooth petal resting against her breast.

An image of her mother flits through her mind. It's there and gone and all is still. Rose closes her eyes, an effort to keep tears of relief contained. She cannot have this release, not yet. Vigilance is required. She opens her eyes. She raises her head.

Vincent is speaking. She feigns interest.

"I'm sorry that we must forego the appetizers and go straight to the entrée. Time is short this evening, thanks to that brother of mine."

Rose says nothing. Apparently, no response is required. Vincent is caught up in plating the meal—lamb, potatoes with rosemary and garlic, and sweet baby peas—all of which he brought to the loft. Where did he go this afternoon? A restaurant? A catering company? Rose doesn't know. And why should she be concerned? It doesn't matter.

Vincent places a steaming plate of food in front of her. Strange that it has no aroma; all Rose can smell is the bouquet of roses, the bouquet *from* the roses. She picks up a fork. She contemplates escape.

Will Vincent leave tonight? He did last night. Will he allow her to change into her jeans before he goes? What if he takes her with him? What if—? She stops. She can't pursue that runaway train of thought. It's Thursday now. The Last Supper night, Vincent called it. Just like Jesus and the apostles. The Last Supper. She's back to thinking about the knife. Should she make another attempt to steal one? How will she scrape that caulk?

While she ponders, she is aware of a constant buzz of chatter from Vincent. A monologue. Is it safe to tune him out? She thinks so. But then he mentions her mother and her sister and his words infiltrate like a virus.

". . . *your* Violet, *your* Margo. *Your* saccharine stories."

Saccharine stories? What does he mean? Truth slaps her and Rose bites back the urge to cry out. How desperately lonely was she that she had spilled treasured details about her family, that she had held nothing back from this man? Shame engulfs her like quicksand and she lets it drag her down, down, until she wonders if she can breathe. Does she even deserve to breathe?

"What of *my* family?" says Vincent. "Your mother was right, you know, in blaming herself."

What is he saying? Rose fights the sinking sensation in her body.

"Perhaps if you had listened to me, you might have ascertained the truth."

A need to know launches Rose to the surface. "I'm listening now." Her voice is soft, ghost-like.

"There are more things in heaven and earth, Horatio . . ." he prods.

". . .than are dreamt of in your philosophy," she whispers, finishing the line.

He nods. "Did you assume I chose those words to impress Rose the English teacher?" He shakes his head. "Such vanity. I was explaining that your beloved mother is at the core of everything."

Rose straightens her posture. "I'm listening now," she says again, struggling to keep her voice even. "What do you know about my mother?"

"All in good time. Need I remind you that you are a captive audience?" He reaches and taps the handcuffs. "You are not the first flower to visit this loft, Rose Harrington. There have been rehearsal flowers—an Iris, a Lily—an inconsequential lot. You and your family, are the main event." He picks up the butter dish and puts two pats of butter onto Rose's peas. "Sufficient?"

Rose has no words.

Shrugging, he places the butter dish back on the table. "First Marigold, then Rose, then Violet. That was the plan. In that order." He lets out a sigh.

Rose stares straight at him. No amount of deep breathing can halt the hammering of her heart. "Where's Margo?" A hoarse whisper.

Vincent wags a finger at her. His face darkens. "It is my family I am talking about. *My* family."

Rose tightens her fingers around her fork and stabs through a potato. An irreverent squeak rises from the meeting of tines and plate.

Vincent grabs her hand. "The china is delicate. Care must be taken." He extricates the fork from her fingers and places it beside her plate. "I need your full attention here."

With every nerve in her body strung tight, Rose waits.

"Your mother was to be the last," Vincent says, his smile fixed and empty. "She was to suffer the loss of her daughters first. Alas, cancer intervened." He sighs. "The best-laid plans . . ." Vincent falls silent.

Rose clears her throat. "I don't understand why—"

Vincent raises a hand, palm toward her. "Ah, but you do," he says, his voice an eerie calm. "I informed you that my father bedded another woman, that my mother died as a result." Vincent leans in, his black eyes boring through Rose. "Who do you think the other woman was?"

Rose blinks repeatedly.

"Not a difficult question, Rose. You know the answer. Go ahead. Say it."

Rose does know. Her mother had had an affair with William Lord, a married man. A married man whose children hated him, whose children sought retribution. Rose flinches as an undeniable truth slams her. She wants to ignore this truth but it persists, repeating and repeating and repeating:

Margo is dead. Margo is dead. Margo is dead.

Rose lowers her head and lets the realization hit home.

"Your mother knew," Vincent says, his tone guttural, victorious.

Rose instantly sits erect. "My mother knew what?"

"About Margo."

"How could she possibly . . . ?"

Vincent reaches across the table and toys with Rose's yin pendant. "How do you think Violet got the yang pendant back? Margo never went anywhere without it."

"You sent—?"

Vincent smiles. "Not me. Gideon. He even sent a note. Sadly, the blow was too much for Violet. I've often wondered what she did with the note."

Rose shakes her head violently. "The yang necklace disappeared with Margo. My mother didn't have it. She would have told me."

Vincent pulls back as if surprised. "You've gone pale, my dear. Perhaps your blood sugar needs elevating."

Abruptly, he clears the dinner plates. He crashes about in the kitchen. In seconds, he returns and places a dish of chocolate mousse in front of her.

Rose blinks at the mound of aerated chocolate. She looks toward Vincent's side of the table. "You're not having dessert?" she asks.

He pulls up the cuff of his left sleeve revealing his diabetes tattoo.

Rose nods. She had forgotten. But is the tattoo real? Is any of this real? Is he afflicted with diabetes? What about insulin? Where does he keep it? Where does he keep syringes?

"You'll never find it. The insulin, if that's what you're thinking." Vincent sighs. "I regret the day I had this done," he says, trailing the fingers of his right hand down the full length of his tattoo. "I lost my MedicAlert bracelet in the garden and opted for ink." He pulls his sleeve down. "Seemed logical. You can't lose a tattoo. Sadly, that has proven to be too true. At some point, I'll cover it with more ink. For now, I just take great pains to conceal it. Except with you, of course." He glances at his watch and taps his fingers on the table.

Rose spoons up the dessert in tiny mouthfuls.

Vincent removes her dessert bowl. "You should rest now," he says. He leads her from the table to the bedroom.

As instructed, she sits on the bed.

He removes her handcuffs and sets them beside her. He stands over her.

Rose's heartbeat thunders through her whole body. If he undresses her, he will find the flower petal which is now sliding in sweat between her breasts.

He shakes his head. "Such a beauty, such a pity."

Rose feels the flutter of his fingers as he lowers the shoulder of her dress. A wave of nausea overcomes her. She retches in dry heaves.

Vincent steps back.

Rose takes note. Vincent won't, *can't*, tolerate the stench and the mess that accompanies vomit. She continues to retch, determined to disgorge the chocolate mousse she just consumed. The vomit is fighting gravity, working its way up through her. She emits a belch. Bile burns her mouth and seeps through her fingers, a trail of it sliding down onto her dress.

Vincent shudders like a dog shaking off water. "Disgusting," he says, taking another step back and pointing a determined finger toward the bathroom.

Rose runs. When she drops and wraps her arms around the cool porcelain, a resounding clink startles her. She lifts her left hand and sees that she is holding the handcuffs. How the hell had she managed to steal the handcuffs? She stashes them behind the base of the toilet, raises the toilet lid and vomits, hugging the toilet with her left arm and releasing the rose petal from her bra with her right. Breaking off a ribbon of toilet paper, she wipes her hands and her breast, removing vomit and sweat and red. She flushes the toilet. Breathing deeply, she contemplates finding a better hiding place for the handcuffs. Where can she put them?

Something *thumps* to the floor beside her. She recoils.

"That's your suitcase," Vincent says. "Clean yourself up." He thunders out.

Rose doesn't waste a second. She unzips the case and hunts for clothes. In the process, her hand falls upon a tiny red leather case. Her manicure kit. She shoves the kit into the side pocket of a pair of cargo pants and struggles into the pants. She manages to do up the zipper but is shaking too much to attempt the button. Heart pummeling, she pulls her dress off, straight up, over her head. She scrambles for the handcuffs and lays them flat on the dress. She folds and wraps, burying the cuffs, obliterating any telltale sound. As she stuffs the dress into the suitcase, she grabs a pair of slip-on sneakers and an oversized T-Shirt. She barely has them on when he is back.

"To the sink." He points.

She steps up to the sink and washes her hands.

He moves his hands to her shoulders and starts to pat her down.

She retches again and veers for the toilet.

Vincent steps back and waits.

When she turns, Vincent is putting on surgical gloves but he makes no further effort to search her.

He pushes her into the bedroom, toward the cage. "Clever, hiding the handcuffs," he says. "However, there are alternatives." He reaches into his jacket and pulls out a zip tie.

Panic seizes Rose. She can't let him use zip ties. Not tonight. He can't bind both wrists tonight. She must escape tonight.

Vincent calmly goes about immobilizing her wrists.

Rose's brain is in a frenzy. What should she do? Flail? Punch? Kick? She vetoes all three.

What about his ego? The girlfriend experience?

She slowly pulls one arm away and looks up at him pleadingly. "Must you tie both wrists, Vincent? Why not just one? You can attach it to the cage wall. A small comfort, but I'd be ever so grateful."

Vincent raises an eyebrow, then relents. "Have it your way," he says, shoving her into the cage, using the zip tie to affix one of her wrists to the wire wall. "I guess you can't gnaw your way out of that." He locks the cage and leaves the room. Rose's heart is thumping, her blood gushing. So loud. So loud. Despite being caged, she feels like singing.

Handcuffed wrists would have been a problem.

Zip-tied wrists would have been a problem.

But one wrist? One wrist connected to the wall of the cage? She can indeed gnaw her way out. She has her manicure kit.

Rose listens. The clink of glassware, the rattle of cutlery, the splash of water. He is cleaning, cleaning, cleaning. Then, footsteps. He is leaving the kitchen. Is he coming to the bedroom?

Rose curls into a comma and closes her eyes, feigning sleep.

He approaches, squats beside the kennel, and sighs. "I'll be back at daybreak, my lovely. Gideon will wait no longer. He wishes me to prepare. Digging is nasty work but your final rose bed must be readied."

Rose opens her eyes. She doesn't move, not yet. She waits for the sounds, the telltale sounds of the locks. Seconds pass. Then minutes. Is he gone? No. Not yet. He is in the closet. That makes sense. Vincent wouldn't dig gardens or graves in a suit. She waits. There are more footsteps. Then the sounds she has been waiting for. The first lock, the second . . .

Click, click, click.

Rose mines the side pocket of her cargo pants for the manicure kit. Out it pops and then it drops to the floor of the kennel. She grabs it and manages to pry out the scissors and snip at the zip tie. The result is a tiny dent, like the imprint of a fingernail. The scissors are sharp, but the zip tie is sturdy. This is going to be harder than she thought.

Determined, she goes at it again.

Fifty-Two

ANXIOUS TO GET ON WITH his mission, Vincent accelerates the Audi, enough to soothe his apprehension, but not enough to attract attention. He is nearing the entrance to the mansion and about to flash his signal indicator when he spots a glut of vehicles and lights and uniforms. In his driveway? It never occurred to him that the sirens he heard upon approach were screaming toward his driveway.

He aborts, driving slowly past the flood of activity. Frustration runs deep. How could Gideon have allowed such an invasion of Mother's garden? She would be appalled at the dirt and the din and the devastation. How could Vincent possibly dig up the rose bed now? And where the hell is that brother of his?

He drives on, creating distance between his car and the obscenity that is occurring at his mansion. He pulls off the road in an area where overgrown cedar hedges eclipse any sign of his car. Bereft, he turns off the ignition and adjusts the seat. He leans back.

The silence is welcome. Contemplation is needed. Vincent longs to protect his mother's garden, longs to fulfill his vow of vengeance. But plans have been thwarted.

An acute sense of loss slams him like a mudslide. Down, down he goes, into despair, all the while remembering the desperation he felt when assailed by his own father, all the while remembering how Gideon would show up to rescue him.

Sometimes one needs an older brother.

"Where the hell are you, Gideon?" Vincent bangs his hands against the steering wheel, repeatedly, until he has exhausted himself physically and mentally. He closes his eyes tight and a childhood image swoops in, that of him, terrified, hiding under his bed, screaming for his mother.

The memory is an assault to body and soul. Vincent buries his face in his hands. From his lips fall his childhood cries, "Mommy, come home! Mommy come home!"

The child Vincent knew that Mommy couldn't come home. The adult Vincent knows that, too. Mommy is gone forever. But perhaps Gideon . . . ?

Vincent dares not open his eyes. He will wait a while and open them at just the right time.

Then Gideon will be there. Gideon will save him.

Fifty-Three

SITTING ON THE STEPS of the mansion, I absentmindedly stroke my chin and am pricked by stubble. How long have I been here anyway? A glance at my watch shows that Friday is almost upon me. I look to the sky. When the heck had darkness unspooled?

The police—both the Vancouver and the West Vancouver departments—have been busy, digging the garden, searching the house. They've called in the Integrated Homicide Investigation Team; it's procedure to bring in IHIT in the case of a suspicious death. Is Violet's death now considered suspicious? Is there another victim here that I don't know about?

All I know for now is that I'm supposed to stay out of the way, but I've had enough of being told what to do. I sneak onto the veranda. No one stops me as I walk around the porch, checking all windows on this level. Not a sign of light from the inside. Blackout curtains? Possibly.

"Flynn?" Lee's standing beside me.

"Just having a look around," I say.

Lee says nothing. Not the expected barb about my being where I'm not supposed to be. Not a word. Nothing.

My gut tells me he's about to speak, though; he's about to discharge a dagger. "Out with it, whatever it is."

"There is a body buried beneath the marigolds. There are a couple of others as well, in other flower beds. IHIT is on the scene. They'll be here for hours. As far as identification . . . we're looking at days here."

I don't need documented identification to know that the body beneath the marigolds is Margo Harrington. I push the knowledge to a back shelf. No time to react. I have to find Rose. "What about inside the house? Did you find any evidence of Rose inside?" I ask, hoping against hope.

Lee shakes his head. "We've scoured the place. You want to come in?"

I'm at the front door before he has time to change his mind.

Lee is on my heels.

The acrid smell of cleaning fluid, specifically chlorine, hits me as soon as I cross the threshold. "Someone's done a major cleaning job here."

"It's mud. Not blood. Already checked."

"What else? Any hidden rooms that Rose could be in?"

"She's not here."

"Are you sure?"

A German shepherd police dog crosses our path at that moment, its handler close behind. The handler looks at Lee, shakes her head, and exits the house.

"I'm positive," says Lee.

"Where else could she be? Any evidence of other property owned by the Lords? What about the yacht?"

"The yacht's been searched. She's not there. To this point, there's no evidence of any other property."

"You mind if I look around?"

He passes me a pair of gloves. "Suit yourself, but stay out of the way of IHIT. Anyone asks, you're with me."

Before he finishes speaking, I'm walking through the hallway, examining every nook and corner. This place has not seen the light of day in a while. All windows have drapes, fully closed. I follow the hall carpet to the kitchen at the back of the house. It's an old design. No island. No backsplash. A teakettle clock on the wall above a circular oak table which is flanked by two rail-back chairs. It's a large room with linoleum floor and little counter space. The cupboards are tall, thin, and painted white. They have locks but every lock is broken, every door stands open. I glance inside and discover nothing but flowered china, an eclectic collection. Evidence of floral obsession is everywhere: wallpaper, art, and bouquets of fresh flowers in crystal vases on every table.

I traverse every room, including the master bedroom, which has two wardrobes, one holding a man's clothing, one holding a woman's. I'm not a fashion-forward kind of guy, but I can see that the woman's clothes are outdated. The man's? High end, contemporary, well-fitted. I examine each suit, checking pockets and lapels and labels. Other than the fact that the wearer has an affinity for Armani, nothing jumps at me.

It's nearly midnight. I'm done and done in and need to move to the next thing. The problem lies in the fact that I don't know what the next thing is. I go to the front exit. There, I pause.

Am I missing something? Is there a room I should go back to? I'm uncertain, but I turn back anyway. In the library, I click on a toggle switch and stare at the brown recliner with a tall lamp at its side. A lamp with a horizontal shade. A reading lamp. A book nook, just like Rose has at her condo. I walk across the room, stand in a corner, and look around.

There's a sense of uneasiness here. Like someone is watching. Reminds me of my Bev Doolittle print, *The Forest Has Eyes*. Do the walls have eyes? Faces? Am I seeing clearly? There's no one here. Was Rose ever here? There's no evidence of it.

From somewhere within the house, a clock chimes. I close my eyes and count. Twelve. It's midnight. Another day. No Rose. It's time to take another tour of the house.

Friday, May 6th

Fifty-Four

HOURS HAVE PASSED. I'M still at the mansion, but I've given up on the interior. I wander to the front porch, around the circular veranda, then down the front steps. The place is whirring with activity. I follow the arc of the driveway. On the far right is something I haven't seen before, a mini parking lot. Eight spots. Why would the Lords have needed eight parking spots? Many vehicles? Many visitors? The parking lot is full at the moment, mostly police cars. My attention is drawn to a white van.

Should I just ask one of the passing officers about it? Maybe, but I can't waste more time explaining my presence. I'm glad the place is lit like Christmas out here because I don't want to drag out my flashlight app. I make a mental note of the license plate which is standard issue. Too bad. A vanity plate would have given me something to decipher. I'm sure the police ran the plate. The van looks familiar. Is it the same white van I saw on Hastings a few days ago? The day I saw the homeless man? Probably not. I circle the vehicle.

"There's mud in it," says Lee, walking up behind me. "And flower petals. No doubt it was used to transport more than plants. Engine's cold. Licensed to Vincent Lord." He points at the plate.

I nod. It's not the plate I'm looking at. I'm looking past the plate at something on the driver side of the rear bumper, something people often ignore — the dealer decal. They're unobtrusive, these stickers, just hints of origin, subliminal marketing tools, often removed at the request of the driver.

Lee has moved on. A glance shows me he's climbing the front steps. A glance in the opposite direction shows that my car is no longer blocked in. I can get out of this place. I sidle up to the rear of the van and pull my cell phone from my pocket. No time to access flashlight app, but I don't need it. There's enough light from my phone screen to show me exactly what I want to see. I do take time to snap a picture. I bring the phone to my ear, pretending to answer it, and then I look at the photo, a finely outlined image of a van with tiny text — illegible — on its side panel. I expand the image. I blink at the text, something connects, and my heart leaps. This is no dealer decal.

Should I report to Lee? Of course, I should. But I've been a jump ahead of the police to now. Is there time to wait for the police? It's the middle of the night. The wee hours of Friday. It's been nearly a week since I've seen Rose. Time waits for no one.

In seconds, I'm in my car. In minutes, I'm off the property. As I shift into third gear, I toy with doubt. Am I right about this? What I saw on the decal was a three-word phrase: *All the Flowers*. Maybe those words have nothing to do with the incessant flower music from Rose's neighbor's condo. My gut tells me they have everything to do with it. Instinct trumps doubt. I accelerate the VW.

I never did get that neighbor's name. But I'm about to.

Fifty-Five

VINCENT OPENS HIS EYES. Where is he? In his car? Yes, he's in his car, hands on the steering wheel. Parked somewhere. But where? The last thing he remembers is pulling off the road, hiding behind cedar hedges. He's still here, in the same place, in the dark. He was waiting for Gideon. Did Gideon show up?

Vincent glances at the dash clock and recoils. Hours lost again. What has happened? His hands are twitching. Twitching, but numb. Why can't he feel his hands?

A familiar ache of helplessness fills him. He doesn't know what has happened, but he saw the lights and he heard the sirens and he's sure police are going to be after him. The police are going to be after him and he can't do a thing about it. So much for all his looks and charm. Charm won't save him now. No one can save him. No one except Gideon. Saving Vincent has been Gideon's job since Vincent was a little boy.

Needing fresh air, needing to get his bearings, Vincent exits the car and stands beside the open door. He inhales deeply, sucking in the scents of sea and cedar, and expels his breath in a harsh whisper. "Where the hell are you, Gideon Lord?"

"The Lord be with you." Gideon's laughter reverberates through Vincent's skull.

Vincent cringes. He has to speak up. He has to state his case. He can't let Gideon bury Rose. Not now. Not ever. The police are trampling the gardens and digging up the flowerbeds. There will be no new bed of roses, no place for a new bed of roses. The garden will be destroyed and Gideon's so-called revenge play will hang, unfinished. He opens his mouth to speak but guttural sobs escape him; he leans against the car in an effort to remain upright.

"Wimp," snipes Gideon from the other side of the car. "Can't do anything without me, can you? You're useless. Once again, it's Gideon to the rescue. Gideon takes care of everything."

Vincent can't deny the truth in Gideon's words and can't control the spasmodic trembling that assails his own body. He has always relied on Gideon. Gideon is the strong one. Vincent isn't enough on his own. He wasn't enough for his father and now he isn't enough for Gideon.

In a last-ditch attempt at strength, Vincent slams his hands on the roof of the car and sends words flying. "Like you took care of Mother's garden?"

"The garden is of no importance now." Gideon's voice is a deathly calm.

"No importance? What the hell will happen to all the flowers, Gideon?"

"They'll be gone." Gideon laughs and breaks into song. *"Where Have All the Flowers Gone?"*

Vincent puts his hands over his ears. "No more singing! Stop the damn singing! Just tell me what happened."

"Rose's private investigator friend has been busy. That's what happened. He found his way here, and he'll soon find his way to the loft."

"Oh my God! Oh my God! What the hell am I going to do now?"

"Stop whining, that's what. Get into the car."

Vincent obliges.

"Take your insulin."

Vincent opens the glove compartment and pulls out an insulin kit. With trembling hands, he loads the syringe. He sits there, shaking, pointing the syringe at his abdomen, unable to execute the next move. He closes his eyes and somehow the needle plunges, finding its mark.

"Now, you are going to finish what we started."

"I can't finish anything." Vincent tosses the syringe to the floor and instantly leans to retrieve it. *A place for everything, everything in its place.* He returns the syringe to the kit and zips it up. Now where was he? "I can't finish anything," he repeats.

"You can and you will. *Tick Tock*, Vincent. You have to get to the loft. It appears that Flynn is not the amateur detective I assumed him to be. You have to get to the loft before he does. You know there's a gun there. Use it."

"Shoot him?"

"Shoot Rose."

"I can't shoot Rose." Vincent isn't lying. He can barely move.

"You are useless," says Gideon.

Gideon is right. Vincent is a weakling. A weakling whose head is spinning. Did he overdo it with the insulin? What if he passes out now, just faints dead away? Would it make any difference? Gideon knows where the gun is. Gideon has access to everything. Gideon will shoot Rose. "Can't we forget this one? Let it be and run away?"

Gideon laughs outright. "Mama's boy," he taunts. "You're right back where you started, wanting to run and hide under the bed. You think I spent all this time cultivating this revenge play just to have you chicken out? That's not happening, you spineless featherweight."

Useless. Spineless. A featherweight. Vincent is slipping away. It's over. He doesn't fight it. He can't fight any longer.

Fifty-Six

CUTTING THE ZIP TIE is an arduous task, one that mangles Rose's manicure scissors. Freed, she crawls from the kennel, unravels to her full height, and then stands very still. Is she alone? Is it safe to turn on the lights?

Vincent said he would be gone overnight. Can she trust that? He said he would be preparing her final rose bed. Beyond sinister, that thought. Rose doesn't dwell. What she is concerned with now is time. How long does it take to dig a grave? It takes a while. He will be gone a while. That gives her time, a bubble of time.

In a few strides, Rose is in the living room. She fingers her breakout tools—maimed manicure scissors and a jagged cuticle pusher—and contemplates: scrape paint and caulking, raise window, and crawl through. But her legs are leaden. It is all she can do to raise an arm to wipe her brow. She catches a whiff of sweat that triggers a wave of nausea. Swallowing hard, she glances toward the door.

When will the jangle of keys assault her eardrums? To this point, she has gotten away with a few tiny deviations from his set of rules, from his idea of perfectionism. But this? This will not go unnoticed. What if she fails? She flinches as she flashes on yesterday: the setting of the table, the misplacement of a water goblet, the blow to her ribcage.

A sob explodes from Rose's throat. How the hell did she end up here? Anxious, she thrusts forward, first one foot, then the other. She is making headway now, inching toward the window, almost there. At the window, she stalls again. What the hell is she waiting for? There is no time for hesitation, no time to question how she got here. But she has to think things through.

With her porthole of time eroding, with every nerve stretched taut, Rose stares at the window.

How long had he hunted her?

A fluttering movement catches Rose's eye—a petal, a single red petal falling from the bouquet of roses on the dining room table. At the base of the vase is a velvet pool of rose petals. As she watches, another cluster of petals rains down.

It's time to go.

Rose lines up her tools on the window ledge. She works feverishly. At first, caulk flies in tiny chips. Then slivers, then chunks. Immersed in the task, fuelled by rage, she has no idea how much time is elapsing; she is only aware that the mound of shavings on the window ledge is growing steadily. When she finally looks at the bits and pieces of caulk forming a scatter graph on the dining room floor, she balks. There will be no hiding this. This is it, the event horizon.

There is no turning back.

Rose drops her manicure tools which clatter to the floor. She plants the heels of her hands against the window casing. She pushes upward. The window doesn't budge. *Damn.* The latch. She forgot about the latch.

Her pulse racing, her muscles taut, she tugs and jiggles the latch. When it doesn't give, she reclaims her cuticle pusher, gouges the paint surrounding the latch, and then jostles the latch a second time. The paint splinters. The latch shifts.

Emboldened, Rose again struggles to raise the window. She pushes, she rattles, she pounds. Still no joy. Sobbing, she draws a sweaty arm across her brow, braces herself, and goes at it again. Nothing.

Propelled by frustration, she grabs a dining room chair and lets it fly at the stubborn window. It hits its mark and bounces back. Rose recoils as the chair crashes to the floor beside her. She checks the pane. Not a crack. Unbreakable, just as Vincent said.

Drained, Rose sinks to a crouch. She cannot stop. She will not stop. But what next? She eyes the victimized chair which lies helplessly on its side. A useless tool, that chair. She scrutinizes its underbelly. Its frame is sturdy; its seat is rigid. Maybe it's not so useless. Perhaps she can stand on it. More height might give her more clout.

Rose scrambles to her feet. She places two chairs side by side, their backs against the window. Then she steps up and positions a foot on each chair. Bending her knees, she plants her hands on the window casing and sucks in a deep breath. One more time, she tells herself. One more time. For Mom. For Margo.

She throws the force of her entire body into thrusting the window upward. Her muscles strain. Lances of pain shoot through her shoulders. From some deep recess of her soul, Rose emits a primal growl. She opens her mouth and the growl grows, rumbling through her like thunder, louder and louder until her breath is spent. Panting, with spasms racking her body, she continues, straightening her knees and pushing until she feels like her bones will snap.

When a brittle crack does sound, Rose freezes in position. Dare she examine the source of the sound? No need. On the heels of the crack, comes a distant sound of a car horn. Dear God in heaven. She has broken the window seal. With renewed strength, she resumes pushing.

The window screeches its resistance but slowly crawls upward. With her breath coming in gasps, Rose continues to push until the window is wide open.

Then she jumps to the floor and shoves the chairs aside. Damn it all. She has done it. She has opened the window.

Night air rushes in, sending a delicious shiver through her. Never has the stench of exhaust smelled so sweet. She leans out and looks around. She knows where she is. An old building in downtown Vancouver. At least six floors up. She's driven past this place countless times. A brick and concrete building. Maybe an apartment block at one time. Maybe a warehouse. She's uncertain. All she knows for sure is that she has spent days here, in the loft of a building located just a few blocks from her own condo.

And beneath this very window? The fire escape. Exactly where she thought it would be.

In minutes she will be free.

Rose throws one leg over the ledge. She pauses. A memory emerges, a moment from childhood, the eight hundred meter race when she wouldn't cross the finish line without her sister, when she went back for her sister.

"Margo." The word is a mere murmur.

If there is evidence about Margo's fate, it is in that concealed room. Rose glances toward the den. Should she go back? Get the evidence before he gets the chance to demolish it?

Rose listens for the clack of the locks. Hearing nothing, she pulls her leg back inside and races for the den.

Fifty-Seven

I USE MY KEY to gain access to Rose's building. On the ninth floor, I head to her neighbor's condo. Curiosity peaks when I notice that the neighbor's door is ajar. Again? In the wee hours? Why hadn't the police locked this place down? I approach. I knock. The door falls in, wide-open. The hallway is empty.

"Hello," I call. "Anyone in here?" My voice echoes back to me. Strange, that. I am about to step through the door, but I hesitate, alerted by the sound of shuffling footsteps from within.

"Mr. Gideon?" Approaching me is the frog-faced woman, the superintendent, carrying a broom. Her lips pull into a frown when she gets to within a foot of me. "You're not Mr. Gideon." She glances nervously around.

I take a respectful step back. "My name is Flynn. I'm a private investigator and a friend of the woman who lives next door—Rose Harrington." I pull my wallet from my pocket and opened it wide so that she can see my ID.

The woman tightens her grip on the broom handle. "What are you doing here? Did they find Rose?"

"Not yet, ma'am. I have reason to believe that the person who lived here had something to do with Rose's disappearance. Did a Mr. Lord live here?"

"Mr. Lord? I don't know no Mr. Lord. It was Mr. Gideon that lived here."

"Mr. Gideon? Was this Mr. Gideon visually impaired?"

"What? Blind? Mr. Gideon was not blind. He could see right well enough."

"Was he tall? Short? Maybe hunched over a bit?"

"Tall and straight as a statue. Quiet as one, too. Never said much of anything. Even up and left without saying a word. I've been up half the night, working myself into the ground, cleaning this place. The owner wants to sublet it again."

The elevator door rumbles open and two uniformed police officers step out. Where the hell did they come from? Is Lee having me followed? I turn, smiling like I was expecting them. "Over here," I say. "Officers, this is . . ." I look at the frog-faced woman. "I'm sorry ma'am, I didn't get your name."

"I didn't offer it. I'm not in the habit of giving that information to strangers, but now that I see you've got the police backing you up, I guess it's okay. I am Mrs. Muriel McConaughey, superintendent of this building." She looks past me into the eyes of the police. "Officers, I'll tell you what I told him. I know all the residents here. The man who lived here was Mr. Gideon. And Mr. Gideon left here in the middle of the night. Just disappeared and took every lick of furniture with him. I just finished cleaning up the place."

"Did Mr. Gideon have a tattoo?" I ask, remembering that she had mentioned it the last time I was here.

"Doesn't everybody?" Muriel yanks back her collar and a sagging monarch butterfly pops into view.

"So that's a yes, then?"

"What's all this about a tattoo?" One of the police officers inserts himself into the conversation.

"Just bear with me a minute, please." I repeat the question.

Mrs. McConaughey scrunches her nose. "Why, yes he did. I remember it exactly. A pretty smart one, it was. He had 'Diabetes Type I' printed in Gothic letters from his elbow to his wrist." She folds her arms and nods her head, obviously pleased with herself.

"Mind if we look around?" I ask.

Mrs. McConaughey shrugs. "No problem, but you won't find nothing. It's clean as a whistle in here. I bleached everything I could."

I step aside so the police officers can go ahead of me. Just as they cross the threshold, the elevator rumbles. I wait for it to open.

Lee emerges and strides right up to me. He gives me a knowing look.

"Following me?" I mutter.

"Under the circumstances . . ."

"I get it." I give him an update and we enter the condo. The first thing that hits me is the smell. Mrs. McConaughey is no liar. The place reeks of cleaning fluid.

"Forensics won't pick up a darn thing in here," says Lee, voicing what we are all thinking.

"Not even a fingerprint," says one of the officers.

"What was it you said the tenant's name was, Mrs. McConaughey?" I ask.

"Mr. Gideon." She nods her head with certainty.

"Did you find that name on the estate anywhere?" I ask Lee.

Lee shakes his head. "We only found Vincent Lord. His parents, William and Annabel Lord, are both deceased. Vincent Lord is an only child." He flicks through his notes. "No mention of a Gideon."

"Do you know the first name of this Mr. Gideon?"

"Indeed I do," says Mrs. McConaughey. "It's Vincent. Mr. Vincent Gideon."

Lee and I simultaneously pull out our phones.

Fifty-Eight

IN THE DEN, ROSE pushes the button, races through the secret door, and runs her hand along the wall to locate the light switch. A simple flick reveals a small room, as tiny as the bathroom in Flynn's tiny house.

The wall directly opposite Rose is curtained, ceiling to floor, in purple velvet. There are two overlapped curtain panels with pleated pocket tops. Rose steps forward, draws the curtains, and steps back to view an arched alcove containing three evenly-spaced shelves, each holding two framed pictures of different flower blossoms. A table sits just below the alcove, a white, semicircular console table on top of which is a wrought-iron, four-tiered votive candle stand.

A sudden coldness hits Rose at her core. Time constraints forgotten, she runs her eyes from the top to bottom of the alcove, reading the names on the brass plates attached to each picture: Lily, Iris, Daisy, Marigold, Rose, and Violet.

It is with dread that she picks up the picture of the marigold and examines the back. Pasted there is a photo of her sister.

The room spins. Rose drops to a squat. She takes several deep breaths and pushes the dizziness down deep. She has to continue.

Opening her eyes, she spots a wall safe beneath the console table, a wall safe with a keypad. Maybe . . . ? She shakes her head. With no hope of access and no time to waste, Rose stands and faces the alcove again. Her hands tremble as she returns the framed image of the marigold to its shelf in the shrine. That's what this is, a shrine. Where are all these women? She shudders, curbs the question, and continues her search.

In the console table, she locates a small drawer which opens with a single tug. A black, leather-bound book lies at the front, easily accessible. She picks it up and riffles its pages. It is a journal, a detailed journal of Vincent's activities. Evidence of stalking and luring. Pictures of gardens and flowers and graves.

And Margo.

And Rose.

Rose's whole body tightens. In a mechanical motion, she reaches to the back of the drawer and pulls out a metal box. No lock. She peeks inside and blows out a gasp. Ammunition. The ammunition she sought is here. She whips the box open and pulls out a single magazine. Is it loaded? Rose examines it. One bullet. And one word etched on the magazine: *Rose*.

Fury leaps into her throat, almost choking her.

Journal in hand, Rose exits the secret room and grabs the gun from behind the painting. Without hesitation, she loads the weapon and shoves it into the back of her jeans.

As she is about to press the button to close the secret panel, Rose hears a familiar click. The first lock. He is opening the first lock. *Damn.* Heart racing, she abandons her task and races for the window.

Another click sounds as she crosses the living room. Lock number two. Or is it three?

She is at the window, through the window and onto the fire escape, which jerks and jiggles at the jolt of her weight, its creaking protests piercing the air. Grabbing the handrail, Rose starts her descent. Down, down. To a landing grate. Around the corner. Down again. On the next landing, she pauses to shove the journal under the waistband at the front of her jeans. A short pause, milliseconds, but long enough to hear her name being called.

Vincent is at the window.

Rose plunges onward, down, down, down at reckless speed. Footsteps pound behind her, the fire escape rumbles beneath her. He's gaining on her.

Relief surges when she hits the last stage of the fire escape, the ladder designed to lower with the pressure of an escapee's weight. Relief is short-lived. The damn ladder doesn't swing down like it's supposed to. She bounces. Nothing. She bounces harder. Still nothing. Rusted? Welded in place? Vincent's footsteps are hammering and her blood is roaring in her ears. How high up is she? Can she land a jump?

She grips the railing.

Rusted metal fragments rip her hands as she flings herself forward. Thoughts race through her head. Did she train as a gymnast for this? Was there some grand design in play? What if she breaks an ankle?

She lands crouched, the journal knifing her gut. Springing to her feet, she tears through the back alley toward the eastern sky, the glimmer of light in the eastern sky.

A green Dumpster looms ahead. Without slowing down, Rose jerks the journal from her jeans and arcs it into the air. It drops into the Dumpster. She keeps running.

She glances back, toward the fire escape. Vincent is almost at the bottom. She picks up her pace, praying that he didn't see her dispose of the journal. How much farther can she run? Where the hell are the police when you need them? She has to get out of this alley. Pounding footsteps are closing in behind her. Rose swerves toward a side street. She doesn't make the turn.

He grabs her, holds her, and twists her toward him. He clutches both her arms and draws her so close she can feel the heat of his breath on her face. Rose meets his eyes full on. In the low light of dawn, she witnesses disbelief in those dark eyes. She spits into those dark eyes.

He tightens his grip on her right arm and raises his free hand, fist clenched. He pauses, hand in mid-air. "It is not for you to challenge me, Rose."

Rose's adrenaline is firing full force. Controlled aggression. That's what she needs. Controlled aggression. The gun she stole is pressing into her back. Her right arm is pinned. She needs that right arm to use that gun. She needs to control the aggression of adrenaline. In an attempt to throw him off balance, Rose collapses into a dead weight.

He responds, releasing her arm. He grabs her again, this time clenching her left bicep in a vise grip.

Rose reaches for the gun. *Your finger is your safety. Do not put your finger on the trigger until you are ready to shoot.* She jams the gun into Vincent's gut and clamps her finger on the trigger.

She pauses. She squeezes.

But she doesn't shoot. She can't shoot. She can't because her split second of indecision resulted in a shifting of power. She no longer has the gun. All that mental rehearsal, all those thoughts about shooting procedure, wasted.

How the hell had Vincent wrestled the gun from her?

"She who hesitates is lost." Vincent points the gun at her heart.

Undaunted, she glares at him. "You can't kill me, Vincent. That's your brother's job. You told me so yourself. Gideon fertilizes the flowers, not you. Gideon."

He steps back, a grin on his face, the gun at his side. "You little fool. You're not dealing with that wimp Vincent now. Vincent has faded away. Permanently. A former part of our psyche. Let me introduce myself." He raises the gun.

"I am Gideon Lord."

Fifty-Nine

IT'S BEEN A LONG night, no sleep. I'm firing on fumes as I speed toward the downtown address that is registered to a Mr. Vincent Gideon. Can it be that all this time Rose has been in some building just blocks away from her own condo? I double park and jump from my VW, leaving the door wide open. I race to the building, an old brick warehouse, and rattle the security grille at the front entrance. It's bedrock solid, designed to protect against burglary and vandalism. The police are showing up in droves, covering the scene like ants. I get the hell out of their way and sprint to the back alley, to the dim back alley, ignoring internal warnings about the level of violence in back lanes in the night. I'm searching for the fire escape. There's one here. I know it.

In the lane, my eyes are drawn past the fire escape to two moving silhouettes, two people, running and running and rounding a corner. The alley is dim and the sirens are screaming and I'm thanking God that Lee had me followed tonight.

I slam toward the images, thoughts changing direction as I veer around the corner. Why didn't Violet Harrington just tell me everything? The last time I saw her, she had Margo's yang necklace in her possession. She should have told me. It wouldn't have mattered. I would have helped. It wasn't her fault that Margo was kidnapped. She blamed herself, but it wasn't her fault. Just a simple choice. A date with a man who turned out to be married. A choice that led to tragedy. I wouldn't have laid blame. I would have helped. I promised. I promised. I could have prevented further tragedy. I could have protected Rose.

I'm close enough now to see outlines of two figures, standing stock still. The tall one is speaking. "I am Gideon Lord," he says as he points a gun at the other.

My adrenaline gushes. No time for thought. I tackle the one with the gun.

We crash to the ground. The gun goes off, a jarring shot into the air. The weapon skitters across the pavement. Then I'm writhing on the ground, wrestling with no one. What the hell? The taut body I just tackled is not with me. I can smell him though; the pungent odor of high-end cologne clogs my nostrils. Is that the only remnant? Where's the damn gun? Crawling, I blindly grope until I locate it. I grab it. I scramble to a standing position, gun at my side. *Jesus*. He's still here, facing me, a few feet from me. A menacing shadow. Why isn't he running? Is he so cock sure I won't shoot him? Sirens are screaming. The police are coming. What is he waiting for? Dawn splits the horizon and sends a shaft of light down the alley and across his face.

And lightning hits me. I know him.

I've been fumbling in the dark for days, sensing his presence, feeling his eyes upon me, even looking at him . . . but not seeing him. Bev Doolittle, master of camouflage art, has nothing on this man. The many faces of Vincent Lord or Mr. Gideon or whoever the hell this is, now emerge in a rush and press in on me.

The homeless man.

The bartender.

The gardener.

Yes, even Rose's neighbor, the "visually-challenged" man whose face I couldn't see.

Rose's neighbor wasn't blind. I was.

And now, Vincent Lord sees it on my face, the recognition. Damn it all. That's what he's waiting for, the recognition. He wants me to acknowledge him. The son of a bitch is enjoying this. He stands straight, a monument of a man, peering down at me. "That gun had only one bullet, Mr. Flynn," he says with a sneer. "Go ahead. Try it." He puts a hand into his pocket. He lifts that pocket, pointing it toward me.

Is that a gun? A finger?

Instinctively, I take aim. Center mass. My heart hammers and my blood pumps and my brain fires danger signals, all urging me onward. But my hand trembles and I hedge. Something in my gut, my trusted gut, detects truth: The gun *is* empty; Vincent Lord is *not* armed. No immediate threat. I make a deliberate show of slowly lowering the gun.

He rips his hand from his pocket, points his index finger at me, and makes a pop sound. Then he laughs, a sinister crow of a laugh.

I watch as he breaks into a run and disappears around a corner. I let him go. The police can deal.

My focus instantly switches to Rose.

"Rose? Where the . . . Rose? Rose! Are you here?" I'm screaming, at least I think I am. I wish those damn sirens would shut up. "Rose?"

I barely turn around when she is in my arms. I feel a sigh of her breath and she morphs into jelly. I sink to the asphalt, cradling Rose. Is she dead? Is she bleeding? Her pulse is pounding. I see no oozing. I don't know what else to look for. And then the ambulance attendants are there. I let out a breath as I step out of the way. If Rose is broken, they can fix her.

Daylight is upon us, and the headlights of the ambulance are glaring into my face, and the EMTs are placing Rose flat on the ground.

"She just flew at me and then passed out," I say.

The first responder nods and checks her pulse and her eyes and her limbs. He's palpating her abdomen when Rose begins to stir. His relief and mine are tangible. "She's coming to now. In shock, and there are minor injuries. We'll take her to trauma. Standard procedure, sir."

"What hospital?"

"VGH."

In a hitching breath, I thank him. When they load Rose into the ambulance, I climb in beside her. "You're going to be fine, Rose. You're going to be fine."

Rose's eyes open slowly. She reaches a hand for me. "There's only one. Only one."

"Yes, I know," I say, sure that she is talking about the bullet.

"Did you get him? Did you? He killed Margo. The loft. Go to the loft." She drifts into unconsciousness.

I stiffen. I look through the ambulance doors and back to the alley, to the building owned by a Mr. Vincent Gideon, the building now surrounded by police cars. I caress Rose's hand. I want to go with Rose, but I know, and I'm sure she knows, that I need to stay behind.

I exit the ambulance and watch as it whisks her away. Then I head toward the building.

The place is a zoo. Cops everywhere. How am I going to get in? There's something there I need to see. I have no clue what that is, but I know it's there. I spot Lee among a group of uniforms. I call and wave. A brisk nod, a few steps, and Lee's at the door. He brushes away the concerns of the uniformed officers. "He's with me." They step aside.

"The loft," I say. "Rose said to go to the loft."

Lee nods and together we walk past shelves and shelves of an eerie collection of movie paraphernalia: statues and hats and wigs and rubber faces. I have much to tell Lee about my encounters with "masked" men, all bent on camouflage. But neither of us comments on anything. We locate the elevator and silently ride to the top floor, the loft.

After we exit the elevator, I wait, as ordered. This time I don't mind waiting while the detectives scour the scene.

"That's the window she escaped through," explains Lee a short time later as he takes me on a tour of the loft. "Careful not to tread on the caulk on the floor. God knows how long it took Rose to claw it out of the window casing, but this was the only way out and she took it. This whole place is locked tight. A fortress. Blackout windows. Light comes in through skylight tubes." He pointed up. "I know she was a gymnast, but there was no way she could access those sky tunnels."

"There's no sign of struggle," I say with surprise.

"No. Everything in here is letter perfect. Obsessive-compulsive disorder perfect."

"But surely her fingerprints . . ."

"Oh, yes. But it's more than that. Brace yourself."

I follow Lee to the den, which has a door to a secret room. The door is wide open. "I'm sure Rose found her way in there. I'm guessing he, that Lord fellow, got back and caught her in the act. When she ran, he opted to chase her rather than seal up his secrets. I don't know how long this building has been here, but there was a major renovation at one time. This room was designed to hide all manner of sins." He stops in the middle of the room, waiting for me to examine, waiting for me to clue in.

I approach the alcove. Six images, all flower blossoms: lily, iris, daisy, marigold, rose, and violet. Lee hands me gloves. I snap them on and pick up the picture of the marigold. I scrutinize it and check the back where I find a photograph. "Margo. Dear God. Three years. Not a trace."

All six flower images have photographs pasted on the back. I cringe at the picture of Rose sitting at a café window, the picture of Violet working in her garden.

"I'm sure that a search will bring up missing person reports on these other women," says Lee. He puts an arm on my shoulder. "You okay?"

I shake my head. "All this time—what the hell happened to these women?"

"I'm guessing the gardens at the Lord estate will reveal that." His phone blares. He steps aside.

I examine the pictures again, scrutinizing the flowers, counting the petals. Something tweaks. I count the petals a second time.

"They found a journal," Lee tells me upon his return. "In the alley Dumpster. Near where you found Rose. This guy left a record of his activities. I'm guessing Rose stole it and tossed it. We'll check security cameras to confirm. Sorry, Flynn, but the guy's in the wind."

I'm silent. I'm thinking about the struggle Rose must have gone through here. I swallow hard.

Lee looks at me curiously. "I know this hits home. But can you have a look at something for me?"

I nod, unable to speak.

"What we don't know," Lee is saying, "is the combination to this safe. Sure we can decode it, but I think you should have a look. Something to do with flowers, no doubt."

One glance at the safe and I'm back on solid ground. Words are easy now. "The combination is related to the Fibonacci sequence," I say, without batting an eye. "But I think the numbers are mixed up."

"What the hell are you talking about?"

"The Fibonacci sequence. A specific series of numbers, each number being the sum of the two preceding it. In progressive order, the numbers are: zero, one, one, two, three, five, eight, thirteen, twenty-one, thirty-four . . . Get it?"

Lee shrugs. "Keep talking."

"I just counted the petals on each of those flowers." I indicate toward the shrine. "The number of petals on each flower is a dead match for a number from that very sequence."

"And you think he would use those numbers *because* . . ."

"Because I saw the gardener punch in a series of numbers at the mansion gate and I recognized the sequence."

"That's how you got through the gate?"

Lee doesn't expect an answer. I don't offer one. "I doubt he'd use the exact same set here but, just in case . . . try one, one, two, three, five, eight."

Lee keys in the numbers. The safe doesn't open. "No worries." He waves a hand in dismissal. "We can decode it later."

"Hold up a second. As I said, the numbers are likely out of order. You're right. The combination has to do with flowers, specifically with the number of petals on each of those flowers." I again point at the shrine. "Top to bottom, left to right, he's positioned the lily, iris, daisy, marigold, rose, and violet. The order of the flowers is deliberate."

"Likely the order in which he kidnapped, or planned to kidnap, these women."

"Exactly. And for some reason, he kept the same order when setting his safe combination. Look closely at the flowers. The lily has three petals; the iris has three; that daisy — your common field variety — has thirty-four; the marigold has thirteen; the rose has five; the violet has five. All Fibonacci numbers: three, three, thirty-four, thirteen, five, five. There's your combination."

Lee blinks in disbelief.

"Three, three, thirty-four, thirteen, five, five. I'm here for a reason. This is it."

Acquiescing, Lee raises a gloved hand to the keypad. He hesitates.

I start in again. "Three, three, thirty-four—"

"I got it. I got it." He keys in the numbers. A few beeps, and the door swings open. Lee reaches in and pulls out four items: a go bag, stuffed with cash and IDs; an insulin kit; and not one, but *two* empty gun cases.

Two guns? I run my hand across my abdomen, checking. Is there some previously unnoticed bullet hole? Did Lord have a gun in that alley? Why didn't he shoot me?

Saturday, May 7th

Sixty

I STOPPED BY MY tiny home yesterday for a shower, shave, and a change of clothes, and I've been on vigil at the hospital ever since. My vinyl chair is uncomfortable as hell, but I'm grateful that they—the doctors, the police—allow me to be here, wait here, to drift in and out of sleep here.

Rose's room is a private room and there is a member of the VPD guarding her door. Security detail. Necessary because they haven't found Rose's kidnapper yet. I have to tell her that. I'm dreading the telling.

With the exception of the capture, the puzzle's complete. The police found Rose's sister—the remains of Rose's sister—in the marigold flowerbed. Three other female bodies were located, one buried beneath lilies, one beneath irises, and the last beneath daisies. Unidentified bodies, but it doesn't take a genius to figure out that their first names are those of flowers.

I'll be a prime witness when they catch him; I stared right into his eyes yesterday. I'm glad I did not pull that trigger. Sure, the gun wasn't loaded, but the whole idea? Deadly force? Not in my wheelhouse. Did I make the right choice in not running after him in that alley? My gut tells me yes. There's no way I could have caught the man. I chase paper, not perps. But he will be caught. IHIT is on this, and the press is all over it. The face of Vincent Lord, a.k.a. "The Gardener" is plastered on every news and social media site on the Internet.

It is four P.M. on my watch before Rose speaks to me. I am sitting in my designated chair, staring out the window. I turn to her just as her eyes open. I lurch to her side. Then gingerly, so as not to disturb the IV needle that pierces her hand, I wrap my fingers around hers. There is no way I can stop the tears that fill my eyes. "Rose," is all I can utter.

She shushes me instantly, putting a finger on my lips. "You don't even have to say it," she says. "I know that Margo is gone. I saw the shrine. Did you catch him?"

"All I care about now is that I found you." I look away from her.

"I know there was only the one. At least I think I know, but the whole thing is so bizarre. Flynn, did Vincent have a brother?"

"Rose, there *was* only one. There was only Vincent. The estate in West Vancouver was his, all his. But the loft was in the name of a Mr. Gideon."

Rose struggles to get words out, but starts to cough. "Water," she says.

I press the call button before I pour water for Rose. She takes a sip and clears her throat.

A petite, brown-haired nurse enters, holding a tray containing a syringe. She places the tray on the bed table.

I step aside.

Rose waves the nurse away. "I'm fine. I'm fine."

"It's time for your medication, Miss Harrington. It won't take long." The nurse smiles tentatively and waits at the foot of the bed.

"Yes, yes, just give me a minute." Rose again turns her attention to me. "Flynn, the last thing that monster said to me was that Vincent had faded away, that he was Gideon Lord."

I move closer again. I lean in. "I heard him. Rose, the police have been through that loft and through the grounds of the West Vancouver estate with a fine-toothed comb. Believe me, the Lords had only one son, Vincent. As for Gideon or Mr. Gideon? A figment of his imagination."

Rose blinks. She tosses off the blankets and sits bolt upright. "He told me he had a brother. I believed it. But I never saw the two of them at the same time. How stupid was I?"

"Mr. Flynn," the nurse says, as she steps in and covers Rose back up, "this patient needs rest now." The nurse injects medication into Rose's IV.

Rose is not done with her protest. "I am absolutely fine and I want to leave."

"You're going nowhere without the permission of the doctor," I tell her.

She grabs my hand. "But—"

"Rose, you're better off here for now. They haven't found him. Vincent Lord got away."

Rose falls back into a supine position, a look of disbelief on her face. In seconds, the medication takes effect and she drifts back into sleep.

Sunday, May 8th

Mother's Day

Sixty-One

I'M IN FLUX. ROSE is still in the hospital. Vincent Lord is on the run. I want to help locate the latter, but that is a police matter now. My other want is to spend more time with Rose. Before I do that, while the police question Rose, I honor a request she made of me. On this day—Mother's Day—I visit her mother's grave.

I don't know why Rose wants me here when Violet Harrington's body isn't. Yes, the authorities will return the remains to this cemetery eventually, after a thorough forensic investigation. The police must determine if Violet Harrington's death was suspicious.

The second part of Rose's request makes more sense. Since I'll be the one to make the arrangements for Margo's funeral, I'm checking out the family plot. The remains of Margo will be buried there, mother and daughter side-by-side.

I visit my son's resting place, too. I rarely do that, and when I do, I don't stay long because the visual evidence of his death gives life to my demons. Today feels different; I don't know why. Yes, today feels different.

"Perhaps I should call your mother," I tell Sanjay as I brush a stray maple leaf from the top of his gravestone. "It's Mother's Day, isn't it?" I stand still for a minute as I digest the significance of the day. Perhaps I should call my wife, check in, see how she's doing. It suddenly strikes me that, until this day, I have never given Amelia's wellbeing a single thought. But Amelia is still my wife, isn't she? What about my promise to her? My vows to her?

I kept my promise to Violet Harrington. Not in the way that I wanted to, but I did learn the fate of Margo. And I managed to help Rose. Yes, I actually kept two promises to Violet Harrington, but I didn't keep my vows to my wife. Navigating the day-to-day marriage stuff was easy, but when Amelia made a simple mistake that led to tragedy? The wound was sudden and deep. A gaping hole that I couldn't look at. Blaming Amelia was a way of muting the pain.

I think about the divorce papers in my office, the meaning of the divorce papers in my office. I am choosing to leave Amelia, to let her dangle the way the dirty laundry dangles in a bag from the ceiling of my tiny house. Is that what I want to do to Amelia? Leave her with no support? Is that what I want to do to Sanjay's mother? I look at my son's grave. I plant a kiss on the tips of my fingers, touch my fingers to the cold stone that marks his resting place, and sigh myself away from the site.

At the hospital, I sit beside Rose's bed again, waiting while she sleeps. There is evidence of visitors, a huge get-well card with many names, among them Marlene and Katie and Jason and Jade, her lunch partners from the Lotus Club. A crop of happy-face Mylar balloons floats above the bed table. I jiggle the attached string and play with the idea, maybe the hope, that these former colleagues of Rose's will become her long-term friends.

It is sudden, Rose's wakefulness. She smiles at the balloons and she smiles at me. For a while, we sit in companionable silence. Like friends do.

When she parts her lips to speak, I sense that what she has to say is prepared.

"I've been too independent for my own good, haven't I?" She waves a hand, dismissing any answer. "He was kind, I thought. I was lonely, desperate really, and he knew it. I think he waited for me to get to that point. Any woman in her right mind would have screamed, fought, and slammed the car door on him. But I just got in." She lets out a long sigh. "In the end, I think I was meant to go with him, to learn the truth."

"He told you about Margo?"

Rose sighs again. "He reveled in the telling."

I reach out and hold her hand.

"I wanted answers," says Rose. "I got answers. I got more answers than I was prepared for. My mother was lonely. She made a choice. She dated William Lord."

"You can't really blame your mother for all this."

Rose looks up, surprise in her eyes. "Blame my mother?" She shakes her head. "Not for a second. How could I? There was no intent to harm anyone, certainly not Margo. Mom made a mistake. Met a man. Trusted that man. A simple choice. A catastrophic choice."

She is silent for a moment, then adds, "How could I possibly blame her when I did the exact same thing? How Mom must have suffered when she realized that she was at the heart of all this." Rose shakes her head. "It must have been agony. In the end, it killed her. The guilt. Killed her. What good would it do for me to lay blame? She's gone, Flynn. She's gone, and she suffered far more than I did." Rose lets out a long sigh. "I loved her. I will always love her. No blame at all."

Rose's hand goes limp in mine as she drifts off.

When I exit into the hallway, Lee is there, telling me Rose is still under guard and that I should go and get a coffee and a bite to eat.

I hedge. "You think she's safe?"

"I'll be here," he says.

Resigned, I nod.

At the coffee shop, I figure that a cup of java will jolt me from fatigue. Not going to bother with food. I have a feeling I shouldn't be away from Rose too long. I get into line, purchase a large coffee, steaming and black, and choose a seat near the entrance to the coffee shop, facing the hospital lobby. I'm people watching as I consider Rose's words, her words about blame.

Rose doesn't blame her mother. Violet punished herself from the day Margo disappeared, until the day of her own death. Rose loved her sister *and* her mother. Rose is empathetic, forgiving a simple, yet costly mistake.

People make simple mistakes, as simple as my wife stopping to notice a pair of shoes, Jimmy Choos, in a store window. I cast my gaze to the floor and watch the shoes that scurry, thump, and click past the coffee shop. I'm considering my life, my soul, my choice to blame my wife, when a particular pair of shoes catches my eye. Shoes that are moving quickly. Shoes worn by a man clad in scrubs over a long-sleeved shirt. I don't care about the scrubs. Scrubs are ubiquitous here.

Instantly, I abandon my coffee and follow him.

He pauses at reception. I step behind a pillar. He moves down the hallway. I shadow him. He enters an empty elevator. I remember the day I was on that elevator, that very same elevator, with a group of doctors in blue scrubs who were talking about a medical problem, a puzzle that was not mine to solve.

This time there is only one person in scrubs entering that elevator, and he is the missing piece of a puzzle that I have taken ownership of. As the doors start to close, my adrenaline leaps into overdrive. I want to jump to the fore, force those doors apart, and render that man inert. Instead, I pull out my phone and punch in a number. I've behaved erratically lately, taking off on my own, but I'm not an idiot.

Lee is on the sixth floor, outside Rose's door.

"The elevator," I say as soon as he picks up. "The perp is on the elevator. He's wearing scrubs."

Sixty-Two

THROUGH THE GAP IN the closing elevator doors, Gideon glimpses a short man, head down, punching a number into a cell phone. Recognition filters in. *Flynn.* A determined man, that private investigator. No doubt summoning the cavalry. Planning an ambush, Mr. Flynn?

As the elevator jerks into motion, Gideon considers the situation. Flynn will definitely move into the stairwell. A fitting venue for a showdown, the stairwell. A *second* showdown.

Though unaccustomed to acknowledging personal error, Gideon sighs an admission. He should have shot Flynn when he had the chance. In the alley. But, even at *that* moment, he couldn't take the private investigator seriously. A mere toy, PI Flynn. Gideon shrugs. A blunder, but not irreparable. When, if ever, has the path to fair maiden been free of conflict? There is always a dragon safeguarding the tower. Gideon will slay this dragon. That's what heroes do.

He presses the button for the fifth floor. There, he steps off. An EXIT sign looms, marking the stairwell entrance. He approaches, depresses the door handle, and pushes through to the landing, navigating the door's closure so that it emits no sound. Deftly, he pulls a gun from the waist pack beneath his scrubs. He pauses. Stairwells are by their very nature noise enhancers. It wouldn't hurt to carve off a few decibels. As he attaches his silencer, he smiles to himself, beaming with pride over his choice of disguise. Scrubs hide him in plain sight. Scrubs conceal his weaponry. Scrubs provide a canvas for blood spatter. No one questions blood on scrubs.

Echoing up the stairwell now are the stomps and wheezes of Gideon's out-of-shape target, PI Flynn. Delight shivers through Gideon. He smirks. This will be too easy. He starts down the stairwell, one slow, silent step after another. So gratifying—the stealth, the thrill, the hunt. He's on the landing beside the fourth floor exit when a door rattles open above him. He instantly halts. What's this? Is the intrusion coming from one floor above? No, two. He waits.

"Flynn?" yells a voice overhead. "Flynn, you in here?"

An easily identifiable voice. The PI's cop buddy. Sergeant Connors. A rush of excitement charges through Gideon, but he remains as still as a sculpture. Listening.

"Down here, Lee," calls Flynn. "Between second and third. Did you get him?"

"Not on elevator. Any sign here?"

"No. No one else entered. Except you."

"Wait there. I'm coming down."

Gideon grins. *Two* dragons? A banner day. Two dragons to kill. First, the cop, the *armed* dragon. Gideon reverses direction, steadily climbing. One step, two steps . . . He raises his gun as he rounds the corner to fifth where he locks eyes with Sergeant Connors.

The cop's eyes widen. Gideon is overjoyed. Such fun, catching people off guard. But he himself must remain wary. Genuine surprise is a fleeting emotion, especially in a highly-trained cop. As expected, the Sergeant's face hardens and he raises his right hand, bringing his weapon into view.

Undaunted, Gideon tilts his head, waiting for the next step in police protocol. The cop parts his lips. Looks like an arrest warning is coming.

Gideon fires, clipping the kneecap of Sergeant Connors, rejoicing in the plunge of the cop, the fall of the gun, the struggle of the cop to retrieve the gun. Gideon ambles toward the writhing sergeant and kicks the gun out of reach. The gun skitters to the edge of the landing and topples over. Not the intended outcome, the loss and clatter of the weapon. Gideon glances over the railing and spies the gun on the second step from the bottom of the stairwell. Near the third-floor exit. Just lying there, waiting for someone to claim it. Will the private investigator find it? Attempt to use it?

Indeed, the footsteps of the mighty Flynn are approaching, a steady crescendo of thunder. An abrupt halt in the ruckus makes Gideon chuckle. He watches as Flynn bends and picks up the weapon. An interesting twist. Inconsequential in the long run. Flynn will not shoot. He has no more guts than that whimpering Vincent who spent a lifetime cowering in closets, hiding under beds. Useless. Imbeciles. Both of them.

Gideon returns his attention to the cop, jamming the toe of his gardening boot into the fresh wound on the Sergeant's knee. The resulting scream sends echoes throughout the stairwell shaft and shivers of satisfaction up Gideon's spine. He slowly brings his gun to the cop's head.

A gun slide clicks into place. But it is not Gideon's gun. The sound comes from behind him. Gideon wheels around.

Flynn stands at the corner of the stairwell, half-hidden, sweating, trembling, pointing the gun at him.

Gideon laughs. "Ah, the mild-mannered private investigator. Come to save the day."

"D-drop the gun, Vincent."

Bile lurches into Gideon's throat. "I am not Vincent. I am GIDEON LORD!" He recoils from the screech of his own voice, but instantly rebounds, reassures himself. Disconcerting, but necessary, that shriek. Gideon must squelch any reference to Vincent. He raises his foot and stomps it, solidly, into the torso of the police officer who is already unconscious. "I am Gideon Lord," he repeats, this time in a controlled monotone. He lets out a long breath. "And you are Shaughnessy Flynn, a featherweight. You *can't* kill me. You surely can't save your friend." He indicates toward the motionless body on the floor. He eyes the shaking gun in Flynn's hand.

"I-I-I'll shoot." Flynn clamps his left hand over his right.

Gideon laughs outright at Flynn's feeble attempt to hold the weapon steady. "You won't shoot. You don't have it in you." He abandons the incapacitated cop and heads slowly down the stairs, gun squarely aimed at Flynn. "You're running out of time, Mr. Flynn."

Sixty-Three

OUT OF TIME. OUT of time. Out of time. My heart is clawing its way through my chest and my breath is coming in rapid gasps. Lee is splayed on the landing, just above. Dead? Alive? Don't know. All I can think about is the spider. Fred. The damn spider that dangles above my head every morning. Can't kill the spider. How the hell can I shoot a man? This isn't the firing range. It's not a paper torso I'm looking at now. It's a human being—towering, threatening, evil—but a human being. I can't stop shaking.

The gardening boots are creeping down the stairs, closer and closer until their wearer is standing inches away. Three steps up. A tall man turned goliath by his position on the third stair. I raise my arm until my gun—Lee's gun—is aimed up, at the giant's chest. Do I shoot? *Can* I shoot? What if I don't shoot? The tremor in my hand escalates. Even with my left hand clamped over my right, I can't hold the gun steady.

"Give in, Mr. Flynn. You're not up to this game."

Damn. Damn. Damn! The harder I try to fix my aim, the less effective I am. The son of a bitch is right. I can't let him be right. My whole body sways like a Weeble toy. Sanjay had Weeble toys. Sanjay *loved* Weeble toys. My vision starts playing tricks. I'm seeing double. Two images of a killer. Which one? Which one? How can I end him when I can't even see him? My blood is pulsing, roaring in my ears and a rush of dread is spinning my brain into a whirlpool. Blackness threatens. I ease my grip on the gun.

"Impotent. Just as I thought."

Drenched in humiliation, I raise both hands in the only solution. Surrender. Instantly, the swaying stops. The two killers in front of me become one again. And I am empty. Hollow.

"Put the gun down gently, Mr. Flynn."

I slowly stoop to comply.

As the gun meets the floor, Gideon Lord lands a kick to my shoulder, knocking me off balance, slamming me into the corner of the landing.

His laugh is a low smirk. "Get up, Mr. Flynn."

I don't move. Can't. "You won't shoot." My words are a wish, not a belief. If I'm honest, they're a plea. Pathetic. But it's all I got. "I'm not a part of your plan. You didn't shoot me in the alley. You won't shoot me now."

"Oh, but I will, Mr. Flynn. You are correct, however. You were not a part of the original blueprint. I am off script but I am quite determined to complete my revenge play. Alas, you have gone from diversion to obstruction. I most certainly will kill you."

"You are one sick son of a bitch."

"I am merely a facilitator, Mr. Flynn. A hero, if you will. A slayer of dragons. Wrinkles and mirrors are dragons. I slay dragons by killing flowers before they fade." He grins. A satanic leer. "And you, sir, are merely a busy little bee that has been flitting amongst my flowers. I have no qualms about squashing insects." He moves down one step. "Now get to your feet."

I struggle to a crawling position. Something falls from my pocket, jangling as it hits the polished cement. On hands and knees, I blink the item into focus. My key ring. I zoom in on Violet Harrington's medallion, the yin-and-yang symbol. The symbol fades, giving way to pictures. First, Violet, a grieving mother pleading for help. Then Amelia, my wife, a grieving mother seeking comfort. Back to Violet. Then Amelia again.

Not one, but two broken mothers. Awareness strikes. I gasp. Dear God. I failed them both.

I promised Amelia I would love and cherish through good times and bad. Outright failure there. I promised Violet I would protect Rose. I thought I had nailed that one. But now? Rose is in danger. Nothing stands between Rose and that maniac in the gardening boots. Nothing but me. Me, and Lee's gun, which rests just inches away.

"Get up, Mr. Flynn. My fair Rose awaits. I will not dash her hopes. Get to your feet. Now." He puts his gun to my head.

I almost laugh. I don't need a gun barrel against my skull to remind me who holds the power. Jesus Christ. I'm going to die here. Inevitable. I get that. I stare at the medallion and I see faces, more faces. Violet and Rose. Amelia and Sanjay. Mother and child. Over and over again. Okay, so it's freaking Mother's Day. So what? Violet and Rose. Amelia and Sanjay. What the hell do they want? What?

A rumbling starts deep in my core and bursts upward and outward, a geyser of release. Strange. Fear's gone. Just like that. Vanished. Leaving me blinking, wondering. When fear's gone, what then? What moves in?

Gideon steps closer until one of his gardening boots nudges my fingers. I inhale, a sharp intake. The scent of cedar floods my nostrils. Bark mulch. Mixed with blood spatter on the toe of the boot.

"Leave the heroic tactics to the heroes, Mr. Flynn," says the gardener. "We can handle them."

A single drop of blood, Lee's blood, lands on my hand.

"Now get the hell to your feet."

This is it. He's going to kill me. When he finishes me, he's going after Rose. My heart is pulsing into my eyes. Sweat is pouring down my face. The medallion blurs before me. Anger curls like a fist in my gut, tighter, tighter.

I don't know how I reach Lee's weapon, but suddenly it's there, in my hand. Adrenaline roars through me as I swerve and fire three rounds into the torso of Gideon Lord.

He drops to his knees. He tilts his head toward me, a look of disbelief on his face. He leans forward. I scramble out of the way and watch him tumble, down, down, to a twisted heap at the bottom of the steps.

By the time I make it up the stairs to Lee's side, help has found us. Noise and confusion crowd in.

All I know is that Lee is alive and Lord is dead.

Sixty-Four

I'M HEADING HOME, TO my tiny house. Rose is resting comfortably; Lee is recuperating from surgery. And I'm whipped. I could have crashed at the hospital but something is pulling me home. Don't know what. Just know I have to go. Home. To nothing. To no one.

It's Sunday, it's late, but it's still Mother's Day. It's Mother's Day and my wife—not ex-wife—my wife is away, visiting her mother.

I'm remembering Rose's words, the truth in Rose's words. Violet Harrington made a simple choice, which resulted in tragedy, in the loss of her child. She suffered for that choice.

What about my Amelia? Did she suffer?

Amelia made a simple choice, a glitch in which, for a mere second or two, she took her eyes away from six-year-old Sanjay. Until that point, even *at* that point, she was a loving mother. Did she suffer like Violet did?

Earlier, at Sanjay's grave, it occurred to me that I never asked. Not once. I've been stuck, lodged like bedrock in blame. Did I express hatred toward Amelia? No. I wasn't that kind. I was cold. Indifferent. The opposite of love is indifference, so they say. The passive aggressive opposite.

When I get home, I will call her and explain my hurt. Am I ready to apologize? Am I ready to forgive? I don't know. Maybe I can try. What about those divorce papers in my office? Am I still choosing to leave Amelia? Don't know that either. I take a deep breath, hoping that some sort of solution is on the horizon.

It's darn near midnight when I pull up to my tiny house. I'm surprised to see Beer-in Hand Burt standing in the back alley beneath the light over the garage. *Damn.* Is he waiting for me? For conversation? I'm just not in the mood. I take my time getting out of the car.

"Good Mother's Day all around, eh?" says Burt. "I see that your wife came home. That's a good sign, Irish. A good sign."

Stunned, I just stand there.

"Surprised, huh? Figured as much. Thought you wouldn't be prepared, so I grabbed this." Burt extends his arm.

In lieu of the usual beer can, he holds a bouquet of red roses. Admittedly not something I want to see right now, but nevertheless . . . I envision my friend Rose to whom I am grateful. My gratitude extends to Burt, my previously-unwelcome snoop of a neighbor.

I take the bouquet. "Thanks, Burt." I don't know what else to say, so I say nothing.

"Go get her, bud!" Burt claps a hand on my shoulder and marches off.

It's been a long day. A long week. I was prepared to call Amelia but am I prepared to see her? I walk toward the big house, measuring every thought, every step. What will I say?

I enter the kitchen of the big house and flick on the light. There's no sign of Amelia, but her keys are on the table. I smile. Intent on doing things right, I place the bouquet beside the keys and proceed to the pantry to search for a vase. As I go past the fridge, I spy a red envelope attached by a yellow clip magnet. On the front of the envelope, in Amelia's cursive, is one word—*Sanjay*. My son's name. My middle name. Only Amelia calls me Sanjay. I don't know why, but the red envelope strikes me as ominous. Vase forgotten, pulse erratic, I reach for the envelope and open it. I pull out a note written on a small sheet of white paper ripped from a square memo pad.

I've tried to forgive myself. I can't.
I've asked you to forgive me. You won't.
I can't be the villain—yours or mine—any longer.

It's then that I become aware of the sound of running water. I charge upstairs toward the source—the bathtub, in the master suite. Gushing louder and louder. I run through the bedroom, tripping over a suitcase, landing prone, arms wide and gliding like a body surfer. Not on a wave, but on a wet area rug. *Jesus.* Slipping and sliding, I scramble to my feet and charge into the locked bathroom door. It doesn't budge so I pound my fist against it. "Amelia! Amelia! Open the damn door!"

Dread builds inside me, and I sure as hell don't want to see whatever is behind that door. But there's no choice here. I kick the door in and everything kicks into slow motion.

Screaming for Burt.

Pulling Amelia from the tub.

Turning off faucets.

The water cascading over the sides of the bathtub is crystal clear. No need to search for wounds. I look for pill bottles and I see them, floating in the pool on the floor.

Burt is on the stairs. "Call nine one one!" I yell. I start doing chest compressions to get her heart started and then I know I must force her to vomit. I'm there, doing what I have to do, praying I'm not too late. Seconds stretch. Sirens scream. Footsteps thunder. For the second time in as many days, I gratefully step aside as first responders usurp the scene.

I'm back at the hospital. *A* hospital. Different from the one I left earlier. No idea how I got here. Only that Amelia is here and I'm waiting.

Waiting, just as I did when my son was transported to emergency. Then, I blamed Amelia. This time I'm blaming no one but myself. If I lose Amelia now, will I get past this? She couldn't get past blaming herself for Sanjay's death. She couldn't because I wouldn't let her.

A doctor, a short man whose face is a deep nut brown hue, walks toward me, his steps crisp and light.

Something rushes through me. Hope, perhaps? Is it malignant, this hope?

The doctor smiles, revealing two even rows of snow-white teeth. He nods, repeatedly. Not a word leaves his lips. I hear something, though. What is it? Not a voice, more like a whisper, that of a page turning.

When my son died, there was no smile, no nod. There was only a taut face with tight lips and steel-gray eyes. That doctor didn't remain wordless; he was explaining and explaining. But I heard nothing. I couldn't move.

Now, with ease, I stand. As I follow the smiling doctor, each step feels lighter than the previous, until I'm almost floating. Freedom. That's what this is. Freedom. I've let go of blame.

I have no idea what awaits Amelia and me. I don't know what the next chapter holds.

I only know that I'm choosing to turn the page.

End

Thank you for taking the time to read *At the Heart of the Missing*. If you enjoyed it, please consider telling your friends or posting a short review. Word of mouth is an author's best friend and is greatly appreciated.

A READING GROUP GUIDE

At the HearT of the Missing

Annie Daylon

ABOUT THIS GUIDE

The suggested questions are included to enhance your group's reading of Annie Daylon's *At the Heart of the Missing.*

Discussion Questions

1. *At the Heart of the Missing* is written from shifting viewpoints, the main one being that of Flynn, the private investigator whose voice is in the first person. Victim and villain also have their say, both in the third person. Why do you think the author chose three viewpoints? Why do you think the author chose present, not past tense, for this novel?

2. Rose Harrington comes from a very close family. What physical symbol does the author use to represent this? Other than family, Rose feels that she is an independent woman who needs no one. But when her sister Margo disappears and her mother, Violet, dies, Rose learns that she is not so independent: she makes a choice that takes her on a tragic path. Why does Rose take such a risk?

3. Violet Harrington keeps a dark secret from her daughter Rose. What physical item represents the secret? Why did the author choose that symbol? How would Rose's life have been different if Violet had simply told her the truth? Have you ever kept a secret from someone you love?

4. PI Shaughnessy Flynn loves puzzles and numbers. How does this come into play in the novel? What, if anything, surprised you about this character?

5. What motivates the antagonist? Do you feel any sympathy for this person? Were there any surprises about him? If so, what?

6. What scene personally resonated the most with you in either a positive or negative way? Why?

7. Do characters experience personal growth in the novel? If so, who and how? What do you think will happen next to the characters?

8. The climax of the book where the story's hero finally comes face to face with his nemesis. In a way, this happens twice in *At the Heart of the Missing*. Why do you think the author chose this "double confrontation" ending? Who really is the hero of the story? Could an argument be made for the story having two heroes?

9. What is the significance of the book's title?

If you have any of your own questions you would like to ask the author, send her an email anniedaylon@shaw.ca. She loves to hear from fans!

Acknowledgments

I wish to acknowledge the assistance of the following people:

Author/editor Ken Loomes for his valuable time and superb skills in content and line editing. I first met Ken while attending a getting-to-know-your-neighbors event. When I mentioned I was starting a writing career, he instantly replied "I'm starting a writing group." I owe Ken a debt of gratitude, not only for his editorial guidance on this novel, but also for years of support and mentorship through the Chilliwack Writers' Group.

Fellow authors Fran Brown and Mary Keane for their insights, edits, and encouragement. I am grateful to be blessed with such giving and talented critique companions.

Consultant Mark Leland for answering questions about police work and guiding me to contact the Vancouver Police Department.

Consultant Nathan Helm, Managing Director of Shadow Investigations, BC for answering questions about private investigator work.

Staff Sergeant Randy Fincham of the Vancouver Police Department for taking time from his schedule to give me a tour of VPD Headquarters. I walked out of that meeting with greater insight into the workings of the department, greater appreciation for the integrity, dedication, and competency of its members, and rock-solid respect for all who choose a career path in law enforcement. (This novel is literary suspense; any inaccuracies regarding the VPD in this novel are mine and mine alone.)

Early readers, avid readers, Lillian Day and Jeannette Lannon for their support, encouragement, and helpful commentary.

My sister Dorothy Lannon for introducing me to the city of Vancouver. I am enamored with this city which serves as setting for two of my novels. I particularly love the West End with its liquid combination of bustle and calm, its abundant diversity of culture and lifestyle, and its proximity to my favorite of all things: the ocean.

My husband David, always David, for his ongoing support as I navigate the world of the writer. David is my rock.

Annie Daylon's exciting novel *Castles in the Sand* examines how one man can have everything he ever wanted in life, only to wake up one day to find he's let it all slip through his fingers and is no longer certain he has the strength to fight for it back . . .

Thirty-eight-year-old Justin Wentworth loses everything when his entitled lifestyle slams into a collapsing economy. Alcoholic, homeless, and living on Vancouver streets, he has one desire: to regain the love and trust of his wife Sarah, and his little boy, Bobby.

Help arrives when twenty-something Steve Jameson, a graduate student researching the homeless, rescues the mugged Justin from a Dumpster and offers food and shelter in return for Justin's story.

As he divulges the tragic details of his life's downward spiral, Justin develops trust for his Good Samaritan. However, he soon discovers that all is not what it seems with Steve. Can Justin persist on his path back to his family, or are darker forces at work against him?

Daylon's poignant, gripping, character-driven novel of tragedy and hope will win the hearts of readers everywhere . . .

Please read on for an exciting sneak peek of Annie Daylon's

CASTLES IN THE SAND

Now on sale in print and ebook!

Winner, Mainstream Genre
Houston Writers Guild 2012 Novel Contest

Castles in the Sand

a novel by

Annie Daylon

"Safe upon the solid rock the ugly houses stand:
Come and see my shining palace built upon the sand!"
~Edna St. Vincent Millay

1

ON THE VERGE

January, 2010

I have to stay on the verge of sleep. Just on the verge. Can't let my body slip over the threshold. Too damn scary.

My long-held conviction—that the homeless are a stationary lot, staking out territory on a corner, steadfast until some third party herds them along—is gone. Vanquished my first night on the street when fear goaded me into motion. Since then, I meander at night, all night, seeking the security of daybreak.

This night, however, is different. Hungover and exhausted, I am motionless, lying on the sidewalk, my very marrow impregnated with cold despite the heating vent beside me. On the verge of sleep. Trying to convince myself that the concrete is a pillow-top mattress, that Sarah is sleeping next to me, and that our Bobby is down the hall, dreaming of Dory and Nemo . . .

"Hey, you! What do you think you're doing?"

My body jumps and my eyes pop open. Some guy in a puffy, white jacket hovers over me. A marshmallow. A goddam talking marshmallow. My heart pounds. *The watch. Do I still have it?* I grab for my wrist.

Yes. Still there. Relief gushes, and I yank at my sleeve until the watch is hidden. *It's safe, my gift from Sarah, safe.* My heart rate slows, but not much; the marshmallow lingers.

I squint to shield my eyes from the streetlight. "I'm trying to sleep. What does it look like I'm doing?"

"Not here, bud. There are shelters, you know."

Great. Another Good Samaritan determined to clean up Vancouver streets. Damn city's going all out to prevent Olympic tourists from tripping over the homeless. I glare at this latest do-gooder and stifle a comeback. Then I drop my gaze to the pigeons strutting the sidewalk. Huh. The little bastards have red feet. Never noticed that before. The way they dart around, seems they'd get crushed by all these people. Yep. The beautiful people are here, scurrying to the office or the Skytrain, or the bus stop. I take a deep breath so I can suck in the Starbucks. Love the smell of Starbucks. The beautiful people all carry Starbucks.

Wind rushes my face as a city bus passes. The bus engine grumbles, preparing to halt at the next stop. *Whooosssssh.* Air brakes.

Damn. The city is awake.

Won't be long before the bolts on the door of the shoe boutique behind me twist open. Three bolts. Every morning. Like clockwork. *Click. Click. Click.* Pretty soon, the whole fleet of designer shops flanking Robson Street will reel in the first cash of the day.

Might as well move. No point in arguing with the marshmallow. Sighing, I scramble to my feet and linger over the heating vent, *my* heating vent that was hard to find, harder to claim.

"Way to go, bud," says Marshmallow Man. "Do you need any help?"

I ignore him. Help, my ass. *Saw the way you looked at me,* bud, *with the corner of your mouth pulled up in contempt. Screw you.* I choke back the urge to spit at him. My mouth is so dry I probably couldn't form a spit wad anyway. I deliberately stick my butt in the direction of his face as I bend over to gather my stuff.

I heft my backpack over my shoulder, turn toward Stanley Park, walk about a block, and then do an about-face. The park washrooms are at least twenty-five minutes away and I need one *now.* I pick up my pace.

Marshmallow Man is still talking at me as I hurry past. Idiot. I push up my tattered sleeve and glance at my watch. Seven-thirty. It's a dangerous time for alleys but my bladder won't wait.

At the next corner, I veer around a bakery and go toward the green Dumpster at the back. I hide behind it, take a leak, and let out a long sigh. Relief doesn't last; as soon as that need is met, before I can zip my jeans, my stomach growls. Time to hunt.

The smell of fresh-baked bread wafts up my nose. My mouth waters. Bakeries throw out stuff. Day-old stuff. Easy pickings. I dislodge my backpack and conceal it in the bushes nearby. Then I scramble up the side of the Dumpster, jump in, and fumble through paper and plastic. At the sound of voices, men's voices, I freeze. *Am I safe here?* The hair on my neck stands up. I slowly lower myself to my haunches and hold my breath. The voices get louder.

"My ex-wife's new boyfriend damn near got himself killed last night."

"How the fuck did that happen? "

"People on bicycles gotta look out for big, red pickup trucks. Hard to see people on bicycles."

"Yeah, right. Especially in that big, red pickup you drive." His laughter rumbles through me like vibrations from a passing freight train. My heart speeds up.

"Shut up, you damn fool. I was with *you* last night, remember?"

"Oh yeah, what was it we were doing?"

A rat scuttles past me and I jump back, splaying my body against the side of the Dumpster. Oh, God. I squeeze my eyes shut and freeze in place, wedged to the wall like a magnet to steel.

"What the hell . . . ? Did you hear that?"

"I don't hear nothing. Jesus, you're jumpier than a . . . "

"Ssssh! Just listen, will ya?"

My heart thunders in my ears and sweat pours off my brow. My lungs are about to explode. Don't breathe. Don't dare breathe.

"Hmmph. Nothing. Probably just a rat. Let's get the hell outta here."

Footsteps pound, thump, then fade. Certain they are gone, I gulp in air. Then I inch forward and peer out. No one in sight. Relieved, I wrap my fingers around the edge of the Dumpster and flip myself over the side with athletic skill bred from chronic fear. I land with knees bent, head down. When I unfold my body, a Goliath fist slams toward me. The stench of stale nicotine hits first. Then bones crunch and pain shoots through my face. Blood spurts into my mouth. I lurch back, bang into the Dumpster, spew teeth, and collapse to the ground.

My body grunts in response to the thumping kicks that land on my torso. Gruff fingers poke and prod, searching. A triumphant "aha!" tells me they have discovered my watch. *Sorry, Sarah.* There is no physical pain now, only crushing sadness. Strange. They pick me up, swing me, and toss me. I am a rag doll, flying. I land with a thud, back in the garbage. Rats scurry over me and up the wall of the Dumpster. Laughter rumbles. Feet hammer. Then . . . stillness.

I want to open my eyes. Can't. Can't move. Know where I am, know what's around me, but can't move. My body is a shell, useless as a flashlight with the batteries ripped out. Maybe this is the end. And maybe I don't give a damn. Bobby. Bobby's castle. What did I do with Bobby's castle?

I must have blacked out completely because the next thing I know I'm on some kind of gurney. Men in uniform are leaning over me. Jesus! Cops. I thrash about like a freshly-landed sockeye. Muscular arms, a whole octopus of them, pin me down.

"Relax, bud," says a voice.

I turn my head. Marshmallow Man. Only this time he's red and white. There's blood on his puffy jacket. Must be my blood. The son of a bitch pulled me out of the Dumpster. I go limp now, allowing the uniforms to stick me and wrap me and wheel me to an ambulance. For some reason, Marshmallow Man stays at my side.

A memory flashes. Bobby's castle. "Backpack," I utter.

Marshmallow Man leans in. "What's that, bud?"

"Backpack. In bushes by Dumpster."

"Oh, yeah, right. I remember your backpack. Listen, the ambulance is going to take you to St. Paul's. I'll look for the backpack and then I'll find you, okay?"

Trust you? Why should I trust you, bud? I struggle to get up but the octopus arms are having none of that.

"Let him get the backpack," says one of the uniforms. "He'll take it to the hospital."

Huh. Guess this guy knows Marshmallow Man. Relieved, I nod. The uniforms lift me and load me onto the ambulance. Safe now—no thugs, no rats, no stench of rotting garbage. The last thing I notice is a nametag sewed onto a uniform bent over me. I focus on it and allow myself to float away . . .

2

ANGEL TATTOO

I jump from sleep, sweating, heart racing. Light glares overhead. Used to that. Always sleep under streetlights. Always wake up cold and stiff, *rigor-mortis* stiff. No comfort on sidewalks. But I'm warm now. Molded to a cloud. I inhale and my nose twitches. Antiseptic. Memory is triggered and my heart rate slows.

"Mister? Are you awake? Mister?" A female voice.

I turn my head and scrutinize her with my one good eye. Middle-aged nurse. Dark hair, streaked with grey. Tattoo on neck. An angel tattoo. Huh. Appropriate.

"What is your name, Mister? Can you tell me your name?" She straps a blood pressure cuff on me and stares long and hard at my arm. Looking for track marks, no doubt. She can look all she wants. None there. "Can you tell me your name, Mister?"

Fat chance. Did I say that out loud? Guess not. She's still staring at me.

"Vladimir," I mutter. I knew a Vladimir once. Liked the man. Liked the name. Means "renowned prince," he told me. I used to be a prince.

"Vladimir, huh?" She raises an eyebrow. "Any possibility you have a last name?"

Rhetorical question. We both know it.

She sighs. "Okay, Vladimir-with-no-last-name, the doctor will be in to see you shortly. You can rest for a while." She touches my hand and I recoil. "It's okay; you're safe here." She reaches for my hand again.

This time I don't pull back. Instead, I look into her eyes. I see compassion there, not pity. Probably no difference to most people. Would have been none to me a few months back before I started living out of garbage cans. But now? Now I think compassion gives hope. And now, as I stare at the nurse with the angel tattoo, I'm sucking in hope like a black hole sucks up light. I want to smile at her. I try, but the pain hits and I remember why I'm here. She withdraws her hand and I am lost, disoriented, like I was cut off in mid-sentence during a phone call. Hope oozes away. Blackness returns and settles in.

"I have to go now. You just rest." She turns and walks away.

Rest. My eyelids droop. One of them anyway. The other is swollen shut. My brain is still. Sounds travel to my ears, hospital sounds. The thud of rubber soles on linoleum, the clatter of trays being loaded onto a cart, the white noise of simultaneous conversations, a moan of pain, a jolt of laughter. Everything feels safe, comfortable. Like listening to a movie soundtrack. Nothing really affects me. It's not like the street where whispers and footsteps can make adrenaline gush. I want to float here for a while, but something niggles at me. What am I trying to remember?

"Hey, bud, I'm back."

That's it. Bobby's castle. My good eye snaps open. My backpack is there, in the hands of Marshmallow Man. I grab it, unzip the side pocket, and shove my hand in.

"Ouch!" I pull back. I try again with my left hand, the one without the IV needle attached to it. I grope. There it is. With the small, plastic castle safely clutched in my fingers, I fall back against the pillow. A deep breath. Feels good. I take another, deeper. Pain slices my ribcage.

"Is that all you wanted, bud? I could have gotten that out for you. They tell me your name is Vladimir? Is that right?"

Annoying little shit. "Get lost. I'm done with you."

"Sorry, bud, I'm not done with you."

Damn. Guess this time I did say the words out loud. The problem with living inside my head is that I'm not sure what leaks out and what doesn't.

"What the hell do you want, *bud?*" I demand.

"The name's Steve. And you're my project."

"Nobody's project. Go away."

"No can do."

"Why the hell not?"

"Need your help."

"Don't need yours."

"You did today."

Couldn't argue that one. "Thanks. Now, get lost."

"Sure." He turns away.

I sigh with relief. But the son of a bitch pulls up a chair and parks his butt in it.

"What the . . . ?"

"Now," says Steve as he pulls a small notebook from his back pocket, "let's talk." He clicks his pen. "Vladimir, huh? How did you come up with that one?"

I open my mouth to lay into him but he grins and I am disarmed. Is there something familiar in his smile? Maybe, maybe not. Maybe I'm just lonely, starved for company, like a prison inmate surfacing from solitary. Maybe I don't want him to walk away like the nurse did. Whatever. I decide to shut up and listen.

"Okay, so, as I was telling you, my name is Steve. Steve Jameson. I'm a grad student, doing research on the homeless for my thesis. Been interviewing people, but can't get the info I want. Seems that street people tell me everything about sex and drug and alcohol habits and nothing about family. Interesting. Why is that, Vladimir?"

Maybe because it's none of your damn business. I shrug. "Don't do drugs." I look straight at him.

The damn fool's eyes light up. He doesn't know I am toying with him.

"Can we skip the alcohol and sex and go right to the family?"

I turn away and an audible sigh escapes Steve's lips.

"Darn," he mutters.

A squeak of rubber sole on linoleum marks the entrance of the doctor. Chair legs scrape the floor as Steve rises and moves both chair and self out of the way.

"Vladimir," reads the doctor from the chart she has pulled from the tray table. "Can you sit up at all?"

I struggle into a seated position. It hurts like hell, but I don't show it.

She pushes a button to raise the head of the bed. I am grateful, but don't show that either. Then she touches my face; I flinch.

"You will need a few stitches above that eye," she announces. "I guess you don't want to tell me what happened."

I look at her. There's no compassion in that face. Silence is golden.

"Fine then. We'll just get those stitches in, and send you to Imaging for a CT scan and an X-ray of your ribs. You'll probably be on your way in a few hours."

I cover my face with my free arm. "On your way." Small statement. Great disappointment. It reminds me of Bobby. Five-year-old Bobby with his little face scrunched up, ready to cry. The time I took him to visit a school friend of his. I got the dates mixed up, and his friend wasn't home. A minor screw-up on my part . . . Lord knows I made far greater mistakes where my family was concerned. But this tiny error stabs me. "This is what disappointment feels like, son," I had told him. I would have given anything, *anything,* to take away Bobby's pain, to feel it for him. Well, I'm feeling it now . . . I'm just like Bobby. A disappointed five-year-old. I don't want to be "on my way." I want to stay here on the soft, clean bed with the bright light overhead.

The doctor lowers my arm and, at warp speed, sews me up. Her shoes whine their way out of the room. The nurse with the angel tattoo reappears.

"Vladimir," she says, her soft, comforting voice sliding around me, like she's wrapping me in a down-filled quilt, "do you know about the homeless shelters? There's one not too far from here. I think you should go there."

I say nothing.

"For the night, at least," she adds, anxiety creeping into her voice. "I know someone over there, and I can phone ahead for you. It is just a few blocks away. What do you think?"

Again, nothing.

"Please, Vladimir." Her voice is a whispered prayer now. Makes me wonder who the other Vladimir is, the one I remind her of.

"I'll take him there." Steve pops into view like a movie star doing a cameo.

Damn it all! Where's the white cowboy hat, Steve?

"That okay with you, Vladimir?" asks the nurse.

I shrug. Somehow, that is enough for her.

"Well, that's settled then." All business now, she helps me into a wheelchair, tucks a blanket on my lap, and we head off to Imaging.

"I'll be waiting," calls Steve.

Don't doubt that for a second, bud.

The wheelchair creaks and rolls, creaks and rolls. To the elevator. *Ping!* The doors slide open and we glide on. The nurse presses the button for the second floor and then stands behind me, leaning on the wheelchair.

I expect conversation—okay, I expect a monologue from my angel companion—maybe some probing. But, no. There is only silence, simple and peaceful, a calming shroud, jostled a bit by the *whir* of the elevator. A short *whir* for a short ride. *Ping!* Damn. Too short.

The doors open and a wall of stifling heat wallops me. We push into it, becoming one with it as we navigate the wide, polished hallway. The angel nurse parks my chair outside a swinging door, locks my wheels and orders me to wait. She disappears then, and I linger, as ordered, and sleep, as needed.

My body jerks when someone unlocks my wheels. A different nurse, male and burly, mutters a hello as he reverses my chair, lines it up with the swinging door and thrusts it through, into the X-ray room.

The whole X-ray/CT scan thing takes a while. Okay with me. The longer the better. At least a couple of hours before the angel nurse comes to claim me. She wheels me back to the ER, removes my IV, and is about to help me up when the PA system barks an order. The only word I make out is "Stat!". Then the nurse is gone. *Pouf!* So much for angels.

I manage to get myself from the wheel chair onto the bed, unassisted. When I realize I'm actually *looking* for Steve, I laugh. Tried to get rid of him and now I'm sorry he's gone. Whatever. I know I'm leaving too, so I pull my shirt from the blue plastic bag on the bed.

"There you are. How are you doing, bud? Want me to help you with that?" Steve barrels in, grabs my shirt, and holds it while I put my arm through the sleeve. Then he does up my buttons.

Jesus! What am I . . . two?

"Where's the nurse? She didn't help you? Well, at least, you got the IV out of your hand. Bet that feels better, doesn't it?"

Maybe I should tell him that if he wants to interview people, he should wait for them to answer his freaking questions. Screw it. Let him figure it out for himself.

"There you go, all done." Steve stands back and surveys the job he did. "Now, do we have to wait for results of X-rays or are we free to go?"

The nurse scurries into the room. "Well, all done. You're free to go."

What was she doing? Standing outside waiting for her cue?

"You will be sore for a while," she says. "Just take care. Steve here is going to take you to the shelter for tonight. Right, Steve? You can't stay there during the day, but you probably know about the library. You can go there in the morning. The library has a nice indoor foyer; it's safe there and you can rest." She insists that I sit in the wheelchair, passes me my backpack, and keeps talking to Steve as she walks us to the exit. Once there, she helps me up and turns around. "Good luck," she says to me. "Thank you," to Steve.

We amble away, Steve and me. He is constantly checking to see if I am there, if I am okay, if I *am* . . . period. Part of me likes being on an invisible leash. Part of me craves being on my own. Since every step causes me to cringe in pain, the leash wins. For now.

I know it's not far to the shelter. Steve mutters something about not having his car. About streets closed preparing for Olympics anyway. About how it's better to use the bus. Or the Skytrain. Yada. Yada. Yada.

Shut up, Steve. Don't care.

It's almost dusk now, and I wonder where the day went. How much time had I spent sleeping, waiting, in the Dumpster, in the hospital? We stop and start, Steve hovering like a nervous new mother. Like Sarah with Bobby. I hold tighter to my backpack and smile on my good side. Steve thinks I'm smiling at him.

"There. That's more like it. You're looking better already. Here, let's sit at the bus stop for a minute or two, just to be sure you're okay."

I oblige. We both sit there, staring at the passersby. Here, at the bus stop, with Steve by my side, I'm a regular person. Almost. Feels good until a homeless man passes, pushing a bulging shopping buggy. My stomach lurches. I used to feel sorry for people like that. Jesus! Who the hell am I kidding? Sorry, my ass. Contempt is more like it. Shiftless vagrants. A blight on the postcard beauty of Vancouver. Scraggly hair, dirty clothes, yellow teeth.

"Hummph!" I hold back a laugh. Stick my tongue into the empty space in the side of my mouth where two teeth used to be. Maybe yellow teeth are better than no teeth. Still, I don't want a shopping cart. There's no hope left when you have a shopping cart. No hope. I don't belong with the shopping cart crowd. "Let's. Get. Out. Of. Here." My body trembles as I spit the words.

Steve rockets to his feet, helps me to mine, and we continue on our way. "After I get you settled in," he says, "I'll go away. But I promise I'll come back in the morning as soon as they open and I'll take you wherever you want. The library works for me if it works for you. We can talk..."

I stop dead. "What do you want from me?"

Steve is still walking. Words still pouring out of him. "... because I don't have classes tomorrow, and I can help..." Yada. Yada. Yada. He's waving his hands around like he's conducting a goddam symphony. He halts abruptly, swings around, and marches back to me.

"What do you want from me?" I demand again.

He is standing about a foot away, looking up at me. I notice how small he is. The man can't be more than a hundred thirty pounds soaking wet. Mid-twenties, I'm guessing.

He runs a hand through his blond brush cut and lets out a sigh. "I want to help. Like I told you, I have to interview..."

"Why me?"

"Don't know." He shrugs his shoulders and shivers.

For the first time, I notice he is not wearing his puffy jacket. A warm January, yeah, but he must be bloody freezing.

"Maybe you just looked like you needed someone," he says, folding his arms.

I narrow my one good eye. Something familiar about that face staring into mine, about the way those arms are crossed. I don't know what.

The only thing I do know is that Marshmallow Man *is a liar*.

Annie Daylon

Annie Daylon is an award-winning author of short stories and novels. She was born and raised in Newfoundland. She studied music at Mount Allison University and education at both the University of Manitoba and the University of British Columbia (M.Ed.). After thirty years teaching, she delved into her passion for writing.

Annie lives in the British Columbia Fraser Valley, with her husband, David, and their dog, CoCo. Readers can learn more about Annie at www.anniedaylon.com.

Made in the USA
Lexington, KY
27 March 2017